A WICKED GAME

KATE McKINSEY

DEDICATION

To my husband, who believed in this story from the start.
To my bestie, Kika, for insisting I could write something worth reading.
To my incredible beta reader hype team:
Julianne, Jenn, and Caitlyn — your support kept me going.
To Emily, a true godsend for your editing skills and fangirling.
And to my parents, for always cheering me on (and for gifting me my very first laptop back in high school). Mom and Dad, please skip a few sections of this book.
Seriously. I love you!

CHAPTER 1

ARIA

The night was heavy with the scent of burning wood and damp earth as Aria stepped into the Sovereign's bedchamber. The grand, decadent room loomed before her, lit only by the flickering fire in the hearth, its warmth doing little to chase away the chill in the air. Shadows danced along the ornate tapestries and high-vaulted ceilings, twisting into unfamiliar shapes, and the silence was heavy and expectant.

Her breath caught in her throat as she hesitated at the threshold. The door closed behind her with a soft click that sounded far too final.

She had been warned that this role was a dangerous one. But of all those she was to tend to, two men had come with the strongest of warnings: the king, of course, and his right hand — the Sovereign Rylik — the most feared archmage in Ravenhelm.

Aria had heard the tales whispered in taverns and inns, in the lower courts where gossip flowed like water. Some said Rylik could command the very shadows themselves, that his power was vast enough to make even the king tread carefully. Legends painted him as a force of nature, a man whose heart was as cold as the magic he wielded. Yet, as she stood there, barely daring to breathe, she couldn't help but think, *Legends rarely live up to the men behind them, do they?*

Blinking against the room's subdued light, she sought the figure seated on the far side. His back was to her, but even in his stillness, there was an undeniable presence. The firelight caught on the crystal glass in his hand, the deep red wine within glinting like blood. He hadn't acknowledged her entrance, but the weight of his attention pressed down on her as though he had.

Nervousness clawed at her throat. Aria forced herself to take a deep breath, willing her hands to stop shaking. She was a healer, after all. She was here for one purpose only, and then after that she could leave. She would likely only deal with him on the rarest of occasions after this.

"Are you going to stand there all night?" His voice, smooth and low, cut through the silence. It was calm, unhurried, but there was a dark edge beneath the casualness that sent a shiver down her spine. "Or are you going to do your job, Healer?"

"I—I'm sorry." Her voice wavered, and she cursed herself for it. She needed to compose herself, not stammer like a frightened child.

Aria took a tentative step forward, her gaze darting around the room as she moved. Every detail here screamed wealth, from the heavy velvet drapes to the gold-threaded embroidery that adorned his bedding. There was nothing out of place, and yet the oppressive atmosphere felt stifling, almost unnatural.

Rylik shifted slightly in his chair, his head tilting just enough for her to see the sharp line of his jaw. His dark hair, tousled as though he had been lost in thought, gleamed faintly in the firelight. When he finally turned his eyes on her, they were cool, assessing. They swept over her in a slow, deliberate motion, lingering just long enough to make her uncomfortable.

"Where—where is the wound?" she asked, trying to keep her voice steady as she met his gaze.

"My chest," he replied with the same lazy indifference, taking another sip from his glass. The flicker of the flames reflected in his eyes, making them seem almost predatory.

Aria hesitated, then cleared her throat. "Would you remove your tunic, Sovereign?"

There was a beat of silence before Rylik set his glass down, the clink of it against the table unnervingly loud. His fingers moved carefully, unlacing his tunic with an exaggerated grace, each motion slow and purposeful. As his fingertips brushed across his chest, just above the opening of his tunic, the touch was soft, almost absent-minded, yet conscious enough that Aria couldn't help but notice. Her gaze followed his hand for a moment, the casual trail of his fingers as they grazed downward.

His eyes never left hers. The fire crackled in the hearth, its heat suddenly thick in the air, closing the space between them. He let his gaze drift over her, an idle sweep that lingered on the curve of her throat, then dipped lower to the swell of her chest before returning to her face.

As his tunic parted, revealing the expanse of his chest, Aria's breathing faltered for a moment. The wound was worse than she had expected. A deep, jagged gash cut across his flesh, red and inflamed, the edges raw and angry. It looked like something had torn through him with brutal force, leaving behind a wound that pulsed with residual magic.

Her stomach lurched. This was no ordinary injury. She glanced up at him, her brow furrowing in concern.

"If you flinch at the sight of a wound," Rylik drawled, his lips curling into a smirk, "you won't last long in this court."

"I'm not flinching," she retorted, though her voice was tight. She couldn't help but think he should be dead, not sitting there sipping wine. "You should be in more pain. This wound—"

"Who said I wasn't in pain?" His eyes were sharp, his tone almost amused.

Aria took a steadying breath and knelt beside him, bringing herself level with his wound. "You have an uncommonly high threshold, Sovereign," she murmured softly, almost as if to herself. Up close, it was even more disturbing, an eerie energy radiating from it like a dark aura. Her fingers hovered above the jagged flesh. This injury itself was horrible, but there was something else beneath the surface that hinted at a problem much worse.

Slowly, she pressed her palm against his skin, and her healing magic flared to life, the familiar golden glow filling the room with a soft warmth. But as the energy poured into him, she felt resistance. Beneath the wound, there was a coldness—an unnatural, biting cold that sent a shiver through her.

Her brow furrowed as she concentrated, her magic pushing harder, probing deeper. The cold fought back, almost alive in its defiance, but she persisted, her hand steady even as her pulse betrayed her.

Rylik's body seemed to ease under her touch, the tension in his shoulders softening slightly, though his expression gave little away. His eyes, hooded and dark, studied her face, tracing the delicate lines of her concentration before dipping to the curve of her mouth, then lower, to where her hand rested against his chest.

Aria said nothing, attempting to keep her focus entirely on the wound. There was something more here, something wrong. And then she felt it—a dark thread of magic, intertwined with perhaps an older injury, pulsing coldly beneath the surface. She could flood it with heat, but it wouldn't completely eradicate it. If anything, it would be like applying a mere balm to alleviate it, rather than curing it.

As she finally withdrew her hand, the wound had vanished, leaving his skin smooth and unscarred, his eyes closed in serene reflection. Yet the icy sensation that had rested beneath her magic now gnawed at her thoughts, stirring darker fears she dared not name.

She drew in a shaky breath as her heart pounded in her chest, a startling realization washing over her. She had only felt something like this a few times before, but it had never been this strong. The Sovereign had to have been struck by an enchanted weapon. One meant to destroy him completely. This was a severe wound, perhaps even a permanent one. If anyone knew about this— if the *Rebellion* knew about this— they would use it against him.

Aria looked hesitantly, fearfully up at him. The unbeatable Sovereign had a *weakness*. She swallowed hard, her heart pounding. And now she knew what it was.

Rylik's blue eyes flicked open, a hint of something dangerous lurking behind them. He knew.

Aria stood abruptly, the sudden gesture betraying her nerves. "I—I hope you feel better, Sovereign. Goodnight."

Before she could reach the door, Rylik moved with inhuman speed, appearing before her in a swirl of shadow. His hand shot out, gripping her wrist. His touch was cold, and the shadows clung to him like a sentinel.

"If you tell anyone," he whispered, his voice like velvet laced with menace, "whatever it is you think you know—I will make sure you regret it."

The faint scent of cedar and smoke lingered between them, rich and sharp, as his grip tightened just enough to ground her in place. His fingers burned like brands against her skin, the heat of him stark against the chill that laced the room.

The threat was soft, but it hit her like a blow. His gaze bore into hers, unyielding, and the tension in the air wrapped around her like a noose. Her heart thundered in her chest as she met his cold eyes, her voice trembling. "I—I wouldn't tell a soul."

His lips curved into a thin, humorless smile. "No, you wouldn't. Because if you did," He leaned in, his grip tightening on her wrist as his breath ghosted over her skin. "You cannot fathom the suffering I would unleash upon every person you love. I would do so unflinchingly."

Aria's pulse raced as she yanked her wrist free, stumbling back from him.

He folded his hands behind his back, watching her with a quiet amusement. She could feel his eyes on her, examining, weighing her as if deciding her fate.

He knew exactly how to hurt her, and worse—he knew she wouldn't defy him. She couldn't win, not against *him*. If the Rebellion was to be believed, he was ruthless. There were whispers of what he'd done—stories that made her blood run cold. Entire villages burned to the ground in the King's pursuit of dissenters, where every soul was wiped out to send a message. Enemies of the crown dragged from their homes in the dead of night, never to be seen again. And those who were captured alive said the Sovereign had ways of making even the most stubborn minds break. Some claimed he could unravel a person's thoughts, turn their deepest fears against them until they'd confess to crimes they hadn't even committed.

She shuddered, her pulse quickening. She had hoped to stay

in his good graces, maybe even remain inconsequential to him, silently healing wounds and hiding away. But now, she could see he was already sizing her up as a foe.

"I don't believe I have ever known of a healer that can heal so efficiently," Rylik said, his voice deceptively soft. "No scars, no trace of the wound at all. And what's more—a healer capable of mending something far worse than any flesh wound. You have proven yourself truly *indispensable* this evening, Aria Thorne."

Her heart sank at the use of her full name, her fingers attempting to smooth a comforting touch over her wrist. He intended to imply that he could make good on that threat to her loved ones. And being *indispensable* is something she would rather *not* be to the Sovereign.

Rylik took a step forward. "Where is your bedchamber?"

Aria blinked, startled by the sudden shift in conversation. "I—I don't think that's an appropriate—"

"I'll have your things moved to the suite adjoining mine."

Aria stared at him, her blood running cold. "You—what?"

He smiled, the faint curve of his lips laced with a quiet, unsettling confidence. "It's prudent," he began, voice low and deliberate, "to keep someone of your abilities close." His gaze lingered on her, sharp and discerning, as if reading her every unspoken thought. "You were told, I assume, whom you were brought here to serve?"

Her breath grew shallow, and she gave a slow, reluctant nod, feeling a chill creep down her spine. "The king, the Shadow Knights, and you, Sovereign. I was informed that the six of you would take precedence over all others here in the palace."

His eyes gleamed with something like satisfaction, his next words hanging heavy between them. "Yes— and having you near will be a comfort, given the constant threat that looms over us." He paused, letting the weight of his presence settle in the air. "In the event that I might require your immediate assistance," his voice dropped, soft but menacing as he added, "I would hate to think of you being needlessly far away from me." His gaze settled on her, unblinking and intent, like a hunter studying its prey—silent, calculating, and entirely in control.

Aria's expression hardened. It was one thing when the king

discovered her healing gift and bound her to his will. It was another when the Rebellion sought to twist that gift to serve their cause. But this—this was different. A darker imprisonment took root within her, deeper than the chains of the crown or the Rebellion. The Sovereign intended to make her a captive of a far more insidious kind. Yet, if she was truly as "indispensable" as he claimed, especially given the darkness festering beneath his skin, then she knew he wouldn't dare harm her. Not yet.

She only needed to play his game.

This was just the beginning, and like any game, the opening moves demanded a strong defense. She could crumble later, in the quiet confines of her room. She could let her fear consume her there, within those four walls. But not here. Here, she would stand before him as if she were unshaken. For if a lifetime of service to this man awaited her, she would meet it head-on, without flinching.

Play the game, Aria.

"That wouldn't be a problem, would it?" he asked, his tone mocking.

She narrowed her eyes. "Do you intend to make me your enemy so soon, Sovereign? I'm here as a healer. To mend the broken. Nothing else."

"'Nothing else,'" he echoed with a cold smile, stepping closer. The space between them shrank, and Aria fought the urge to back away. "You come from a part of the kingdom where the Rebellion has a foothold. This fact seems to have eluded His Majesty, given his preoccupation with your *unique* skill set. But I am a cautious man, Aria." He leaned in, his breath warm on her skin. "I don't trust you. And I won't. But you are as valuable as His Majesty assessed. And when I find something of such value, I don't let it out of my sight."

Her heart pounded in her chest, her mouth dry as he leaned back, his eyes glittering with silent command.

"Follow me," he murmured, his gaze assessing her one final time before he turned away and led her to the other side of the room.

Rylik stood still, his back to Aria as he reached for the handle of the door connecting his suite to the adjoining one. The creak of the hinges seemed louder than it should, breaking the silence like a crack through the tension hanging between them. He pushed the door open, the two of them walking across the marbled floors of the bathing room and opening the final door that was to be her new suite. He paused deliberately before glancing back at her, his eyes catching hers for one last, measured look.

"Your things will be brought up shortly," he said in a low tone. "You're to remain in this suite unless otherwise instructed."

Aria clenched her hands at her sides, trying to steady her trembling fingers, trying to hold her expression together, as though her composure could mask the storm raging beneath her skin. She gave a stiff nod, more out of reflex than understanding, her throat too tight to speak.

Without another word, Rylik stepped into his own room, leaving her alone with the echo of his presence like a haunting shadow. The door closed softly behind her, but it felt as final as a prison gate.

She let out a slow breath, turning to survey the lavish surroundings. The suite was beyond anything she had ever imagined for herself—a world of polished marble floors, velvet drapes, and ornate furnishings that belonged in stories, not her reality. Each detail spoke of wealth, of power, of a life that was leagues apart from her simple village home.

She crossed the room on unsteady feet, her eyes tracing the delicate carvings on the furniture, the shimmering silks draped over the bed. It was all untouched, pristine—so unlike the small, worn-down house she had grown up in, where her mother's voice hummed from the kitchen and her father mended tools by the hearth. She had never needed extravagance, never wanted it either.

Her fingers brushed the edge of a gilded chair as she circled the room, but her mind was elsewhere, clouded with the weight of what had just happened. Rylik's power hung heavy over her, but there was another more dangerous presence that loomed overhead—the king.

She shuddered at the thought of him. King Kaldros. A name that carried fear across the kingdom like a cold wind. He had ruled for as long as she could remember, longer than she had even been alive, his reign more like a suffocating fog, creeping over everything it touched and choking the life from it. Stories of his cruelty spread through the streets like a murmur carried on the wind, tales of innocent lives destroyed in the blink of an eye, of entire families erased from history on a whim. He was a man who thrived on control, who delighted in the suffering of others, and unfortunately, she had landed in the center of his court. She had never met the man, but knew it was only a matter of time before she would have to. She had only been brought to the palace this morning, and already she was in over her head. *I would have taken the first boat out of here if I'd known I was to be a prisoner*, she thought bitterly.

But she hadn't tried to run. And she knew why.

Her hand tightened against the back of the chair. *Leon.*

If it hadn't been for Leon, she might have run far from this place while she still had the illusion of the chance, far from the king, far from the danger that now curled around her like the bars of a cage. She could almost picture it—a quick escape, disappearing into the anonymity of some distant town. But Leon had always been there. He had been a constant in her life for as long as she could remember, a presence that made her feel safe, even when the world around her didn't. He had always been that good friend she could lean on, the one she could count on in ways that no one else could. Or at least, that's what she told herself.

A pang of doubt tugged at her, though she couldn't place why. Hadn't he always been there for her? There in the village, when they were just children playing in the fields, there after her healing powers had awakened and he joined the noble cause— the Rebellion. He was still there as things got harder, darker. He was dependable, a protector. But in the back of her mind, something nagged at her, a feeling she couldn't quite shake—was it really friendship that bound him to her? Or something else? She couldn't remember the last time he had truly listened, the last time he had asked her what *she* wanted. It had always been about the Rebellion, about the cause. She swallowed down the creeping realization, pushing it aside for now.

Still, despite everything, she couldn't forget that feeling—that warmth that had always flickered between them, even if Leon had never acknowledged it. Perhaps he couldn't feel it, and that was her burden to bear. *A one-sided love,* she thought with a wry smile. She was too smart to let herself fall into something like that, wasn't she? And yet here she was, entangled in a dangerous game because of it. Because he had asked her to stay.

She sank into the plush chair by the window, staring out into the vast, glittering landscape of Ravenhelm that sprawled beyond the glass. The weight of it all pressed against her—Leon's distant affection, the king's looming menace, and the Sovereign's cold, controlling presence. They were all tangled around her now, pulling her in different directions. And somewhere in the middle of it all, she was supposed to make sense of her life, of her choices.

But all she could think about was the one undeniable truth: no one would protect her but herself. The game had begun, and whether she liked it or not, she was now a player in it.

CHAPTER 2

ARIA

Morning light streamed through the vast windows of Aria's new suite, spilling across the stone walls and glinting off the polished wood and untouched furniture. The golden glow softened the edges of the room, making it feel almost peaceful. From the bathing room connected to the suite, the sound of water gently lapping at the edge of the tub was the only interruption to the stillness.

Aria sat immersed in the warm water, her thoughts drifting as the quiet solitude of the space surrounded her. The scent of lavender lingered in the air, a reminder of the lavish accommodations she had yet to fully claim as her own. But even as the beauty of the morning tried to coax her into ease, the weight of the previous night remained. The luxury surrounding her was in stark contrast to the tense grip of fear still wound tightly in her chest.

Rylik's words haunted her, his threat a constant murmur in her thoughts. She had replayed his voice again and again, the way he had measured every word, knowing exactly where to wound her without ever raising a hand. *But I'm still here.* Despite the tension in her shoulders and the lingering unease in her gut, she had awoken unharmed, her breath still warm in her chest. The night had passed in silence, and that small mercy was something she clung to, even if the relief was delicate, like a thread ready to snap.

She sighed, rubbing her temples as the soft morning air drifted through the bathing room, carrying the faint scent of jasmine from the courtyard below. The warm water embraced her, its heat seeping into her muscles, easing the tension that had gathered overnight. She leaned back, letting the stillness of the moment settle over her as she closed her eyes, enjoying the calm isolation. For the first time in hours, she felt the tension in her body begin to unwind. The heat seeped into her skin, unraveling some of the dread from her muscles as she let herself sink deeper into the tub.

Her thoughts wandered as she stared at the intricate mosaic lining the walls of the bath, the tiles glittering faintly in the daylight. She thought of Rylik's cold, penetrating eyes—how they seemed to see through her. Every move he made had carried a quiet menace, a controlled power that felt like a wolf's breath at her neck.

Once finished, she stood and stepped out of the bath, reaching for the towel draped over a chair. The soft linen brushed against her skin as she dried herself off, her damp red hair falling in loose curls over her shoulders. The familiar scent of lavender clung to her now, a faint reminder of home—of a time before all of this. For a brief moment, she allowed herself to relax. *I'm alone. I'm safe for now.*

She stepped into her room, her eyes settling on the small suitcase perched on a stool by the bed—the only belongings she owned, delivered the night before by a servant who hadn't even glanced her way. A single bag. It held everything she had brought from the village, but it felt like it belonged to a different life now. As she looked around the grand room—the rich sage curtains, the plush bedding, the hand-carved furnishings—she was reminded how far she had come from her humble beginnings. The luxurious suite was more opulent than anything she had ever lived in, far grander than her small room back home, where her parents still lived in quiet simplicity.

She wrapped the towel tighter around herself and padded toward her large window, gazing out over the sprawling palace gardens below. The flowers were in full bloom, a burst of color that almost made her forget the fear gnawing at her insides. If this was to be her prison, she could at least appreciate the view.

Aria took a deep breath, forcing herself to focus. Whatever the future held, whatever dangers awaited her in this palace, she would face them directly.

Suddenly, the door to her suite creaked open.

Her heart leaped into her throat. She gasped, clutching the towel to her chest as she whirled around.

"Sovereign?!" she exclaimed, eyes wide in shock.

Rylik stood in the doorway, his expression cool and entirely unfazed. His gaze swept over her leisurely, taking in her disheveled appearance—the towel clutched tightly around her, her tousled red hair still damp from the bath. A smirk tugged at the corner of his lips before he turned his back to her with deliberate nonchalance.

"Good morning, Healer," he said, his voice calm and smooth, as though this was the most natural of situations. "Slept in, I see."

Aria's shock quickly turned to anger as she darted across the room to hide behind her changing screen, her hands fumbling with the fabric. "It is customary to **knock** before entering a room, especially one with a woman inside!"

"Relax, dear." Rylik's tone was dismissive, his amusement at her expense obvious. "You're one of us now—a valuable asset to the Shadow Knights. We're going to be working very closely from now on, so you'll need to get used to my coming and going as I please."

Her hands trembled with frustration as she hurriedly dressed behind the screen, her voice strained as she called out to him. "You surely don't intend to imply that this sort of behavior will be commonplace?"

"No, of course not."

Aria paused, peering around the edge of the screen, her eyes narrowing suspiciously.

Rylik glanced over his shoulder at her, his smirk deepening. "I'm asserting it. There's no implication here." His gaze met hers with a flash of cold amusement. "I don't want you getting too comfortable."

Aria's face flushed with both embarrassment and anger as she ducked back behind the screen, quickly lacing up her corset. *How can he be so arrogant?* She fumed, struggling with the laces. She could hear him moving behind her, his presence filling the room.

Suddenly, the shadows seemed to shift, and she gasped as Rylik appeared just a few steps away from her. His approach was casual, but the dark energy that followed him was anything but.

Her heart lurched, and she backed up instinctively, still only half-dressed, her corset barely tied and her skirt falling loosely at her hips. "I swear I won't tell a soul about your Frostwraith Blight," she blurted, her voice rising in panic. "Please, I beg you, stop terrorizing me—"

Rylik stepped closer, his icy blue eyes locking onto hers, calculating. "You're more informed than I gave you credit for," he said, his tone cold, his gaze narrowing in suspicion.

Aria stumbled back, her hand reaching out to stop herself as she crashed into the stool behind her. She cursed herself inwardly as she felt her voice begin to tremble. *Oh, gods. My voice is practically squeaking. I need to get it together!*

Rylik paused, his eyes fixed on her unkempt state. For a brief moment, something in his expression shifted—his shoulders eased, and he sighed, his gaze sliding away from her.

"One of the Shadow Knights, Thorian, sustained an injury on a mission last night. He's in need of your services this morning. You're required immediately. Time is of the essence."

Aria blinked, caught off guard by the sudden change in subject. She stared at him for a moment before her frustration bubbled to the surface.

"With all due respect to Thorian's injury," Her tone was clipped, her anger barely contained. "I am *clearly* not dressed." She gestured to her state of undress with a sharp wave of her hand. "I'm sure he can survive another five minutes while I put on a proper dress and some boots."

Rylik's lips curved into a knowing smile, his eyes gleaming with mischief. "If you were not so exceptionally gifted, I'd say you were being careless," he remarked, his voice lilting with a hint of challenge. "But, in the future, you'll need to respond a little faster. I don't want my men getting the wrong impression of you."

"The wrong impression?" she retorted, her irritation boiling over. "They'll get the 'wrong impression' of me when I show up indecent to treat their wounds. I am a healer, not a tavern wench."

Rylik's smile deepened, his eyes trailing over her once more before he turned sharply on his heel and headed toward the door. "Five minutes," he called over his shoulder. "Make haste."

Aria stared after him, her hands clenched into fists, her body vibrating with anger. She glared at the back of his head, wishing for nothing more than to drive her boot straight into it as the door closed behind him.

* * *

When they arrived at the Shadow Knight's room, it was drenched in soft hues of blue, creating an inviting atmosphere that belied the tension of the moment. Aria knelt before the knight, Thorian, as she tended to a severe gash that marred his calf muscle.

The muted blue of his tunic paired with the black armor that fit snugly over his lean, well-built frame, hinting at his strength. She focused intently on the wound, her golden magic glowing softly through her palm.

As Aria's magic flowed into the injury, she felt the familiar warmth radiate from her hand. With each passing moment, the gash began to close, his dark skin returning to its unmarred state. She looked up just in time to catch the look of relief in Thorian's deep brown eyes. A smile spread across her face, and she couldn't help but feel a rush of satisfaction. *My favorite part.*

Thorian's eyes widened with surprise as he stood from his chair, testing his newfound mobility. "That is incredible." His voice held a note of awe as he marveled at her work. "Gods, what are you?"

Aria chuckled, the sound light and free in the cozy room.

Across the chamber, Rylik stood with his arms folded, his presence looming like a storm cloud. Dressed entirely in black, his ominous armor glimmered with threads of silver, the long cape cascading down his back. His pale blue eyes, sharp and piercing, scrutinized her as if assessing her worth.

15

Thorian, undeterred by Rylik's foreboding demeanor, jogged in place, flexing his calves and radiating enthusiasm. "Come on, Sovereign, even you have to admit this is amazing. Seriously, I don't think I've ever felt this good." He glanced down at Aria, excitement shining in his eyes. "Could you do this to my whole body?"

Aria laughed again, enjoying the lightheartedness of the moment.

Rylik's expression remained dim, unamused. "The lady has other matters to attend to today, Thorian."

Thorian shrugged, his playful spirit unyielding. "Well, if you change your mind," He winked at Aria, a mischievous glint in his eye. "I'll even slip you some extra gold."

With a swift motion, Rylik secured an arm around Aria, gently steering her toward the door. "That will be all, Thorian," he said over his shoulder, his tone brooking no argument.

Aria pulled away from Rylik as they exited the room, her eyes flickering uncomfortably back at him as they walked down the long hallway.

"Are you always so formal?" she asked, trying to fill the silence. "Even with your Shadow Knights?" She couldn't imagine working daily with the same people and never building camaraderie together.

Rylik, seemingly annoyed, ignored her question entirely. "We are going to visit the royal apothecary today, where you will be spending most of your time." His tone was clipped, giving little room for further discussion.

"An apothecary?" Aria's eyes became lively, excitement bubbling just beneath the surface. "With potions?"

Rylik noted her interest with a subject lift of his brow, but kept his tone neutral. "Yes. That is generally where potions are kept."

A smile crept across Aria's face. She had always loved and admired potion-making. Though it wasn't something she practiced herself—her healing magic was enough to help those in need—she adored the artistry involved in creating potions. To her, it was a craft filled with creativity and wonder.

Rylik observed her, his expression unreadable. "You will be meeting the Potion Master, Maven Feya. She is a fellow

16

court healer, and you will be working closely with her." They continued walking, and he added, "Your gifts are extravagant, but we do not always need extravagance. It would be unwise to let you lounge about all day simply because you're only needed some of the time."

As they stepped through the large double doors leading to the outer bailey, Aria scoffed quietly to herself despite the beautiful scenery surrounding them. *Yes, what a shame it would be if I were to "lounge about"*, she thought to herself. *It's not like every single day of my life has been filled with grueling housework and the constant flow of the infirm needing healing.*

She admired the vibrant flowers lining the trimmed garden, their colors vivid against the lush green foliage. As her gaze drifted up, she caught a glimpse of Rylik's face, finding a similar expression in his eyes as he looked at the blossoms. She quickly looked away, dismissing the notion that he might share in the beauty of the moment, convinced that such a serene expression was likely linked to some fresh kill he was reflecting on.

They soon arrived at the apothecary, a quaint yet cluttered space that felt warm and inviting. The air was thick with earthy scents, the mingling aromas of herbs and potions swirling together in a way that both comforted and inspired her. Aria breathed in deeply, savoring the view before her. Shelves lined the walls, brimming with an array of colorful glass vials and jars filled with vibrant liquids, each labeled with delicate, handwritten notes that hinted at their magical properties. Some glowed faintly, while others appeared murky and mysterious, catching the light in ways that made them seem almost alive.

In the center of the room, a sturdy wooden table bore the marks of countless experiments, its surface scattered with dried leaves, half-finished potions, and an assortment of mortar and pestles. Above, dried herbs hung from the beams of the ceiling, swaying gently like pendants, their scents releasing subtle hints of lavender, rosemary, and something more exotic that Aria couldn't quite place. A large window at the far end allowed sunlight to pour in, illuminating the dust motes dancing in the air and creating a warm, golden glow. In the corner, a cozy fireplace crackled softly, and for a moment, Aria felt a familiar sensation, as if she were home.

Maven entered the room mid-conversation, laughter spilling from her lips. With dark skin and long black hair braided elegantly down her back, she exuded a striking beauty. "I've already given you my answer," she said, clearly amused.

A man slipped in after her, his flirtatious aura drawing immediate attention. "But you gave it so fast, my love! Did you even consider it?" He was undeniably handsome, with light skin and long brown hair pulled into a topknot, clad in armor that combined black and gray with undertones of red and purple.

Maven swatted away his advances, her expression firm. "I am a healer, not a noblewoman. I will not be in attendance." Her gaze shifted to Rylik and Aria, and she paused, her smile brightening. "Oh! Visitors! Hello, welcome to my apothecary. As always, a pleasure to see you, Sovereign." Rylik acknowledged her with a slight nod.

Maven turned her attention to Aria, her expression shifting to curiosity. "Is this the Imperial Healer I've heard so much about?"

Aria was taken aback, surprised that the Potion Master appeared so young—seemingly her own age. She opened her mouth to speak, but Rylik interjected.

"This is Aria," he said, turning his head toward her. "Aria, this is Maven. You'll be spending most of your time here as an assistant to her. Treat her as your superior."

Maven stifled a faint smile, as if she were entertained by a private joke.

Rylik's tone sharpened as he directed his gaze to the armored man beside the healer. "Sylas. You wouldn't be bothering Maven, would you?"

Sylas straightened, a hint of unease creeping into his demeanor as he forced a smile. "Well, I—"

Hands clasped behind his back, Rylik lifted his chin. "I trust you are prepared for the meeting."

Sylas stiffened. "Of course. Absolutely, Sovereign. Definitely."

Rylik's gaze turned unamused as he saw through Sylas's poorly executed attempt at deception. "Prepare yourself, Sylas. Go."

With a bow at his waist, Sylas cut a sidelong glance and a smile toward Maven, who rolled her eyes in response, before he left the room briskly.

Rylik's gaze returned to Maven, serious now. "Don't let this one out of your sight, Maven." His eyes flicked to Aria, lingering for a moment as he cast her a smothering look that seemed to convey all the same warnings of the night before. Without another word, he turned and walked away, leaving the two women alone together.

Aria let out a soft breath, her shoulders relaxing slightly as the tension in the room began to ease.

Maven, watching the black-caped figure of the Sovereign retreating into the distance, remarked, "Sovereign's in a cheerful mood, I see."

"Is he always so," Aria hesitated, struggling to find the right word without being rude.

"Moody?" Maven guessed, a smile creeping across her face as Aria turned to meet her gaze. They shared a moment of cautious amusement. "Yes, he is often like that. And I suppose he has good reason to be, but," She shrugged. "Anyway, it's very nice to meet you, Aria."

Aria smiled back at her, warmth radiating from her. "And you as well, Lady Maven."

"Please, just Maven will be fine." The potion master sighed and turned away, walking toward her table cluttered with bottles and herbs. "Also, please disregard the Sovereign's order about treating me as a superior." She grabbed a bundle of herbs and placed them into a wicker basket, her laughter ringing softly in the air. "I hardly think that's appropriate, and I'd be uncomfortable with it." She glanced over her shoulder, her expression one of easy familiarity. "We are just two healers in the king's court. Nothing more, nothing less."

Aria felt a sense of relief wash over her at Maven's words.

Changing the topic to keep the atmosphere light, Maven asked, "So, how has your stay been so far?"

Aria approached the table, absently helping Maven put the dried herbs into the basket. "I'm enjoying my suite. I've met a couple of nice people already."

Maven eyed her slyly, a soft laugh escaping her lips. "I think it will be refreshing to work with someone so optimistic."

Aria hesitated, her fingers grazing over a bundle of herbs as she sensed a deeper current beneath Maven's cheerful demeanor.

"King Kaldros has a way of getting the finest talent in the kingdom, does he not?" Maven's purple eyes held a barely masked sadness, which she quickly breathed away. "I am glad to hear that you can find things to be happy about. That mentality will serve you well here."

A brief look of understanding passed between them. Aria wondered if Maven had been plucked from her village just as she had been, if she too missed her family in the same way. Placing another bundle of herbs into the basket, Aria cleared her throat, attempting to shift the topic. "So, um, who was that brunette man that was in here before? The one the Sovereign was chiding?"

Maven let out a soft huff, a hint of mild agitation lacing her voice but softened by a half-smile. "That was Sylas. He is one of the Sovereign's Shadow Knights. But don't let his demeanor fool you. He is lethal and terrifying in combat." She shook her head as if to dispel the image from her mind. "All four of them are, actually."

Aria's eyes widened in surprise. "I met another one of them this morning. One of the Shadow Knights, I mean. Thorian, I think his name was."

Maven laughed, rolling her eyes playfully. "Oh, gods, that's the worst one."

Aria felt her brows furrow in shock at Maven's candor.

Maven smiled cheekily. "That's my cousin."

"Really?" Aria was astonished.

"Yes." Maven's expression softened. "And he was in rough shape when I last saw him. If you've met him, you probably fixed him up. Thank you." With a nod of appreciation, she grabbed her basket of herbs and walked away, leaving the room to head outside.

Aria followed Maven, her footsteps light as she moved quickly to keep up. Suddenly, she collided with Maven's back, startled to find her halted, her focus fixed ahead.

"I'm s-sorry?" Aria stammered, peering around Maven to see what had caught her attention.

Maven was staring at a handsome young man framed in the doorway. He had tanned skin, trimmed blond hair, and glittering hazel eyes that seemed to catch the light in a way that made them sparkle. His broad, muscular frame was silhouetted against the brightness behind him, and he wore a loose tunic in neutral browns and grays that revealed a hint of his chest—undoubtedly a soldier in the king's army.

Aria felt her heart flutter involuntarily. "Leon."

CHAPTER 3

ARIA

Maven glanced back at Aria before turning her gaze back to Leon standing before them, a sheepish smile tugging at her lips. It almost seemed as if his presence had stifled her chatter completely away, but Aria didn't have time to ruminate on that observation for long before Leon spoke. "I need to borrow Aria," he muttered politely. "Please excuse me."

Then, without hesitation, he stepped inside, grasping Aria's wrist and pulling her gently but firmly away from Maven.

They slipped around the back of the apothecary, where the shadows of the outbuilding offered a moment of privacy, and Leon cast wary glances around them as he moved.

Leaning in closer, their bodies nearly touching and enveloped in the discreet shadows by the forest's edge, Leon asked in a low voice, "How are things proceeding?"

Aria took a deep breath, her heart racing as she reminded herself that his closeness was merely a necessity of their covert mission. He would never corner her for anything romantic. This was, and would always be, for the cause. "Nothing is proceeding, Leon." She sighed, the weight of her words heavy. "I've only been in this castle for maybe twenty-four hours."

"The Sovereign—you met him." He urged, his gaze intent as it searched hers for confirmation.

Aria felt a chill at the memory of their encounter the night before and averted her eyes. "Yes," she replied, discomfort creeping in.

"Have you learned anything?" Leon pressed, leaning in further.

Aria stiffened, unwilling to whisper even a hint of the Frostwraith Blight that plagued the man. Revealing his weakness would be a death sentence. "No. Like I said, it hasn't been that long—"

"What of the others? The knights? The king?" His questions came rapid-fire, each one a reminder of the urgency they faced.

"I've met half of the knights. Thorian and Sylas," she said, trying to maintain her composure. "I haven't met the other two yet, and I certainly haven't met the king." She hesitated, feeling the weight of Leon's expectations. "You have to give me time. Not everyone is just going to divulge their deepest secrets to me right away."

Leon scratched his head absently, stepping back from her to regain some space. "You're right. It will take time. Sorry."

"It's alright." Aria breathed out, relieved by the distance but wishing they could discuss something other than the Rebellion for once. Since Leon had joined the Rebellion five years ago, their conversations had become so burdened with tension that they rarely felt light anymore. He had infiltrated the king's army as an informant, a decision that ensured their lives would never return to what they once were.

"Orren is just really nagging at me," Leon said, his gaze scanning the back of the apothecary, always alert for potential threats. "He wants updates, and I feel bad when I don't have any for him."

Aria felt a wave of annoyance wash over her at the mention of Orren, the leader of the Rebellion. She had only met him a few days ago when she was informed that the king wanted to make her his imperial healer, her miraculous abilities drawing unwanted attention. "Well, he will have to learn patience," she said, crossing her arms defensively. And perhaps he would have to settle for useless information, because if the Sovereign's threat was to be believed, she would be taking his secret with her to the grave. She didn't trust Orren. She hardly trusted the Rebellion, but that's beside the point.

"Alright, well. Stay sharp." Leon nodded at her, his expression resolute as he turned to leave, mindful of their shared cause.

Aria watched him walk away, a glum feeling settling in her chest. *Not even a 'how are you?' or well wishes of any kind?* Frustrated, she turned back toward the apothecary. Why had she gone through all this trouble for him? He could at least feign concern for her. But she reminded herself that he was busy, weighed down by his own stresses. Perhaps later he would be more cordial.

* * *

As the sun dipped lower in the sky, casting a warm golden hue across the landscape, Aria and Maven enjoyed each other's company, and Aria couldn't help but feel that, one day soon, they would become good friends. Time seemed to slip away as they delved into discussions about healing techniques and the intricacies of potion-making, the atmosphere in the apothecary growing more familiar and inviting with each passing hour.

Just as the day began to give way to twilight, the Sovereign made his appearance, ready to escort Aria back to the main castle. With a gracious nod, he beckoned her to follow him, and together they strolled along the winding paths, the soft rustle of leaves accompanying their footsteps as they left the apothecary behind and returned to the confining walls of the castle.

The grand corridor stretched ahead of them, lit only by the wavering light of a torch every few feet. Aria's steps echoed faintly alongside the Sovereign's, her mind churning in the silence. The air felt thick with his presence, as though his mere proximity sought to unravel her defenses. She quickened her pace.

"I don't need an escort back to my room, thank you," she said, failing to suppress the tension rising within her.

Rylik, walking with infuriating ease beside her, replied without even a hint of yielding. "I'm simply being thorough."

Aria's gaze darted up to him, her lips pressing into a thin line. "By smothering me with your presence?"

The moment she said it, she regretted it. His cold blue eyes slid down to meet hers, the weight of his gaze oppressive. A tightness formed in her chest as she swallowed, forced to drop her defiance.

"Sovereign," she murmured, barely audible as her eyes cast downward.

They reached her chamber door, and Rylik opened it for her as if it were his right. With a hesitant glance, she stepped inside, but any relief at being back in her quarters vanished as he silently followed, closing the door behind him.

Her heart raced, unsettled by his persistence. Turning, she glared at him over her shoulder, her voice strained with unease. "How long do you intend to follow me around like a shadow?"

Rylik's expression remained impenetrable, though there was an undercurrent of amusement in his words. "Long enough for you to let down your guard, I suppose."

"I won't tell anyone about your secret. I swear it!" Aria's voice sharpened, her desperation clear. "I have no intention of turning my life into chaos. I want a simple life with good pay so I can take care of my family. Why would I ever jeopardize that?"

Rylik's lips curled faintly into a half-smile, his gaze predatory as he stepped closer. "That's what I intend to find out. You already know more than you should, and I've learned better than to place trust in something as fickle as a person's word."

Aria instinctively stepped back, her heart hammering in her chest. Her body tensed as his cold presence loomed over her. "It won't last, you know," she said quickly, her voice trembling despite her best efforts to sound steady. "The effects of my healing on your blight will fade."

"I am aware," Rylik said, his voice smooth, almost indifferent. His piercing gaze remained fixed on her. "I feel it slowly returning, covering my blood in ice." There was a pause, his eyes watching her closely. "But, you will heal it again. As many times as necessary."

"Of course," Aria murmured, swallowing hard as she braced herself. "I am the healer to the king, to the Shadow Knights, and to you, Sovereign. If there is anything that ails you it is my obligation to heal it."

"So it is," Rylik agreed, the cold intrigue never leaving his face.

"I will," Aria gathered what little courage she had left, squaring her shoulders as she met his gaze. "I will take care of you, Sovereign." Her tone was firmer now, though the nervous tremor in her hands betrayed her.

Rylik's smirk deepened, as though he found her defiance diverting. "Will you?"

She clenched her fists, struggling to hold her ground under the weight of his scrutiny.

Rylik exhaled softly, straightening his posture. His voice shifted, now tinged with the authority that came so easily to him. "Be in my room in two hours."

Aria's eyes widened, her concern immediate. "For what purpose?"

"As you so astutely pointed out, I require your additional services," Rylik said with casual detachment.

Her legs shifted uneasily beneath her as she murmured low, "Services?"

"Healing," he clarified, though there was a hint of roguishness in his eyes as he added, "What other services would I require of you?"

She felt an unbidden wave of heat flush her cheeks and she glanced away from him.

Intrigued, he drew closer, a taunting expression playing across his features. "Unless, of course, you have other services in mind?"

"No," Aria chirped, the rising panic in her chest making her voice tight. "And to assume anything otherwise would be improper and scandalous—"

"Settle yourself," Rylik's voice cut through her protest with a smirk. "My, you are rather fiery, aren't you?"

Aria clenched her jaw, clearly wanting to say more, but instead biting her tongue.

"Stay in this room for the next two hours," Rylik ordered, his tone laced with calm certainty. "And then come to me, promptly."

Aria hesitated, her gaze lifting cautiously toward him. "I'm tired. What if I'm asleep by then? Can it not wait until morning?"

A shadowed smile curved his lips as he stepped closer, his form looming over her, watching the way she subtly leaned back in response to his presence. "I do not wait. I take what I want at precisely the time I want to." Rylik's voice was low as he reached out, his hand grazing the loose strands of her spiraling red hair. He took a lock of it between his fingers, the faintest tinge of devilry in his eyes as he held it. "So, if you are not in my bedchambers in two hours' time, then I will drag you from your bedsheets, nightgown and all, and you'll remain in my suite until morning, little Pyra."

Aria felt her heart racing at the brief touch and the accompanying threat. With a panic, she jerked her head away, pulling the strand from his grasp. "I'll be there," she snapped, her voice dripping with exasperation. "On time, Sovereign."

Rylik only smiled, his eyes tracing her a moment longer before he turned sharply on his heel, the door closing behind him.

CHAPTER 4

RYLIK

Rylik stepped into his suite, the heavy wooden door clicking softly behind him. The room was grand yet severe, much like its occupant—bathed in deep hues of red and gold, with heavy drapes hanging at the tall windows, partially blocking out the golden light of dusk from outside. Embers glowed faintly as the fire murmured in the hearth of his fireplace, filling the air with a comforting stillness. The furnishings were simple but elegant, each piece meticulously chosen: a large bed with dark, intricately carved posts, a long wooden desk, and small table framed by two chairs before the fireplace.

Rylik unclasped his black cape and draped it across the back of the chair as he crossed the room. He lowered himself into the seat, the leather creaking slightly under his weight. His head fell back against the cushioned rest as he exhaled, the tension in his chest easing, if only for a moment. His thoughts drifted, settling on the name that had begun to haunt him. *Aria Thorne.*

His eyelids fluttered open, the glow of the fire reflecting in his pale eyes as the memory of the previous night flooded back— her arrival in his chambers, her quiet presence. The first thing that had struck him was her beauty, unexpected and understated in the simplicity of her appearance. But it wasn't her looks that troubled him now. It was the way she had so effortlessly calmed the Frostwraith Blight that chilled him to his core. That magic—her magic—had seeped into him, warmth flooding the icy void that always plagued his chest.

Instinctively, he raised his hand, fingers brushing the black armor that still covered him. His chest still ached with the familiar cold, creeping back in where her touch had banished it, if only for a short time. His fingertips traced the outline of his breastplate, nails faintly scratching at the surface before drifting upward to his lips, deep in thought.

Rylik's thoughts wandered back to that fateful day, etched into his memory like a scar. It had been years since the battle, a day when the glory of war had nearly swallowed him whole. He had led a battalion of the king's army into the fray, cutting down one of the king's greatest enemies, a battle that should have been his triumph. But the victory soured when the defeated duke, desperate and cornered, unleashed a weapon that had been his final, vicious defense—a jagged, icy blue blade, glowing with the dark magic of Frostwraith.

The enchanted weapon had cut through Rylik's chest as though his armor were nothing more than paper. The pain had been unlike anything he had ever known, a cold that burrowed into his bones, freezing him from the inside out. Though Rylik struck back with a fatal blow, ending the duke's life, the damage had already been done. The satisfaction in the dying man's eyes had haunted him ever since—he had known, with terrible certainty, that he had left Rylik with a curse, one that would not kill him swiftly, but would gnaw at him, day by day, year by year.

For a lesser man, the Frostwraith Blight would have been a death sentence within hours. But Rylik had refused to die. His rage, his relentless will to survive, had kept him alive when the cold had threatened to claim him. He had endured it, fought against the blistering freeze that settled in his chest like a parasite, weakening him with every passing moment.

His gaze found the corner of the room, where shelves held rows of neatly assembled potions, the only reprieve from the curse that had plagued him for a decade. Hidden behind those cabinets was the elixir that had become his lifeline. Derived from

Volcanis magic, it was a searing, liquid fire that burned as it coursed through him. The pain of consuming it was sharp, but it was nothing compared to the icy grip of the Blight. Without it, he would have succumbed long ago.

He savored the memory of the warm, intoxicating heat Aria had bestowed upon him, an ember of relief that still flickered within his mind. It was a sensation he craved like a drug, a peace that had eluded him for far too long. Now, it was embodied in the form of a young woman whose power resided just beyond his reach in the adjoining suite. He hungered for her gifts, a desperate need gnashing at his insides. Yet, he could not allow her to see the depths of his longing; he had to remain formidable, a figure of fear and authority. She must understand her place in his world. To lose her now would be to expose his weakness — not merely a flaw, but a chink in the armor of his ambition. With her at his side, he could wield unparalleled power, and in the treacherous game he played, vulnerability was an invitation for defeat.

Rylik's grip tightened on the arm of his chair as he rose, determination igniting within him. He strode to his shelves, opening one of the cupboard doors with a swift motion, his eyes narrowing as he selected a small vial filled with a shimmering orange potion, its contents glistening like molten gold in the firelight. With a practiced ease, he uncorked it and tilted it back, the burning liquid pouring down his throat like white-hot flames, searing a path into his chest and soothing the blight with its fierce embrace. A breath of relief escaped him, fleeting and hollow compared to the healing Aria had granted him with a mere touch.

His pale blue eyes hardened, now fixed with a calculating clarity. Her gift was extraordinary, a treasure that could reshape his very existence. He understood why the king sought to keep her close, yet he was certain the monarch failed to grasp the full extent of her capabilities. To pacify a wound as fatal as his was a feat that seemed impossible — yet she had done it. Though still shackled by his injury, she possessed the power to restore him to his former glory. He needed that restoration; he was far from finished in this palace.

He strode purposefully to the door of his adjoining suite,

pacing before it as if commanding it to yield. The Volcanis Elixir could offer him only a fleeting reprieve. While it would alleviate his cold for a few hours, nothing could compare to the sensation of Aria's hand pressed against his heart. That touch would grant him relief that lasted until morning, just as it had when he awoke hours earlier, the sounds of maids bustling about as they prepared her bath in the bathing room.

A smirk curled his lips. She likely had no inkling it was his bath, which explained her ease in allowing her guard to drop, traipsing about naked without a care. He studied the door, as if he could pierce through its barrier. He had nearly given in to the temptation of interrupting her bath, drawn by the melody of her soft humming that floated through the wall, accompanied by the gentle splashes of water as she moved. An intoxicating curiosity brewed within him, imagining how she might appear with her defenses stripped away.

He had waited until she was safely in her room before emerging to greet her. He could have lingered a little longer, after hearing the soft creak of the door as she entered her suite. He could have given her time to dress, but he wasn't a gentleman—and she must not mistake him for one. Comfort, he thought, would be a luxury she could ill afford. He recalled the sight of her fondly, when he had seen her by the window, enveloped in the soft morning light. Her red curls were damp from the bath, and the towel she wore clung to her form, revealing more than it concealed.

Approaching the door, he found his thoughts spiraling into the depths of desire with every step. Was it merely her power that ensnared him, or was there something darker at play, a twisted longing he was reluctant to confront? He turned away, his attention drawn to the window as the sun dipped slowly behind the mountains.

Rylik sighed as he approached his desk. Another dinner tonight, another tedious procession of sycophants, filling the table with the same dull faces, the same endless praise and pointless exchanges. He could already picture it—himself standing behind the king, a silent shadow as the man prattled on to his favorites. Lord Orren Soltren would no doubt be there, leaning in with his ever-smirking face, grasping every chance to ingratiate himself further. And Rylik, as always, would watch from his post, alert yet utterly disengaged, masking his boredom behind the facade of vigilant guard. It was a familiar role, but one he could do without tonight.

His fingers absently brushed over a small signet ring resting on his work desk, its polished black stone gleaming in the firelight. The silver symbol etched into the tarnished obsidian band—two crossed swords over a crescent moon—was jagged, split by a crack running through it. He picked it up, turning it over in his hand with a wistful expression before sliding it into a drawer and shutting it with a soft snap.

He had only two objectives for the evening: Suffer through the king's dinner, and then return to his room to be graced by Aria's healing presence.

* * *

The grand dining hall was alive with revelry, the low thrum of laughter and conversation blending with the lilting music of the bards. Their harps and lutes sang of old conquests, a soundtrack perfectly attuned to the king's tastes. Firelight glinted over the polished marble floor, radiating a warm, amber glow over the dark wood table crowded with gleaming plates and brimming goblets. Servants bustled in and out, keeping the nobles' wine refreshed, while the smell of roasted meats and spices hung heavy in the air.

At the head of the table sat King Kaldros, his broad chest and powerful build filling the space with an imposing presence. His dark brown hair framed his head like a lion's mane, thick and wild, while his equally formidable beard curled over his chest. He looked every inch the ruler, but any semblance of elegance was lost in his approach to his meal. Grease glistened on his fingers, and every bite he took was punctuated by a loud, hearty chew. A young woman, all soft curves and doe-eyed adoration, perched on his knee, slipping grapes past his lips between bites. She was one of his latest indulgences, her silken gown clinging in all the right places as she leaned in to brush his lips with each offering, her laughter blending with the clink of goblets around the table.

Standing behind him, Rylik observed the scene with a blank, disciplined face. To anyone watching, he was merely a loyal shadow. But inwardly, he felt a simmering disapproval. This messy display, this show of power through indulgence and cruelty—it was, in a word, distasteful. The king savored his own excess as if each sloppily eaten bite somehow reinforced his authority.

"Ah, but Eldric," the king was saying, his voice carrying over the music, thick with cruel enjoyment. "He sang like a bird for me when I broke his fingers." He barked a laugh, taking another grape from his mistress, who giggled obediently and stroked his beard, whispering some encouragement into his ear.

Lord Eldric, once a nobleman who had sat proudly at this very table, had fallen from grace when his ties to the Rebellion were exposed last year. Since then, the king had made a game of the man's suffering, using him as a source of information and toying with him like a cat with prey. Eldric's weak constitution meant he needed little persuasion to talk, but that hardly stopped Kaldros. The king was a man who savored pain, who took grim pleasure in breaking others. Rylik didn't fault him for his brutality—he was no stranger to ruthless measures himself. But there was a time to be cruel and a time to be tactful, a balance Kaldros had never learned to strike.

The king turned to Lord Orren, his closest advisor and loyal flatterer. "You should've seen him, Orren. A man of his station, begging like a dog. It would almost make you pity him—if it wasn't so pathetic."

Orren chuckled along, leaning forward with an eager gleam in his eyes. He was a muscular man of similar age, his red beard thick and well-kept, his hair framing a face as sharp as his tongue. "Your Majesty," he said, voice dripping with admiration, "it is your unmatched wisdom that brought him to his knees. Who else could command such fear and loyalty with only a look?" Orren's voice was soft, reverent, as though he were speaking to a god instead of a man dripping wine onto his own tunic.

The other nobles echoed Orren's praise, nodding with enthusiasm, vying for the king's attention. Goblets clinked, compliments were lavished, and beneath it all was a desperate eagerness to remain in the king's good graces.

Orren, like many seated at the king's table, was as cunning as he was ruthless. If there was anyone worth watching closely, it was him. He had been an advisor to the king for years, an elitist who reveled in the rigid hierarchy, taking pleasure in seeing peasants far beneath his boot. To him, wealth meant worth, and the noble class belonged firmly at the top. Rylik suspected that Orren harbored ambitions for the throne himself, though only time would reveal whether he'd dare risk it. Kaldros, after all, was no ordinary ruler; his mastery of magic made him formidable. He could control time in brutal ways, suspending an attacker mid-motion, savoring violence against them in repeated, twisted loops until he grew bored.

Orren, like those closest to Kaldros, was a formidable man himself, though the full extent of his magic remained a mystery. Orren was secretive by nature, sharing little of his power or past victories, but his reputation was enough—no opponent had bested him in combat, or so he claimed. Rylik, however, harbored suspicions that Orren's victories were built on more than skill alone.

"When do you plan to put the traitor out of his misery, my king?" Orren inquired, a spark of intrigue gleaming in his amber eyes.

Kaldros chuckled, leaning back as his mistress fed him another grape. "I imagine when his cries are no longer quite so *amusing*."

The nobles around the table joined in laughter, as if the king had shared some private, twisted joke.

Rylik stood unyielding, noting every gesture, every exchange. The king, for all his brute strength and regal bearing, had a twisted affinity for these hollow praises and flaunted his mistresses like prized possessions.

A brief flare of agitation crossed Rylik's mind, unnoticed behind his stoic expression. If he were in charge, he'd cut through this wasteful excess, trade the shallow loyalty for something earned, something honest. But here he was, watching the king devour his meal as carelessly as he toyed with his subjects, a man who gloried in his own power and savored the fear he could command.

"Your Majesty, when will you finally introduce us to your new healer? We've all heard tales of her miraculous abilities," one of the noblemen inquired, inclining his head respectfully. At the mention of Aria, Rylik's attention sharpened, though he maintained his impassive stance behind the king's chair.

Kaldros reclined, a lazy smirk on his face. "All in due time. I haven't even met the woman myself," he replied, his tone as casual as if they were discussing the weather.

Another nobleman, Lord Clarence, hiccupped as he finished his drink, leaning forward in his chair with enthusiasm. "I've seen her, actually. It was only in passing—I was at the apothecary for my medicine—but I caught sight of her. For a commoner, she's easy enough on the eyes."

The king's eyebrow arched with interest. "Is that so? Describe her for me."

Rylik kept his expression steady, though he loathed the turn this conversation was taking. Clarence, swaying slightly from drink, made a crude squeezing motion with his hands, evoking laughter from the table. "She's got a good set, Your Grace, and red hair you'd want to wrap around your fingers."

Rylik's gaze darkened, settling coldly on Clarence, a man who might soon require a lesson, one of swift and bloody persuasion.

The king's smirk deepened as he took a slow sip from his goblet, his expression contemplative. "I rarely lower myself to consort with commoners, but, if she is as appealing as you suggest," his voice trailed off as his mistress leaned in, whispering something into his ear, her words eliciting a glint of crude interest in his eyes. "But for tonight, gentlemen, I'm already occupied with a most enticing beauty."

The men raised their goblets in approval, toasting as the king rose, taking his mistress's hand with a pleased smile. He cast a dismissive glance back at Rylik, offering a curt nod before exiting the hall.

Rylik mirrored the gesture, bowing in acknowledgment, but instead of relief, a shadow of unease settled over him. Aria should never have been a subject of entertainment for these men.

"Maybe I ought to visit the lady in the apothecary myself, tonight," a nobleman murmured to Clarence, chuckling as he tipped back his glass of wine.

Clarence smirked, his grin stretching lazily from the effects of the wine. "She's likely already in bed—maybe I'll just summon her to mine instead."

"You're incorrigible. She's a healer," his friend snickered. "She's not a whore."

"She will be when I'm done with her," Clarence laughed and made a crude gesture, drawing another chuckle from his companion. Their conversation was mostly swallowed by the lively hum of minstrels and other voices, yet Rylik, listening nearby, missed none of it.

He allowed himself one last, dismaying glance at the room, the unsavory sense that keeping Aria from the reach of these nobles, and perhaps the king, would prove to be more difficult than he'd anticipated.

* * *

Later that night, Rylik stalked through the dim, winding corridors of the palace, each step driven by a brooding displeasure from the evening's revolting display. He'd had his fill of the king's tasteless indulgences, and the thought of returning to his own rooms was a relief—a place where he could shed the day's frustrations and steel himself with Aria's healing touch. The burning torchlight cast his shadow along the stone walls as he finally reached his door, his hand tightening around the handle with an exhale of anticipation before he pushed it open and stepped inside.

His eyes caught immediately on Aria's wild, curling red hair, gleaming in the firelight as she stood by the hearth, dressed just as she had been when he'd left her only hours before. She looked over her shoulder at him, a hint of hesitation in her gaze. "You're late," she said, her voice a soft reprimand. He smirked at her remark, locking the door behind him as he approached with deliberate steps.

"Late, am I?" A dark part of him had relished in the hope that she might defy him tonight—a twisted impulse to drag her from her bed as he'd threatened, picturing her in nothing but a nightgown, vulnerable and pliant.

"Yes, it's quite late, actually," she retorted, edging back as he closed the distance. "You should've been here at least an hour ago. I've been struggling to stay awake." Her words held a bite, but he only gestured smugly toward his bed, noting the wrinkle in her brow as she resisted the invitation.

"You need healing, right? Let's just get it over with." She extended a shaky hand, hovering it near his chest but hesitating.

"Are you nervous?" he asked coolly, relishing her unease. He ached for her touch, yet he wouldn't let her see it.

"Of course I am," she murmured, "You're the Sovereign. You have a reputation, and I'm not about to be the next victim on your list of kills." There was a slight slur in her words that he hadn't noticed when she'd first spoken.

His eyes flitted to a wine glass on his small table, a small bead of merlot at bottom. A smirk curved at his lips as his attention drifted back over to her, noting the pinkness in her cheeks, the unsteadiness in her balance. She had been drinking, though clearly not enough to have taken away her ability to speak and stand. She was nervous, perhaps hoping to dull the edge of her fear by helping herself to his personal collection of wine.

He reached out, capturing her hand and pressing it firmly against his chest. "I can assure you," he murmured, voice low, "there is nothing you could do to find yourself on my 'list of kills,' Aria. Need I remind you of how indispensable you are?" Her flinch only deepened his satisfaction, his smirk turning cruel. "Play your role to my satisfaction, and we'll get along just fine."

"I'll try to do that," she muttered, her eyes gleaming a soft golden hue as she summoned her magic.

As Aria's energy flowed into him, warm and vibrant, Rylik felt the familiar, painful chill recede. It was a welcomed reprieve, and in that moment, he allowed himself to bask in the warmth of her power. He exhaled slowly, feeling his shoulders relax as the healing took effect. His typically sharp features softened just a fraction, revealing a glimpse of tranquility that he rarely permitted himself. Here, in the solace of her touch, he found a brief sanctuary from the encroaching cold that haunted him.

Yet, as Aria's energy waned and she withdrew her hand, a sense of desperation clawed at him. The warmth faded too quickly, leaving behind a seething anger at what he knew would bring the inevitable return of his affliction by morning. He felt greedy—insatiable. He opened his eyes, his gaze locked onto her, measuring the distance she had created.

He could keep her here. She was entirely at his mercy, after all, and the thought of several advantages to having her in his bed was enticing. He imagined that warmth nestled against his chest through the night, a comforting heat that would last until morning. His mind drifted back to the noblemen's crude remarks at the dinner table, their shameless speculation about her. And yet here she stood, barefoot in his suite, close enough to hold—to savor. She was drowsy, her balance faintly swaying; a few more sips of his prized wine might make her a little less guarded. A little more persuadable. He closed his eyes, temptation pulling at the edges of his control.

"Goodnight," he said, his voice calm, betraying none of the turmoil beneath his composed exterior.

Aria paused, wavering as she regarded him. Her eyes narrowed slightly, warily assessing his expression to no avail. "Goodnight, Sovereign," she replied, her tone subdued, before turning to leave the room, her movements unsteady and uncoordinated.

Rylik stared lazily into the fire of his hearth, the sound of the door's latch clicking into place with Aria's departure. His fingers lightly traced the spot on his chest where Aria's hand had been, and he exhaled slowly. The warmth he felt now was almost foreign, a stark contrast to the chilling numbness of his blight.

Damn. I haven't felt this revitalized in years. How can she do in a moment what the Volcanis Elixir cannot? The fire's blaze seemed almost alive, a vibrant testament to the healing she had bestowed upon him. He knew the sting of his affliction would deepen by morning, and no amount of prolonging her touch would prevent that. Even so, he wanted it. He knew he could order her to heal him whenever he pleased. She was his captive, and it wasn't her place to deny him.

He stood up, the weight of his thoughts pressing down on him. He turned away from the fireplace, his fingers sliding over one another in a restless gesture. He had been close to making a very poor decision born of his own desperation. He wasn't quite the lecher that the king was, but he did enjoy a woman's company as much as the next man. Aria was beautiful, but more than that she was a necessity. Sharing her with anyone – including the king – was simply something he could not allow. And if she was to belong to anyone, she would belong to him alone.

He cast one final glance toward the door to her suite, his gaze fixed as if he could still sense her warmth on the other side. But there were other matters to attend to tonight—one, in particular, that might ease his frustrations. Turning on his heel, he strode across his room, his steps measured yet darkly intent, until he reached his own door.

Waiting far beyond it was someone whose insolent tongue had earned him a place on Rylik's list. Tonight, he would see to it that the impudent lord met with an unfortunate accident, one that would silence him—permanently. With his well-known lechery, there wouldn't be a single woman in the palace who would mourn him. Rylik's hand tightened on the doorknob, a smile curving at his lips as he savored the promise of retribution.

CHAPTER 5

ARIA

The next morning, Aria sat rigidly on her sofa, her arms folded tightly across her chest as she stared at the door. *I woke up at dawn, had the fastest bath of my life, and got dressed in record time.* Her gaze fixed on the door as if willing it to open, she continued to brood. *I will not let him catch me half naked ever again. What time did he even come in here yesterday? Will he make a habit of it, I wonder?* The thought of walking into his room and catching him half naked flickered through her mind, and she quickly shook her head, a faint blush creeping across her cheeks. *Get the mental image out of your head, Aria!* She groaned softly, trying to banish the unwelcome thoughts.

The door to her room swung open, and Rylik entered with his usual confident stride. His presence filled the room as he approached her. "Good morning, Pyra. I'm glad to see you're prepared for the day ahead."

Aria stood reluctantly, her nerves on edge. "Is there a reason I have to be up so early? Will you always be here this hour?"

Rylik's eyes gleamed with a hint of playfulness. "I will make it a habit moving forward to not follow a predictable pattern, lest you grow to anticipate my moves with any sort of accuracy."

"But I've told you, I won't tell anyone about the—"

"So you've said." Rylik glanced back at her as he walked toward the door. "I'll ensure that your loyalty toward me remains unwavering."

Aria's unease deepened, her thoughts racing as she followed him. The weight of his words hung heavily in the air, a constant reminder of the precarious balance she was forced to maintain.

The long stone corridors of the castle echoed with murmurs as a cluster of maids stood gathered just ahead, their voices low but unmistakably animated.

"Did you hear?" one woman whispered, eyes wide.

The other nodded, leaning in. "About Lord Clarence? Yes! Just this morning."

"I know he's a boorish drunk, but I can't believe he'd be so foolish as to fall off a turret," the first maid muttered, pulling in close as if her body was enough of a sound barrier.

"If you ask me, the scoundrel had what was coming to him—"

"Shh, Marie!"

"Why, it was only last week that he forced Reina to—"

"Marie! Hush!" The second woman hissed, her expression shifting to alarm as her gaze fixed on Rylik and Aria approaching. The maids dropped into polite bows before hastily dispersing down the hall, their conversation stifled to a whisper that faded into the distance.

Aria, however, was hardly paying attention. Her mind retraced the events of last night, replaying moments she could barely recall with clarity. Nervous about facing him, she had indulged in two glasses of wine to calm her nerves, only to wonder now if she had perhaps loosened her tongue a bit too much in his company. She stole a glance at him as his cape swirled around his frame, his gaze fixed straight ahead, seemingly oblivious to her disquiet.

They emerged into the sunlight of the outer bailey, the warmth of the day brushing over her. Her anxiety began to ease—if she had overstepped last night, he hadn't mentioned it. Their exchange had been direct, almost clinical: he'd asked for her healing, received it, and dismissed her. Could their arrangement really be so simple? A cold exchange of secrecy for service? And if that was the case, she found herself uneasy with her own complicity.

A pang of guilt gnawed at her. By keeping his condition a

secret, was she betraying the Rebellion? His blight—this hidden weakness—could shift the tide in the struggle against the king's forces. Rylik's strength was nearly mythic; his command of the crown's defenses unassailable. The Rebellion's greatest weapon against him might be a simple truth. Yet, here she was, protecting it—aiding it, even.

As they continued down the garden walkway, her eyes strayed to his back. His dark hair caught the sunlight, its sleek strands gleaming like polished obsidian. He moved with the ease and grace of someone who sensed every subtle shift around him. She felt a chill of doubt, her gaze tightening as if seeking an answer in his stride. Escape seemed nearly impossible, yet her thoughts drifted there more and more.

But even the thought of whispering his secret to Leon made her chest tighten in dread. Rylik's warning hovered like a blade's edge over her family, the implied threat casting a shadow over her every impulse.

Without warning, Rylik turned to face her, and she realized she'd fallen behind. "Are you tired?" he asked, his voice carrying the faintest note of sarcasm.

Aria's pulse quickened, and she hurried her steps along the cobbled path to close the distance. "No," she muttered, though she was far from fine.

She bristled hurriedly past him and toward the apothecary in the distance. Behind her, his footsteps had resumed, engulfing her stride and effortlessly closing the gap between them. She quickened her steps toward the apothecary's door, feeling a surge of relief as she finally reached the threshold. Crossing into the room, she was instantly comforted by the fragrant air, thick with the scents of dried lavender, rosemary, and the earthy tang of various roots and herbs.

The scene inside was lively: Maven, sleeves rolled to her elbows, hovered over a broad-shouldered man seated before her. She had a flush across her cheeks, whether from the warmth of her work or from irritation, Aria couldn't tell. Strands of hair had slipped loose from her braid, framing her face as she carefully wound a fresh bandage around the man's abdomen. Aria didn't recognize him, but judging by his physique, she could assume he was a soldier or a knight. He looked formidable, with muscular arms and a rugged face marked by scars that told a story of countless battles. His dark hair, cropped close, highlighted his intense brown eyes that held a sharp but weary glint.

"I've told you," Maven said over her shoulder to Sylas who was approaching her from behind, "I will not be going." Her voice sharpened with frustration as she continued to mend the knight in front of her. Sylas, oblivious or simply undeterred, leaned in with a relaxed charm that bordered on pestering, one brow arched as he persisted.

"Oh, come now, Maven. You'll be missed if you don't go. A shame, really," he urged, his gaze trailing over her with a practiced calmness.

"No, and please stop asking," Maven insisted, her tone growing more dismissive as she half-heartedly waved Sylas away.

"Gods, Sylas," the wounded knight muttered, "How many rejections do you need? At this point, I'll just be your date to shut you up."

Sylas smirked, sparing the knight a look. "You wouldn't look nearly as good in a dress, Kaelith." He laughed under his breath.

Rolling her eyes, Maven gave Kaelith's bandage a firm pat, perhaps a little harder than necessary, as she finished up. "Please, get some rest for that wound." Her words were more gentle, though her impatience with Sylas hadn't faded. Just then, she looked up, noticing Aria and Rylik standing quietly in the doorway. Maven's lips parted in surprise, her annoyance replaced by a look of relief.

"Oh, Aria! Fantastic timing!" she exclaimed, brushing an errant strand of hair back from her forehead as she straightened. "I wish you'd been here ten minutes ago. Where have you been?"

Rylik's gaze darkened as he watched Kaelith, who was awkwardly pulling his shirt over the fresh bandages, a faint hint of color in his cheeks as his eyes kept drifting toward Maven. "Kaelith," he said, his tone smooth but edged with steel, "the Shadow Knights have a new healer for injuries like that. You have a mission tonight, and I can't afford to have you lagging behind."

Kaelith grumbled, glancing at Maven as he fumbled to sheath his blade at his side. "I have my preferences," he muttered as he turned away, face flushed with what Aria could only assume was fondness for the healer.

"Your preferences in women do not supersede the requirements of your duties," Rylik replied sharply, barely keeping his patience in check. Kaelith's brief blush deepened, and with a small, sheepish nod, he reluctantly moved away from Maven, his shoulders hunched slightly as he did.

Meanwhile, Maven, already weary from the bustle of the apothecary, didn't notice Kaelith's reluctance to leave her side. She was already moving across the room, her attention pulled in every direction but toward the men who hovered too close. Her irritation grew as she sensed Sylas still trailing after her, his flirtatious persistence wearing thin.

"Leave the healer alone," Rylik ordered, his voice a low, dangerous murmur. "As she said, there are other ladies you could ask."

Sylas hesitated, his easygoing charm faltering under the weight of Rylik's unrelenting glare. He offered a halfhearted shrug, raising his hands in reluctant surrender. "Is it my fault that there are so few women who meet my standards?" he muttered as he turned, snatching a vial from the table and striding away with a begrudging swagger. His head was still half-turned over his shoulder, lost in a parting smirk, just as he nearly collided with another figure—Leon, who was just entering.

Leon's entrance was like a shift in the room's center of gravity. His stride was purposeful, his build solid and steady, carrying an air of command even before he spoke. He stopped sharply, eyes narrowing as he shot a glare at Sylas, the flicker of restrained irritation clear. But with a quick breath, Leon recalled himself, his hazel eyes flicking downward as he clenched his jaw.

"Excuse me, Sir Knight. My apologies. Should've been looking where I was going," he muttered, his voice clipped, though his tone remained respectful.

Sylas, hardly seeming to notice or care, tossed a final glance at Maven—a somewhat self-satisfied look—before he slipped out of the apothecary, leaving a faint trail of tension behind him.

The room settled, but not entirely. Leon's presence carried an undercurrent, subtle but distinct, that didn't go unnoticed by Maven. She stood at the herb-laden table, her usual poise slightly faltering, her fingers moving faster than necessary as she ground herbs together. Her face had taken on a shade of red that Aria hadn't seen on her before. It was as though his arrival had unsettled her careful composure. Though, perhaps she was still a little ruffled by Sylas's advances.

Aria moved closer to the table, hoping to settle the energy in the room, even as her attention drifted toward Rylik, whose presence at the door held its own magnetic pull.

"Anything I can help with?" Aria asked Maven, hoping to bring a semblance of normalcy back.

Maven let out a breath, her fingers pressing the herbs into the mortar with a little too much force. "Yes, you can find a date for Sylas so I'll have a moment's peace around here," she replied, her tone laced with irritation.

Leon's brows lifted as he stepped up beside Aria, his voice steady but curious. "A date for what?" he asked, his eyes fixed on Maven with an intensity that felt more than casual.

Maven bit her lip, her gaze darting away from his, clearly avoiding his direct look as she replied, quieter this time, "A date to the ball, of course."

"Oh?" Leon's tone softened, a playful note entering his words. "Are you not going? Are healers not allowed to attend?" His gaze remained on her, and though Aria's attention kept slipping to Rylik by the door, Leon's focus on Maven was unmistakable.

"I mean, I could go if I had a reason to," Maven admitted, her words hesitant as her fingers continued to fidget with the herbs, not meeting his gaze.

Leon's grin brightened, a familiar boyish charm he wore effortlessly. "I hope to see you there," he said, his voice gentler, as if the moment held something unsaid. Maven's cheeks flushed deeper, and she managed a shy, coy smile, a nod barely containing her own uncertainty.

"Perhaps I'll go after all, Leontias," she replied softly, her voice almost catching on his name.

"Leon, please." His correction was warm, his gaze flourishing with open admiration as her blush deepened.

Aria felt a small pang of jealousy in her chest, but dismissed it just as quickly. She had seen Leon flirt with women before, but it never led anywhere. He was practically married to the Rebellion, and he had no time for lovers. She looked over her shoulder toward Rylik. His attention was fixed on Leon, his arms crossed, assessing the interaction with a sharp eye.

"Corporal," Rylik said smoothly, a cold look in his eyes.

Leon stiffened, swallowing down a lump of air as he looked to the Sovereign in response. "Yes, Sovereign?"

"A moment with you, outside." He said gruffly. Leon reluctantly gave a nod to Maven and Aria, then stalked away.

The room quieted for a brief moment, a rare lull settling as Leon followed Rylik out, his posture stiff and cautious. The last echoes of his footsteps faded beyond the door, leaving a stillness in the apothecary, almost soothing against the morning's chaos. The soft scents of lavender and sage hung in the air, the gentle clinking of glass vials as Maven adjusted a few bottles on the shelves adding a calm, rhythmic cadence.

Aria let herself relax, finding some peace in the fleeting calm. But just as she began to focus, another presence disturbed the quiet.

"Is he gone yet?" Thorian's familiar voice rang out as he leaned out from the doorway of an adjoining room, his tone loud and casual, breaking the stillness like a pebble cast into a pond.

Maven spun around, visibly bristling. Her usual patience had finally run dry, and her glare could have burned through iron. "My god, Thorian, you're *still* here? Go!"

Unfazed by her irritation, Thorian strolled in, ignoring the mounting tension as he cast a quick, almost conspiratorial glance at Aria. "I only wanted to talk to Aria without being chided by the Sovereign. He doesn't like when people talk to her," he said, moving closer to Aria.

Maven intercepted her cousin, blocking his path and nudging him firmly by the arm. "No, he doesn't like when his Shadow Knights waste her time," she corrected, her voice cold as she directed him toward the back of the apothecary, clearly done with any further distractions.

Aria's gaze followed them, a touch of mirth mingling with curiosity as their voices began to fade toward the back of the room.

Maven's voice grew sharper as they neared the rear door. "For the last time, no. I will not talk to her about it. And neither will you. *Go.*" With a determined push, she reached for the door, gesturing pointedly for him to leave.

Thorian hesitated, turning back with a pleading expression. "He's practically your father, too, Maven—"

"Then he can do this himself," she cut him off, her tone steely as she shoved him outside and shut the door with a decisive click. She turned the lock with a swift, practiced motion, her exasperation evident.

When she returned to the table, Maven's expression had softened but only slightly. Her forced smile held a hint of weariness as she looked at Aria. "No, I don't want to talk about any of it. Please grab me the pestle behind you."

Aria offered a polite smile, sensing Maven's barely restrained irritation. She nodded, moving to the shelf without a word, her fingers reaching for the pestle. Glancing out the nearby window, her eyes landed on Rylik and Leon, standing just outside. Their silhouettes shifted as Leon turned and began heading toward the barracks, while Rylik stayed a moment longer, arms crossed as he watched the Corporal depart.

A small worry pricked at Aria's thoughts. She made a mental note to speak with Leon later, curious about what Rylik might have discussed with him and whether it held any bearing on her or the quiet but growing tensions with the Rebellion.

CHAPTER 6

ARIA

Several hours later, the afternoon sunlight fell gently over the bustling courtyard of the castle, coating the cobblestones in a warm, golden hue. The courtyard was alive with the clamor of daily activities, the air filled with the din of distant conversations and the clatter of horses' hooves. Off to the side, where the crowd thinned out, Aria and Leon stood close together, their conversation seemingly casual but laden with an unspoken tension.

Aria carefully applied her magic to the small cut on Leon's hand, the soft glow of her power betraying nothing of the distress twisting inside her. Her touch was gentle, deliberate, even as her pulse raced beneath her calm exterior.

"I had wanted to get you alone, but your—" Leon hesitated, his eyes scanning nervously around the bustling courtyard. "Your guardian is ever-present today."

She nodded, her voice barely above a whisper as she finished healing him, the radiance of her magic fading. "I haven't seen him since this morning."

"That doesn't mean he isn't nearby," Leon grumbled, forcing a strained smile as he waved to a passerby. His body was tense, but Aria could tell he was too guarded to let his fear show.

"What did you and him discuss earlier?" She asked, concerned, but keeping her face impassive.

"It was nothing." He whispered, "He asked me about my duties and then encouraged me to get back to them. It doesn't seem like he wants me around you."

"Is it too late to leave?" Her voice was softer than she intended, nearly swallowed by the hum of the courtyard. She didn't mean to sound so desperate, but the question clung to her throat.

Leon's gaze cut to her, but his watchful eyes swept the crowd as his growing unease crept into his posture. "Leave?" he repeated, his confusion evident.

She shifted uneasily, her fingers tightening around the fabric of her dress. "The palace. Ravenhelm."

Leon froze. His eyes sharpened as they met hers, his jaw tightening. He rubbed the spot on his hand where her magic had sealed his wound, as though feeling the tension in the healed skin. "You'd abandon us?" His voice, though low, carried an edge of indignation.

"No, that's not—"

He cut her off, his expression hardening with insult. "I know you're scared, Aria, but you have to be stronger than this. This is bigger than either of us."

Her eyes darted to the people milling around them, the weight of the courtyard pressing in. She leaned closer, her voice barely a breath between them. "I don't know if I'm cut out for this, Leon. I think I'm in over my head."

"You've been here *one* day," he hissed, stepping closer, his presence suffocating. His hand gripped her shoulder, firm but not comforting, as he leaned in, his breath brushing her ear. "You will have to find your strength at some point, Aria. Do not be a coward."

Her teeth sank into her lip, a sharp pain to hold back the sting of tears. She wouldn't cry here. Not now, not in front of him, and certainly not in front of these strangers. "I'm not a coward," she forced out, her voice shaking with the effort to remain steady.

Leon pulled back from her, his hand brushing her face with a tenderness that was meant to reassure, though his expression remained distant, almost mechanical. "You can do this," he said, but the words felt hollow in the cool air between them.

Aria's eyes shifted away from his, surveying the courtyard for the presence she could almost feel nearby. Though she couldn't see the Sovereign, she worried he was there, watching from the shadows. Her gaze flicked back to Leon's hazel eyes, and she willed herself to find comfort in them, but all she saw was the reflection of a past that was long gone. She wanted to tell him— wanted to make him understand—that wanting to leave wasn't cowardice, it was survival. She was being practical, not weak. She didn't want to die.

Leon misread her silence as acceptance, his familiar smile creeping across his face. It was the smile she remembered from sunlit afternoons in her village, back when they were younger, back when he still cared. Without thinking, Aria moved in and hugged him, tighter than she intended, as if hoping to find some fragment of the safety she used to know. But deep down, she knew—he couldn't save her. He wouldn't save her. His refusal to entertain her plea for escape had sealed that truth. Yet still, she clung to him, desperate for the comfort she knew he couldn't give.

Ever since her powers had surfaced, everyone looked at her like she was a tool, something to be used. Even the king had claimed her; it had been inevitable.

Leon patted her back in a way that felt more dismissive than comforting, his sigh barely audible as he gently peeled her away from him. Aria swallowed her emotions, forcing her features to harden as her tears threatened to betray her. She kept her chin up, meeting his gaze as he tucked a stray curl behind her ear. "Any news?" he asked, his voice casual, as if the weight of her world didn't hang in the balance. "Anything useful?"

Her jaw clenched, and for a brief moment, her resolve wavered. But no, she would never tell him what she knew—not here, not in the open, and maybe not ever. "As you said," she replied, her voice cool and edged with bitterness, "it's only been one day. I'll let you know if anything comes up."

Leon nodded, already losing interest, his thoughts elsewhere. "Fine then," he said, his gaze drifting to the distance as if she was no longer there. "We'll talk later."

She watched him leave, the familiar ache settling into her chest.

That prickling feeling crept up her spine again, the sensation of being watched. She scanned the courtyard, but nothing was out of place. No shadow lurked in the corners, no eyes peered from the crowd. Shaking off the chill, she turned sharply on her heel, heading toward the garden walkway that would lead her to the apothecary. She still had work to do, and if anything it might keep her mind off of the fact that she was trapped.

As she stepped across the threshold of the healer's quarters, the familiar scent of dried herbs wrapped around her comfortingly. The quiet hum of the space was a welcome reprieve from the bustling courtyard and the tense conversation she'd had with Leon, though she paused in mild surprise to find a man already inside, sitting casually in chair by the fireplace. He was familiar, and she recognized him as one of the Sovereign's Shadow Knights.

He straightened at her entrance, his broad shoulders widening as he flashed her a roguish smile. His brown hair was neatly pulled into a topknot, and his warm, chocolate-colored eyes sparkled with an easy charm. "Ah, Aria, isn't it?"

Aria tilted her head, curiosity softening her features. "Yes. And you're Sylas, aren't you? One of the Shadow Knights. I don't believe we have formally met yet."

He nodded, "That is correct. My apologies for that, as I tend to be a little single-minded and fixated on another healer most of my days."

Aria smiled at that, glancing around the room, noticing that Maven wasn't around. "You were waiting for her, I take it?

He gave a short laugh, a touch of embarrassment coloring his tone. "I was hoping to ask her to the ball. Again. Though I'm fairly certain she'll turn me down. Again."

Aria couldn't help the gentle expression that tugged at her lips. "How long have you had feelings for her?"

Sylas rubbed the back of his neck, glancing toward the shelves as though seeking refuge from the question. "A while," he admitted, his voice quieter now. "Ever since she was appointed as a court healer. She patched me up after a skirmish—pressed a bandage to my arm—and I've been pathetic ever since."

"That's very sweet," Aria said, her smile softening as she tried to offer some comfort.

"Not to her," he sighed, his shoulders slumping slightly. "My persistence comes off as annoying—and maybe it is."

"Or maybe she's just a little shy. You shouldn't give up hope yet." The words came easily, though Aria wasn't entirely sure why she felt the urge to console him. She barely knew him, but perhaps her pity was a reflection of her own heartache. She knew all too well the sting of unreturned affection, the quiet ache of longing for someone who couldn't—or wouldn't—feel the same.

"You're kind to say that," He snorted, shaking his head with a lopsided grin.

"If it doesn't work out, you're very handsome. I'm sure you'll find someone who will love you back." The words escaped her before she could think to hold them back. She winced inwardly, aware of how they might be taken—how they sounded like a coy murmur of flirtation when that couldn't be further from the truth. She hadn't meant to flirt. She was grasping for solace, using him as an anchor in her own storm. A foolish, desperate attempt to soothe the ache of knowing she would never earn Leon's love.

His brow lifted slightly at that, and he scanned down her frame with a mixture of fascination and intrigue. "Are you suggesting I adjust my sights?" he asked, a coy half-smile pulling on his lips. "Perhaps toward another beautiful healer?"

Her face flushed pink in abashment. Was he seriously alluding to her? She doubted it was anything he truly meant as anything but a joke. Sylas struck her as the flirtatious type, someone who enjoyed a laugh more than he intended to be taken to heart.

"I'm teasing," he chuckled. "Don't worry. You're safe from my advances." Then, with a wink he added, "for now."

Aria tucked a loose curl behind her ear, her fingers trembling slightly as she struggled to process the unexpected attention. Flattery and flirtation weren't things she was accustomed to, and the nervous laugh that escaped her lips only heightened her frustration with herself. He was bound to misinterpret her reaction, and the thought of drawing even more attention—especially the kind she neither wanted nor needed—made her chest tighten.

He stood with a sigh, stretching his arms before a faint grimace crossed his face. He pressed a hand to his thigh and groaned softly.

"What's wrong?" Aria asked, the apprehension she had felt from his playful overtures suddenly dissipating with her concern.

"Nothing serious," he replied, brushing it off with a dismissive wave. "Just sore. It's been bothering me for a few days now, but it'll pass."

"I could help with that," she offered, her tone gentle but firm as she approached him. "If you don't mind. All I need to do is touch wherever it hurts and you'll feel better. It only takes a moment."

His grin returned, teasing. "Can you heal through clothes, or should I remove my trousers?"

Aria barely stifled a nervous laugh. "Not unless you want to. Skin-to-skin contact allows for a deeper healing, but I'm sure yours might not be that serious."

"Good to know," he said with mock relief, sinking back into his chair. "Alright then. Go ahead, miracle worker."

She stood beside him, her hand hovering briefly over his thigh before resting lightly against it. Her yellow eyes radiated with light as she summoned her magic, soft and golden as it emanated from her palm. The warmth spread through the fabric, and as she worked, she felt his gaze on her.

Glancing up, she met his eyes for a brief moment. His expression was unreadable—focused and intent. There was something in his gaze that gave her pause, though she couldn't quite place what it was. It left her faintly unsettled, and she looked away quickly, returning her attention to the magic flowing through her hand.

After a moment, the light faded, and she withdrew. "It was just a pulled muscle," she said, brushing her hands against her skirt. "You should be fine now."

Sylas stood as if to test her words, rolling his shoulder back and stretching his leg. A broad smile spread across his face. "Incredible. You are every bit as good as people are saying. Thank you."

The door to the apothecary opened with a raspy groan, and Maven stepped inside, her dark braid swaying as she carried a tray of herbs.

Sylas immediately turned to greet her, his grin bright and

expectant. "Maven! Just the person I was hoping to see. About the ball—"

"No," Maven said, her tone polite but firm, the barest hint of irritation in her eyes.

Sylas sighed dramatically, placing a hand over his heart as though wounded. Then he glanced back at Aria, flashing her a conspiratorial smile. "Thank you again for the healing. Hope to see you at the ball."

With that, he strode out, leaving behind the faint scent of leather and steel in his wake.

* * *

The evening settled quietly over the castle, the usual clamor of the day replaced by the subdued hush of night. The door to Rylik's suite creaked as Aria pushed it open and stepped into his room, her presence a stark contrast to the shadowed ambiance. Rylik didn't look up immediately, sitting quietly with his gaze fixed on the dancing flames, as if caught in a daze.

He sipped from a glass of wine, the rich liquid contrasting with the stark stillness around him. After another moment, he looked up from his contemplative trance, his expression shifting from introspective to alert.

"Pyra," he greeted, his voice smooth but with an edge of amusement. "Good evening."

Aria glanced around, her eyes catching the flicker of the firelight, before meeting his gaze. "I noticed I was lacking a shadow today."

Rylik's lips curved into a faint smile as he rested his wine glass against his lips. "Good. If you noticed me, that would be a problem in my profession."

Aria stiffened, a knot of apprehension forming in her chest. *So he's been there all the while, watching? Did he see me with Leon? Did he hear what we talked about?* The questions swirled in her mind, but she kept her voice steady. "What can I do to convince you to trust that I won't tell your secret?"

Rylik's silence stretched on, a cruel game he played as he sipped his wine, his lips curling faintly. The tension pressed on

Aria, winding her nerves tighter with each unbearable second. She shifted in place, the crackle of the fire doing little to disguise her growing discomfort, which only seemed to please him more. "I don't mean to sound paranoid, but I would rather not spend the rest of my life looking over my shoulder."

His gaze turned sharp, his eyes narrowing slightly, the name rolling off his tongue with derision, "Corporal Leontias Valenforth."

Aria's heart skipped a beat.

"What is the nature of your involvement with him?" He asked coolly, eyes intent on her form.

She felt the flush of heat rising to her cheeks. "I don't see how that pertains to—"

"You want me to trust you," Rylik interrupted, his tone hardening, "yet you can't tell me what your relationship is with a member of the Royal Guard?"

Aria swallowed, trying to steady her voice. "I—He had a wound, and I, um—" She took a deep breath. "Leon and I knew each other when we were younger. He was always like an older brother to me. When he told me he had a wound, I thought it prudent to—"

Rylik cut her off, his voice cold and adamant. "You belong to His Majesty and to the Shadow Knights, and as such, you belong to *me*." He fixed her with a piercing gaze. "He has access to any of the royal healers below. Just because you are old friends does not mean he should also benefit from your expertise. He doesn't have clearance for that."

Aria's posture stiffened. "Sorry. It won't happen again, Sovereign." Her eyes were cold, the hint of defiance evident. "I didn't realize you were such a strict rule follower. Is it not also customary to let your superiors know when you have life-threatening ailments?"

Rylik stood, his full height imposing as he approached her, lifting his hand as if to pin her between him and the hearth. Aria froze, her gaze faltering under his intense scrutiny. He set his wine glass down behind her on the mantle, the sound faint but deliberate.

His eyes never left her as he continued. "I suppose *some* rules can afford to be broken."

Aria's shoulders tensed briefly, almost imperceptibly. "If I hadn't arrived when I did, Sovereign, how much longer do you think you really would've made it? Your blight has progressed to such a degree that this is the worst I've ever observed."

Rylik's gaze remained steady, but there was a hint of curiosity in his tone. "How many people do you know that have received such a death blow like mine? I am curious as to the company you keep, Aria. Nearly as curious as I am about you altogether."

Aria's voice was firm. "I am merely a healer. A great many people have made my acquaintance. I've never felt the need to inquire about anyone within my clientele. They are passersby. But, you and the other Shadow Knights, I will gain much familiarity with your ailments. It is to your benefit that I know more and not less. I can help you."

Rylik's smirk was faint but significant. "Hm, can you now?"

"I could heal your blight over time," Aria replied, "which could take years. However, if you divulge more about how you received it, I could easily hasten that healing time because I would know what additional measures to take."

Rylik raised an eyebrow, his tone skeptical. "I don't mean to call into question your miraculous abilities, little Pyra, but your hubris is rather impressive. I will admit you provide extensive relief, but this is something no mere healer can fully eradicate."

"I can," Aria said firmly. "If you still had the blade you were struck by, I could remove the enchantment from it, releasing you from its curse."

He hesitated a moment, as if truly assessing her words. "That blade," he began quietly, as if entrenched in the memory, "is likely still abandoned on that battlefield, buried under the bones of those who died in that attack. It is untraceable. And even if it weren't, I highly doubt you could resolve such formidable, eternal magic."

She lifted her chin nobly, a firmness in her tone as she replied, "I could."

Rylik studied her, his gaze unreadable. "Your confidence is admirable. But, in the absence of such a miracle," he paused as he opened his tunic shirt, revealing the expanse of his chest. "I'll settle for a temporary release from my agony."

Aria's breath caught in her throat, a blush settling over her cheeks. She reached out, her fingers trembling slightly as they made contact with his bare skin.

Rylik closed his eyes as her magic flowed into him, his breathing slowing, a visible relaxation settling over him. As she pulled her hand away, a flicker of urgency appeared in his eyes. He clasped his hand over hers, preventing her from fully withdrawing.

"Is something wrong?" Aria asked worriedly, her anxiety evident.

Rylik's eyes met hers, a moment of awareness passing between them. "No. You've done adequately. Thank you."

Aria's small smile was a blend of relief and triumph. "That's a first."

Rylik looked at her, puzzled. "Excuse me?"

"You thanked me," Aria said with a chuckle. "I didn't think you knew how to say such a thing."

Rylik's agitation was masked by a forced smile. "Well, I won't let it happen again."

Aria's smile widened, her eyes sparkling playfully. "Is that a joke?"

Rylik seemed to be taken aback by her warm demeanor. He receded a step away from her, regaining his former passive composure. "I am fully capable of having a sense of humor, Pyra. Just because I operate in murder and deceit doesn't mean I don't know how to have a good time."

Aria laughed softly, her expression a mixture of bemusement and mild annoyance. "Well, it's refreshing to know that when you aren't stalking me or terrorizing me, you find yourself having a *good time*."

Rylik's smile was sly. "On the contrary, stalking and terrorizing are among my favorite activities, and therefore I am enjoying myself quite a bit."

Aria's head tilted just a fraction, her smile gentle but fleeting. "Hn."

Rylik observed her for a moment, then turned away. "Well, it's late. You should get some rest before the dawn."

"Goodnight, Sovereign," Aria said softly, turning to leave.

"Goodnight," came his cool reply, just as she closed the door behind her, relieved he couldn't see the newly forming blush creeping across her cheeks.

CHAPTER 7

RYLIK

As Aria closed the door to her suite, Rylik sank back into his chair by the fire, his thoughts swirling with a tempest of disquiet and unbidden emotion. He recalled with irritation how he'd impulsively snatched her hand, trapping it over his heart as if to claim her in that fleeting moment. What had he hoped to achieve? Surely nothing substantial. She had administered the healing, and there was nothing more for her to do.

With his jaw clenched, his gaze bore into the flames, their flickering light dancing like the turmoil within him. He conjured the image of Aria from earlier that day, leaning toward the Corporal, their intimacy barely concealed amid the bustling crowd. The way she leaned into Leontias, desperation in her features, made the world around them fade into a blur. They were close—too close—sharing secrets in hushed tones, the air thick with unspoken tension. It was an intimate tableau that ignited a dark spark of envy within him, smoldering like the embers in the hearth.

His grip on the armrest tightened until his knuckles turned white, the wood pressing painfully against his palm as he recalled Leontias whispering something into her ear, his voice low and conspiratorial, his hand resting possessively on her delicate shoulder as if claiming her. How close had they been? The very thought twisted in Rylik's gut, a searing reminder of the intimacy he so desperately craved but felt eternally denied.

He recognized his ignorance regarding both of them, yet he would uncover their secrets soon enough. He always did. He was relentless in his pursuit of information, for he understood that even the slightest oversight could unravel him.

Aria had kept his secret, that much was certain. But how long could she maintain that silence in the presence of a lover? The mere thought of Leontias being her lover pierced him like a shard of ice, one that not even her healing touch could alleviate. His expression grew cold, a wall rising behind his eyes as he unwillingly envisioned her in the Corporal's arms, both entwined in a shared fervor. He shot to his feet, urgency propelling him, as if he could physically banish the image from his mind.

He crossed the length of his room and turned the handle of the balcony doors, stepping out onto his terrace, letting the quiet of the night settle over him. He needed to sever that bond between his healer and the Corporal. For the sake of his secret, of course. He could not permit his vulnerability to become fodder for idle whispers in the Corporal's bed.

Rylik reached beneath the loose stone tucked in the railing, fingers brushing the cool leather spine of his hidden sketchbook. The familiar feel of it calmed his edge, and he slipped it out with a quick glance over his shoulder, though he knew no one was watching. Stars scattered in the sky above like scattered gems, bright and defiant against the stretch of deep, inky blue. Each one gleamed as if daring him to name it, to track it, to capture it in lines on paper. His mind wandered to Aria again, knowing that he would have to tighten his grip on her. She would know no moment of privacy with that soldier again. He would see to it. If she were to share whispers with anyone, it would be him.

With precise movements, he opened the book to a clean page, letting the night air steady his focus. He squinted, marking the brightest stars, noting their positions in his own quiet, calculated shorthand. The moon, waxing just enough, would be full in three nights, perfect for his ascent to the highest turret in the palace. There, above all else, he could drink in the night without interruption, letting each detail slip into his chart. His lips pressed together, the sharp prick of his jealousy slicing through him as his thoughts drifted back to earlier in the day.

For a brief, intoxicating moment, he imagined his own hand resting possessively on Aria's shoulder as Leon's had been, his breath warm and tantalizing against the delicate shell of her ear. The image of her small arms encircling him flooded his senses, pressing her soft body against his, just as she had done so easily with the Corporal. He could almost feel the gentle flush of her skin beneath his fingertips, the rise and fall of her breath mingling with his own. The thought took root within him, defying his better judgment and igniting a fierce longing that he struggled to suppress. He knew it would haunt him through the night, lurking in the shadows of his mind.

He drew his gaze upward, regarding the vastness of the sky above him. The stars were his constant. Some private ritual to escape the mounting frustrations of the palace. His hand moved smoothly, sketching each star's place in a swift, familiar rhythm.

He was aware of his possessive nature regarding the things he desired, yet he had never coveted a person before now. He knew it was because of the blight that twisted within him; Aria provided a sweet relief from the agony that had become his continual companion. How could he not yearn for her? Yet, as his mind dwelled on her, the fleeting memory of moments before when he had her pinned between him and the mantle of the fireplace surged within him, and an ache blossomed in his chest. He wanted more than just her gifts. He wanted *everything*.

* * *

The morning light trickled through the tall windows of Aria's room, bathing her figure in a golden glow. She slumped in her chair, lost to the quiet of her thoughts, her posture languid, almost defeated. Her copper hair tumbled in soft, tousled waves, catching the light with a muted shine, and her dress had shifted awkwardly around her form, giving her an air of vulnerability she rarely displayed. Oblivious, she didn't stir as the door creaked open behind her.

Rylik paused at the threshold, his sharp gaze sweeping over her. A flicker of amusement danced in his eyes as he observed her unguarded state, wholly unaware of the predator in the room. He took his time, savoring the rare sight of her undone, the one moment where her defenses had dropped. It was a sharp contrast to the disciplined, wary creature she usually became around him.

He'd heard her earlier that morning, the telltale splash of water signaling her early rise for a bath. She had been meticulous lately, carefully timing her preparations, always ready, always concealed behind the drab armor of modesty. It had already been a week since their first meeting, and since that day he had caught her in a towel, she had been guarded. Each day, she greeted him already dressed, hiding beneath neutral, boorish dresses of brown and tan, desperately trying to erase any shred of vulnerability. There had been no misstep, no accidental glimpse of her perfect body outlined by little more than her corset. A wry smile tugged at his lips, spite having spurred him to arrive late today.

He wanted to catch her with her guard down. He wanted to see her undone once more. He craved it. He liked the look of fire in her eyes when she felt cornered, and the way she struggled to bridle her tongue in her efforts to force the distance between them. Lately she had been so careful with him, trying to be cordial and professional, despite his many attempts to push at her boundaries. Yet, he could hardly resist the urge to press and prod her.

He reveled in this small fleeting moment when he could strip away her control. He wanted to see her laid bare, to catch her in the act of being human. It was not affection that drove him, no. It was a darker hunger, a fascination that bordered on obsession. Nobody had ever known his secret, and so there was a deep-seated desire within him now to uncover her secrets as well. If he was to be made vulnerable before her, then he would make her equally so.

He stepped closer, his boots barely making a sound on the polished floor. His gaze swept over her figure, admiring the quiet rise and fall of her breathing, the way her red hair spilled over her shoulder like molten metal. He imagined her in something finer, something that suited the fire hidden beneath her composed exterior.

Instinctively, his hand reached out, fingertips brushing the air just above her wild curls. For a moment, he waited, close enough to touch, close enough to seize control. His fingers twitched, curling back into a fist before retreating to clasp behind his back. Straightening, he breathed deeply, his presence finally breaking the stillness.

"Good morning, Aria," he murmured, his voice a velvet command, rich and insidious, filling the quiet room. He waited, relishing the moment before she would realize he was there, savoring the knowledge that for now, in this breath of time, she was still at his mercy.

Aria blinked, the sound jolting her from sleep. Her eyes snapped open, her heart racing as she shot upright. "S—Sovereign!" she stammered, "What time is it?!"

Rylik, calm and unaffected, merely replied, "It's eight in the morning."

Her eyes widened. "But, aren't you usually here as early as seven?"

"I often am." He gave a casual shrug. "But, like I said, I do not intend to fall into a predictable routine for you to follow. I'd like you to stay alert and cautious."

Aria straightened up, trying to hide her annoyance. Even standing at her full height, she was still dwarfed by him, his presence looming and unwavering.

"There are several noblemen and women that need tending to today," Rylik continued, his tone matter-of-fact. "The healers will need all the extra help they can get. You'll offset their workload today, but this will not be commonplace for you."

"Why? What's so different about today in particular?" Aria asked, eyeing him suspiciously.

"Tonight is a royal ball," he explained, his tone edging toward boredom. "The king is hosting a celebration for his achievements of the year, and he has invited every nobleman and woman in the kingdom to attend. Those living in the palace will be extra needy today, likely bothering the royal healers for insignificant matters like healing acne or covering liver spots." He sighed, the annoyance clear on his face. "An obvious waste of their talents, but they need assistance, as per His Majesty's request. It would be untoward to send away the nobles, but we cannot neglect the guardsmen. You'll be attending to the more serious matters."

Aria nodded, though a flicker of apprehension shadowed her expression as she seemed to turn the day's events over in her mind. Her eyes darted toward him, wary, as if she were caught in a dangerous thought she hoped he hadn't noticed.

Rylik's expression was calm as he watched her. "This should only occupy your time for a few hours at most. Afterward, you'll visit the royal tailor for a fitting, and then spend the rest of your time being prepared for the ball."

Aria froze, her eyes wide. "Excuse me?"

He met her surprise with cool indifference.

"I am to attend this ball?"

"Yes," Rylik confirmed, his tone devoid of any elaboration.

"Are you expecting that I will have to deploy my services at this event?" she asked, still reeling from the shock.

"The only services I anticipate you rendering will likely be dancing, I assume. Perhaps some idle chatter. Ballroom activities, in general." He watched her, catching the subtle shift in her posture as she tried to process his words.

"What? Why? I'm not a noblewoman," Aria said, her voice tinged with confusion.

"Not in the slightest, no." A faint sigh escaped him as he regarded her. "Thankfully," He cleared his throat, regaining his usual composure. "But I am required to be in attendance. And I would just hate," he said as his gaze locked onto hers with a pointed stare, "to think of you missing out on all the festivities this evening. I wouldn't want you to grow bored in my absence."

Aria's eyes narrowed as she stared back, and he mused to himself at the sharp expression. She knew he didn't intend to let her out of his sight. He had been diligent this week in his efforts to be a smothering and constant presence. Tonight would be no different.

"Do you have a color preference?" Rylik asked suddenly, his voice seemingly cutting through her wandering, agitated thoughts.

Aria furrowed her brow. "Um?"

"For your dress," he clarified. "I'll be speaking to the tailor shortly, and I can have him acquire fabrics in the color of your choosing."

Her swallow was small but telling, a hint of hesitation slipping into her posture. It was clear she had never worn a ballgown before, let alone attended a ball. Judging by her current wardrobe, it seemed unlikely she had ever worn anything other than muted tones, let alone discovered what truly suited her. Clearing her throat, she muttered awkwardly, "Uh, I guess any color would work—"

"Teal," Rylik interrupted, his tone resolute as he stepped closer to inspect her more carefully in the soft morning light. His gaze swept over her pale skin, her fiery red hair catching the light. "I think the color would look elegant with your complexion— accentuate the red in your hair in a way that might make you look," he paused, smirking, before adding, "Captivating."

Aria blinked, taken aback by the sudden compliment. A faint blush colored her cheeks as she met his gaze, momentarily lost for words.

Rylik's eyes settled on her delicate features, noting the soft pink that bloomed over the freckles on her cheeks and the way her eyes widened in tentative appreciation. Perhaps compliments on her appearance were a rarity. He mused that he would have to offer them more often, if only to coax out that lovely expression. If Leontias wasn't offering her such praise, then he was clearly failing as a lover. A wry smile tugged at Rylik's lips, satisfied with how he had managed to keep them apart all week. The Corporal had been noticeably flustered by the interference, a fact that pleased Rylik immensely. He stepped back, his expression returning to practiced nonchalance.

"What color will you wear?" she asked, her voice softer than before.

"Black," he replied, the corners of his mouth lifting into a faint, almost mocking smile. "Naturally." Without another word, he turned and walked toward the door, leaving Aria alone with her thoughts.

* * *

Rylik made his way through the palace halls with measured strides, his exterior calm and steady, though something restless stirred beneath it. He had a great many objectives to accomplish today and the royal tailor's chambers awaited him first—a task that should have felt mundane, yet he found it surprisingly absorbing.

Rylik turned the corner and pushed open the door to the tailor's suite. His sharp eyes scanned the walls draped with rich fabrics and intricate dresses, a visual feast of color and texture.

The tailor, a man of modest stature but overflowing with the art of his craft, bowed low. "Sovereign, good morning."

"To you as well," Rylik said, his voice smooth and controlled, his hands clasped behind his back. "The lady should be fitted into something teal. Though you're welcome to provide any other colors you think might suit."

The tailor nodded swiftly. "Yes, Sovereign," he said, motioning toward several half-finished dresses, each one a vision of luxury.

Rylik's gaze moved over them idly, his expression unreadable, though his mind was less disengaged than it appeared. The tailor eagerly gestured toward a few of the dresses. "Any of these styles you think would be best for your lady?"

Rylik admired the gowns, his imagination conjuring the image of Aria draped in the silken fabric. He chose a few of the more daring, sensual designs with a casual wave of his hand, though he knew her modesty would ever allow her to be so bold. He smirked, already picturing the flush that would rise to her cheeks in embarrassment. She would have a hard time slipping away from him if she became the center of attention.

"Have the rest prepared for her to try. I'll pay for all of them, whichever she chooses," he added, the casualness of his tone betraying no real concern over the cost.

The tailor beamed, bowing again, grateful for the generous patronage. "Of course, Sovereign. The finest craftsmanship, as always."

Rylik nodded once before turning to leave, his mind briefly drifting to his own motivations. *Is that the only reason I want her to stand out? To make sure she has no room to squirm away and reveal secrets?* His steps echoed in the corridor as he turned another corner. *Or do I simply want her in my sights the entire night, to merely enjoy the view?* He smirked inwardly. *Both, I suppose.*

Rylik strode through the palace corridors, the golden glow of morning light streaming through arched windows and pooling on the cold tiles. The rhythmic click of his boots was steady, unhurried, a perfect mask for the irritation simmering beneath his cool facade. The king's summons felt unnecessary, another tedious game he was obliged to play despite knowing the outcome would be the same. His fingers brushed idly against the hilt of his sword as he approached the ornate double doors, a habitual gesture that brought him a faint sense of focus. Without hesitation, he pushed them open, stepping inside with an air of detached confidence.

"Morning," Kaldros greeted as he saw him enter, his voice gruff but calm as he approached Rylik.

Rylik gave a curt nod, his expression as cool and controlled as ever.

"There's a matter that requires your attention," the king began, his tone laced with intrigue as he continued to speak in lowered tones. Rylik listened, his mind dissecting each word with sharp precision.

Ah, he mused silently as the king spoke, *the king's plans for the day—a meeting with a group of rival nobles who have been encroaching on his territories. They'll need to be "dealt with" before tonight's celebrations.*

A ghost of a smirk played at the corner of Rylik's lips. *For all the king's faults, I have to admire his ruthlessness. Even on the day of a grand ball, he conducts his business with the same cold efficiency as any other day. In that, we are alike.*

The king's voice droned in his mind as Rylik strode out of the chamber, the details of the assignment already committed to memory and swiftly discarded as irrelevant beyond their execution. By the time the carriage wheels clattered over the cobblestones, the rival lord's name and the expected body count were little more than facts in a growing ledger of service. His gaze drifted to the passing countryside, his thoughts unbothered by the task ahead; it was a predictable cycle of politics, treachery, and violence. Killing was easy—cleaner than the king's endless scheming—and he had no illusions about which of the two he preferred.

The air in the rival manor was tense, the heavy scent of desperation lingering as Rylik stood at the king's side, watching the gathered nobles with dispassionate eyes. Their posturing had grown predictable, their threats empty. Rylik remained bored and passive as the conversation circled, their words little more than the prelude to the inevitable.

When it came time for the escalation—when the threat of violence was made clear—Rylik moved first, stealing his opening. He summoned the Veil, assuming a cloak of shadows as he bent the world to his will. When summoned, it allowed him to slip from one place to another, unseen and unheard, leaving no trace behind.

His shadows flickered across the room, his blade flashing between obsidian mists in an arc too swift for the naked eye to follow. Two men dropped before they even had a chance to inhale their last breath. Another followed swiftly, then another. It was over in moments, the room suddenly filled with the sharp scent of blood, staining the floor where they once stood.

Rylik's hands remained steady, his heart unchanged. Killing, like everything else in life, was a task to be handled efficiently. No hesitation. No second thoughts.

The king's dark eyes gleamed with satisfaction as he nodded approvingly. "Excellent work as always, Sovereign."

Rylik gave a brief nod in return, but his thoughts were already wandering to the evening ahead. His tasks for the king were done, the weight of his obligations lifted—for now. There was only one thing left to draw his attention, and for once, it was something he found himself anticipating.

A rare, fleeting smile tugged at his lips as he strode away from the bloodied manor, leaving the aftermath of his work behind like a shadow in his wake. By the time they returned to the palace, he and the king parted ways with little more than a nod, their purposes already diverging. Rylik's path led him to the apothecary, his steps unhurried but deliberate as he reached the healers' quarters.

His gaze found Aria almost immediately. She was bent over a soldier, her hands glowing faintly with magic as she worked to seal a wound. The soft light played against her face, and though her focus was fixed on her task, she still managed to radiate an air of quiet defiance. Leaning casually against the doorway, he didn't bother to hide his presence. He wanted her to notice.

The corner of his mouth curled as their eyes met, her gaze betraying that familiar flicker of annoyance and dread.

Yes, I think I'll rather enjoy the evening.

CHAPTER 8

ARIA

The royal tailor's suite was a swirl of fabrics, colors, and fine stitching, the room filled with an air of opulence and expectation. Aria stepped inside, her fingers fidgeting nervously at her sides. The atmosphere felt heavy with opulence, a stark contrast to the more modest life she had led up until recently. As much as her day had felt very commonplace, as it used to when she healed the people in and around her small village, this experience did not. Her station in life had never afforded her the luxury of fine clothing, much less an experience like this one.

The tailor greeted her with a professional smile. "Lady Aria, we've prepared a few selections for you." He gestured towards a row of elegant gowns hanging neatly. "You may try on whichever you wish."

Aria's eyes followed the tailor's gesture but froze when they landed on a figure in the back corner of the room. Rylik. He stood brooding, arms folded, silent as a shadow. Her heart thudded in her chest, a mix of nerves and something else she couldn't quite name. How long had the Sovereign been standing there? Was he simply making sure she arrived here per his expectations?

"Come, see which you'd like," the tailor encouraged, oblivious to her internal turmoil.

Taking a deep breath, Aria pushed down her unease and approached the first dress. It was a gown of rich teal, its material shimmering as it caught the light. *Teal*, she thought with faint wonder, remembering Rylik's mention of the color earlier that morning. She had assumed it was just a passing observation, but here it was, the color he mentioned now manifested in fine silk and delicate embroidery.

She shot a glance at him, trying to gauge his reaction. His face remained unreadable.

"Shall I assist you with the fitting, Lady Aria?" the tailor asked, snapping her attention back.

Aria nodded, and moments later, she was in the changing room, her mind racing as the tailor helped her into the gown.

When she stepped out, she hesitated before facing the mirror, anxious about her reflection. But when her eyes finally met the glass, she was surprised. The woman staring back at her looked different, almost regal in the teal gown. Her gaze flicked to Rylik, who was watching her from his darkened corner, a subtle smirk tugging at his lips. His approval was unmistakable. She realized he liked it, and though it shouldn't matter, she couldn't help but feel her cheeks warm at the thought.

The tailor clapped his hands once, clearly pleased with his work. "Beautiful, my lady. Truly exquisite. Would you care to try another? You can try on as many as you like."

"I—I don't know if that's necessary—" Aria began, but the tailor quickly cut her off.

"Your benefactor has approved any dress you wish, as many as you wish. Does that change your mind?"

"My 'benefactor'?" she echoed, her tone dubious. Her eyes slowly drifted back to Rylik, who was already striding out of the room noiselessly. The door closed with a soft click behind him. Aria swallowed, her cheeks now a deep shade of red. It was obvious that he was referring to the Sovereign, but she couldn't puzzle out why he would pay for these. What would he gain from this?

Her mind raced with possibilities, each one more unsettling than the last. Was it some form of control? A way to bind her even closer to him, to make her indebted to him in some subtle, unspoken way?

"My lady?" the tailor's voice interrupted her spiraling thoughts. He looked at her expectantly, waiting for her decision.

She blinked, shaking off her confusion. "Sorry, lost in thought with all of my options."

The tailor smiled, clearly used to such reactions. "Understandable."

"Are there any dresses here that my 'benefactor' showed interest in?" she asked, her voice hesitant.

The tailor's eyes gleamed at the question, clearly pleased at the prospect of a larger sale. "Several, yes. You should try them all."

Aria offered a nervous smile. "Yes, and my benefactor—you're obviously referring to—?" She didn't utter a name, hoping he would offer it. Instead, the tailor raised a brow in confusion, and Aria quickly waved it off. "N—nevermind. It's not important."

"Very good, my lady." The tailor nodded smoothly. "Let's begin."

* * *

The corridor was narrow and dimly lit as Aria made her way back to her room. She had chosen only one dress—the teal gown Rylik had shown interest in—and now her mind buzzed with conflicting concerns.

Had she chosen wisely? Her fingers fidgeted at her sides as she mulled it over, her steps quickening. It just wouldn't be wise to test the boundaries of his supposed benevolence. Maybe this was a test, she reasoned. Maybe he wanted to see how positively audacious she would be with his pocketbook. She sighed, feeling a knot of tension grow in her stomach. Or perhaps it was something else entirely.

The thoughts continued to twist inside her, troubling her as she turned down the next hallway, her gaze distant. Purchasing gowns was the act of a lord courting a lady, that much she could posture. But, why? Was it some sort of head game?

Before she could dwell further on it, a door she had just passed creaked open behind her, too quietly to notice. Without warning, strong hands clamped around her, one arm snaking around her waist while the other covered her mouth. A startled cry died in her throat as she was yanked backward into a dimly lit room, the door closing swiftly and silently behind her.

Aria stumbled as she was thrown inside, her heartbeat roaring in her ears. But the familiar face that greeted her quickly switched her fear to relief.

"Leon!" she gasped, her voice an unrestrained gasp.

Leon was close, his wide eyes urging her to keep her voice low. "Shh!" he hissed, pressing a finger to his lips. "Keep your voice low, Aria."

She swallowed thickly, her breath still catching in her chest. "Sorry, I—"

Leon cut her off, his hand firm on her arm, his agitation evident in the ragged whisper of his voice. "You have been impossible to corner of late!" He stepped closer, his grip tightening just a fraction. "That Sovereign has been glued to your side nearly every waking moment."

Aria nodded, unsettled by the accuracy in his words. "I know," she murmured, her voice barely audible. "I'm sorry. I just think he suspects me is all. He's very wary of me." Her stomach twisted again, this time at the thought of Rylik's intense, calculating gaze always following her. Even in this small room, she wouldn't dare utter a word of the Sovereign's blight. Just thinking about his threat from their first night together made her regret ever aligning herself with the Rebellion in the first place, no matter how much she also despised the king's tyranny.

"There's been no time to tell you today about our plans for the evening," Leon continued, his voice dropping even lower.

Aria's head tilted slightly as she studied him. "The Rebellion is planning something for this evening?"

Leon's expression darkened. "We shouldn't be, but, yes." He glanced around nervously, as if the walls themselves could listen. "I believe we still are. Some significant allies of ours were killed mere hours ago in a private meeting with the king." His eyes met hers, grim and tired. "Even so, Orren thinks it would still be wise to proceed with our endeavors. That is, if the Sovereign is not present."

Her brows furrowed. "How are you going to pluck him from

the king's side? And even so, the Shadow Knights will also be in attendance, and I can assure you that they are quite formidable as well—"

Leon waved her concern away. "We already have plans in place for them. They aren't our primary concern. No, our main issue is that *monster* you've had to suffer as your shadow for more than a week." He shook his head, a look of frustration crossing his face. "He's too perceptive—too impossible. We need him gone, just for a little while."

Aria swallowed, her voice barely more than a breath. "Yes, so you say. But you haven't said how."

Leon hesitated, eyeing her uncomfortably before he spoke again. "Have you considered, Aria, that his fixation on you is more than just cautious behavior?"

A flush of heat crept into Aria's cheeks, though she quickly shook her head. "No. No, I think that is all it is. Just wise caution." She narrowed her eyes at him. "And what's more, I hope you are not implying that *I* should be the one distracting the Sovereign from the ball?!"

Leon's eyes widened in alarm, and he quickly clamped his hand over her mouth again. His eyes darted to the door, listening intently for any movement before slowly pulling his hand away. "You," he said as he shifted awkwardly. "You could be capable of disarming him in a way the rest of us in the Rebellion simply can't."

Aria's glare turned icy. "What are you suggesting, Leon?"

He grimaced, discomfited. "It's Orren's idea. He thinks the Sovereign might be soft on you. You could use your *feminine charms.*"

Her jaw tightened, her eyes narrowing into sharp slits. "Orren can use his 'charms' on the Sovereign. I am willing to be a healer and informant for the Rebellion, but one thing I will not compromise on," she leaned in for full effect, "is to be some kind of whore. I do have my pride after all."

Leon observed her now closed off frame, arms crossed over her chest, as he looked away. "I knew it was a bit of a stretch," He sighed, running a hand through his hair. "I told him that he had to have been mistaken, anyway. Why, the kind of women that keep the Sovereign company are likely very experienced, suave ladies of the court who are very practiced in the art of romance and seduction. While you—" He glanced at her and back away, giving a half-hearted chuckle. "You're *just* Aria. I'll just tell Orren that you're not—"

Aria's expression turned steely. "I'll do it."

Leon blinked, confused. "You—What?"

Her eyes flashed, annoyance and determination gleaming in them. "I'll get the Sovereign alone with the use of my *feminine charms*." Her lips curved into a sharp, irritated smile. "I do possess them, after all, and I am perfectly capable of luring a man in if I so desire."

Leon stared at her for a moment, contemplative. "Alright," he said slowly, a smile crossing his face that made Aria wonder if he'd goaded her into it. "I'll let Orren know that we will proceed as planned. Thank you, Aria." He clapped her shoulder, his grip meant to be firm and reassuring. "Wait a few minutes before leaving, just to avoid suspicion."

With that, he slipped out of the room, leaving Aria standing there, staring at the closed door in disbelief.

Did I just agree to play the part of some painted-up harlot to steal the Sovereign away from the ball? Her face burned as her mind whirled with the absurdity of it all. *Oh, god! What was I thinking?! I couldn't possibly! I mean, hell, I've been trying to use my stupid "feminine charms" on Leon for years, and the poor sod still has no idea that I'm even interested in him! Worse, still, he has no interest in me!* She groaned inwardly. *So little interest, in fact, that he would brazenly assert that there is no way the Sovereign could be interested in me romantically!*

She stood abruptly and began pacing the floor, flailing her arms in frustration. The fact that he would even suggest what sort of women might keep the Sovereign's company was a step too far.

But then, her shoulders slumped in defeat, her steps slowing. She didn't actually know what kind of women he liked. If she had to guess, he'd probably want a woman much more sure of herself and confident in her skin than Aria. Someone, maybe, who knows what color of regal dresses best suit her.

With one last defeated sigh, Aria groaned and opened the

door, stepping into the empty hallway.

Well, it doesn't matter now, does it? She bit her lip as she started walking. *I told Leon I would distract the Sovereign.* She sighed heavily. *Damn my wounded pride.*

CHAPTER 9

ARIA

Aria stood at the entrance to the grand ballroom, fidgeting nervously as the two knights escorting her took their posts by the door. The heavy wooden doors had already swung open, revealing the glittering scene beyond. The swirling colors of gowns and tunics, the sounds of a string quartet, and the hum of low conversation reached her ears.

The maidservants had spent hours preparing her for this night. *This* night, where she was to pretend to be someone she was not. She absentmindedly touched the jewels in her hair, her fingers tracing the soft curls that framed her face. They took such care in making sure her wild hair looked effortlessly elegant.

They had it pinned up in a loose arrangement, held in place by sparkling teal jewels, with delicate curls teasing her neck. Her gown, dark stormy teal and dangerously low-cut, clung to her figure before sweeping to the floor in a cascade of silk. Tiny gems adorned the fitted sleeves and the bodice, shimmering faintly in the light.

Aria hoped this would be enough to pull him away. She scanned the room, suddenly aware that heads were turning her way. Whispers fluttered around her, indistinct but growing. She didn't know what she ought to do after getting him alone. Her heart raced, heat creeping up her cheeks. She could easily venture a guess at what might preoccupy him, but her mind could hardly conjure the unwelcome images.

Suddenly, a familiar voice broke into her thoughts.

"Aria!" Maven called out with a bright, welcoming smile, drawing her attention to the side. She was dressed in a deep purple gown that clung gracefully to her curves, the rich hue of the fabric accentuating the violet gleam in her eyes. Maven's smile widened as she approached, her arms open for a warm hug. The sweet scent of jasmine drifted from her hair, mingling with the air around them. Tonight, she looked every inch the lady — far removed from her usual appearance in the apothecary, where practicality reigned over such elegance. "You look absolutely incredible," Maven exclaimed, her tone overflowing with genuine admiration.

Behind her, Thorian made a low, appreciative whistle as he approached, his attire a striking blend of gold and blue. His expression softened into a polite smile when Maven turned her attention toward him. "You clean up well, cousin," he remarked with warmth, then cast his gaze toward Aria, his smile deepening. "And you, Aria, look especially stunning this evening."

Aria, a bit flustered by the attention, returned the smile, dipping into a shy curtsey as he bowed in her direction. "Everyone really does look amazing," she murmured, her voice tinged with bashfulness.

"Indeed, we do," Thorian agreed with a playful twinkle in his eye, extending his hand toward her. "May I have this dance?"

Before Aria could make any response, Maven's hand shot out, taking his instead. She gave him a pointed look, a subtle but unmistakable warning, and then gently steered him away. "I think she has far better options awaiting her this evening, Thorian," she said, her voice laced with a touch of mischief.

"I just wanted to talk to her," Thorian muttered, his voice trailing off as Maven guided him toward the growing sea of dancers. Sylas approached them, prompting Maven to duck behind Thorian in a futile effort to avoid him. Aria's attention flickered their way, but before she could attempt to follow the sound of Thorian's words, another voice — this one deeper and far more commanding—interrupted her thoughts.

"Aria," Leon's tone was low, almost hesitant, as he approached behind her, watching her turn to face him. His eyes raked over her, surprise plain on his face. "I didn't know you, um—" His voice stuttered into silence.

Aria allowed a small smile of triumph to tug at her lips, feeling a bit more confident.

"You look really good," Leon said awkwardly, finally meeting her eyes.

"Thanks," she replied, satisfaction humming beneath her calm exterior. She wanted to bask in the compliment from her beloved Leon, but her nerves couldn't seem to allow it. She glanced around again, searching for the man who had dominated her thoughts all day. Where was the Sovereign? He didn't bother her while the maids prepared her, and he didn't escort her to the ball either. Likely he was meant to escort the king, but still, the mystery remained.

"Would you care to dance?" Leon's question brought her attention back to him.

She blinked, startled by the unexpected invitation. "Alright." She took his outstretched hand, a small surge of warmth spreading through her. She supposed it couldn't hurt to have one dance with Leon, to imagine what it might be like after all this Rebellion nonsense was finally over.

As they stepped onto the dance floor, the attention they drew was undeniable. Whispers followed them, though Leon seemed determined to ignore them.

"You look nice," she said, her voice light.

Leon chuckled, though it was a bit strained. "Thanks. This tunic is about the best I could manage. It's going to allow me to maneuver more easily before we, well, you know."

Aria's stomach tightened. She didn't know, actually, because she never asked what the Rebellion had been planning. "What is happening tonight?" she asked, her voice low.

Leon's eyes flickered with a shadow of tension, but he spoke quietly, leaning in as they turned. "Nothing large. We don't have enough forces for that. We just need the Sovereign distracted long enough to sneak someone out."

Aria stiffened. "Who?"

Leon exhaled sharply. "One of ours. He's been detained for nearly a year now. The timing of this ball is perfect for his escape. We are going to cause a brief distraction, while you have your 'target' preoccupied. You'll need to keep him busy even after that distraction occurs."

Her heart thudded louder. "How long do you need?"

"Ten minutes." His voice was barely a whisper, his eyes darting around them. "Maybe more."

Her cheeks flushed. *Ten minutes? There's no way I'll last that long.* She swallowed, forcing a smile. "I'll do what I can."

Leon's gaze softened with gratitude. "Thank you, Aria." But then his expression faltered, his face paling suddenly as his eyes shifted over her shoulder.

Rylik moved toward them like a wraith through the crowd, his eyes cutting to Leon with cold precision, then moving onto Aria's hand in Leon's. A smirk tugged at the corners of his lips, a dangerous, knowing curve.

"Evening," Rylik said, his voice smooth but edged with steel. "May I interrupt?" It wasn't a question, even if it was phrased like one. That much was evident in his commanding demeanor.

Leon was a mere soldier and therefore his subordinate, and so immediately he released her hand, offering a stiff bow before making a hurried exit.

Aria remained rooted in place, her heart stuttering at the sight of Rylik. He stood before her, imposing in his attire, a dark figure of authority wrapped in shadowed elegance. His black armor gleamed with an understated sheen, perhaps needlessly worn despite the assumed safety of the ballroom, a testament to his ever-present readiness. Silver threads wove through the edges of his cloak and along the intricate engravings on his chest plate, catching the faint light in subtle glints.

The crimson accents, barely visible beneath the silver filigree, hinted at something darker, restrained yet simmering just beneath the surface. The polished black of his boots and gauntlets completed the look, regal and commanding, a reminder that even here, among the glittering finery, he was a knight—always vigilant, always in control.

His eyes swept over her, slow and savoring. When he spoke, his voice was a purr. "Well, little Pyra," He took her hand, his cool fingers brushing against her skin as he lifted it to his lips, placing a kiss over her knuckles. "You look..." He paused, letting the moment stretch. "Captivating."

Aria's face heated, her heart pounding. She couldn't look away, no matter how much she wanted to.

Pleased by her reaction, Rylik pulled her into the dance, his hand pressing firmly against the small of her back as they moved together.

"You dance?" she stammered, struggling to keep her thoughts from scattering.

"Shock and horror," he murmured with a smirk. "The murderous Sovereign can dance."

Despite herself, a grin broke through, defying her restraint. "I didn't mean to dig at your pride." She glanced up at him, catching his eyes. "I'm just surprised, is all."

Rylik's steps were effortless, guiding her with such ease that it was as though they had rehearsed it. "Once upon a time, I had other hobbies," he said, voice smooth. "Before my current occupation, of course."

"You haven't always been the Sovereign?" she teased.

"Believe it or not, I was once a child," he quipped, though his eyes remained serious.

Aria laughed, the melodic sound of it fading as the dance carried them through the crowd. Whispers followed their movements, eyes watching their every turn.

"You're an enigma," she murmured, "that can dance, apparently. And quite well, might I add. You're leading so well that one wouldn't even be able to tell that I don't know how to dance."

Rylik's smirk deepened. "Well, it helps when you have someone who knows how to lead."

Aria flushed at the insinuation. "Leon isn't a nobleman. He dances well enough."

"Hn." His voice lowered, a keen glint in his gaze. "You're protective of your 'older brother,' aren't you?"

She stiffened subtly.

"No, I suppose that's not accurate," he mused. His words slid between them like a knife. "He may think you a little sister, but you do *not* see him as an elder brother, do you, dear?"

Aria's heart thudded painfully. *Either he really is that perceptive, or I'm that obvious.*

"Do not pity yourself for lacking his attention, especially not after tonight when no one in this room could possibly see you as anything but," His eyes darkened with intent as he added, "some kind of temptress."

For a brief moment, she was taken aback by the compliment.

As the song came to a close, Rylik slowed their dance, his hand gentle at her back before he took her hand again, lifting it to his lips once more. His gaze locked with hers, holding her in place with an intensity she couldn't escape.

Then, with deliberate grace, he turned to walk away, only pausing at the sound of her desperate plea behind him.

"W—wait!" she stammered, her voice barely louder than a whisper as she reached out toward Rylik. *Why do I sound so winded?!* Aria swallowed, struggling to keep her voice steady, every syllable strained as she spoke. "Would you accompany me to—" She faltered, shutting her eyes briefly to steady herself, trying to gather the courage she needed to speak, "the courtyard?"

Rylik's eyes shone with quiet satisfaction, the corners of his lips curving into a slow, knowing smile. "The courtyard?" he asked, stepping toward her, his voice smooth, teasing.

She squirmed slightly beneath his gaze.

"Are you aware," Rylik murmured, his tone playfully conspiratorial, "of the things that typically occur in the courtyard, Aria?"

Of course, she was aware. The very thought of it was what crippled her now. Her throat tightened, but she refused to let her discomfort show. She lifted her chin.

"Scandalous, little Pyra," he added, clearly enjoying her struggle.

"I scarcely think it's a scandal to take a leisurely walk through the courtyard," she replied, her voice firmer this time, though her confidence was fragile.

Rylik chuckled, the sound deep and indulgent, as if he found her innocence amusing. "Is that what you think happens in the courtyard on the eve of a ball? Walking?"

A new song had started in the ballroom behind them, the delicate sound of instruments swelling, but they were the only ones not dancing. Aria fidgeted again, painfully aware of the weight of his stare on her.

"Do we not walk together enough in the daytime to please you?" Rylik asked, his tone laced with mischief.

Embarrassment flooded Aria, burning hot across her cheeks. "I'll walk by myself. I need the fresh air anyway." She spun on her heel, determined to flee the situation. *Oh, please god, follow me. Let your annoying paranoia of me spilling your secret compel you to follow me, you damn Shadow.*

CHAPTER 10

ARIA

Aria rushed through the ballroom doors, the crisp night air catching her in a sudden breath. For a moment, the silence of the courtyard enveloped her, and the gravity of her boldness settled on her chest. She couldn't help but wonder if she had overplayed her hand.

A voice cut through her thoughts, smooth and casual. "I'd advise you against your course of action."

Aria turned sharply to see Rylik leaning against the entranceway to the courtyard, his posture relaxed but his eyes sharp.

She was somewhat relieved that his back was to the ballroom now. Perhaps if she could keep him distracted out here, Leon and the others might accomplish their aims. "I'm not allowed to walk by myself now?"

He pushed off the wall and strolled toward her with an easy grace. "You're in a beautiful dress for a reason, dear. You should be dancing in it."

Her heart thudded harder, and she forced herself to find some semblance of resolve. "Why did you tell the tailor you would buy whatever dress I wanted? However many I wanted?" The words spilled out before she could think better of them, and her stomach clenched with anxiety.

Rylik stopped a few feet away, angling his head as he regarded her with interest. "Is that what this is about?" A playful note colored his tone, hinting at something unspoken. He took another step forward, eyes never straying from hers. "Are you," he began tentatively, "are you under the impression that I have any sort of romantic interest in you?"

Her face flushed deeply, and she took an involuntary step back, words failing her.

A low chuckle escaped him, dark and rich. "Oh, I see. That is what you thought."

Her throat closed as she looked down, mortified. *Oh, if only I could crawl into a hole and die,* she thought miserably.

Rylik's voice softened, though his delight was unmistakable. "You are a healer in the palace—*My* healer. And you'll be employed here for the rest of your life, I'm certain. A trophy, no doubt, for the king in some ignorant quest for immortality. You'll attend a great many balls. You will require a great many dresses. And as much as the king may be paying you, it's certainly not enough of a salary to afford taking care of your aging parents and buying luxurious dresses." He leaned closer, his breath warm against her ear. "Since I have a keen interest in keeping my eyes on you at all times, I might as well enjoy the view."

Aria's blood hummed, her heart thundering in a frantic, dizzying rhythm. Was this a rejection or a confession? She pulled back slightly to meet his gaze, her thoughts a tangled mess of confusion and hope.

Rylik's smile was confident, his presence imposing as ever.

If it was the former, she was used to that. But if it was the latter, she was far outside of her depth. She hesitated with trembling fingers as she reached for his hand. If he was interested in her, then there was still a chance that she might not fail this objective – an objective which she was now finding herself far too invested in.

Rylik's gaze flickered in surprise at her touch, though he masked it quickly. His lips curled into a wry smile. "Careful, Pyra."

Aria's breath stilled as his eyes scanned her face, taking in the sight of her beneath the soft glow of moonlight. His fingers trailed up her arm, the heat of his touch seeping through the fabric of her sleeve. Slowly, they grazed her cheek, brushing aside a curling lock of hair.

Her heart pounded violently in her chest, a mix of excitement and nerves rendering her almost breathless as he leaned in closer.

Suddenly, a commotion broke out near one of the side entrances—a clatter of dishes and the sound of raised voices. Several guests turned to see what was happening.

Aria gasped. Was that the distraction Leon was talking about?

Rylik's head snapped in the direction of the noise, his body tensing instinctively. Before he could move, Aria's hand flew to his cheek, and she pressed her lips against his own in haste.

For a heartbeat, Rylik froze, caught off guard by the suddenness of Aria's lips on his. The softness of the kiss was a jarring contrast to the tension that had hung between them moments earlier. His surprise sparked briefly in his eyes, but it melted away quickly, replaced by something darker, more intense.

Then, without hesitation, he returned the kiss—deeply. His hand slid to her waist, gripping her with a strength that sent a shiver through her body, as though he were claiming her, pulling her into him with a possessive urgency. His fingers splayed across her back, pressing her flush against the solidity of his chest, the heat of his body seeping into her.

Aria's mind reeled, the kiss knocking the breath from her lungs. Startled by the depth of it, she instinctively leaned into him, her hands grasping his shoulders for balance as the world around her blurred into nothing. There was nothing but the taste of him, the way his tongue moved against hers with a fierce, controlled hunger. Her pulse raced, her heart thudding so loudly in her ears that the clatter from the disturbance in the courtyard had faded into a distant hum.

She hadn't meant for it to feel like this. She had intended it to be a distraction—something quick, something fleeting—but the warmth of his mouth on hers made her head swim. Her body responded to him on its own accord, a strange heat unfurling low in her stomach. It was intoxicating, dangerous.

Rylik's grip on her waist tightened momentarily, as if he, too, was caught in something unexpected, before his touch shifted, growing more forceful. His free hand cupped the back of her neck, fingers tangling in the loose strands of her hair, deepening the kiss with a slow, deliberate pressure.

Then, just as suddenly as it began, he pulled back. Aria gasped, her lips parted, the taste of him still on her tongue. Her head was spinning, her legs weak beneath her, and she clung to him, trying to steady herself.

Rylik's eyes were dark, his lips curving into a slow, knowing smile that sent a chill down her spine. He didn't speak immediately, only watched her for a long moment, as if savoring the look of surprise and confusion on her flushed face. "Please excuse me." His voice was low, amused, as he vanished into the shadows, leaving her standing alone.

Aria's face flushed with heat as she gasped for air, her mind racing after Rylik had so unceremoniously abandoned her. "Wait!?" she whispered, her voice trembling.

She had failed. He was going to catch them.

Aria rushed back into the ballroom, her heart racing as she scanned the room, her eyes darting from one guest to another, searching for any sign of calamity. But the festivities appeared undisturbed, the grand hall filled with laughter, conversation, and the lilting strains of the orchestra. Nothing. There was no commotion.

Her hands trembled slightly as she grabbed a glass of wine from a passing servant's tray, downing the entire glass in a single gulp. The alcohol burned as it slid down her throat, but it did nothing to calm the anxious storm churning inside her. Several minutes passed in agonizing uncertainty.

Suddenly, she felt a firm hand close around her wrist. She gasped, spinning around to see Leon standing behind her, his face tense, eyes darting about to ensure they weren't overheard. Before she could say anything, he tugged her to the side, away from the crowd.

"It's ruined," Leon said, his voice thick with frustration. His jaw clenched, his brow furrowed in anger. "The Sovereign found the man we were trying to smuggle out." He swallowed hard, his throat tight. "I wasn't directly involved in this one, but, the news is spreading. Fast."

Aria felt her stomach twist. "What happened?" she asked, her voice barely a whisper. Her heart pounded so violently she thought it might burst from her chest.

Leon's face darkened with a mix of defeat and rage. "The others—the ones trying to smuggle the defector from the cells—they didn't even have a chance to fight back." His words were bitter, clipped. "He took them all down. Quietly. Hastily. No one out here even noticed."

Aria's mind reeled, the room tilting ever so slightly as she struggled to process the news. "And the defector?" she asked, her throat dry.

"Back in the dungeons." Leon's hands clenched into fists at his sides. "The Sovereign was too fast. No one stood a chance." He shook his head, bitterness heavy in his voice. "Thanks for trying." Without another word, he pulled away, disappearing into the crowd as quickly as he'd come.

Aria stood there, fixed to the spot, her breath coming in short, ragged bursts. She grabbed another glass of wine, drinking it down just as fast as the first, her mind swirling with fear and shame. *Does he suspect me? Will he?* Her heart skipped a beat. *I kissed him! I kissed the Sovereign, and for longer than I should have.* The realization crashed over her, heat rising in her cheeks.

And I—I enjoyed it.

The shame of it made her want to sink into the floor.

Her gaze drifted across the room, landing on a familiar figure standing near the king—Rylik. He was whispering something into the monarch's ear, his expression composed, his manner calm, as though nothing had happened.

The king's face turned more serious as he listened, but after a moment, he nodded, forcing a polite smile for the guests watching him. Rylik, his task apparently complete, withdrew silently into the shadows, moving with a grace that kept him largely unnoticed by the rest of the crowd.

Aria's blood ran cold. When had the Sovereign slipped back into the ballroom? Her panic grew. He was too perceptive. He would know, undoubtedly now, that she was involved. Her thoughts spiraled into dread over her family's safety.

The instinct to flee overwhelmed her, and she turned toward the door, ready to bolt from the ballroom and the scrutiny of his all-seeing eye. But something stopped her. She hesitated, a sudden tightness gripping her throat. If she left now, it would only make things worse. It would make him suspicious.

She stood frozen in place, forcing herself to breathe, to calm the rising tide of panic. Closing her eyes, she willed her pulse to steady, fought the urge to run. She would have to stay here for the rest of the night and act like nothing was wrong.

Opening her eyes, she straightened her spine, forcing her body to move with the same casual grace as the other guests, despite the terror lurking just beneath her skin.

She was trapped. For now.

Aria set her emptied wine glass onto a passing servant's tray and swiftly lifted a fresh one. Perhaps a bit of intoxication would serve as her shield, should the Sovereign choose to interrogate her later. Although, there'd be no easy defense for kissing him. The thought alone exhausted her—she couldn't even begin to imagine a plausible lie. How could he possibly believe she'd developed a sudden infatuation with him? He knew, as well as she did, that he was her captor, her keeper, binding her to a life of reluctant servitude. People didn't simply fall into the arms of their jailers and embrace them with long, passionate kisses.

She took a long swallow of her wine, letting out a quiet, defeated sigh as the liquid burned down her throat. Across the room, she caught sight of Leon dancing with Maven. He was probably only doing it to avoid suspicion, but still, the sight pierced her. She wasn't possessive of Leon, and nor could she be, but something about the way he looked at Maven stirred a sour pang of jealousy within her.

Another swig, and her glass was empty again. Despite herself, she reached for a fourth, ignoring the inner voice urging restraint. There was a restless desperation clawing at her tonight—a bitterness that refused to be quieted. She'd kissed her enemy, failed her mission, and somehow still couldn't manage to catch Leon's attention. The sharp taste of wine filled her mouth once more as she tipped back another glass, then wandered unsteadily to the outer edge of the ballroom, where she found refuge in an empty, plush chair.

The night drifted on, one dance blending into another as she watched miserably from her secluded spot. Men approached her a handful of times, but she turned them all away with curt refusals. Had she been standing, anyone could have seen her growing inebriation and taken advantage, yet she remained tucked away, slouched in the safety of her seat. Four drinks, yet she knew they were four too many.

By the end of the night, her limbs felt loose, her vision blurred, and her legs barely managed to hold her as she wobbled down the corridors. If not for the guards who accompanied her back, she might very well have collapsed somewhere along the way.

As Aria entered her room, she exhaled a shaky sigh of relief. The guardsmen who had escorted her bowed slightly and closed the door behind her, leaving her in solitude. She moved to her vanity mirror, her steps heavy with exhaustion and emotional turmoil.

Sitting down in front of the mirror, Aria began methodically removing her hairpins and jewels. Each delicate piece of adornment was set aside, revealing her hair—once elegantly arranged—now cascading in tousled curls over her shoulders. She stared at her reflection, the image before her a stark contrast to the poised figure she had been just hours earlier. Her hair, now undone, framed a face that looked both disheveled and desperate.

Absent-mindedly, her finger traced her lips as if trying to hold onto the memory of their kiss. The sensation of Rylik's lips on hers replayed in her mind with vivid intensity. She couldn't shake the feeling, the way he had held her in that moment, his touch both fiery and consuming.

She was certain that she had never been kissed like that before. She blushed, her heart pounding at the memory. It was unlike anything she had ever felt, as though he might have consumed her very soul, and she would have offered it willingly. The thought was absurd, but perhaps her drunkenness had allowed her to briefly overlook the absurdity. She couldn't possibly like him, because she feared him. The last thing she should be doing is thinking fondly of his lips pressed against her own, especially when that moment didn't even achieve its purpose. Worse, still, the only thing it had accomplished was to ruin her emotional state, which was already fragile, and make her look even more like an untrustworthy traitor in his eyes.

She sighed helplessly, her thoughts a tangled mess of regret and fear. He had eagerly returned her kiss—her blatant attempt to distract him—and then he immediately left to go silently stalk and kill members of the Rebellion. He did that. And then, just as casually, entered the ball again as if it hadn't happened.

In a flustered movement, she stood abruptly, rubbing her anxious hand across her face. She would have to run away. She would have to talk to Leon, who would talk to Orren, and they would get her smuggled out of the country, with her parents, and they would live on a different continent, very far away. Yes. That was what she needed to do. She groaned, the weight of her situation crashing down on her as she moved to her bed. She collapsed onto it, her body sinking into the mattress in an effort to seek solace from its comforting embrace.

"I've drunk so much wine," she whimpered softly into the pillows. She closed her eyes wearily, the remnants of the night's events swirling in her mind. *Please, god, let this night have been nothing more than a nightmare I can awaken from in the morning.* She lay there in silence, the room around her dim and quiet, her thoughts a chaotic mix of despair and the desperate hope for a different reality.

CHAPTER 11

RYLIK

Rylik sat alone in his dimly lit chamber, the moonlight filtering softly through the gauzy curtains that framed the windows. The flickering firelight danced across his face as he lounged in an armchair, absently toying with his signet ring. His eyes, though focused on the flames, were distant and troubled, a mixture of frustration and intrigue simmering beneath his stern exterior.

The events of the evening replayed in his mind—Aria at the ball, her presence like a vivid flame amidst the grandiosity of the event. Her unexpected kiss was now seared into his memory, a poignant moment that both sent a thrill coursing through him and a deep aggravation at the same time. He muttered a curse under his breath, the sound barely more than a whisper against the crackling fire. *She's muddying my senses,* he thought, his agitation palpable. *I ensured she looked so deeply "captivating" that even I fell victim, and lost sight of my own objectives, even if just for a moment.*

He glanced down at the ring twirling between his fingers, a silent reflection of his inner turmoil. *How is it that she has such an effect on me? He* wondered. *Am I so starved for human connection? Or simply starved for the touch of a beautiful woman?* He clenched the ring tightly in his fist, and his gaze remained fixed on the fire. This should've been an easy night, watching her in that dress and making the room tilt in her direction. He had just wanted to enjoy the view.

Rylik sighed deeply, drawing his fist up to his lips, leaning heavily on the arm of his chair. Leontias was quick to snatch her into his arms, which he had assumed might happen. He allowed a smirk to curve his lips. He supposed now that was more for her benefit, so she could see that while her love may be unrequited, the man was not blind. He was thankful, though, for the admittance from her lips that the Corporal was no lover to her and never had been. But even so, it still pleased him to take her so easily from Leon and watch that wonder fill her eyes.

He recalled her smile and the fleeting moments of laughter they had shared, the way her eyes had sparkled when he had guided her across the dance floor. The signet ring now rested lightly on the bend of his index finger as he pressed it gently to his lips in thought. Maybe Leontias really is blind. How do you miss such a beauty, when she is standing right in front of you, looking like *that*? He found himself smirking again, the memory of her kiss mingling with his thoughts.

The taste of her had been intoxicating—sweet and rich, leaving him hungry for more as her warmth enveloped him. Whether she had intended to prolong it or not, he seized her with unforgivable possession. He had claimed her in that moment, savoring every second as her mouth melted against his, surrendering to him. His palms ached as he remembered how he had threaded his fingers through her wild curls, pulling her closer, as if he could fuse their souls together.

Rylik couldn't decide if her actions then were merely a woman desperate for his affection, or if she had some role to play in what followed. It was well-timed after all, and up until now, she had made concerted efforts to be distant from him. Was it an inevitable surge of desire that had fueled her? Or was it a ploy to distract him? She certainly had returned his passion with her own enthusiasm, which brought him unparalleled satisfaction.

His chest squeezed at the thought of her tongue mingling against his own, allowing himself a moment to give way to dark reveries. Again, he felt that unrelenting surge of need that left him breathless. Every part of him surged with a desperate hunger, the impulse to consume her, to mark her as his. He could feel her yielding all the more beneath him, and it only fueled the flames of desire that roared through his veins.

He wished, now, that he could've pressed her into the shadows, leaving her gasping between him and the stone walls of the courtyard. She wouldn't have been able to slip away. Barely a word would've escaped her lips as he sought to claim all of her, and he would've *savored* it. He clenched the ring into a fist again, standing abruptly from his chair as if jolted by his own thoughts. He cursed softly under his breath, the turmoil evident in his features.

Rylik walked over to the mantle and grabbed a glass of wine, tilting it back in a single swig.

I must be losing my mind, or simply losing my edge. He had been so careful to keep his distance from her after the incident. The prisoner—none other than the disgraced nobleman Eldric—had been so terrified when Rylik had thwarted his escape attempt. It was a carefully constructed plan by the Rebellion, but, obviously not careful enough. Had he arrived any later, though, they might've slipped away into the night.

He recalled how swiftly and quietly he had dealt with the Rebellion's members, their screams unable to reach their throats before the life left their eyes. He had locked Eldric back in his cell with ease, and the whole thing had been finished in mere moments. His gaze absently wandered to the door connecting his suite with Aria's.

Rylik wondered if it would be wise to distance himself from her. His own momentary lapse of judgment could have cost him a valuable informant. And while the night was largely uneventful after that, she truly had been somewhat resigned, drinking far too much wine for a woman of her size. So much, in fact, that he had ordered his most trustworthy guards escorted her back to her room. Anyone could see that she was drunk, and the noblemen in the room had practically descended upon her like vultures.

Still, she refused them, much to his delight, making the night at least easier in that regard. She did seem to be pouting, though. Perhaps she was disappointed that he didn't return to the courtyard to finish what she had started.

Rylik looked away, down at the fire once more, as though it might offer clarity.

I have half a mind to enter her suite and…

He swallowed hard, forcing the thought away. *Do **not** finish that thought, Rylik.*

He moved to his desk, grabbing the bottle of wine and refilling his glass. He sighed deeply, the weight of the evening pressing heavily on him. He needed to compose himself. This would not do. He took another drink, more passively this time, the bitterness of the wine offering a temporary respite from his agitation.

She is nothing more than my prisoner. She will heal my blight, keep my secret, and remain firmly under my thumb for as long as I wish her to. And if she has feelings for me, then, he became reflective, pensive. *Then I'm sure there's no harm in obliging her desires.* He wasn't foolish enough to push away a beautiful woman. He would just have to keep his wits about him and not get too close.

With that dark thought, he placed the signet ring on the table, the firelight pulsing across it like a warning. A question, unbidden, gnawed at the edges of his mind.

What if she used me? He couldn't ignore it. The fervor in her kiss had seared into his memory, yet the timing of it whispered betrayal. He narrowed his gaze, a steel-cold resolve hardening within him. He was not a man who allowed himself to be ruled by faith or foolish optimism. No, suspicion had always served him well.

Straightening, he set his sights on her suite door. If she truly was a loose thread, one that posed even the slightest risk, he would handle it swiftly. A well-placed reminder of who held the power was all it would take. As his gaze darkened, shadows swirled around him, rising in smoky coils, and in a breath, the darkness swept him from sight as he passed through the Veil.

In the next instant, he stood in her bedchamber. The room lay in quiet, undisturbed silence, bathed in moonlight spilling through the tall windows, painting silver pools across the polished marble floor. His gaze roamed over the scene, his shadow slipping ahead of him like a prowling creature, dark and watchful. A faint sound broke the stillness, and he slowed, halting as he caught the softest murmur.

A whimper drifted from the bed, and his brow furrowed. He inhaled abruptly, his attention sharpening as he watched her, as if caught in some haunting dream. Her bare thigh shifted, ghostly white against the midnight teal of her gown, and he noticed it was no dream she was caught up in. Her fingers were between her legs and pressed low against herself, eyes closed, as she drew in steady, even breaths. He stood in raptured silence, a figure melded into the shadowed canvas of her room, his sight held captive on something he was never meant to witness.

The question of whether to leave or stay rooted him in place, an indecision rare for him yet impossible to shake. Slowly, he turned aside, as if his presence alone threatened to fracture the stillness.

Then, a soft, breathy whisper drifted through the room, stilling him at once.

"Sovereign," The sound of his title, so faint yet unmistakable, made him halt.

Had he been noticed? His eyes narrowed, every sense sharpened, as shadows coiled protectively around him, cloaking him in obscurity. He slipped forward, gliding closer through the darkness, his presence a mere ripple against the silence as he neared her bed. She couldn't have seen him. No one ever had—not truly—and she would be no exception. Yet there it was again, his title on her lips, as if summoned in desperation.

He watched her closely, his gaze intent as her fingers deftly massaged herself in the safety of her satin sheets

Another soft, tremulous gasp slipped from her, followed by a pleading murmur, "Sovereign."

It was both an invitation and a mystery he found himself utterly powerless to resist. His eyes widened, realization striking him with sudden clarity—she was thinking of *him*. A slow, devilish smile began to spread across his lips as he savored the notion.

Another moan escaped her, serene and uninhibited, as if she was slipping deeper into her own satisfaction. An insatiable curiosity ignited within him, stirring a dark fascination to see her fully surrender, to witness her crossing the threshold of pleasure. His gaze fastened on her, her silhouette partly veiled in shadow yet no less enticing for it—an erotic vision that left little to his imagination. She called out for him again, her voice a frantic whisper trembling in the silence.

He clenched his eyes shut, fingers curling into fists at his sides. What was he doing? He had come here to confront her, to level his suspicion, not to watch her indulge some wild fantasy of him. A sudden, painful swallow constricted his throat, his pulse hammering as he forced himself to step back, each soft gasp she made clawing at his restraint.

He had to leave—*now*—before he became too invested in her fevered dream and decided not to leave at all.

In a silent sweep of shadows, he melted from view, only to reappear in his suite by the fire, where the embers flickered a haunting glow over his figure. His trousers felt noticeably tighter, his breath now uneven for reasons he was unwilling to confront.

She wanted him.

He glanced once more at her door, a single heartbeat away from crossing a line he knew could unravel him. With a rough sigh, he forced himself back into his chair, fingers gripping the armrests as if anchoring himself to reason. Could she truly have harbored a desire for him all this time? Why? How? He had been cold, ruthless, a shadowed threat when they'd first met, his intentions laid bare without mercy. When had her feelings shifted, and how had he failed to notice?

Women often wanted him, yes—but not women he'd blackmailed, not women he'd forced into silence. A rare, dark amusement tugged at the corner of his mouth, and he raised a hand to his lips, as if to hold it back.

She wants me.

He relished the thought, tasting the sinful decadence of it. The passion of her kiss had burned through him and now she wanted more, just as he did. He stood to his feet in a futile attempt to soothe the tightness he felt surging low within him, suddenly desperate to reenter her room. He wanted to hear the climax of her reveries, to touch every smooth part of her, to have his fingers trace the same pattern she had. How saturated would that dress be now?

A dark, frustrated growl rumbled low in his throat as he stormed toward the door at the far end of his room, his body taut with unspent need and agitation. He couldn't remain here, trapped with a temptation that clawed at his deteriorating restraint. This was one kiss—one brief, reckless kiss—and yet it gnawed at him, seeping into his mind like a poison. Letting it unravel him was weakness; succumbing to the fevered visions that crept in would be foolish. It was madness. And if he stayed in this room a moment longer, he'd risk committing sins he was barely prepared to name, let alone resist.

* * *

The soft glow of morning light crept through Aria's window, casting golden hues over her rumpled bed. She lay tangled in her ballgown, its rich fabric twisted and riding up her thighs, her fiery red curls fanning wildly across the sheets, tousled and unkempt. Her chest rose and fell in the peaceful rhythm of sleep, completely unaware of the shadow that moved silently through the doorway.

Rylik stepped into her room without a sound, his gaze drifting over her sleeping form. He paused at the foot of her bed, intrigue flickering in his eyes as they roved over the scene before him.

All at once, the memory of her shallow breaths in that very bed assaulted him and he closed his eyes, attempting to steel himself against it. He had spent the better part of the night distracting himself, but now here he was, already crumbling at the mere sight of her. *Pitiful,* he scolded himself.

He sighed, his hand moved almost of its own accord, brushing a lock of her wild hair away from her face as if she was his alone to touch. He paused, admiring the delicate features of her face, the slope of her cheekbones, the fullness of her lips. She *was* his, whether she realized it or not. His fingers hovered for a moment longer before he slowly withdrew, tucking his hand at his side as he took a couple of steps back, giving her space before his voice cut through the quiet.

"Aria?" he spoke softly, but with an edge of authority. "Are you going to sleep all day?"

Her eyelids fluttered open, dazed and confused at first, her mind struggling to catch up with reality. But when she saw him standing there, she bolted upright, only to wince in pain.

"Ungh," she groaned, rubbing her head, undoubtedly hungover. As he observed her, he noted the way that her eyes slowly began to widen, likely recalling each memory of the evening, one by one until she finally glanced up at him with worry.

Rylik's lips curled into a knowing smirk. "Sleep well?"

Her face betrayed a raw panic as she grappled with the vivid echoes of the night before. "I could use more sleep, honestly," she spoke low, her voice still groggy as she reached for any semblance of an excuse. "I may have overdone it with the festivities, I think. The wine, specifically."

He said nothing, only watched her, his amusement clear.

Aria swallowed, her nerves rattling beneath the surface, but not invisible to him. "Surely I'm not needed for anything important this morning, am I? I mean, all that happened was a ball last night. How much could I possibly be needed today?"

Rylik clicked his tongue and casually clasped his hands behind his back. "There was a commotion that occurred while we were in the courtyard last night. That commotion left a straggler in its wake, consuming much of the remainder of the night, unfortunately."

He stepped closer, his movements slow and deliberate. "However, that's not why I'm here." His voice dropped as he casually sat on the edge of her bed beside her, his gaze locking with hers. "It seems last night, in the wake of the disruption, we both forgot about something important."

Rylik began to unlace his tunic, his fingers moving with an almost maddening precision over each tie. Aria's breath quieted, her widened eyes betraying her unease as he tugged the laces loose, the silence between them stretched taut. The fabric parted slowly, revealing the chiseled contours of his chest, and without hesitation, he leaned closer. His hand found hers, firm but unhurried, guiding her trembling fingers to rest against his bare skin. She flinched at the contact, but he held her there, the gesture commanding yet oddly gentle, as if daring her to pull away.

"Why are you suddenly so frantic, dear?" he murmured, amusement playing in his eyes as he held her hand in place. "I only need you to heal my blight."

Her mouth fell open in dumbfounded realization, though her cheeks flushed with nerves. "Right! Of course, that." She swallowed hard, trying to regain her composure. "Sorry, I'll go ahead and," She trailed off, exhaling deeply as her eyes glowed with the soft gleam of golden magic, her healing powers flowing into him.

Rylik breathed slowly, his chest rising and falling as the relief from the blight washed over him like a long-awaited balm. The familiar warmth spread through his veins, easing the cold that had gripped him for so long. He closed his eyes, allowing himself a moment to fully savor the sensation, the tension in his body melting away. For a brief second, it was as though nothing else existed but the soothing heat. When he reopened his eyes, his gaze fell on her once more, this time softer, yet more pensive, his thoughts turning as he studied her in silence. He wanted more. He *needed* more.

"My—my hand, Sovereign," she reminded him, her voice quiet as she began to pull back.

Rylik's lips curled into a dark smile, but he released her hand reluctantly, watching her shrink back slightly.

"I also feel the need to apologize for last night," Aria said suddenly, standing and putting as much distance between them as she could. "I think I've given you the wrong impression."

"Oh?" His voice was unhurried, his eyes following her every movement as she tried to gather her composure.

"I—I have feelings for Leon," she blurted, her back to him. "I think you know that. I was trying to make him jealous."

Rylik's eyes clouded over, a faint glimmer of disbelief crossing his face. *This* was her excuse? "An act of jealousy, was it?" he asked, his voice deceptively calm as he stood, moving toward her with slow, predatory steps. He looked her over, eyeing her fingers as they clenched around her skirt, unabashedly recalling how last night he'd watched those same fingers move provocatively in the moonlight.

"Yes." Her voice wavered in her lie, "And I'm sorry. It was childish of me. It won't happen again."

He stopped inches from her, close enough to feel the heat from her skin. He reached for her chin, tilting her face toward him.

"You kiss very passionately for a woman trying to make a man jealous," he murmured, his voice smooth but edged with a dark amusement. "I'm either naive to your feminine wiles, or you're lying to save face."

Her heart raced, her eyes wide and conflicted as they met his.

"Either way," he continued, his lips curling into a smirk as he leaned closer, "I don't mind if it isn't genuine. In fact, the less sincere you are, the easier it will be for me to take advantage of anything you offer up."

She stared at him in shock, her mouth slightly agape. He could see the effect of his words pouring over her. He wasn't merely *implying*, he was outright *saying* that he could continue in romantic affairs with her with no attachment. He reveled in her ire.

"You are a *rake*, Sovereign," she hissed, scowling.

A wicked grin crossed his face, thoroughly amused by her frustration. "And you are a desperate *whore*," he replied, his voice as smooth as it was cutting.

Her cheeks flared with anger, her hand twitching at her side, likely desperate to slap him. But she knew better than to retaliate. His lips curved in a manner that dared her to respond.

In a flash, her palm connected with his cheek, sharp and swift. He blinked, stunned, his head jerking slightly to the side from the force of her slap. For a moment, silence hung between them, heavy with tension, as he slowly turned his gaze back to her. Then, his lips pulled into a slow, unnerving grin, the glint in his eyes cold and dangerous, promising she'd regret it.

Her eyes widened, and she took a hesitant step back, as though she truly had anywhere to run from him. He tilted his head, his gaze dark with satisfaction, relishing the quiet tremor in her frame that she tried so hard to suppress. The fear in her eyes was a temptation he savored, a silent acknowledgment of the control he could wield with nothing more than a look.

He clicked his tongue softly, his eyes dark with mischief and something far more dangerous as he whispered, "Not the wisest move, Pyra." He advanced on her with measured steps, his movements calm yet commanding. Her retreat was instinctive, stopping only when she collided with the solid surface of the wall, leaving her caught in his looming shadow.

"You must think I'm someone who tolerates such things," he murmured, his tone low and calm, prolonging the moment for his own amusement. He leaned in just slightly, his voice lowering to a teasing, almost seductive purr. "Just this once, for *you*, I'll let it slide," he said, his lips brushing the edge of her ear. "But if you try to do anything like that again, I won't be so forgiving. You'll regret it. Though, not in the way you might think."

She swallowed, her gaze slipping to the side as she instinctively sought to distance herself. He caught the subtle shift and, with a knowing grin, took a slow step back.

"Please leave my room," she bit out, her voice sharp. "Now."

Rylik chuckled darkly, folding his hands behind his back. Even after his warning, she dared to issue a command? He stood firm, unmoving, fully intent on offering her no satisfaction.

"I need to get dressed for the day," she said stiffly, lifting her chin defiantly. "You might have noticed I haven't changed from last night."

His eyes wandered slowly over her, committing the sight to memory. The fabric of her gown, once pristine and elegant, was now creased and bunched awkwardly from the night's events, drawing attention to the way it clung snugly to her hips, accentuating the curve of her figure in ways that felt both unintentional and arousing.

Her hair, a striking red, had come undone from its careful styling, now falling in wild, unruly curls around her face like a fiery halo. Each curl framed her delicate features in a disarray that only heightened her beauty, giving her an untamed, almost vulnerable look, as though the chaos of the evening had stripped away her carefully maintained composure. His smile widened, clearly pleased. "It would seem you look the very same, yes." *And yet, somehow far more enticing right now*, he couldn't help but to think.

Aria's blush deepened as she shifted, uncomfortable under his gaze, seemingly gesturing for the door. "If you would please—!"

He almost pitied her, he mused with a dark smirk. He'd insulted her, threatened her, and yet her only weapon now was that sharp tongue of hers. Mercy wasn't something he typically indulged in, but perhaps he'd make an exception—this time. He'd never deny his enjoyment of others' discomfort, but even he could see Aria was teetering on the edge this morning. After the night she'd indulged in, who could blame her?

Rylik's pleasure lingered as he slowly walked past her. "I'll be just outside your door."

She exhaled shakily. "Other than the healing just now, what else am I needed for today?"

He paused at the door, glancing back over his shoulder. "I haven't decided yet," he said with a passive, pleased smile. "Perhaps I'll have you accompany me into town."

"For what?" she asked, her tone laced with dread.

But Rylik only smiled wider, leaving the room without another word, the door clicking softly behind him.

CHAPTER 12

ARIA

Aria's mood had soured that morning, her usual composure frayed by Rylik's presence. She avoided his gaze, trailing a few steps behind as they moved away from the carriage that had taken them into town. Each step into the capital was an effort to keep her growing irritation at bay, but her mind wouldn't let go of the sting from earlier. Her eyes bore into the back of his head, imagining the satisfaction of seeing him flinch—though she knew he wouldn't. Rylik was unshakable, always so smugly composed, and it only deepened her annoyance.

Last night had been a mistake. A series of mistakes, it would seem. Not only had she kissed the Sovereign – regrettably enjoying it – but she had fallen victim to a chaotic, beautiful, wicked dream of him. The shame pooled low inside of her as she steadied her breath, clumsily watching his cape billowing just paces in front of her. The dream had awoken her with such a violence of emotion, leaving her weak and sodden with a desire she could hardly bring herself to acknowledge.

She could recall his tongue in her mouth, undoubtedly a leftover remnant from the reality of that kiss only hours prior to her slumber. Her throat constricted, and she pulled a hand up to her chest, resisting the pull to touch her own lips. *This sinful hand.* She looked at her fingers in spite, lowering them back to her side, squeezing the material of her dress into a tight bundle against her palm.

She had been intoxicated, she reminded herself. She wasn't fully in control of her actions when, bleary-eyed she had awoken from her twisted reveries of the Sovereign in the middle of the night. It was hardly her fault that her mind had entertained such a lurid incitement. He was undeniably attractive, and it was futile to ignore both that fact and the effect he had on her heart. Truly, their kiss under the stars had been blissful, but to think of him the way she had in that dream, it was unforgiveable.

Her heart wrenched against itself, recalling all the places his touch had been on her body, the way his tongue had felt against her bare skin. She had been insatiable, clawing at him to please her so fully as she had never been pleased before. She wasn't completely ignorant to sex, she knew. The functions of it were simple and basic, and she had tried it out once.

The act had been enjoyable, though it seemed to lack finesse — but whether the fault was hers or that of the man she'd chosen, she could never be sure. Men and women alike had hailed it as the ultimate experience of euphoria. And perhaps it was, but she had only found such satisfaction on her own. She could only concede that a man was necessary for one particular trait inherent to his body — a trait that carried with it a delicious depth and force.

Pressing her lips together, she let out a slow exhale to center herself. She should not be thinking about that particular trait where it concerned the Sovereign. The problem was surely that she was still frustrated with Leon. He had never indulged her, even for a moment, despite how outwardly she had attempted to be affectionate with him. He wasn't interested. He was so disinterested, in fact, but she had found solace in his friend's arms one particular night.

Even now, she could not recall his name. He had expressed interest in her before, and doted on her, and she was so very exhausted with Leon's rejection that she caved into the fleeting temptation of release. The night had been forgettable in a lot of ways, but not unpleasant. It was nice to feel wanted, but the moment had been largely devoid of significance. Had it not been her first time—and *last* time—she might've forgotten it entirely.

For now, she could only settle for the unbidden dreams that would come to her on rare occasions. Had she been a little less drunk, she might've thought better of her actions last night and refrained. But, for some nagging reason, the thought of Leon didn't set her body aflame as it always had. She swallowed at the memory of Rylik's haunting blue eyes gaping at her in the shadowy courtyard. No, unfortunately, it was another man entirely that was affecting her. She fixed her eyes on his back, wrestling inwardly with thoughts she knew she shouldn't entertain.

He was dangerous, and possibly the purest form of evil incarnate. He was the enemy. He was lethal and merciless. This senseless fixation on him would have to end, sooner rather than later. She had no doubt that logic and rationale would outweigh the insatiable urge to pull him into a darkened alleyway and claim those lips again.

This man had threatened her and her family. He was a menace, not only to the Rebellion, but to herself. Their relationship was surely warden and prisoner, at best. Hope for anything more than that would be foolish. To *want* for anything more than that would be insanity. If there was anything she truly wanted, it was to be continents apart from him.

Because the longer she stayed in that wretched palace, the more the lines between Rebellion and loyalty were beginning to blur. She was supposed to be against all of this—a hidden thorn in the Sovereign's side. And yet, she felt herself becoming just another cog in the king's cruel machinery. She needed to sharpen her mind, not lose herself to girlish, wistful, drunken fantasies of the Sovereign late into the night.

His murderous proclivities aside, how could she even think of him as any sort of suitor at this point, especially after his little remark earlier? It had been snide, cutting, likely in response to her own barbed comment and it still clung to her thoughts. It had been a petty exchange of insults, nothing more. Yet, she couldn't shake the irritation that he'd retaliated at all. Perhaps he had a right to be offended by her cold dismissal of him, but still, there were better ways to handle such things. Then again, he was the Sovereign. Moral compasses and decency were not traits he concerned himself with.

As they continued with their morning, Aria steeled herself, masking her frustration beneath a carefully crafted facade of neutrality. She would banish her lewd thoughts of him and set herself straight upon a course that served the Rebellion and not her own self-gratification.

The streets of the capital buzzed with life as Rylik led Aria through the winding alleys and bustling squares. The vibrant marketplace stood in stark contrast to the solemn halls of the castle, and Aria, unused to such vibrancy, felt a thrill of excitement coursing through her. Colorful stalls lined the streets, and lively street performers captivated the crowds. She cast sidelong glances at Rylik, who moved with purpose, seemingly unperturbed by the sights and sounds around them.

It feels so good to be outside the palace, she thought. Aria's eyes darted to a group of musicians playing an upbeat tune in the corner. The melody was light and enticing, stirring an old yearning within her, though she quickly pushed it aside. She had never explored the capital before. Though she doubted she would have the chance today. She pouted slightly. "I assume this isn't a leisurely visit?"

Rylik glanced at her, a small half-smile playing on his lips. "You assume correctly. I have business to attend to."

Her expression fell, glum yet resigned, as she stole one last look at the musicians before they rounded a corner.

As they turned, a small, nondescript shop came into view. Above the door, a faded sign read *Alchemical Wonders*, and the glass windows were fogged, obscuring the treasures within. Rylik opened the door, gesturing for her to enter.

Inside, the air was thick with the scents of herbs, oils, and something slightly acrid. Shelves lined the walls, filled with vials of every size and color, each containing swirling liquids and powders. Aria's curiosity piqued immediately, her eyes darting over the strange concoctions.

Rylik observed her with casual detachment, leaving her to explore as he approached the counter.

An old man with a curved spine and wiry gray hair emerged

from the back, his eyes glinting with suspicion as he looked Rylik over. "Ah, hello, Sovereign. Are you here for the usual?"

"Not this time," Rylik replied, glancing over his shoulder to ensure Aria was properly enthralled by the displays. "I no longer have need for my usual elixir. I'm here for the special request I mentioned a week ago."

The potion master nodded, producing three small vials from beneath the counter. One shimmered with a pearlescent white liquid, the one in the middle a deep crimson, and the third a dark sapphire blue, each one almost glowing in the dim light of the shop.

"What are those for?" Aria asked, suddenly at his side, her interest piqued.

Rylik, perhaps momentarily surprised by her sudden appearance, quickly recovered. "Just a few things to help with court matters. You needn't be interested."

She shot him a speculative glare, annoyance flickering in her eyes. The red one looked like a love potion. But the other two were unfamiliar to her. She was insatiably curious, but not brave enough to inquire about any of them.

Rylik paid the potion master swiftly and slid the vials into his coat. "Ready?"

"Lead the way," she replied, her tone laced with sarcasm. She doubted she had any real choice in the matter.

As Rylik moved toward the door, he paused when he noticed Aria admiring a display of tiny, delicate vials.

She reached out to gently touch one, her expression softening as she regarded the craftsmanship. "These are beautiful. I've never seen anything like them. I didn't know potions could be," she paused, searching for the right word.

"Artistic?" Rylik raised an eyebrow, a hint of amusement in his voice. "Even alchemists have their vanities, it seems. Did you want to buy one?"

Shaking her head, Aria replied, "No, I don't think I could afford anything in this shop. And I don't even know what this potion does. It's just pretty."

"That potion in your hand is a Whistling Wind Draught," the potion master announced, his voice bubbling with enthusiasm as he appeared from behind a shelf, startling her.

"Wh—what does it do?" Aria asked, her curiosity ignited.

"It conjures a soft, enchanting breeze that follows you, whistling delightful tunes whenever the air caresses them. The melodies shift with their surroundings—epic symphonies atop mountaintops or gentle lullabies by serene streams."

Aria's eyes sparkled with wonder. "That sounds utterly whimsical!"

Rylik observed her delight, a flicker of intrigue warming his gaze.

"What about this one?" she asked, pointing to a vibrant vial glimmering in the light.

"That is a Potion of Playful Shadows," the potion master explained, adjusting his spectacles with a twinkle in his eye. "It allows your shadow to dance to its own tune for a brief time, mimicking your movements with exaggerated flair, or even engaging with the shadows of others as if in a lively conversation or a little waltz."

Aria laughed, genuine amazement lighting her features. "I had no idea such potions existed! That's simply charming!"

Rylik blinked, seemingly caught off guard by the warmth of her laughter, feeling an unexpected enchantment envelop the moment.

"The one beside it is an Elixir of Rainbow Veils," the potion master continued, his enthusiasm radiating. "After you sip this, faint, rainbow-colored veils will trail behind you with every move, like wisps of colorful smoke that dance and vanish in an instant. It transforms even the simplest gesture into something magical."

Aria was entranced. "These are so inspired! Do you create all of these yourself?"

The potion master beamed, pride sparkling in his eyes. "Indeed, my dear. Each one is a labor of love."

"You're incredibly talented! These potions are fabulous!" Aria exclaimed, her voice bright with admiration.

"Allow me to show you another," the potion master said, guiding her to a nearby shelf. Aria cast an expectant glance at Rylik, waiting to see if he'd allow the indulgence. He gave a casual nod, paired with a half-smile. She grinned, then turned her attention back to the old man. He selected a potion, placing it delicately in her palm. "This is a Potion of Reflection. It grants you a fleeting glimpse of your future. A favorite among my patrons! While it may not always be accurate, it could pique your interest."

Aria's eyes widened with excitement, then shadowed with concern. "Oh, I'm sorry. I don't think I can afford—"

"Take it," the potion master insisted, gently closing her fingers around the vial. "It's been ages since anyone has come in here with such joy for the craft. It has warmed an old man's heart, I suppose." He chuckled, clearly delighted.

Rylik cocked a brow, a subtle shift in his expression as he observed the man.

"I couldn't possibly—" Aria started, her resolve wavering.

"Tut, tut!" The potion master waved his hands dismissively, a mischievous grin spreading across his face. "I insist!"

Aria's smile bloomed like a flower in spring. "You are too kind, sir. I will cherish it. Thank you!"

"You have a rather enjoyable young lady here, my lord," the potion master remarked, casting a knowing glance at Rylik. "If you're not careful, I might be tempted to steal her away from you."

Rylik smiled, though subtle agitation flickered in his eyes. "Not until my last breath."

Aria stifled a snort, covering her mouth. *To anyone else, that could sound romantic. But I know it's because he considers me little better than his lifelong prisoner.*

The potion master laughed heartily. "Oh! How I love seeing a young lad in love."

"Actually—" Aria began, but Rylik cut her off, putting an arm around her possessively.

"Thank you for bestowing a little joy on my lady's face this morning," he said, his tone firm yet oddly protective.

Aria felt her cheeks flush at his words, the warmth of his arm around her shoulder, and the scent of him so close. The fact that he referred to her as his "lady" sent her heart racing for reasons she didn't want to understand.

Soon after, they stepped out of the shop and back into the bustling streets, the vibrant life of the capital enveloping them once more.

As they strolled down the cobblestone road, Rylik glanced sideways at Aria. "Remind me to bring you every time I need to visit that potion master. In all my visits, I have not once received a free item. Had I known it was as easy as batting my lashes and fawning over him, I'd have been doing that from the start."

Aria chuckled, watching him give her a half-sneer. "I'm sorry, are you jealous that I got something for simply being excited about his beautiful potions? I certainly didn't think my enthusiasm was going to win me anything!"

Rylik's amusement was tinged with agitation. "It's not merely your 'enthusiasm' that he admired. Undoubtedly, you are a vision of youth and beauty he hasn't seen in a long time, and he merely wished to see you keep smiling for him as long as possible. You do not know the effect you have on people, it would seem."

Her cheeks flushed at the compliment. "Well, I hardly think my appearance had anything to do with it. I liked his potions. I think they're magical and wonderful and sweet. It's precious that there is still a little charm and sweetness left in the world."

Rylik sighed, mildly pleased, then looked away from her. "So, are you going to use your potion? Curious about your future?"

Aria glanced down at the vial in her hands, wonder sparkling in her eyes. "I have to admit, I am a little curious."

"Go on," he urged, shrugging casually.

She couldn't help but wonder, would she see Leon and herself, old and gray, huddled together in their cozy future home? Would the world finally be peaceful around them? Tension built within her, her lips dry and parched as she gathered her resolve. With a decisive tilt of her wrist, she poured the potion's contents into her mouth in one swift gulp. A warm tingle rumbled over her skin as she looked at her arms.

"Well? Do you see anything yet?" Rylik asked, his scrutiny evident.

"No, just feeling a warm tingle, is all. Maybe it takes a moment to work?"

Either that or the old man swindled you with a dud, came Rylik's voice, threaded with sarcasm.

She turned to Rylik with a sigh, "He wouldn't do that."

"What?" he asked, furrowing his brows.

"Didn't you," she inquired slowly, "say something just now?"

"No," he said, tilting his head.

"But, I—" she began, but then her voice dropped off, noting his attention shifting away from her to the people passing by them. "Huh," she muttered, shrugging her shoulders, "I guess it was a passerby. Sorry."

Rylik glanced down the street. But again, Aria heard his voice. *It may be most advantageous to hail a carriage back into town if we stay around much longer.*

She looked up at him, surprised when he turned his head to the side, his lips unmoving, yet words still flowed into her ears.

His thoughts continued aloud for her as he met her eyes. *Why is she staring at me?* "Do you have a question, Aria?"

Swallowing, she hesitated. "No. Sorry, I just—I saw my future." She knew she needed to cover this whole thing up with haste.

Rylik's brow raised, intrigue replacing skepticism. "Oh? And what did you see?"

"I saw myself. I was old and weathered—happy, even." She attempted a smile, but her thoughts raced. That sly old man must've given her a potion to hear inner thoughts. If it wasn't presently happening, she'd scarcely believe such a thing was possible. This couldn't be any ordinary potion. It likely cost a lot of money.

"Living into your old age, hm? Well, that must be a comfort." He smirked, looking aside again. *At least it wasn't a dud. Regardless, those fortune-telling potions are mostly harmless apparitions of hopes for the future, rather than anything truly revealing.*

Cautiously stepping up beside him, Aria kept her revelation quiet. "Well, where to next, Sovereign?"

"I was finding it difficult to concentrate earlier on our ride into town, on account of your rumbling gut. So, perhaps we should get you some food before heading back?"

Her embarrassment washed over her. Cutting remark aside, she was quite hungry. She had skipped breakfast on account of trying to hurry out the door to keep up with his schedule.

"Do you have a food preference?" he asked. "At this hour, it's mainly breakfast treats, but I'm not sure if—"

"I would love to visit a bakery! Do you have one you like?"

Rylik hesitated, commenting to himself, *Well, I don't believe I've ever seen her so excited.* He gave a small smile, replying aloud, "I don't frequent many bakeries, but I am told there is one in the square that is quite popular."

"Lead the way, Sovereign." She eyed him slyly, delighted at the prospect of eavesdropping on his thoughts for every minute of that walk.

Rylik eyed her before turning away, beckoning her to follow him. As they walked, Aria buzzed along excitedly. Since she didn't know how long she would have until the potion wore off, she figured she should be advantageous and ask extremely probing questions. "Sovereign, why are you so paranoid about me? Why can't you just trust that I won't tell anyone what I know?"

He didn't look at her. "This is your idea of light conversation?"

"I'm not trying to keep anything *light*. I just don't understand why you have to be lurking in every dark corner behind me. I can be trusted, you know."

He let out a soft scoff. "You know too much to ever not be a liability. Trust isn't something I can afford with you, nor will I."

Aria stared up at him, willing him to think any thoughts. Frowning, she looked away.

Suddenly, a passerby's voice pierced her thoughts. *My god, what a woman.*

Startled, she searched for the source, finding a man leering at her as he walked past.

I'd like to get her alone and—

His words jumbled into noise as she simultaneously picked up Rylik's inner thoughts, resulting in a chaotic cacophony of sound. She winced as she plugged her ears to no avail.

Rylik saw the man, jaw tightening in annoyance, subtly shifting his cloak so that his dagger was easily visible. The man, sensing the obvious danger, scurried away, muttering curses under his breath.

With a satisfied smirk, Rylik turned to face ahead. Aria

instinctively pulled a little closer to him, unease creeping in as the gawker moved further away.

"It would be wise, especially as we get closer to the square, for you to stay close to me," Rylik said, pulling her in so that her arm was interlocked with his own.

Nodding, she braced a hand against his bicep, looking around dubiously for anyone else who might approach too closely.

Gods, if she squeezes me any tighter, I might—

Rylik groaned inwardly. *Do **not** finish that thought, Rylik.* Agitated with himself, he glanced at her.

Startled, Aria looked up, intrigue flickering in her eyes.

Great. Now she's staring again.

She hesitated at his thought, then looked away, feeling needlessly challenged by the mind-reading task she was fumbling through.

A group of women passed, their eyes on Rylik, thinking scandalous thoughts. Thankfully their words came jumbled and largely unintelligible, but she could gather they were interested in him.

Embarrassed, Aria squeezed him again, half in shock, half in annoyance.

I will not survive this walk if she keeps clawing at me like this, he thought, exasperation flooding him. *I would've thought after her obvious lie earlier this morning that she would at least attempt to act as detached as she now claims to be toward me.* "Careful, dear, I'm not a pin cushion."

Her brows furrowed at his accusation. Was the 'obvious lie' he was referring to the one she'd told him this morning? When she had said she kissed him to make Leon jealous? Was he truly so perceptive?! Aria's frown deepened as she pulled away entirely.

"You didn't need to pull completely away from me, you know," Rylik said, watchful.

Aria winced at the noisy thoughts of the crowd. "Can we go somewhere private? Somewhere quiet?"

Rylik chuckled, a hint of amusement in his eyes. "What's this now? You want us to steal away alone?" *I won't survive much more of this.*

"Yes! Please! Just for a few minutes." Aria's agitation built as she spoke.

With a teasing smile, Rylik pulled her down a side alleyway, the bustling noise of the marketplace fading into distant chatter. "Is this better now?"

Aria breathed out in relief, leaning her back against the cool stone wall and closing her eyes. "Yes. Much."

His hand rested lightly on her waist as he leaned closer, a provocative glint in his eye that startled her back into awareness.

"Sovereign?" she gasped, heart pounding as her thoughts flickered to the dream she'd had the night before—and the unsettling similarity to her current predicament.

"Yes?" His gaze was piercing, unrelenting.

"What are you doing?" she asked, her voice shaded with both confusion and the stirrings of her resurfacing imaginations.

Rylik's eyes roamed over her. "What am *I* doing? You just begged me to take you somewhere private to be alone with me. What are *you* doing?"

Her face flushed. "I was only wanting to stifle the noise! Of the people, I mean."

He raised an eyebrow. "There were hardly any people. Not enough to have overwhelmed you so."

"Well, I needed distance from it! And I needed *you*—" Aria's voice was firmer than she felt, suddenly realizing how that sentence came out, unable to save it in enough time before losing her words completely.

Rylik's interest piqued. *A confession*, he mused within his thoughts.

"No—" she stammered, "I mean, specifically I wanted to be alone with you. Because—no, that's not what I meant to say—"

He watched her stutter, a wry smile playing on his lips. *Adorable*, he thought to himself.

Aria's throat constricted, her heart fluttering at the unspoken comment.

How long will she pretend to deny her interests, I wonder? His eyes were content on her, challenging her.

"I wasn't lying this morning," she blurted, fuming. "I did kiss you to make Leon jealous. I meant that. So, whatever you think is still going on here between us, it is entirely in your head."

His smile turned dark as he leaned closer, the heat from his body enveloping her. His hand, firm against her waist, pressed her gently yet insistently against the cold stone wall, creating an abrupt contrast that sent shivers down her spine. *I should kiss her,* he thought with a tinge of mischief, *and see if that tongue of hers can continue to protest.*

Aria's heart thudded in her chest, each beat echoing in the stillness, leaving her utterly speechless. The intensity of his gaze held her captive, making the air thick with his hungry, unspoken words.

His lips brushed near her ear, sending a warm thrill through her as he whispered, "So, if I were to kiss you right now, you would push me away, right? Because Leon is nowhere in sight, and there is no one to incense."

Her mind spun from the closeness, the warmth and pressure of his hands anchoring her in place, while the cool stone pressed into her back, grounding her in a way that both excited and terrified her. There was hardly any space to breathe between them, the world outside fading away, leaving only the two of them in this charged moment.

"Well, I'm waiting. Push me away, like the vile reprobate you know that I am." His lips hovered tantalizingly close to hers, their warmth almost brushing against her own, yet never quite connecting.

She's waiting for me to act, is she? He turned the thought over in his mind.

Aria felt dizzy, swept up in the intoxicating mix of desire and defiance. She *did* want him to act, and she didn't want to question herself as to why. The tension crackled around them, wrapping her in a cocoon of urgency, leaving her unable to concentrate, lost in the magnetic pull of his presence.

Gods. If I start now, I won't stop, he reflected bitterly.

Aria exhaled a shaky breath, weighing the notion with cautious excitement.

Rylik finally pulled back, clasping his hands behind his back, but not without a lasting intensity in his gaze that kept her pulse racing.

"Yes, I can see it now. It's all in my head," he mused, a teasing edge to his tone.

She opened her eyes to meet his, the fire of embarrassment igniting in her cheeks while anger simmered just beneath the surface. It was a potent blend of emotions that left her reeling, the line between attraction and enmity blurring in the wake of their confrontation.

Oh, now I've aggravated her, he considered silently, a triumphant look on his face. *Perfect.*

Aria pushed herself off the wall with an aggravated shove, striding down the narrow alleyway, each step a testament to her frustration. Her thoughts raced, mentally chiding herself, and her stride faltered, bringing her to a hesitant stop. She glanced back, torn between her emotions and the connection she had with him. She could still read his mind. She still needed to keep him away from others, so that she could hear him clearly. But, she wasn't sure *how* to keep him alone without making him believe that she actually wanted any of this romantic nonsense. With a sharp turn on her heel, she called out, her voice firm, "Sovereign."

Rylik's voice came from behind her, calm and unbothered. "Yes, Aria?"

Closing the gap between them, though keeping enough distance to feel safe, she looked at him with a cold stare. "How long are you going to follow me around, watching my every move? The rest of my life?"

Without missing a beat, Rylik replied in his usual, passive tone, "Yes."

The simplicity of his answer startled her. "What?"

He turned his head, amusement tugging at the corners of his mouth. "My, such dramatic questions today. If I didn't know any better, I'd say you slipped me truth serum to ensure I gave you honest answers. But, you can rarely anticipate that I would ever give you an honest answer, dear, unless I stood to benefit from it."

Aria's eyes narrowed as she stared daggers into the back of his head, falling back into step behind him. "Did you mean what you said this morning when you called me a whore?" Her hand clenched at her side. She didn't know why she cared, or why she felt compelled to ask such a thing. She should be thinking about the Rebellion, not his words.

Rylik glanced back at her with a smirk. "No, a whore would take care in being subtle and professional in her dealings with men." He turned away again, his thoughts flickering in her mind. *And you are thankfully anything but subtle. And I love it.*

Aria froze for a moment, his words shocking her into silence. She was unable to comprehend the sheer arrogance of his statement, her mind spinning from the mixture of his words and his thoughts.

Love? Rylik continued walking smoothly, lost in his musings. *Am I really using the word 'love' in the same context as her? I'm no better than the potion master, clearly getting overtaken by her innocent ploys. I need to focus.*

Aria remained fixated and interested, hovering close behind him as she concentrated on his thoughts.

Rylik still had his back still to her as they walked. *Though, she is rather spirited today. I wonder why she keeps pulling and prodding me. Is she trying to make me lose my composure? It's obvious she is attracted to me, but likely resisting due to the fact that I hold her fate in my hands.* He smirked to himself at the idea. *Such a defiant little prisoner. If I wasn't so keenly aware of how inexperienced she is, I'd have forgone the trip into town and instead taken her to bed.*

Without warning, Aria collided into his back, lost in his thoughts and unaware that he had stopped. The impact sent a jolt through her, and she groaned, rubbing her nose in frustration.

Rylik peered over his shoulder, a teasing smirk playing on his lips. "Are you caught in a daze?"

Aria looked away quickly, attempting to hide her embarrassment. He had wanted to take her to bed? She was indignant that he did seem to think of her as no better than an escort! She swallowed her discomfort, fumbling for her words. "I—yes, a daze. Sorry," she muttered, her voice disgruntled.

Rylik's gaze pressed her. "Do I need to carry you?"

Her body stiffened at his suggestion. "I am perfectly capable of walking." She pushed past him with a burst of stubborn determination.

"Good." He let out a playful chuckle, his tone laced with teasing. "I was beginning to worry that hunger had overtaken you and made you weak at the knees."

Aria spun around on her heel, jabbing a finger into his chest. "I," her voice faltered, catching in her throat. She swallowed hard, the words escaping her as she was met with his triumphant smile.

It's adorable how she keeps trying to have the last word. Rylik mused, his satisfaction evident.

Aria pulled her finger back, exasperated, and turned away from him again, running a hand down her face in melodramatic frustration, wishing she'd never drunk that potion. Knowing his thoughts had only caused her to embarrass herself repeatedly in front of him. She sighed, feeling the weight of his perceptive gaze on her. He had her pegged with such accuracy that it infuriated her.

She didn't have much time to dwell on her thoughts as Rylik's arm slid around her, gently guiding her back toward the bustling city. "Let's get you something to eat. Can't have my healer passing out from hunger, now, can I? What good would you be to me then?" His smirk was infuriating, but she allowed herself to be led, too tired to resist.

As they stepped into the throng of the city streets, the noise swelled around them. The unpleasant mixture of hundreds of thoughts bombarded her mind, and Aria winced, her head throbbing as she tried to block them out. She staggered, the pressure overwhelming her.

Rylik glanced down at her, concern flickering in his eyes. "Are you alright, Aria?"

The world spun as her vision blurred, and the last thing she felt was the warmth of his arms catching her before darkness overtook her.

CHAPTER 13

ARIA

The scent of freshly baked bread and sweets greeted Aria as she slowly opened her eyes, the stillness of the room contrasting sharply with the chaos she had just left behind. Her surroundings came into focus, and she realized she was lying across a comfortable sofa in what appeared to be a bakery.

Rylik sat a short distance away, his back to her, arms folded as he gazed out the window. When he noticed her stirring, he turned, his expression softening from concern to calm amusement. "If I'd known you were so hungry you'd faint, I would've given you something to eat before we took that carriage into town. How are you feeling?"

Aria paused, listening for the hum of thoughts in the room of maybe five or six people.

Nothing. No outside thoughts.

She breathed a sigh of relief. "Better. I'm feeling better, Sovereign. Hungry, though."

Rylik stood and gestured to the table beside him laden with pastries and sweets. "I didn't know what you would like, so I bought one of everything. Take what you want."

Aria's eyes widened as she took in the assortment, her spirits lifting with unexpected excitement. She couldn't help but smile, her fingers brushing her lips in a childlike gesture of delight. She eagerly grabbed the first treat that caught her eye, barely able to contain her enthusiasm as she scarfed it down.

Rylik chuckled softly at the sight. "You act like a starved peasant child."

Her cheeks flushed with embarrassment as she quickly brushed the crumbs from her lips. "It's really good. You should have some, too. You did buy them, after all."

"I've already had breakfast," he said with a shrug, but when she gestured to the table again, he sighed. "Which one do you recommend?"

A smile tugged at her lips as she picked up a sweet roll and held it out to him. "This one."

Rylik's fingers brushed against hers as he took the roll, his touch lingering longer than necessary. He scrutinized the pastry for a moment before taking a bite, his expression shifting from indifference to pleasant surprise. "Hm. That's actually not bad at all."

Aria's heart skipped a beat, surprising her. *Oh, gods. Did I just think his smile was* **endearing***?* She hurriedly grabbed another treat, mentally swatting away the thought.

As Rylik finished the roll, he looked her over with a casual gaze. "It was a good recommendation. Thank you."

Her smile was candid, despite the odd tension between them. "I can't finish all of these myself," she said lightly. "Come on, help yourself."

Rylik shook his head. "I bought them for *you*, not for myself."

Aria rolled her eyes with a soft laugh. "Then I'm going to need a basket to take these back to the palace. You were a bit overzealous in your attempt to appease my hunger, Sovereign. It's already bad enough I had to faint in your arms and likely be carried in here by you like I was useless sack of potatoes. Truthfully, I'm a bit embarrassed."

Rylik's smile was knowing. "Don't be embarrassed. I didn't mind it."

Her cheeks burned with the weight of his words, and she glanced away, chortling softly. "You didn't mind me passing out? You're more vindictive than I gave you credit for."

He was clearly amused. "It was honestly nice to have a reprieve from your mouth for a bit."

Aria shot him a sharp look but couldn't help the sly grin tugging at her lips. "My mouth? I believe yours is the one that could use a reprieve."

He raised an eyebrow, his grin growing more mischievous. "Huh. That's not how it seemed in the alley. In fact, I think you wanted my mouth. Did you not?"

Aria's face flushed as she remembered the cold stone wall at her back, and the heat of his breath and fingertips threatening to consume her. He knew she was thinking of it too, now, no doubt. *Insufferable ass.* She grabbed another treat and bit into it with frustration. "A basket," she demanded, gesturing to the counter. "Perhaps you might put your mouth to good use and ask the clerk for one." Then, with half-hearted regret, she added, "please."

With a satisfied smirk, Rylik rose to do as she asked.

He was back moments later with a basket, catching her attention as it drifted out the window to the plaza. She was smiling broadly as if it were the most pleasant thing she had seen all day aside from the enchanting potions in *Alchemical Wonders*.

"You really like the capital, do you?" He asked her passively.

"I've never really been to the capital—not until today," she said shyly, "and we only passed through it when I was brought here to serve the King." She looked back to him with bright eyes, shrugging her shoulders. "I like what I've seen so far. I love how everything is so lively and exciting. It's so different from my village and from the castle as well."

"I see," he mused with a kind expression, kinder than even she could believe given his usual ominous countenance. "Well, we'll have to come back another time then."

"You mean that?" She asked brightly, not bothering to hide her enthusiasm.

He gingerly picked up a roll from beside the basket and took a small bite, nodding. "Yes, I don't see why not."

Her eyes softened at the thought. To him, perhaps it was truly a simple thing, and barely worth the level of ardor she was gleaning from it. But, such a small gesture meant a lot to her, more than she was ready to admit. It wasn't simply that she had given up somewhat on a normal life once becoming inducted into the palace, but rather that she doubted she'd ever have the liberty to venture outside of the palace walls ever again. This was a strange sort of miracle, and one she was more than happy to revel in.

* * *

Hours had slipped by since morning, and the memory of her day in town with Rylik had blurred, swallowed by the monotony of her tedious work alongside Maven in the apothecary. The moon hung high in the night sky as Aria walked along the garden path, her footsteps muffled by the lush greenery surrounding her. The crickets' steady chirping blended into the soothing hum of the night, though her thoughts were far from quiet. She found herself begrudgingly reminiscing about her morning with Rylik.

While she'd enjoyed it more than she cared to admit, the latter half of her day had been consumed by helping Maven. She had even unintentionally convinced Aria to stay longer than necessary, gathering herbs and mixing potions long into the evening.

But now, as exhaustion pulled at her, all Aria wanted was the comfort of her bed.

The moment my feet cross that threshold into my suite, I'll crumple into a heap before I even make it to the mattress.

Suddenly, the sound of footsteps echoed behind her. Aria sighed, expecting the source.

"Sovereign, I know you're there, creeping in the shadows," she called out. "If you're going to follow me, you might as well talk with me."

A low chuckle answered her, but it wasn't the one she expected. "Is that so?"

Aria's heart froze, the voice unfamiliar. She whirled around, only to be grabbed by a pair of strong arms. Before she could scream, a rough hand clamped over her mouth, muffling any sound.

"Stop struggling, healer," the man hissed into her ear, his voice sharp and menacing. "There's no use in it." With brutal force, he dragged her off the path and into the shadows where three more figures stood, waiting by horses. Their eyes glinted with malicious intent.

"Is that the fastest you can move, man?!" one of them barked. "Hurry up!"

The man holding her adjusted his grip, lifting her off her feet. Aria kicked and flailed, desperation clawing at her as she tried to fight him off.

"Help!" she screamed, her voice raw with fear.

"Get her on the horse, quickly!" one of the rogues shouted. "Before he shows—"

Suddenly, one of the men crumpled to the ground, a knife protruding from his back. The others spun in alarm.

A disembodied voice drifted through the darkness, cold and taunting. "Now, now, gentlemen. That one isn't yours to take."

Terror gripped the remaining rogues as they scanned the darkness. A sickening crack filled the air as another of them fell, his neck twisted at an unnatural angle.

"Show yourself, coward!" the third man roared, drawing his sword with trembling hands.

A chuckle echoed in response. "Am I the coward? You're the one targeting and abducting a woman walking alone at night."

The rogue's eyes darted wildly around the garden, his grip tightening on the hilt of his sword. "Are you afraid, Sovereign?! Come out of hiding!"

"Very well." Rylik emerged from the shadows, his form shrouded in a misty darkness, tendrils of power swirling around him. "Though, I think you will find it makes no difference in your fate this evening," he taunted. His expression was calm, but there was a cold cruelty in his eyes. The remaining rogues stood frozen, paralyzed by the sight of him.

One of them, still holding Aria, pressed a knife to her throat in a panic. "I'll kill her!" he threatened, his voice shaking.

Rylik's gaze flicked lazily to the man, unimpressed by the threat.

"I swear I'll do it!" The rogue's voice cracked.

Another man shouted desperately, "We can't kill her, you idiot!"

"Leave now," the one holding the blade stammered, "or she—

"

Before he could finish, Rylik was behind him, moving faster than the eye could follow. With a swift, ruthless motion, he drove a blade into the man's back, wrenching him away from Aria in one brutal pull.

"No one takes what is mine." His voice was low and venomous as the rogue collapsed, lifeless, at his feet.

Aria stumbled forward, gasping for breath, her eyes darting frantically to find Rylik again. But he had already melted back into the shadows.

"You," Rylik's voice drifted through the darkness once more, addressing the final rogue. "I suppose I'll keep you alive—for *now*. I got carried away, it seems."

The remaining rogue was trembling, his eyes wide with terror as he glanced from his fallen comrades to the surrounding darkness. "You think I'll tell you anything?!"

"I should hope with enough persuasion, you might be inspired, yes." Rylik's voice was calm, even bored, as he reappeared, plunging a knife into the man's side with clinical precision.

The rogue let out a guttural groan, collapsing to the ground, clutching his side as blood spilled through his fingers.

Aria stood frozen, her mind reeling from the stark contrast between this man—the one she had bantered with just this morning—and the merciless figure now looming before her.

Rylik circled the wounded rogue, his expression cold and detached. He kicked the man onto his back with a swift, casual motion, standing over him as though he were nothing more than an insect.

"How interesting that you knew lady Aria walks this path each evening," Rylik mused, his voice a deadly whisper. "And that I would be occupied with other matters. You were well informed. Who sent you?"

The rogue spat blood onto the ground, his face contorted with pain. "You really think I'd tell you anything?"

Rylik's gaze flicked briefly to Aria, his voice softening as he spoke to her. "Look away, little Pyra."

Aria swallowed hard, trembling as she slowly turned her back to him. She didn't want to see what was coming next, though the sounds—those grotesque, cracking and squelching sounds—made it all too clear. She flinched, trying not to conjure an image.

"Who sent you?" Rylik asked again, his tone unchanging as if he were inquiring about something as mundane as the weather.

The rogue's defiance crumbled as his body convulsed in pain. "Please!" he gasped, his voice breaking. "Just let me die!"

Rylik's gaze darkened. "What do you want with my healer?"

The rogue whimpered, gasping for air. "The general—he needs her."

Aria winced at the groans that came pleading from the man as another crack echoed in the clearing.

Rylik sighed, sounding almost bored. "Who is your general?"

The rogue's breathing grew labored, his voice fading. "You," he choked out, "You can't keep her forever."

Rylik crouched down, his voice barely a whisper. "The healer is mine. Your general could send an army in your stead, and I would slaughter them all without hesitation. If you weren't on the brink of death, I'd let you tell him this yourself. But I suppose this massacre will convey the message well enough."

The rogue groaned, blood bubbling in his throat. "Watch your back. Or there will be a knife in it."

With one final, sickening gurgle, the rogue was silent.

Rylik clicked his tongue in irritation. "Such melodrama."

The garden was quiet now, save for the distant chirping of crickets. The moonlight gleamed off Rylik's blade as he calmly wiped the blood away, his expression unreadable.

Aria stood frozen, still unable to turn and face him, her heart pounding in her chest.

Rylik's presence materialized beside her, his arm coiling gently around her shoulders. "It's over now, Aria," he murmured, his voice almost tender. "Allow me to escort you back to your suite."

* * *

The walk back to the castle manor was steeped in silence, with each step echoing against the quiet of the night. Aria's mind swirled in disarray, thoughts colliding and twisting about Rylik. How could one man be so utterly terrifying yet unexpectedly kind? She was grateful to him for saving her, but an unbidden fear crept in—a fear of ever being caught in his vengeful path. The weight of his power hung in the air like an ominous cloud.

Who were those rogues that attacked her, and what had they wanted from her? Would this happen again? Could she even be safe again after this? The questions were a grievous onslaught, tumbling one after another in a chaotic discord in her mind.

When they reached the entrance to her suite, Rylik paused at the threshold, his tall frame silhouetted by the dim light of the manor. He watched as she walked inside, his expression unreadable.

"Will you be alright?" he asked, his voice softer than usual, as though testing the words.

Aria hesitated, her body tired but her mind racing. "Yes. I just think that I could use some sleep." She moved further into the room, but her hands trembled slightly, betraying her shaken composure.

Rylik stepped inside without invitation, his concern apparent in the brief glance he gave her as she sat down on the edge of her bed.

"Would you like me to keep you company?"

"No, that's alright." Aria kept her gaze down, unwilling to meet his eyes, her hands resting limp in her lap. The horrors of the night weighed heavily on her.

Rylik nodded, his tone almost gentle. "Well, I should endeavor to keep such *unpleasant* things further away from you in the future." His expression softened as he glanced aside, placing his hands behind his back. "I acquired a peculiar vial today. I had wanted to surprise you with it this evening, but you were running later than usual." From his pocket, he pulled out a small glass bottle and moved to sit beside her, holding it out.

Aria looked at the vial in his hand, her weariness momentarily forgotten as the swirling emerald and gold liquid inside glowed in the firelight. "What is it?"

A somewhat gentle expression touched Rylik's lips as he admired her curiosity. "It's another oddity from the potion master's shop. This one is called a Firefly Glow Tonic. Supposedly, it will cause tiny glowing lights, like fireflies, to hover around you—casting a warm, magical glow. These lights flicker and twirl in response to your emotions."

Aria marveled at the vial, her thoughts briefly drifting away from the earlier violence as she took in the beauty of the potion. The memory of the attack seemed to soften in the presence of the tonic's wonder.

"Would you like to try it?" Rylik asked, a glint of hope in his eyes.

Hesitant but intrigued, Aria nodded and carefully uncorked the bottle. Her fingers shook slightly as she raised it to her lips and drank. A warm hum filled the air as the liquid coursed through her, settling over her body like a blanket of soft light. She glanced at Rylik, and suddenly, tiny gold and green lights began to blink and glitter around them, like delicate magical sprites.

"It's beautiful," she whispered, her voice full of awe, eyes reflecting the soft glow dancing around them.

Rylik watched her face closely as a sort of childlike wonder filled her large yellow eyes. Absently, he smiled. "Quite beautiful, yes."

Aria's eyes shone with curiosity and wonder as she looked up at him. "When did you buy this?"

Rylik leaned back, clearly pleased with her reaction. "After you passed out on me this morning, I carried you to the bakery. I paid a young boy handsomely to go buy me all the vials of interest in that potion master's shop. He may have kept one or two for himself." A sly smirk crossed his lips. "But he still supplied me with a wide assortment of charming potions. I thought you might like this one tonight."

Aria blushed, touched by the unexpected gesture. She looked down at her hands, a small smile creeping onto her lips despite herself. "You probably shouldn't have done such a thing, but thank you. That was very thoughtful."

Rylik huffed a quiet laugh, the warmth in his eyes barely hidden by his usual cold demeanor. "Don't mention it." He stood, smoothing his tunic. "Alright, I think it's for the best I let you retire for the evening. Goodnight, Aria." He moved to leave, but before he could take a step, Aria reached out, grasping his arm.

"Wait."

Rylik paused, glancing back down at her. The firefly-like lights still hovered around them, casting the room in a soft, magical glow. "Yes?"

"Your blight," she whispered, compassion softening her features.

Rylik mused over her expression, then reseated himself beside her. "I wasn't going to press you, but, if you insist." With a casual ease, he unbuttoned his tunic, revealing the pale skin of his chest.

Aria gently placed her hand over the afflicted area, her eyes glowing softly with her healing magic. A warmth spread through the room, and Rylik breathed deeply as the firefly lights around them flickered brighter, reacting to the surge of her energy. The glow intensified, illuminating her features, making her appear almost ethereal.

When the healing was complete, the light around them began to fade, and Aria withdrew her hand, her eyes returning to their usual hue. She smiled. "Does that feel better?"

Rylik, still lost in the daze of the moment, recovered quickly, his smile returning with a wry edge. "Yes, thank you, Pyra."

Aria's expression shifted to one of curiosity. "I've been meaning to ask you—what does Pyra mean?"

Rylik seemed subtly amused by her innocent question. "It's Ancient Greek, meaning 'fire.' I couldn't help but think it suited you well. After all, my blood is ice. And your touch—a *flame*."

Caught off guard, Aria blushed deeply, unsure of how to respond.

Rylik rose, his demeanor softening once more. "Anyway, have a good night. And sleep in tomorrow morning. I think you'd benefit from the extra rest." With that, he turned and left, his steps soft against the floor.

The soft firefly glow still lingered in the room as Aria watched Rylik approach the door, the golden and viridian lights flickering softly around her.

"Sovereign," she called, her voice tentative, barely louder than a whisper.

Rylik paused, a sigh escaping him. His broad shoulders sagged slightly as he turned his head, glancing over his shoulder. "Yes?" His voice was low, carrying a hint of weariness.

She hesitated, her nerves tightening in her chest. "You," Aria's voice faltered, her fingers brushing lightly over the soft fabric of her dress. "Thank you for saving me tonight. I—I hope you'll only ever play the role of protector, where it concerns me."

His gaze darkened, a slow smile spreading across his lips, unreadable and slightly dangerous. "You are invaluable, Aria," he murmured, his words curling through the air like a quiet threat wrapped in silk. "If anyone seeks to take you from me, their lives will be forfeit. I will play any role necessary to ensure that you remain mine alone."

A gasp lodged in her chest. The firefly glow surrounding her dimmed to a muted green as she sat there, a strange mix of emotions swirling inside her. There was fear, yes, but also a peculiar sense of relief, and a feeling of safety she couldn't fully understand.

Rylik's voice softened, almost soothing despite its chilling edge. "Please, do not worry for your safety. You will never find yourself as anything but the one I will protect."

As though responding to his words, the firefly lights flickered back to gold and green, casting a warm, magical glow around her once more.

Without another word, Rylik turned back to the door, pulling it open. He stepped into the hall, leaving quietly, the soft click of the door the only sound left behind.

Aria remained where she sat, mesmerized, her mind swirling as the soft firefly glow sparkled faintly in the quiet room for long after he had gone.

CHAPTER 14

RYLIK

Rylik sat in his bedchamber, the soft glow of firelight gently illuminating his room. Papers shuffled under his hand, one after another, a sea of intelligence reports and intercepted letters strewn across the desk. His face was impassive, eyes scanning the documents as though each one carried the weight of a mundane task, rather than the very secrets that had confirmed the existence of a traitor in his ranks.

Thorian Dregane. The man had been sloppy. Rylik wasn't surprised by the betrayal—it was the nature of power to invite envy and ambition—but rather irritated by the clumsy execution. He had always known that someone within his Shadow Knights would turn. People were so quick to betray one another, after all. Though, out of all of his knights, he had thought better of Thorian. He couldn't help but wonder if perhaps his opinion of him had merely been bolstered due to his appreciation of Maven.

Rylik's fingers tapped idly on the edge of the desk, his thoughts as cold and calculated as ever. There was evidence of communication between Thorian and a mysterious man who signed his letters as "H", and now he at least knew the man to be a general. Though, of all the neighboring kingdoms of generals, it would be hard to pinpoint which one exactly was guilty.

He glanced at the scattered papers—correspondence between Thorian and his contact, coded but not beyond Rylik's ability to decipher. There was no mention of Aria in the messages, save for one reading with the words: *"I need time."*

And time, he would give to the traitor. He at least knew the game that was being played, and he knew how close to watch him.

Rylik leaned back in his chair, picking up a sweet roll wrapped in parchment. The scent of sugar and cinnamon wafted into the air, reminding him, briefly, of the trip into town with Aria. She had looked at the world with such wide eyes, full of wonder at the simplest things—a marked contrast to the grim reality of the court and its constant intrigue.

He took a bite of the roll, the very same variety his little Pyra recommended to him, savoring the sweetness on his tongue. She had been so captivated by the bakery, her bright-eyed fascination palpable. For a moment, she had been someone else—free from her fears and concerns in her new role as court healer. He found himself wondering now, with idle curiosity, what she might do if he took her to the Festival of the Sun and Stars. There was no better time to view the capital than during such a grand annual celebration in the plaza.

Rylik leaned forward again, pushing the papers aside, his mind returning to the matter at hand. When the time came, when Thorian foolishly dared to act again, he would strike. And it would be final. Brutal. There was no room for mercy in these matters, even if it might break Maven's heart. Though, he couldn't fully absolve her of involvement, either. They were family, after all. He would have to have her watched as well.

He took another bite of the pastry, gaze wandering to the window where the morning sun would soon crest over the mountains. The maids would be in her bathing room shortly, clattering with basins and hot water, preparing for the day.

He wondered if they would wake her. He wondered if he should stop them. The night before had weighed heavily on her; the violence and death had left her shaken. A cold knot tightened in his chest as he remembered her pale face in the moonlight, terror stark in her features. His grip on the pastry tightened as the memory from the capital flashed again in his mind—the way her eyes had sparkled with childlike wonder when they shared sweets at the bakery. Those rogues had tried to steal that innocence from her, hadn't they?

He looked down, his gaze darkening, a rare ember of guilt burning in him. Last night's bloodshed had been merciless—a brutal, raw expression of his rage unleashed on her attackers who'd dared to hunt her with such cruelty. He'd cut them down with cold precision, indifferent to their lives, too blinded by fury to see anything beyond the offense they'd dared to commit. How dare they try to take what was his? *Aria was his.* Yet, was she not also his to protect?

The guilt burrowed deeper. There was something at stake now—something fragile in her, some lightness that might not return. He thought of her earlier awe, the way firefly magic had danced around them, glowing in soft emerald and gold in response to her delight. She had brightened the room with her joy, a joy he hadn't seen dimmed by shadows or danger. That was the part of her he had to shield—the part still capable of finding beauty in the simplest things. He clenched his jaw. He couldn't allow her to witness such savagery again. But in this court, violence was woven into the very fabric. Protecting her from it would mean fighting inevitability.

A faint rush of water and the muffled sounds of movement reached him through the wall, pulling him abruptly from the spiral of his thoughts. He welcomed the distraction, anything to break the unsettling tide of guilt creeping into his mind. The rising burden of moral obligation pressed down on him, a weight he wasn't used to carrying. Was this really a feeling he would continue to entertain?

With a long exhale, his stare settled back over the papers of treachery strewn about his table. Rylik was nothing if not patient, and patience, as he knew, was the key to winning any game. Finishing the last of the roll, he wiped his hands clean on the parchment, carelessly crumpling it and tossing it aside. He stood, rolling his shoulders as if shedding the weight of his thoughts. There were other matters to attend to, and he would deal with Thorian soon enough.

For now, he would at least intercept the maids and tell them to go. His healer needed rest, and he wouldn't have her be disturbed. With a commanding push, he shoved the door open to the bathing room and turned his attention sharply to the side.

Before the words of dismissal could alight his tongue, he froze. Aria stood naked mere paces away, her figure bathed in the soft reflections of the water like a Grecian statue come to life. Her long red hair cascaded in loose curls down her back, glistening as it clung to her damp skin. It was clear she had only just stepped into the bath.

She turned at the sound of his entrance, mortification in her eyes when she saw him, instantly letting out a shriek as she dropped like lead into the water. It splashed out into the marble floors, glittering in the morning sunlight. "Sovereign?!"

Rylik bit the inside of his lip, eyes feasting on the sight without restraint. He wanted to feel shame, but instead his interest was clearly painted across his features. "Good morning," he said, a wry smile curling at the corners of his lips, as if he were savoring a secret only he could know.

"What are you doing in here!?" She asked, horrified in her embarrassment. "Get out! Now!"

Rylik felt his weight shift more firmly into his boots, spite compelling him to walk toward her. He would not be commanded by his own prisoner. "This is *my* bathing room, Pyra," he informed her coolly, watching her panic as she made useless efforts to cover her ample breasts under the water. "If anything, *you* shouldn't be in here," he said in accusation, brazenly towering over the edge of the tub. "Shall I now hoist you out of there with the same ferocity that you dared to order me?"

Her face was pink with shock and rage, and he found he dearly loved the sight of that. "I did not realize," she bit out nervously, "that this was your bathing room, Sovereign."

"And I have been so kind as to share it with you. Perhaps some gratitude is in order, is it not?" he mused. He was enjoying this far too much at her expense, he knew, but he couldn't stop himself.

Aria shifted under the scrutiny of his gaze, squeezing her two perfect ivory thighs together as if to make herself smaller and invisible under the crystal clear surface. A low thrum of desire stirred within him, conjuring dark fantasies at the sight. He felt his breath catch, a hunger pulling at his insides, spreading warmth into his depths. Closing his eyes, he stilled himself, realizing their predicament.

Turning abruptly on his heel, he muttered over his shoulder, "the bath is yours in the mornings, Aria. I have no intention of keeping you from it. I only came in here because I thought the maids would disturb you." His pulse raced, his entire body urging him to turn around and drag her from the water.

"Thank you," came her sheepish reply behind him, "Sovereign."

Forcing a sharp exhale of breath, he crossed the floor with steady, controlled steps, ensuring his emotions remained hidden in his graceful movement. The door closed quietly behind him, and the moment he was alone in the privacy of his room, he inwardly groaned.

An obscene curse fell quietly from his lips as he ran his fingers through his hair in maddening anxiety. He wanted desperately to turn back around. It was *his* bathing room, after all. She was naked in *his* tub. It was his *right* to view her, was it not? No prisoner should dictate what he was allowed to do in his own quarters.

Opening his eyes, seemingly aghast with his own lurid thoughts, he let out another sharp curse as he strode to his desk and leaned against the chair. He was not disillusioned with himself. He was hardly a man of honor. But, she wasn't the same as the lovers he had taken to bed in the past. She was a needlessly pure thing, with enough pride to feel shame in her nakedness in front of a man. He could respect that, even if the very thought made him want her all the more.

With a grievous inhale he prowled across the floor and snatched his cape into his fingers, draping it over his shoulders with poise. He would take a walk. A long, long walk. Because if he remained in this room any longer, the urge to turn around and walk back through that door would become impossible to resist.

CHAPTER 15

ARIA

Light streamed through the windows of the bathing room, illuminating the soapy water with a soft glow. Aria lay steeped in her bath, eyes closed, her long hair fanning out in the water like a silken blanket. It had taken maybe ten minutes after the Sovereign had left the room for her to relax. She thought she had heard his door close some time ago, signaling his departure. When enough time after that passed, she figured she was safe to unclench.

She was mad at him, and she was trying hard to cool her head to no avail. He had seen her stark naked and his first reaction was to stare. Hard. Irritation boiled in her throat and she muttered a curse under her breath. Was he simply surprised? Unable to tear his gaze away due to his bewilderment at a naked woman standing in his bath?

She puffed out a soft sigh. It was partially understandable. He hadn't expected to see her, and that was evident. However, the ease with which he had fastened his eyes upon her and sustained them on her bare figure was entirely unforgivable. While he might hold the chains of her servitude here, that should not also give him the right to look freely at her nude form. There were boundaries. These boundaries should not need to be defined, either. And perhaps he thought better of his actions, when he had turned around and left the room after letting her stay there.

Aria hoped that some part of him felt a crawling guilt at his own behavior. If for no other reason than to make it easier to believe that he might be capable of being a decent person.

A peaceful sigh escaped her lips as she recalled the night before, when the enchanted fireflies had floated around her, drenching her suite in a resplendent, ethereal glow. How is it that such a harrowing night had ended with such magic? She smiled softly. It was a wonder she ever fell asleep with all those beautiful little sparkling lights around her. She hadn't wanted to rest for fear of waking up and finding them gone.

For once, she had been allowed the luxury of sleeping in, and had it not been for the maids bustling through her room, she might've been successful. She didn't mind, though. It gave her time for a morning soak. And had the Sovereign not shown up, it might've been wholly peaceful. As the soothing water lapped at her skin, she trailed her hand over her arm, washing away the last traces of soap, lost in thought.

I wonder why the Sovereign was so gentle with me yesterday, she mused, remembering how he had let her hold his arm when they walked through town, how he had taken her to the bakery and bought her sweets and potions. Was he trying to lull her into a false sense of security? She blushed, the heat rising to her cheeks as she considered the alternative. *Or, like he accused the potion master of, am I affecting him in ways I don't yet realize?*

A soft hum escaped her as she pondered the thought, though a pang of guilt soon followed, the image of Leon and the Rebellion resurfacing in her mind. *What am I doing?* she thought bitterly. *Am I seriously fawning over him in my imaginings? Leon would be ashamed of me. He would tell me that I'm betraying the Rebellion, aligning myself with the king.*

If anything, she was only gathering even more information about the Sovereign, wasn't she?

And by the time I reveal it—

The thought trailed off as fear gripped her. She froze, nervous, the memory of Rylik's brutality in the gardens flashing before her eyes. She exhaled shakily, trying to calm herself.

*I won't. I won't **ever** tell,* she reminded herself.

Because, she couldn't, and most of her reasoned that she didn't have to, not really. She had never sworn any allegiance to the Rebellion. She hadn't even wanted to be tangled in this web of danger and chaos. But Orren had pressured her into it the moment the king sent out his decree to "offer her the job."

She scoffed at the memory of those words. As if it were truly an offer. The king wanted her as his imperial healer, and if she hadn't accepted willingly, he would have withdrawn the monetary promises and taken her by force. Refusing would have been foolish—especially with her family so dependent on the income.

Until that fateful day, she hadn't even met Orren; she'd only heard of him from Leon, who spoke of him as both a nobleman and a favorite of the king. No doubt, that favor granted him access to secrets others couldn't even imagine. Their meeting was brief; Orren had come to her home under the cover of night, cloaked and severe, with Leon at his side. She had been grappling with the thought of her future slipping from her control when they arrived to "discuss" her role. Orren was all confidence, spending no more than ten minutes convincing her parents that she could serve a noble cause.

The cause. She scoffed to herself.

Orren hadn't truly asked her. He had merely instructed, framing it as a duty, a natural obligation, simply because she had occasionally offered her healing services to support the Rebellion's efforts. She had never imagined that small kindness would drag her into their fight. She had only wanted to help those she respected, in the name of a cause she respected—not to become its pawn.

A long sigh escaped her as she stared up at the ceiling, frustration bubbling up inside her. She did hate the king, but she never bargained to risk her life in an effort to bring him down. She had the most terrifying man in the world as her shadow now, and if she breathed a word of his weaknesses to Orren, everything would fall apart.

Her eyes hardened as the truth she'd been avoiding settled in. Would she have even agreed to this terrible plan had it not been for her interest in Leon? Would Orren even have pressed if he didn't know she had such deep feelings for Leon? She wondered, shame pooling in her chest.

Truth be told, Leon was thrilled when she had agreed that night to help serve the cause. It made her heart flutter then, to see that she had brought a genuine smile to his face. For a moment he might've even been *proud* of her.

She groaned inwardly at the memory, running a hand down her face. How utterly ignorant. How could she agree to something when she didn't understand how dark this world really was? Nearly everyone in the palace was deceitful and conniving, and there was hardly anyone above reproach. Why would Leon have ever been happy for her to throw her life into harm's way? She knew he didn't love her, but this bordered on apathy.

The sadness that followed was heavy, but Aria couldn't deny herself the question: *Does anyone actually love me, I wonder? I suppose my parents do, yes, but, why did no one stop this? Why did the Rebellion use this forced employment as an opportunity for them to expand their reach? Why am I just always being exploited?*

As if refusing to think about it any longer, she slid beneath the water, holding her breath, allowing the muted, deafening silence to take over as she sank deeper into the tub. For a few blissful moments, the world outside ceased to exist.

But air soon became a necessity, and Aria emerged from the water with a gasp, leaning heavily over the edge of the tub, droplets running down her face and pooling on the marble floor. Her gaze drifted to the vanity, where the vial of firefly glow tonic sat like a trophy. A small, soft smile tugged at her lips.

He didn't have to do that, she thought, staring at the empty vial. *But he did.* A part of her clung to that gesture, to the faint glimmer of kindness hidden beneath the Sovereign's cold, calculating exterior. She supposed his reasons were his own. Part of her would rather assume the best rather than the worst. But she'd like to think that maybe he didn't want her to have to go to bed scared of losing her life last night. Perhaps he wanted her to feel safe, even if it wasn't tangible. She'd like to think it was in compassion. And she wasn't sure she could accept any other reality without almost completely crumbling within herself.

With a sigh, Aria climbed out of the bath, toweling off before setting her dress over the back of her vanity chair. She dressed slowly, her thoughts a jumbled mess as she laced her corset.

Just as she was starting to hum to herself again, the door to her chambers opened without warning.

"You've got to be kidding me!" she breathed, a curse slipping past her lips. "How can this happen *twice*?"

The Sovereign stepped into the room with his usual casual smirk, his eyes scanning her over with a pleased glint. Her damp red hair, half-dried and tousled into unruly curls, tumbled over one shoulder in a cascade of fiery strands. The ivory corset cinched tightly at her small waist, accentuating her bust shamelessly, and his gaze rested there a moment too long before flitting up to her golden eyes. All too soon, the memory of him staring at her in the bath came flooding back and hit her with a wave of abashment. "Hello again, Aria," he greeted smoothly, "did you enjoy your soak?"

Flustered, she scrambled behind her vanity, trying to shield herself. "Seriously, you *have* to start knocking!"

He strolled closer, as if unbothered by her embarrassment. "I would, but then I'd miss out on what color corset you're wearing for the day."

Her cheeks flushed a deep crimson and her breaths came in quick, heavy bursts, each rise and fall of her chest betraying her mix of embarrassment and anger. "That's not something you need to know!" she protested. "And besides—" she added, grabbing her dress and pulling it over her head in a rush. She gasped when she realized he had closed the distance between them, standing much too close. "Eep!"

Rylik's smirk deepened as she stumbled back against the wall. "And besides?" he prompted.

She swallowed nervously, holding a hand out as if to push him back. "And besides," she gritted, "I only have the one."

"Tsk. Oh, that simply won't do." He took a step back, looking her over with amusement. "You need variety."

Her eyes widened in disbelief.

"There's a boutique in town," he continued nonchalantly, "we ought to visit it together. The dressmaker there sells a wide array of colorful corsets and undergarments. " He swept his gaze over her once more, an undeniable glint of seduction in his eyes, before finally locking onto hers with a playful grin. "We could get you one in every color."

Aria's face burned in embarrassment as she shoved past him, hastily lacing up her dress. "*Sovereign!*" she fumed. "I know you're fond of teasing, but please! Take pity on my inexperience, at the very least."

He released a soft, mischievous chuckle, his voice rich with amusement, as he clasped his hands behind his back, allowing his broad shoulders to relax into a casual yet confident stance. "I *do* take pity on you, dear," he replied, "If I didn't, my behavior would be far more brazen."

She shot him an exasperated glare and pointed toward the door. "Exit. Please. I'd like to finish preparing for my day without an audience."

With a feigned sigh of disappointment, Rylik approached her once more, brushing his fingers against her damp hair. "How will you arrange your hair today?"

She pulled her hair away from him, scowling. "Not that it matters, but probably a braid. Why?"

His smirk returned. "Your hair will be a cascade of waves by this evening, then, when you're in my bedchamber."

Her face turned scarlet, her eyes wide in shock.

Rylik's voice softened with amusement as he stepped back. "To remove my blight, dear. What were *you* thinking of?"

Completely aghast, she pointed to the door again, her voice high with frustration. "If you *please*! The *door*. Walk through it."

Still chuckling at her expense, Rylik exited the room, closing the door behind him with a quiet click.

* * *

Aria worked quietly in the castle's apothecary, side by side with Maven. The rhythmic grinding of her mortar and pestle filled the room as they tended to their duties. Maven, glancing over at the vials strewn across the table, sighed in frustration.

"Ah, would you hand me that vial over there? The one I

grabbed is not big enough," she said, gesturing across the cluttered workspace.

Aria obliged, passing her the empty vial before resuming her task. Her teeth pressed together in frustration, cheeks still burning from the teasing she had endured with Rylik earlier. *Gods, he escorted me all the way here to the apothecary and teased me nonstop. Was it not enough that he saw me naked already this morning? For a man so deathly terrifying and practically evil, he certainly knows how to make jokes at my expense.* The memory of his smirk fed her aggravation as she ground the herbs more forcefully.

"Oh," Maven's soft voice snapped Aria from her thoughts.

The woman flushed a deep red, her eyes brightening as she looked past Aria, a wide smile spreading over her face. "Good morning, Leon," she greeted, dipping her head with a hint of demureness.

Aria turned, her pulse hitching as she caught Leon's gaze fixed warmly on Maven, his expression softening as he took her in. "It is now," he replied with a warmth that sent a strange prickling down Aria's spine.

Was he *flirting* with Maven? The realization stung, a faint bristle stirring in her chest as she watched the gentle ease between them. Her fingers clenched a bit harder around the pestle, grinding the herbs with a sharper pressure than intended.

Leon's hand dipped into his pocket, pulling out a small, colorful handkerchief that he held out toward Maven. "You left this last night," he said, his voice a quiet note of intimacy that made Aria's chest tighten.

Maven's cheeks deepened into a rosy glow as she reached to take it, her eyes soft with memory, as though recalling a private moment the night had held for them. "You didn't need to return it," she murmured, her fingers brushing against his palm for just a second longer than necessary.

Aria's thoughts tumbled in a spiral, tangled between questions and quiet envy. How long had this connection been blooming between them? She'd seen them dancing at the ball, yes, but this was a different kind of closeness. It hadn't occurred to her that it could grow so quickly. She'd been so preoccupied with her own struggles that she hadn't seen it—or perhaps she hadn't wanted to see it. A bitter twist knotted her chest, jealousy flaring quietly as she watched them, their conversation becoming a distant hum in the growing din of her own thoughts.

A gentle touch on her shoulder startled her, Leon's hand grounding her in the present. She looked up to see him watching her with a questioning look. "Where is your shadow today, Aria?"

The words seemed innocent enough, yet she felt the pointedness behind them, his careful phrasing aimed at drawing her back toward matters of the Rebellion. She recoiled, wanting nothing of the sort—especially not after last night's attack, nor after the humiliating role the Rebellion seemed determined to cast her in. For a fleeting second, a deep weariness settled in her, the constant push and pull fraying her patience.

Forcing herself to remain calm, she replied, her voice a touch stiff, "Looming, as usual." She knew he'd pick up on her reluctance, the subtle chill in her tone.

Leon's expression darkened slightly, a flicker of concern passing through his eyes as he reached to touch her hand, his tone dipping low. "Can we go somewhere in private?"

Aria's resolve faltered for just a breath, but frustration crept in, tugging her patience dangerously thin. With a long, exasperated sigh, she set her tools down and gave him a reluctant nod. "Fine."

Her gaze darted back to Maven, who was already turning away, a dreamy smile gracing her lips as she pressed the handkerchief to her mouth, her eyes softened by a quiet happiness.

Leon led Aria into a small storage closet, shutting the door behind them. He lowered his voice, speaking in a hushed whisper. "There's been a rare opening recently that we need to exploit. You see, a member of the royal guard—"

"Let me stop you right there, Leontias," Aria interrupted, her voice cutting through his hurried explanation.

Leon's brows furrowed.

Aria's eyes hardened, and she folded her arms across her chest. She only used his given name when she was especially mad, but she didn't care that he knew she was upset. Because she *was* upset. "Do you know what I was doing last night on my walk back to my suite?" she asked coolly, her eyes locking onto his. "I was attacked. Some men—I still don't even know who they were—came out of the shadows and intended to abduct me and take me to someone's general."

Leon's face remained disturbingly impassive. "Hm, interesting. Who was the general? I assume from a neighboring kingdom? Did you find out which one?"

Aria's eyes widened in disbelief, her anger bubbling over. "That's your takeaway? I was nearly captured, a knife to my throat, and you want to know what information I gathered?"

Leon stammered, sheepishly running a hand through his hair. "Aria, I—I'm sorry. I only meant—"

"I'm going to need about ten percent more compassion from you," she snapped, her eyes burning with unshed tears. "Seeing as we have been friends for ages. I nearly lost my life, and you look like you merely stepped on my toe just now."

Leon's eyes softened. "Aria, it's not like that—"

"No, it is," she cut him off, her voice cold. "It is like that. I know you've committed your entire life to this—" She hesitated, glancing around before lowering her voice to a whisper, "uprising. But I didn't. Sure, I share your same sentiments, but I do not share your same conviction. You all are borderline religious fanatics hellbent on suicide missions. I will *not* indulge in this sort of careless activity. My life is more valuable to me than that."

Leon's face twisted with frustration. "And what life is that? Living under a tyrannical king, taking his gold while the good people of our kingdom are left to starve and—"

"Spare me your speech." Her eyes were icy, her tone final. "I'm no self-sacrificing hero like you, it would seem. I do have a sickening desire for self-preservation, after all. My parents are old and impoverished, but I can make their lives better in this position. And maybe, in time, in small ways, I can help others. But I'm going to help my own first. And if you can't understand that, then we have even less in common than I thought."

Leon's gaze darkened, his anger simmering just beneath the surface. "To hear you speak so apathetically—"

"Apathetic, am I?" Aria snapped. "It's one thing to be willing—even longing for—sacrificing your own life for the sake of the "greater good", but another thing entirely when you make that same judgment call for me." Her eyes were glossy, refusing to cry, and she continued through angry, tight lips, "I could've said no to Orren, I suppose, when he pressed me to supply the Rebellion with information. But you were so persuasive, preaching to me about the illustrious wonder that awaits me to be willing to give everything away—my life included—in an effort to make the world a better place for the next generation. Well, what about *my* generation? What about my parents? What about—"

Leon's voice turned cold, his tone biting. "You want out, Aria?"

Her gaze didn't falter. "I was never truly 'in,' but yes. I want out. Having my life nearly come to an end almost a week after agreeing to work with the Rebellion, was far more than I bargained for."

A chill swept through the small room as Leon's eyes narrowed. "This wouldn't have anything to do with the *Sovereign*, would it?"

Aria lifted her chin defiantly. "Oh, the cold and sadistic murderer who carries out the king's every order? Are you suggesting I'm aligning myself with him?"

"That's not all I'm suggesting," he said coldly, his eyes probing hers for any hint of truth.

Her cheeks flushed with a mix of anger and embarrassment. "Are you insinuating that I'm engaged in some sort of romantic affair with that merciless man?"

Leon's lips twisted bitterly. "I saw the dress you wore at the ball. The way you danced with him. You seemed all too willing to distract him for us. Maybe it's because you *feel* something—"

Before he could finish, Aria slapped him hard across the face, her hand stinging from the impact. Her lips trembled with restrained fury as she bit down to keep from saying something worse.

Leon kept his gaze averted, half in shame, his cheek reddened from the blow.

"This conversation is over," Aria hissed, her voice shaking with emotion. "My helping the Rebellion is over."

Leon barely looked up. "Did it ever really start?"

Her jaw clenched as she let out a frustrated growl, storming out of the storage room and slamming the door behind her.

CHAPTER 16

RYLIK

Rylik stood in the king's private study, hands clasped behind his back, posture composed yet betraying the edge of boredom. His eyes, cool and calculating, feigned attention as the king droned on.

"Alright, Sovereign," Kaldros said, waving a dismissive hand, "that's all for today."

Rylik gave a respectful nod but did not move to leave. "If I may, Your Majesty, it's about the imperial healer, Aria."

The king's eyes flicked up, a glimmer of interest sparking beneath the royal lethargy.

"I've kept matters discreet," Rylik continued smoothly. "Had the bodies removed under cover of night to ensure no one knew of the disturbance. But she was targeted in an abduction attempt last night. Her life was also threatened."

"By whom?" The king's tone shifted, more attentive now.

"I don't know yet." Rylik's sharp eyes remained unreadable. "And until I do, I'll need increased security around her, to ensure her protection at all times, even when I cannot watch over her."

"That's understandable." Kaldros waved him on. "You may have what you wish. She is in your adjoining suite, is she not?"

"Not at present, but yes," Rylik replied calmly, his gaze steady.

The king sighed, stroking his beard as if a thought had suddenly occurred to him. "This is a good time to broach another topic with you, I think." His eyes gleamed with intrigue. "I have an interest in her."

Rylik raised a brow, his face a practiced mask of stoicism.

"I'll admit I hadn't given her much thought, given her social standing," the king mused, his voice laced with indulgence. "But, having seen her at the ball, well, I'd be remiss if I didn't indulge in such an exquisite beauty."

Behind his composed facade, Rylik felt the flare of violent disapproval, his hands curling into fists where the king couldn't see. Still, he remained silent, expression neutral.

"I could hardly keep my gaze off her the night of the ball. I'd intended to order her to my bedchamber that same evening, but that *incident* with Eldric occurred, and it left me on edge." Kaldros continued, his tone now tinged with annoyance. "I was thinking I might call her to my bedchamber this evening, and imploring her to become one of my concubines." The king chuckled lightly. "Not that she could refuse me, of course. But that's neither here nor there."

Rylik's mind ignited with a violent image—the king's filthy hands on Aria's delicate frame, a visceral affront that sent a shockwave of fury through him. His jaw tightened, teeth grinding against the rising tide of rage that surged beneath his calm exterior. Each heartbeat drummed with the urge to act, a primal instinct to protect what was his, and the simmering anger crackled in the air around him, poised to erupt.

"The only thing holding me back," the king continued, leaning forward slightly, "is your intentions for her. As you know, Sovereign, I hold you in the highest regard. You have been my loyal right hand for years, unwavering in your fealty. So, if *you* want her for your own, then," he sighed, continuing, "I am obliged to concede. After all, I wasn't the only man eyeing her at the ball." The king's eyes narrowed, watching him closely.

Rylik held his breath, the tension coiling tightly around him as he fought to maintain his composure, but he was a mask of calm before the king's scrutiny. Finally, he spoke, his voice low and measured, each word laced with intent. "Oh, my king, I can't say I'm not tempted, but, I hesitate." The weight of his reluctance hung in the air, sharp and electric, a dangerous game played with a poised dagger.

The king's brows knitted. "Why?"

"Your Majesty, if I may speak candidly," Rylik began carefully. "In my due diligence to ensure we were acquiring a healer of such high quality, I learned that she carries the Dread Curse."

The king's eyes widened in concern, his posture stiffening slightly.

"Now, it's no concern for you or me, as it doesn't affect her ability to heal or the quality of her health," Rylik added, voice low and grave. "However, it's said that those who deign to take her to bed are haunted by a dark aura, experiencing unsettling nightmares and an overwhelming sense of dread. It has driven her few past lovers to madness—even unto death."

Rylik's expression darkened as he locked eyes with the king, his voice laden with warning. "Beautiful, though she may be, sire, I would hate for you to suffer such consequences, should you consider drawing her into your *intimate* circle."

Kaldros blinked, visibly unsettled. His eyes darted aside, a flicker of panic in them. "That is highly disconcerting. I wish you would've told me sooner."

"I apologize, Your Majesty. I did not think it pertinent at the time, as I was unaware of your interest in her," Rylik said smoothly.

The king sighed, nodding slowly, disappointment etching itself across his face. "Right, right. Yes. Well," he waved the thought away with a dissatisfied flick of his hand. "You may have your extra security for her. She is undoubtedly one of our most valuable assets and needs to be protected."

"Thank you, Your Grace," Rylik responded, his voice measured and polite.

With a final wave, Kaldros dismissed him. Rylik turned and walked out, his steps calm and methodical. As soon as he left the room, his composure fractured. His fists clenched tightly, his eyes steely with controlled rage.

The king was a superstitious man, prone to gossip. Ever more so when that gossip came from Rylik, since he had rarely ever steered him wrong. He was happy to feed him false information today, though he knew it wouldn't keep the king at bay for nearly long enough. His thoughts churned darkly as he turned a corner, heading down a stairway toward the lower floor. His gait remained smooth, unhurried, despite the roiling anger within him. The thought of the king's disgusting hands on Aria's body made Rylik want to rip the man's head from his shoulders and impale it on a spear.

He breathed out, forcing his rage under control once more. Rylik was not unwise. Kaldros wasn't *asking* for permission to make her his concubine. He wasn't concerned about Rylik's interests. Everything was a game. Kaldros thought to lay a snare for him, to test his loyalty to him, and the boundaries of his affection for those he might seek to use against him. One whisper of Rylik's interest in her, and the king would gain a foothold.

Stepping out of the palace manor and into the outer bailey, Rylik took in the surroundings, his mind already shifting to other matters. He straightened his tunic, adjusted his sleeves, and rolled his neck, expelling the tension. That lie would hold until the king began to think better of it. And when that time would come, he would need to have a plan. His gaze drifted toward the gardens. A small, almost imperceptible smile tugged at the corner of his mouth. He was ready now to engage in more interesting matters.

* * *

Rylik walked through the garden pathway, the afternoon sun high overhead and shining over the apothecary in the distance. The scent of blooming flowers filled the air, though he barely noticed as his thoughts churned, heavy with frustration from his talk with the king. His eyes swept over the vibrant foliage, until his gaze fell on a familiar figure ahead, her presence drawing his attention like a magnet.

He came to a halt, hidden by the shadows of the garden trees, with his gaze fixed on Aria moving along the walkway. He watched the frustration in her steps, the way her body stiffened with each one. Something had clearly unsettled her—perhaps an argument with the Corporal? He had been admittedly less vigilant in keeping them apart when he'd learned they weren't lovers. The tension in her shoulders spoke volumes, and though she wiped her tears hastily, he didn't miss the subtle tremor of her hands.

His eyes trailed after her, noting how her attention drifted to the broken flowers at her feet. The irises, once vibrant, now lay trampled and crushed, remnants of the chaos from the night before. He could see the change in her as she stared at them, the momentary break in her defenses. She didn't need to say a word for him to understand what she was thinking. The haunted look in her eyes, the way her lips trembled—it was clear the memory of her near-abduction haunted her just beneath the surface.

Her fingers dug into her arms as she crossed them tightly over her chest, a futile attempt to hold herself together. He could almost feel the weight of the moment pressing down on her, see the flood of emotions that she was trying so hard to contain. The tears that slipped down her face, unchecked this time, told him more than anything else.

There was a strange pull in his chest as he watched her. He approached her slowly, intent to not call attention to what he had witnessed. He could let her have her pride after all.

"Such a waste of a perfectly lovely batch of Moonveil irises," Rylik remarked as he stepped beside her, his sudden presence making her flinch. She hadn't noticed his approach. His gaze was already on the damaged flowers, and with a soft click of his tongue, he shook his head in quiet disapproval.

Aria hastily wiped at her face, trying to hide the evidence of her crying. "You know what kind of flowers they are? Are you secretly a botanist when you're not the Sovereign?"

Rylik smirked, the playful edge in his tone catching her off guard. "I'd wager I might actually know more about plants than you do, Aria. Though no, I am no botanist. I'm merely an enthusiast at best."

"For flowers?" she asked, surprised, her fingers still trembling as she hoped he hadn't noticed her tears.

"For plants of all kinds, yes." He pointed toward the plants beside the ruined irises. "You see those? They are Bloodroot Camelias, though you wouldn't know it because they aren't quite in bloom yet. They should start flowering in late autumn. They provide shade to the irises, allowing them just the right portion of sunlight. Our gardeners always ensure there's something in bloom all year round, not only for visual appeal, but also so one flower complements the other."

Aria blinked at him, a disbelieving smile tugging at her lips. "How do you know so much about such a thing?"

He smiled down at the flowers. "There was a time I studied them. I took great interest in plants of all kinds, grew impassioned with how to cultivate them, fascinated to watch them grow to their fullest. I don't have time for such hobbies now, of course." His eyes dimmed slightly, the brightness fading. "So, I'm more of a useless encyclopedia, filled with trivial knowledge of plant life and no one to bore with it." He glanced at her with a wry smile.

Aria watched him in careful silence before smiling deeply. "You can consider me your captive audience, Sovereign."

"I often do," he teased, his smile growing.

Her eyes softened, but the moment didn't last.

"I come with news." He turned to her fully, his hands resting behind his back. "His majesty has approved of you having semi-permanent guardians to keep a close and careful eye on all that you do, all the day long."

Aria's hopeful expression faded. "Somehow, with your demeanor, I was expecting good news. But this is just more of your damn paranoia, isn't it?"

Rylik's smug grin widened. "I'd be lying if I said I didn't have ulterior motives, dear, but I do have my limitations as your shadow. I should've been at your side last night, but I wasn't. Now, moving forward, someone *will* be. At nearly all times. It's mainly for your protection, I assure you. The added surveillance is but an additional benefit for me."

Aria sighed, turning away from him. "Well, I suppose I should be grateful for the added protection. I'll choose to ignore the benefit you glean from it."

Rylik followed her without missing a beat, his demeanor calm and casual. "That's the spirit."

"Tch." She glanced sideways at him, a faint smile breaking through her irritation. "Your lack of pretense is refreshing,

Sovereign."

He met her gaze, his expression knowing. "And your outwardly defiant remarks are equally so."

She bit back a chuckle, her fingers trailing through the ends of her braid. "So, will you be stalking me the rest of the evening? Or do you have more exciting plans?"

"I merely came to tell you the good news, and to walk with you through the garden, it seems. But yes, I do have other matters to attend to." He smirked, stepping in line with her. "However, you won't be alone. Your attentive chaperones should be here within the hour, ensuring you have all the comforting protection you need."

"Delightful," she muttered, rolling her eyes. "Thank you."

Despite the sharp edge of her sarcasm, she seemed more at ease now — perhaps even grateful, though he doubted she would ever admit it aloud. With a subtle nod, he turned and left her standing at the apothecary door, a quiet hope stirring that the remainder of her evening might be kinder to her than the day had been.

* * *

It was hours later when Rylik finally concluded his tasks for the day and made his way toward his suite, the burden of the king's desires only mildly displaced for now. His footsteps echoed softly along the stone corridor, his mind already drifting toward the quiet solitude of his room. As he approached his door, his hand reached for the latch, eager for the reprieve that awaited him beyond it.

The fire roared in the hearth, the first sound to reach him as he crossed the threshold. Candles flickered on various surfaces, creating a soft, almost intimate atmosphere. Almost at once, he noticed a familiar figure silhouetted in the light and he froze when he saw a small black ring pinched between her fingertips. He shut the door behind him, nearly startling Aria into dropping the heirloom.

His gaze was glued on the ring in her hand, but he masked his discomfort with a calm, playful tone. "Snooping around in my quarters, Pyra?"

Aria's laughter was soft, almost distant, as she drew near, her gaze settling on the ring in her hand. "This is a beautiful ring, Sovereign, but there's a crack running through it." She tilted her head, studying the damaged band with curiosity. "Why haven't you repaired it?"

His eyes were fixed on the ring as she offered it back, her fingers hovering inches from his. "Some things," he replied, voice low, "are better left broken."

She paused, her expression searching his face for some trace of humor or jest, but found none. "Why is that?"

He reached for the ring, his fingertips brushing the curve of her palm. "If we fix everything that breaks, Aria," he said softly, "we might forget to learn from our mistakes." The familiar chill of the ring rested in his hand, solid and unyielding. "I like to carry my failures with me, to remember what I can't afford to repeat."

Her brow furrowed as she watched him. "And what failure is held in that crack?" Her voice was barely above a whisper, but he could see the sincerity in her eyes, the unguarded curiosity.

"The failure of my father," he answered, a cool edge to his tone. She already knew his darkest secret—he'd unwittingly taken that risk once before—so this, too, he would allow her to hear. "He trusted his closest friend, and that trust led to betrayal. That betrayal led to his death. He was executed for treason against the crown, condemned by the one he thought he could trust."

Her face softened, a glimmer of sorrow pooling in her gaze as if she could feel that loss through him. Her lips parted, and though he expected no comfort from her, her gentle words touched him unexpectedly. "I—I'm so sorry, Sovereign."

He let the words settle around him, their warmth fighting against the chill that was always with him. It had been his burden to bear alone, yet, in that brief moment, her sympathy felt easing. The words could hardly reach him, but he appreciated hearing them nonetheless. He closed his hand over the ring, lowering it to his side as a quiet sigh left his lips.

"I understand now why you wouldn't repair it." Her voice was gentle, cautious. "Sometimes, living with our scars is a reminder.

Though, is it worth the pain of reliving them?"

He shook his head, a faint pity in his eyes for her innocence. "Of course it is. Reliving these memories makes sure a new one doesn't replace it."

"But the lesson you take from it," she persisted, her brows drawing together as she looked up at him, "is to be alone? To never trust anyone?"

Her words fell into the silence between them. He walked past her, feeling the weight of her question as he placed the ring on his desk with a heavy sigh. "It is better to be lonely than to be dead."

Behind him, her soft footsteps drew closer, her presence a warmth against his back. "Not everyone is a supreme evil, Sovereign," she murmured, almost imploring him to believe her. "Some people can be trusted."

His gaze lifted, catching hers over his shoulder, a glint of bitter amusement in his eyes. "I am pleased for you, Pyra. I am glad that you have not yet experienced how cruel a person can truly be." He offered a slow, dark smile, his voice softening with a touch of regret. "Present company excluded."

Yet she didn't shrink from his words; if anything, her gaze held a gentle, almost aching sympathy. "I'm sorry—truly, I am," she whispered. "I wish I could convince you that there are decent people in this world."

"I agree that there are," he mused, almost wistfully. "But they behave no differently than those who seek to harm."

She looked up at him, a desperation in her eyes, clearly reaching for some spark of hope in him. "Surely, someone like you can discern the difference."

"No." He extended his hand, wrapping it gently around her arm as she settled beside him. "The ones who betray you are often the most convincing." He pulled her closer, his fingers firm but unhurried, as if testing her resolve. "They are practiced in deceit, and they wait, hidden, until the moment is right. But I'm never caught off guard." His tone deepened, his gaze unwavering. "When they raise their sword against me, I am already behind them, my own blade at the ready."

He felt the slight tremor in her as she swallowed, struggling to keep her composure, but he welcomed it. Let her feel that sliver of fear—it would only reinforce the cost of betrayal, should she ever be tempted to waver.

"That is a harsh reality to live by, Sovereign," she murmured, her voice barely a whisper. "No one can live so guarded, shutting out affection or love."

"Love," he repeated, the word tinged with quiet derision. "I can easily do without. And affection," His fingers tightened just slightly around her arm, a hint of his strength behind the touch. "Affection is easily rendered if I want it."

Her gaze fell, sliding to the window as she turned her head away. "I," She hesitated, her voice faltering. She swallowed, willing her tone back to steady. "I actually put something together for you today." Her words were brighter, an obvious attempt to change the subject—a shift he allowed, if only for the moment. Perhaps that was for the best, as his mind was beginning to spiral with visions of what *affections* he'd like Aria to render to *him*.

"It's nothing grand, really," she said, a tentative smile lifting her lips. "But I thought you might appreciate it." She gestured toward his windowsill, where a small planter box sat nestled in the light. "I hope you don't mind."

Rylik's eyes widened, a rare look of genuine surprise softening his features. "So, here we have a Luminara Bloom on the left. It enhances mental clarity and focus," Aria explained, pointing to each plant in turn. "In the middle, a Whispering Willowroot. It sharpens intuition and foresight, which I thought you'd find useful. And finally, the Firesong Fern. It radiates warmth, and if you steep the leaves in tea, it produces a warming effect throughout the body. Even if I'm not healing you directly, maybe this will provide some comfort."

She sighed softly, catching his sharp gaze. "And you already knew what all of these were, didn't you?"

Rylik's smirk returned. "I did."

"So then, I suppose I don't have to tell you how to care for them."

His smile grew wider. "You do not."

Aria chuckled, shaking her head. "Well, I hope you find that you now have a little time to tend to a very, very little garden." She smiled at the box, then at him. "They're just sprouts now, but they'll bloom soon."

Rylik's gaze softened. "Indeed, they will."

He glanced down, noting how her hair had loosened from her braid, soft waves cascading down her back. His fingers ached to touch her again, but he clenched his fists, resisting the urge.

Aria raised her hand, wiggling her fingers with a playful smirk. "Your blight, please, so I can go to bed."

Rylik untied his tunic, baring his chest with ease as he watched her approach. Her fingers touched him with familiar precision, her golden-hued eyes glowing softly as she healed his blight.

As her hand withdrew, Rylik grasped her wrist, startling himself with the intensity of the motion.

"Is something wrong?" she asked, her eyes wide.

Yes, his mind screamed. *You're leaving me again.*

The unexpected thought sent a shock through him. He let go of her wrist, clearing his throat as he looked toward the window. "I just wanted to thank you for the kind gift you assembled. You clearly took great care to choose flora that would be of the utmost interest and usefulness to me. Startlingly, I'm amazed that you would even know where to begin. I look forward to watching them bloom."

Aria blushed, her face lighting up with satisfaction. "Well, after the kindness you've already shown me, despite everything, I wanted to extend my gratitude."

Rylik's expression darkened slightly. "Kindness?" He felt an inner turmoil begin to unfurl within him.

Aria's smile faltered at the change in his tone. "Good night, Sovereign." She turned to leave, but Rylik reached out, grabbing her wrist again. This time, he tugged her back toward him.

She staggered back a couple of steps, looking up at him, her face flushed. "Sovereign?"

Taking a deep breath, Rylik's hand found its way to Aria's face, his fingers tracing the line of her jaw. His thumb hovered over her lower lip, the warmth of her skin igniting a flicker of heat within him. "You think that I have been showing you *kindness*?"

Aria's eyes widened in astonishment, a deep flush creeping across her cheeks, a mixture of memory and his words igniting something raw between them.

"Everything that I do is for my own benefit," He said sharply as he pulled her closer, fingers weaving possessively through her hair, the tension coiling like a spring between them. Caught in the moment, Aria stared up at him, eyes wide with surprise and something deeper—a vulnerability that mirrored his own. His words should've made her recoil, but instead she seemed to soften under his touch.

His lips hovered tantalizingly close to hers, the world around them fading into a blur. Time seemed to stretch as their breaths mingled, a tantalizing promise hanging in the air. Yet, with a sudden rush of clarity, he closed his eyes, frustration crashing over him like a cold wave. He released her, stepping back as if the very act of pulling away could quell the storm raging within.

"I don't know what came over me. I'm clearly very tired." His voice was a strained whisper, the tension hanging between them like a fragile thread, threatening to snap.

Aria, cheeks still flushed, gaped at him in silence, struggling to find her words.

"You should go." He attempted a smile, then turned his back to her.

She hesitated for a moment longer before shuffling out of the room, closing the door behind her.

Left alone, Rylik hunched over his desk, heart racing with vexation. *I was mere moments away from dismantling the contents of my desk by splaying her body over top of it, pressing her, kissing every inch of her. Gods, what is happening to me?!*

He looked at the budding plants on his windowsill, reflecting on her use of the word "kindness". It was laughable that she thought any action he had taken with her thus far could've ever been merely done in "kindness". As if he had ever done anything at all that had not directly benefited him. How naive she was. Frustratingly naive. Swallowing hard, he pushed away from the desk and strode over to his chair, slumping down into it, brooding.

Trust leads to ruin.

He closed his eyes, willing himself to remember the day he had found his father's signet ring, their family crest broken and stained with blood—His father's blood. The sound of his father pleading for his life echoed in his mind as the axe fell. What a horrid lesson to learn—what a brutal way to discover that even the best of friends would betray you for glory.

But, she's not like that. He opened his eyes. *Is that what my father thought? Before he was betrayed?* He stared into the fire, irritation bubbling beneath the surface. *But Aria is different, is she not? She's not part of this world—this sickening collection of twisted souls vying for power, greed, and glory. Try as I might, I can find no fault in her.* He glanced toward the window sill. *And that's far more concerning, I suppose.*

Rylik rose to his feet, his jaw tight, the restlessness coursing through him. People, he knew too well, could betray—even if they began with the purest of intentions. And Aria, bound in her own fragile state, was balanced precariously on a thin, delicate thread between fear and desperation. He was not blind to her predicament, to the frailty of her position. One misstep could send her plummeting into darkness, pulling him down with her. She was frightened, cautious, so painfully vulnerable to any force that might twist her circumstances to its own ends.

Kindness. Again, that word plagued him.

What sort of *kindness* might someone offer her, only to snare her within a trap? What *kindness* might fray that delicate thread, snapping it and letting them both fall? Though she lacked the coldness he expected in others, she was impressionable, susceptible to threats, and others could use that against him. Worse, it was only a matter of time before she realized she could free herself if the right opportunity arose.

He tightened his hand into a fist. There was no question—he *needed* her. But worse than that, he *wanted* her. And beyond chaining her to his side, he had no guarantee she'd stay. If she fled, he would chase her. If someone sought to claim her, he would eliminate them. This possessiveness unsettled him, yet he found himself wanting her to know it, to fear it. Fear was a powerful force, one that could bind her to him—but at the same time, he found himself drawn to something softer.

The delicate plants on the windowsill caught his eye, mocking him with their simplicity, the gentle care they represented. She had thought of him. She had chosen to see something in him, something that shouldn't exist. And he liked it—he liked knowing she thought of him fondly, liked that he was somehow worthy of any trace of affection from her. This was never the plan; he had never anticipated that his fixation on her would shift toward something so warm, something achingly fragile.

He knew well enough that fear could enforce loyalty, but there was a gentler way, too—one that he wasn't blind to. Manipulation was familiar to him; he had wielded it often, pulling strings to suit his needs in the court, playing on people's insecurities, their eagerness for praise. It should be easy with her, and yet, he was playing a dangerous game. He was too invested in her every little reaction, too attuned to the subtle shifts in her expression, the blushes and defiant quips, the anger that flickered through her eyes. She was maddeningly *adorable*.

Annoyed with himself, his jaw clenched in reaction to his own foolish thoughts. Perhaps he couldn't stop this pull toward her; perhaps he didn't need to. But one thing was clear: he couldn't let her go. The king's leering gaze was already circling her, and if he didn't continue to intervene on her behalf, she would be taken. And that, above all else, was something he could never allow.

*She is **mine***, he thought bitterly.

Taking one final look at the planter box bathed in moonlight, he felt a swell of emotions he'd rather not identify. When he had seen her tears earlier today, standing in the very spot she had been dragged through the night before by rogues, he had felt a pang in his chest not unlike wrath. Pain and anger were familiar and comforting feelings, but the tinge of something more—it was unsettling. A deep sigh escaped him, refusing to dwell any longer on it. He steeled his resolve, determination hardening like iron in his chest.

He couldn't afford to make mistakes where it concerned her. He *owned* her. Every breath she took, every flicker of defiance in her gaze—those belonged to him, tethered by the bond he'd imposed and the power he wielded. He was the puppeteer here, was he not? The Sovereign, ever powerful, ever in control, the master of her fate and her fears.

He would keep her bound to him in whatever way he saw fit, pulling the strings as he pleased. She would not escape. Not from him. And if anyone dared try to sever that bond, he would show them what it meant to cross the Sovereign's will—swiftly and without mercy.

CHAPTER 17

RYLIK

Rylik stood by the windowsill of his bedchamber, sunlight streaming through the glass and casting a warm glow on the budding sprouts nestled within the planter box that Aria had given him. He poured water over the tiny plants, a soft feeling blossoming in his chest, one he refused to acknowledge.

I wonder if Aria might like to join me tonight, he mused, setting the now-empty cup down on his desk. *The moon will be bright and every star illuminated. It would be nice, for once, to share in the majesty of the night sky with another person.* He sighed, shuffling papers around on the cluttered surface. Having her company would be like a reward for having survived the day. He had been so content recently that he hardly noticed what time of year it was.

He gathered the scattered papers and arranged them neatly into a black leather-bound book, the familiar motions grounding him. The Summit of Realms was drawing closer, that annual farce where the king would flaunt his authority before the provincial lords, their attendance bought with forced tributes and shallow praise. Each year, it was the same tiresome display—a hollow show of unity, a staged assembly meant only to serve the king's insatiable hunger for power and admiration.

At the summit, each provincial lord would be summoned,

ushered into a grand hall draped in banners proclaiming royal supremacy. They would offer gifts meant to reflect their "loyalty," but these tributes were mere tokens—a demand wrapped in tradition, extracted with thinly veiled threats of consequence for any lack of enthusiasm. The lords would bow and feign respect, reciting oaths they surely loathed but dared not refuse. The king would address each province in turn, his words rich with hollow encouragements to obey and flourish under his watchful eye. Any grievances raised would be swiftly redirected or dismissed, the complaints drowned beneath layers of politeness and pretense.

Rylik let out a sigh, imagining how different such a gathering could be under a more discerning rule. If he held such power, the summit would have purpose beyond sycophancy, each gathering a chance to create genuine alliances and address issues rather than dismiss them. The provinces would be heard in earnest, their voices respected, and their concerns met with actual solutions, not empty rhetoric. Respect, after all, could be earned without demanding submission through these gilded decrees.

He closed the book, his gaze darkening. Perhaps, one day, the Summit of Realms could become what it ought to be—a council of equals, each voice valued rather than silenced. But that vision demanded a change that he could only entertain in silence, an ambition that lurked in the shadows of his thoughts. For now, he would settle for the role he played, but he couldn't suppress the sense that the day would come when these empty shows of power would meet their end.

He tied the leather book with a string to secure the pages, glancing toward the adjoining suite door where Aria was likely waiting. The memory of the previous night flashed in his mind—when he'd nearly lost his composure and almost pulled her onto his desk for something far more sinful than he cared to admit. A smirk crept onto his lips.

He opened his door smoothly, the cool air rushing in as he stepped out. His near-pitiful desire for her presence was a growing problem, but since last night he had resigned himself to accept his desires for her. She was a woman. A beautiful woman, but a woman nonetheless. And he was aware of the effect she had on him.

It was quite likely, he had reasoned, that the more he indulged in her, the less desirable she would eventually become to him. After her effects on him waned, he could then focus more on the practical side of their connection: she healed him, and therefore she must be a constant in his life. There was no need for her to be anything more than that.

"Good morning, Sovereign." Aria stood to his left, just outside her own door, looking at him with an uncertain expression.

Rylik blinked in mild surprise. "Aria, I would've thought you'd be sleeping." He let a hint of mischief slip into his voice. "Or at the very least, lacing up your corset about this time."

She looked aside, a blush creeping onto her cheeks. "I got up early. Didn't sleep well."

"I'm sorry to hear that. Why are you loitering in the hallway?" He looked her over, then cast a casual glance around. "Where are your chaperones?"

Aria met his eyes briefly before shifting her gaze away. "I told them I didn't need their presence this morning because I thought you and I might walk together?"

Rylik's lips curved into a slow smile. "What's this? You *want* to walk with me? That's new. I had intended to give you a small reprieve from my presence this morning."

A hint of sweetness mingled with playful annoyance flickered across her face as she soothingly rubbed her arm. "I thought I might pick your brain about some species of plants. There are some potions that need reworking, and I had some ideas that I might run by you, see what you think. Given that you're somewhat of an expert on plant species."

He took a step closer, pleased. "That is something I would very much enjoy doing with you."

She hesitated, a nervous energy flickering between them. "I feel a 'however' forming next."

"Yes, it would seem you've picked a morning that I cannot be at your side." He closed the distance between them, easing her back against her door with his towering presence. "Perhaps we could reconvene this evening?"

"Well, naturally, yes," she said casually, before asking, "Will you be otherwise engaged all day? Will I have no shadow at all?"

"Sadly, no. I have an audience with the king and various matters to attend to that will require my full attention."

Biting the inside of her lip, she let a sly smile play on her lips as a thought seemingly crossed her mind. "So, you're saying if there was ever a day to consider escaping the palace to find my freedom, today would be the day?"

Rylik's expression suddenly turned serious, his eyes darkening. "You think I would ever allow you to escape?"

Swallowing uneasily, she attempted a smile. "I was teasing, of course. I'm not trying to say that I'd—"

In a swift motion, he opened the door to her room, pushing her inside with a firm but gentle shove. He closed the door behind him, his gaze sharp as he watched Aria stagger, eyes wide with a quiet but unmistakable unease as her steps faltered in the open space.

"You ought not," He flashed a dark smile, his blood feeling colder at the thought of losing her, "jest about such a thing."

"I didn't realize I could unnerve the fearsome Sovereign with such a half-hearted joke," she murmured, trying to keep her tone innocent.

"I am not unnerved." He loomed over her again, his gaze sweeping over her as the sunlight streamed in, highlighting the golden glint of her silhouette. "I am cautious. And if you have thoughts of running away from here, jesting or otherwise, then perhaps," His hand found her arm lightly, leaning in close to whisper, "I will have to put shackles on your feet."

Rylik could sense Aria's heart thudding in her chest, the quick tempo of her breaths betraying the tension twisting within her. He felt the warmth radiating from her as his fingers traced her sleeve, nearly desperate for the fire in her blood to quell the ice in his own. He steadied his breathing, pulling back from her, though his blood still felt cold.

"I'm not going anywhere, Sovereign." Aria found his gaze as he withdrew, trying to appear fearless, but he could easily discern her unease. "I wouldn't risk the failure," her voice was hushed, though she made an effort to lend it firmness, "Do you really think that I would even try?"

"I think you would." A dark, knowing smile returned to his

lips, his vulnerability caged behind a cold façade as he added, "and I would savor the hunt."

She looked aside, unable to hold his gaze, feeling the weight of the moment.

"Perhaps you should get going to meet with His Majesty." She moved to walk past him, eager to break the tension. "I don't want you to be late on my behalf."

He clasped his hands behind his back as he turned to look at her over his shoulder, his expression shifting slightly. "I'll find two guardsmen to walk with you just to ensure you're not left alone."

Annoyance flared in her features as she opened her door and swiftly walked out, shutting it softly behind her.

* * *

Sunlight streamed through the tall, arched windows of the grand dining hall, casting a warm glow over the long oak table set with polished silverware and an array of vibrant fruits, the air thick with the rich aroma of freshly baked bread, roast chicken, and brewing coffee. At the head of the table, the king sat leisurely, cutting into the meat of the roasted bird. The scrape of his fork against the plate echoed through the otherwise quiet room, each bite savored as if it were a luxury he had all the time in the world to indulge in.

Rylik stood off to the side, hands folded behind his back, his face impassive as he waited for the king to finish his meal. Inside, his thoughts churned, *I'll admit, I was a little too harsh with her. I didn't anticipate her to strike such a nerve within me. It's as if she found my weakness and drove a knife in.* His eyes flicked to the window, his expression remaining stony. The thought of not having her around to heal his blight was more than just life-threatening in its implications. But, she wouldn't dare step out of line. She was too terrified to cross him, he had made certain of that. And even if she did act in such foolish desperation, he would catch her with ease and drag her back to his suite, make her bonds a little tighter. His icy blue eyes were cold and resolute.

The king dabbed at his mouth with a napkin before casting a

glance at Rylik. "The Summit preparations," he said, his voice carrying an air of authority as he dropped the napkin beside his plate. "I trust everything is in order?"

Rylik inclined his head slightly. "Of course. The gifts have already begun arriving, and everyone has given notice that they will be in attendance."

The king chuckled happily, stabbing his fork into a piece of chicken. "I do so look forward to the Summit."

Rylik's lips curved in a faint, nearly imperceptible smile, but his eyes remained cold.

"There is another matter I've been considering, Sovereign." He set his fork down, chewing and swallowing down a lump of meat as leaned back in his chair, folding his hands over his stomach. "It concerns the imperial healer, Aria."

Rylik's posture remained unchanged, but his attention sharpened at the mention of her name. "What about her, Your Majesty?"

The king picked up his goblet, swirling the dark wine inside, his eyes focused on the liquid as if it held some answer. "I've had some of my best men look into it, trying to confirm the rumors of her unfortunate condition. The stories about her previous lovers are," he didn't bother to hide his shudder as he finished, "truly disturbing."

Amusement flickered briefly in Rylik's eyes, though his face remained carefully neutral. *Well, it seems my threatened connections took care of his predictable snooping around. It's unlikely he will investigate any further on this matter.* "Yes, well, it is a grave concern, but so long as she is not sharing your bed, your majesty, you do not have to suffer the fate of her dread curse."

The king's expression sobered. "Indeed. I have no shortage of women to warm my bed, but that's not what concerns me most." His eyes narrowed as they flicked to Rylik. "The town she's from is crawling with Rebellion sympathizers. More than any town of its size should have."

Rylik remained quiet, though his gaze darkened. His suspicions were not surprising, but the sudden caution from him could complicate things. "That is curious, indeed, my king."

"Curious, yes," Kaldros echoed, his voice edged with suspicion.

"Do you think it's possible she's involved?"

Well, of **course** *she is,* he thought to himself. Rylik's gaze turned hard, though his voice was smooth when he replied, "I'll look into it, Sire. If there's any connection to the Rebellion, I'll find it, and I will sever it completely."

The king leaned forward slightly, his gaze sharp. "Good. I trust you'll handle it with the same *thoroughness* that you handle everything else."

"Without hesitation," Rylik promised, inclining his head slightly.

Satisfied, the king waved a dismissive hand as he returned to his plate. "That's all, Sovereign. You may go."

"As you wish, Your Majesty." Rylik gave a small bow, then turned and left the room, the door closing softly behind him.

He passed silently through the castle halls, his footsteps a ghostly whisper on the stone floors, until he emerged into the bright expanse of the outer bailey. The sunlight did little to warm his bitter expression as he crossed the courtyard, his eyes narrowing as they settled on the distant figure of the apothecary.

There, in the shade of the hedges, Leon stood, tense and uneasy. His gaze was locked on Aria, who was hanging dried herbs beside Maven and a few other healers.

From a distance, Rylik observed the scene with cold calculation. *Valenforth.* The surname was a flimsy cover for whatever his true name might be. Rylik had long suspected Leon was tied to the Rebellion, but the man held no real power. He was merely a cog in a larger machine, albeit a cog that could ruin Rylik's plans for Aria if not dealt with properly.

Sinking into the shade under the trees of the garden walkway, Rylik's gaze followed Leon as he hesitated near the apothecary. His fingers twitched at his sides, and after a moment, Leon seemed to lose his nerve. He turned on his heel, retreating quickly.

Rylik's voice cut through the air, smooth as silk. "Lovely morning, isn't it?"

Leon nearly stumbled backward, startled as he whipped around to find him. "Sovereign?" he stammered, his face paling as he recognized the figure leaned against the tree, nearly melting into the shadows.

Rylik's smile was dark, unsettling. "Do you often spend a lot of time over here?" he asked, his tone deceptively casual.

Leon fumbled for a response. "I—uh, no. Only when I need something medicinal. Or just a walk."

Rylik's eyes gleamed as he stepped forward, his gaze never leaving Leon's. "I see, and are you well?"

"I'm fine, I assure you." Leon's reply was sharp, though his anxiety bled through. "I was just getting some fresh air."

"No need of a healer today?"

Leon's expression tightened. "Is there a point to your prying—" He quickly caught himself, adjusting his tone with forced reverence. "Sovereign."

A flicker of satisfaction crossed Rylik's features. He walked toward Leon, his presence predatory. "Corporal Valenforth," he began, his voice smooth as ever, "I've heard impressive things about you from your superiors. It would seem you are rather skilled with a blade on the battlefield. I should like to see that some time."

Leon's face remained unreadable, though tension simmered beneath the surface. "I should like to show you," he said, his tone guarded.

Rylik's smile grew sharper, more dangerous. "You are due for a promotion, are you not?"

Leon hesitated before replying quietly, "I am."

"The Valenforth house is a strong one—a noble one, at that," Rylik said, his voice low as he began to prowl around Leon, his gaze never wavering. "I imagine it wouldn't take much to ascend the ranks with that name alone on your resume."

Leon eyed him warily, the unease in his chest growing with every step Rylik took. "I don't think I understand what you're getting at, Sovereign. My family name is hardly a concern. If I ascend the ranks, it will be on my merit alone and not my name."

Rylik's eyes gleamed with subtle delight. "Yes, but what a fortunate name it is."

Leon tensed. "If you're implying anything, Sovereign—"

"Whatever would I be implying?" Rylik began with mock sincerity, "Surely not that you stole a good surname to ensure your rank of Corporal."

Leon's frame went rigid with the words.

Rylik chuckled softly. "Oh, relax, I don't care how you rise through the ranks, boy. If anything, I admire your gall." He placed a hand on Leon's shoulder, gently turning him. "You are so very careful, Corporal, and so very guarded in all that you do. I admire your ability to stay focused on your goals and to pursue whatever means necessary to get what you want."

Leon followed Rylik's lead reluctantly, his body tense as the Sovereign's hand remained on his shoulder.

"Though it seems your pursuits are becoming somewhat misguided of late," Rylik added, gesturing toward the apothecary where Aria was now alone, plucking dried herbs from the line above their porch.

Leon's jaw clenched. The unspoken threat in Rylik's words hung heavy in the air. "I'm simply keeping an eye on things. Of course, naturally, I'd keep an eye on an old friend. The kingdom has its fair share of unrest these days, doesn't it?"

"Unrest?" Rylik's voice dripped with mockery. "Oh yes, we've seen whispers of that. A few discontented souls who think they can change the world by gathering in secret and stirring the pot. Funny, don't you think? How easy it is to get caught up in someone else's mistakes." His grip on Leon's shoulder tightened as the Corporal tried to step away.

Leon's heart raced, but he kept his expression neutral. "Mistakes can be dangerous, that's true."

"Indeed." Rylik's tone darkened. "Especially for those caught in the wrong place, at the wrong time. Or worse—with the wrong people." He let the words linger, their weight pressing down on Leon's chest. "I imagine it would be particularly devastating if someone like Aria found herself entangled in such a mess."

Leon's fists clenched at his sides. "Aria's a healer. She has nothing to do with politics."

Rylik's voice turned soft, almost sinister. "Ah, but healers have a way of becoming involved in things whether they like it or not.

Especially when others have taken a keen interest in them." His gaze bore into Leon's. "She's valuable. And fragile. It would be a shame if something happened to her because of someone else's recklessness. A shame if something happened to *you* as a result, Corporal."

Leon's throat tightened as he fought to keep his composure. "I don't speak to her much these days, Sovereign. I doubt she wants much to do with me anymore."

Rylik released his grip, watching as Leon instinctively stepped back. "That's likely for the best," he murmured. "After all, I'm sure you wouldn't want to be the reason she's caught up in anything *unpleasant*." He paused, letting the silence stretch before adding, "keep your distance from her."

Leon swallowed hard, his mouth dry, feeling the command like a punch to the gut. He forced himself to nod. "Of course. I understand."

Rylik's smile returned, cold and sharp. "Good. I knew you would." With that, the Sovereign turned and strode away, his black cloak billowing behind him like a shadow.

CHAPTER 18

ARIA

Sunlight streamed through the narrow windows of the apothecary, catching in the floating specks of dust and casting a warm glow across the rows of glass vials and jars. The gentle aroma of crushed herbs mingled with the rich scent of freshly ground roots, filling the air with an earthy fragrance. The rhythmic sound of a mortar grinding against a pestle blended with the soft chatter of birds outside, creating a peaceful backdrop to the busy workspace.

At the workbench, Aria stood with practiced ease, her fingers deftly mixing a concoction of wildflower essence and feverfew, though her mind was elsewhere. The frustration of her encounter with Rylik earlier that morning was pulsing through her as she worked. *I can't believe that I thought for a moment this morning that I was going to enjoy a walk with him! That was clearly a moment of insanity for me! Because, I'm an imbecile! Idiot! Naïve! I'm his prisoner, and this is no budding friendship or—god forbid— romance!* She was trapped here for the foreseeable future with no end in sight. She was clearly desperate for camaraderie. So desperate that she'd been willing to befriend her own jailer.

Sighing, she wrestled with her thoughts. *I really am a fool. Of course he doesn't see me as any kind of friend. Why did I even give him that planter box?* Miserable and embarrassed, she thought of her role as a healer. *I need to just keep my role simple: heal his blight and shut my mouth.* Memories of the firefly tonic's beautiful gold and green glow washed over her—how magical it had felt with him seated next to her in that gentle light. She recalled how kind he had looked last night when she had given him the planter box, how they had nearly kissed, and how she had not resisted. *Foolish to think I was anything but trapped.*

Beside her at the workbench, Maven moved with quiet precision, measuring out dried lavender and nettle leaves. The two women worked in silence until Maven glanced over, her eyes catching the slight tension in Aria's hands as they moved a little too briskly, a little too harshly.

"You've been quiet today." Maven's voice was gentle but probing. She set down her bundle of herbs, her gaze resting on Aria's strained expression. "Is everything alright?"

Aria's brow furrowed as she kept her eyes on the mixture before her. "It's nothing," she muttered, her tone carefully controlled. The tension in her hands, however, betrayed her emotions. She could almost hear Maven's unspoken doubt. *It's not really worth our time to talk about it,* Aria thought to herself. *She doesn't need to know.*

Maven wasn't so easily deterred. "Nothing, huh?" Her voice was kind, yet persistent. "It wouldn't have anything to do with the Sovereign, would it?"

Aria stiffened at the mention of Rylik, a reaction that didn't escape Maven's notice.

"I've had my fair share of dealings with him," Maven continued, her smile soft but knowing. "I used to be a preferred healer for the Shadow Knights, so I had plenty of time to make small talk with them. The Sovereign included." She paused, carefully arranging sprigs of thyme. "He might seem cold— unfeeling, even—but I don't think he's as heartless as he appears. There's a bit of kindness there, buried deep down."

Aria couldn't stop herself from scoffing. "Deep, deep down. Very deep, Maven."

Maven only shrugged, her smile never faltering. "It's hard to see sometimes, I know. But it's there. He's not as unpleasant as he seems."

Aria rolled her eyes. She had witnessed those rare moments when Rylik's icy demeanor thawed, but they were fleeting. Whatever warmth he possessed, it was buried so far beneath his armor that it seemed almost nonexistent after this morning.

The two women lapsed back into silence, the sound of grinding herbs filling the quiet. After a while, Maven's voice broke through again, softer this time, hesitant.

"Speaking of difficult men," she began, her fingers nervously playing with the edge of her apron, "Leon was supposed to meet me for lunch today, but I haven't heard from him since last night. I am wondering now if I said something to upset him."

Aria shook her head, partly in disbelief that she was being pulled into a conversation about the only other man she disliked more than Rylik. "You think you've upset him?" She paused, a wry smile tugging at her lips. "Maven, he's borderline obsessed with you. If anything, he might only be keeping his distance because of me."

Maven stare faltered slightly, her gaze dropping as she fiddled with the vials on the table. "He did say that you once had feelings for him. I have been wondering if perhaps—" her voice fell silent.

Aria's puzzlement deepened. "Wait, Maven, are you really thinking for even a moment that he'd be interested in me?"

Maven's sheepish expression and awkward silence said it all.

"Oh, God," Aria sighed, her tone softening with sympathy. "Leon and I are as platonic as brother and sister. He's right, though, when he told you that I used to have feelings for him. But, those feelings are," She hesitated, her voice growing quieter. "He and I will never be anything at all." The finality of that sentence made her heart sting a little, but she tried to brush it away. "So, trust me, if he's being distant today, it's likely just because he and I are fighting. I'm sure you'll find him quite pleasant if you can corner him alone later."

Maven's blush deepened, her relief evident with Aria's reassurance. She hadn't noticed the hint of regret in Aria's voice, the unspoken weight of what could have been.

Aria's thoughts drifted as she returned to her work, her hands moving automatically through the familiar motions. If Maven only knew the truth about Leon—how cold he could be, how detached. But, even so, she couldn't really blame the woman for developing feelings for him. She understood the draw. But, with everything that's happened recently, she couldn't really find the reasons why she liked him anymore.

Her hands stilled for a moment, the silence pressing down on her. The anger she'd been carrying lately felt like a heavy cloak, weighing her down, suffocating her thoughts. *I wish that I wasn't so angry.* Because she was so often angry lately. At herself, at Leon, at the Sovereign; at this strange new life that had taken her away from everything she knew, and had made her a prisoner within these walls.

But as the anger boiled, a deeper thought bubbled up from the depths of her mind, quiet yet insistent. She didn't want her life to be over, or for it to be defined by this palace—this new identity forced upon her. She didn't want to be resigned to bitterness and helplessness, not when there was still so much left to live for. How could she tell Leon she wanted to live her own life, but in the same breath be willing to give up what little she had left of it? If she was going to give up on her life, then she should've stayed aligned with the Rebellion and thrown her life away at her own discretion. But, that's not what she wanted.

Reaching aimlessly across the table for anything to grasp onto, she let her mind continue to grapple with her emotions.

I don't want to be angry anymore. She couldn't stay angry forever. She needed to be more resilient. She needed to focus on the good. That's what had gotten her this far in life. Her parents, though poor and simple, had always adopted a positive mentality. They taught her that looking for the beauty in small moments was a way that she might always see the good in the darkest of times. *I can't forget that now, not when that's the mentality I need to adopt in this dark future that awaits me,* she thought, a seed of resolve taking root within her.

The payment she had received from the king was generous. Her family, once struggling, was now well taken care of. Her suite, grand and spacious, was larger than the house she grew up in, with windows that offered views she never could've dreamt of having before now. Learning potion making alongside Maven was incredible in its own right. She was becoming more of a true healer every day, doing something that brought her so much joy to learn. And there had been a few pleasant moments here — experiences she never would've had as a poor commoner.

Aria's gaze softened as she considered her situation. *So, the Sovereign has made me his prisoner. But, honestly, it could be worse.* A soft sigh escaped her lips as she mused. If she had to be here against her will, then at least she had already known a handful of beautiful, unexpected moments. And if she could use a little tact, she could have a lifetime more. She resolved, her heart stirring with a quiet determination.

Taking a deep breath, she let the tension ease from her shoulders. She glanced at Maven, who was still carefully sorting herbs beside her, unaware of the storm of emotions swirling within Aria.

Aria straightened, feeling a small, determined warmth spread through her. She would make the most of this life, this strange, gilded cage. She would find her place, even if it meant treading carefully around the Sovereign, even if it meant navigating the complexities of her heart and the shifting allegiances that bound her.

If this is my life now, Aria thought with quiet conviction, *then I'll make it mine.*

And with that, she turned back to her work, a newfound strength burgeoning in her chest, ready to face whatever came next.

* * *

Aria stood outside Rylik's door, her hand hovering just above the surface, fingers trembling slightly as she hesitated. The cool evening air slipped through the hallways, but it was the nervous flutter in her stomach that truly unsettled her. Taking a steadying breath, she knocked.

"Enter," came Rylik's voice, muffled but clear.

She stepped inside, her eyes immediately drawn to the Sovereign seated by the fireplace, a glass of wine in his hand. The flickering light cast shadows across his face, softening his usually stern features. Aria's gaze drifted toward the planter box on the windowsill, and her expression faltered for a moment—bittersweet, though she couldn't place why. Collecting herself, she folded her hands in front of her skirt and walked over to him.

"Evening, Sovereign," she said softly.

Rylik looked up at her, a smile playing at the corners of his lips. Without a word, he reached for a glass on the side table, one she hadn't noticed before, and handed it to her. "Join me, won't you?"

Aria hesitated, eyeing the glass for a moment before accepting it. She took the seat opposite him, the fire's warmth barely touching her growing unease.

"I'm pleased you made it through the day without attempting to flee," Rylik said, an amused edge to his voice.

Aria frowned subtly, the comment pulling at her patience. "I told you, Sovereign. I wasn't being serious."

Rylik exhaled, the sound dismissive as he sipped his wine. Aria's gaze shifted to the flames, her thoughts wandering as the silence settled between them. She raised the glass to her lips, sipping slowly.

"Do you ever stargaze?" Rylik asked, his tone shifting abruptly, casual as if they weren't sitting in a moment heavy with unspoken tension.

Aria blinked, startled by the sudden change in topic. "No, I can't say that I have. I mean, I've seen stars, of course, but I wouldn't classify it as stargazing. Why?"

Rylik's gaze remained on the fire. "There's a certain vantage point at the top of the castle, in one of the turrets. The view of the night sky is clearest there. I go sometimes to be alone, to track the stars. Would you care to see it for yourself?"

Aria hesitated, her heart skipping at the unexpected invitation. Perhaps she shouldn't just jump at the opportunity to be alone with this man in the darkness of night. However, it was safe to say that she was far too valuable to him alive, and so it was unlikely he would throw her from the turret. And besides, was this not exactly the sort of thing she had told myself she wanted to start doing, making the most of her new life? When would she ever have another chance to see the night sky from the top of a castle? She downed the rest of her wine in one gulp, setting the glass down with a soft clink. "Fine. If I am to be a prisoner, I might as well enjoy the perks."

Rylik chuckled softly at her candor, rising to his feet. "Very well. Let's go."

As they navigated the dimly lit stone corridors, Aria followed closely behind Rylik. He moved with purpose, leading her through the narrow passageways that twisted like a labyrinth, the air thick with the scent of aged stone and the faint hint of night-blooming jasmine from the garden below.

Aria couldn't help but steal glances at Rylik, whose demeanor was steady and composed, a stark contrast to the fluttering nerves dancing in her own stomach. As much as she didn't care to admit it to herself, she was a little nervous to be making a nighttime trek through the castle with the Sovereign, especially with his sustained silence. The flickering torches cast long swatches of light along the walls as they ascended higher, each staircase bringing them closer to the rooftop.

Finally, they reached a heavy wooden door, worn by time and the elements. Rylik pushed it open with a deliberate motion, the creaking sound reverberating through the stillness. As they stepped out onto the turret rooftop, the cool night air enveloped them, carrying with it the soft melody of crickets chirping.

A gasp caught in Aria's chest as she gazed upward, the night sky stretching endlessly above them, a canvas painted with stars twinkling like a sea of diamonds. Each point of light seemed to pulse with its own energy, illuminating the darkness in a mesmerizing dance. Beneath them and far in the distance, the sprawling capital city shimmered with life, its lights flickering like fireflies caught in a gentle breeze. She looked around them with wide, enchanted eyes, the grandeur of the moment wrapping around her like a warm embrace.

As she gazed out into the vastness, a quiet thrill coursed through her veins. The stars felt within reach, and the world below seemed to pulse with possibilities. In that moment, atop the turret, she was not just a girl entangled in the intricacies of court politics; she was a part of something much larger, woven into the very fabric of the night sky.

"This is incredible," she breathed, awe filling her voice.

Rylik stepped up beside her, sharing the view. "It truly is."

"I can see why you like it," Aria said, turning her gaze toward him. "Do you come here every night?"

Rylik's eyes met hers, hesitating a moment as he looked her over. He cleared his throat and looked away from her as if dispelling a thought. "I come here as often as time allows. I find it especially comforting after a long day to clear my mind. The air is a little crisper up here, and the sky seems to be vast enough to make my musings feel insignificant."

Aria watched him with quiet awe. She had only known Rylik to be intense and distant, but this version of him—wistful, almost vulnerable—was a side she had begun to crave more of. She looked up at the sky again, sharing the moment with him. "Sovereign, botanist, and now astronomer?" she teased lightly.

Rylik scoffed, though it was more amused than defensive. "I'm not nearly as studied on the stars as an astronomer. I do find them captivating, though. I am merely content to stand under them."

Aria smiled, letting the warmth of the moment envelop her. "I understand why. I've never seen a grander view of the night sky than this. And the capital," her voice trailed off as her eyes dropped to the distant city. "It looks like a dream."

Rylik observed her closely as he spoke. "At night, oftentimes it is lively in the square. People gather to drink, to eat, to dance, and to purchase needless wares, late into the evening," he said, watching as her expression softened.

"It sounds wonderful," Aria murmured, her voice filled with quiet longing.

"It can be," Rylik admitted, his tone casual. "But, it can also be deadly. When there is too much liquor to drink and enough rowdy men, even an innocent evening can take a turn for the worst."

Aria's brow furrowed slightly. "Does that happen often?"

"Often enough to be of concern," Rylik said with a shrug. "But it's the capital. It has a reputation for both beauty and violence."

A flicker of sadness crossed Aria's face, dulling her smile.

Rylik's eyes softened as he watched her, a wry smirk tugging at his lips. "Perhaps I'll take you there one day. You needn't worry about your safety as long as I'm with you."

She glanced at him, a playful glint in her eye, and she teased before she could stop herself, "Not afraid I might run, Sovereign?"

In an instant, the playful atmosphere shifted as Rylik's hand reached for hers, his grip firm, his eyes hard as he gave her a look that sent a chill through her. "Are you trying to make me lock you away, Pyra?"

Aria froze, captivated by the desperation in his eyes—an urgency in them she hadn't perceived until now, and had likely missed this morning when he cornered her in her suite. A chilling realization washed over her: he was afraid.

She swallowed, unable to dismiss the pity welling up inside, despite herself. She didn't want to pity him. He didn't deserve it. But, she could understand it. The Sovereign was afraid of losing his life to the blight. Whatever method of healing he had used before meeting her was clearly nothing he wished to return to. It likely did very little to stave off the icy cold.

The weight of his vulnerability pressed down on her, igniting a sense of responsibility she couldn't shake. She shouldn't have to care about what happens to him. If he died from the blight, she might very well be free. She winced, hating herself as her power thrummed through her fingertips in anticipation, as if rebelling against her better judgment.

Without a single word, she reached for the ties of his tunic, her fingers moving deftly to loosen the fabric. Rylik's hand fell away as he watched her, his breathing shallow as her fingers grazed his skin.

The moonlight bathed them in a soft glow, the tension between them thick but not hostile. Rylik closed his eyes, relishing the warmth of her touch, the heat from her magic slowly spreading through his chest. Her fingers pressed him gingerly in a futile attempt to thaw every bit of coldness inside him. It would never be enough.

After a long moment, Aria sighed, allowing the golden light of her magic to dissipate. Her hand remained firm on his chest, her touch gentle. "I won't tease you about it anymore, Sovereign," she whispered.

Rylik opened his eyes, and for a moment, they stood in silence, the softness in his expression mirroring the quiet vulnerability of the night.

CHAPTER 19

ARIA

Aria pulled her hand away from Rylik's chest slowly, a small smile tugging at her lips as she turned back to the view of the capital. She rubbed her arms, the night air finally reaching her.

Rylik casually removed his outer cape, draping it over Aria's shoulders as if it were the most natural thing in the world. He didn't draw attention to the gesture, even as she looked up at him, surprise flickering in her eyes. "They make fresh batches of cakes and pastries in the evenings, on the weekends. You can smell the sugar for miles."

Aria felt her cheeks warm at the idea, "Careful, I might force you to take me there tonight." She rubbed the thick fabric of the cape now enveloping her arms, relishing the warmth it provided.

"Ah, but then there would be no fresh cakes." Rylik's tone was playful, his gaze steady. "It's a weekday, after all."

"Then, I suppose I'll have to wait." She sighed, a tender smirk playing on her lips.

With a reassuring smile, he looked away, his gaze drifting up to the stars. "Well, don't sound so defeated. Perhaps I'll take you there tonight."

She eyed him, suspicion mingled with hope. "You—you would do that?"

"I don't see why not," he mused. "Or we could go in the morning, if you prefer. I could gather you at dawn."

"Dawn??" She groaned, "you're going to expect me to get up that early?"

He let out a soft huff of breath, mirth dancing in his eyes. "If you want the freshest rolls, you'll have to rise early. And if you can't, I could always pull you out of bed. Which I would be more than happy to do, of course."

"I'm content to wait for a visit to town on the weekend. Maybe this weekend or next? And, I don't need you seeing my nightgown, either, so there is no reason to surprise me at dawn." She waved him off dismissively.

Rylik feigned surprise. "Well, I don't believe I've ever seen one of your nightgowns."

"A nightgown is a nightgown. And I only have the one." She knew better than to make eye contact with him, since he was surely making some unforgivable sly expression.

"By the gods, one corset. One nightgown. You are a lady in the palace now, Aria. You need much more than that." His tone was playful, begging her attention.

Aria flushed, the heat creeping up her neck. "I am not a noble lady, Sovereign. I am a healer, and I have no use for multiple undergarments for the sake of variety."

His tone turned serious, eyes glinting with lightheartedness. "Your wardrobe is severely lacking. I should send for a tailor to visit with you. Perhaps I will arrange for a full closet fitting." He tapped his chin thoughtfully, as if contemplating the logistics.

Closing her eyes in embarrassment, Aria thought, *Just take it in stride. The man is offering to buy you an entirely frivolous wardrobe.* When she opened them, she caught the mischief glimmering in his eyes. *And perhaps he should, seeing as I am his imprisoned healer for eternity. I should get to enjoy it.* She sighed exasperatedly, looking up at the sky. "Fine. Buy an entire wardrobe for a simple healer. Enjoy your absolute lack of gold when you're done."

"Lack of gold?" Rylik chuckled softly. "I doubt I will ever know what that feels like."

"Good god, Sovereign. How much does the king pay you?"

"Well enough, I suppose," he offered a casual lift of his

shoulders.

Aria huffed, shaking her head. "I should ask for a pay raise."

"Right, because he's known for being charitable." His grin was entertained, teasing.

"Oh, yes." She agreed sardonically, a smile breaking through as she dropped down to the turret floor, lying on her back, gazing up at the stars.

"Aria? What are you doing on the floor?" He observed in bemusement, his eyes narrowing. "Dirtying my cape?"

Blushing, she sat upright, pulling at the cape. "Sorry! I wasn't thinking! I just wanted to lay down and look at the stars. I'm so sorry that I—"

"Please, you act like I have only one cape." He sat down beside her, readjusting the fabric around her before lying down with an arm behind his head, the other resting on his stomach, both of them now sharing the same space beneath the canopy of stars.

Aria's eyes widened in disbelief. "You have more than one cape? Are they all black?!"

"Most of them are." He relaxed, clearly teasing her with a deadpan expression. "I have one in dark gray."

"Tsk," Aria began in mock derision with her best masculine accent, "oh no, that simply won't do. You need variety."

Stifling a chortle, he glanced at her, an amused expression dancing on his lips. "Is that what you think I sound like?"

"My voice isn't nearly as deep as yours, but the smug tone is spot on." She looked at him, sniggering before returning her gaze to the sky.

Rylik's expression remained soft and unreadable as his gaze swept over her before drifting back to the heavens, a flicker of amusement playing across his features.

"Wow, look at that bright red star over there. I don't think I've ever noticed it before." Aria pointed excitedly.

He turned his gaze upward, a sly grin forming on his face. "That is a part of the Serpent's Path. If you look around that star, to the right of it, there is a little winding trail of smaller stars surging along behind it in a bit of an S-curve." He pointed, pulling his head closer to hers to direct her eyes.

"I see it!" she exclaimed, her excitement infectious.

"The red star is the head of the serpent, and the stars behind it are its body." Lowering his hand, he admired the formation. "It represents wisdom and deception. It is said that those born under this constellation are clever but often walk the line between truth and lies."

In awe, she turned to another formation—a graceful arch of stars with a line stretching vertically beneath it, forming the shape of a harp. "What about that one? Does it have a name too?"

"Indeed." Rylik looked up calmly. "You have a good eye. That is a constellation known as The Silent Harp, and it's usually not very bright this time of year. It is associated with peace, healing, and harmony. It's believed to be the constellation that brings calm after storms." He glanced at her. "Both literal and emotional."

Aria smirked, the corner of her mouth lifting. "Not an astronomer, hm?"

Rylik rolled his eyes, turning his attention back to the stars. "I've enjoyed this view my entire life. I found patterns eventually."

"Downplay it if you want, but I think if you weren't the Sovereign, you might've been a scholar." She shot him a cheeky smile.

"It would've been a welcomed alternative." His tone was casual, so casual that it surprised her. He glanced at her, amusement lacing his voice. "But then perhaps I would've missed out on all the murderous fun his majesty presents to me."

She made a face, disapproval etched on her features, but only for a moment. "Regardless, it's fascinating that you know so much about constellations."

"So much?" he let out a dismissive laugh. "I pointed out exactly two."

"That's two more than I knew about." She half-shrugged, pointing to another formation, leaning her head close to Rylik's. Unaware of his subtle surprise, she inquired, "What about that one?"

"That one—" He felt her soft hair brushing against his forehead, swallowing briefly to moisten his dry throat. "Is the Dreaming Tree." His gaze softened. "It symbolizes growth, patience, and hope. It's seen as a reminder to nurture one's dreams and to trust in slow, steady progress."

"Pfft." She looked at him, skepticism tinging her tone. "Are you making this up? Are you trying to impress me with your knowledge, knowing full well I won't know otherwise?"

He met her eyes, their foreheads almost touching. "You think I would care to impress you?"

Realizing their proximity, Aria's cheeks flushed, yet she didn't move her head. "Well, maybe. Maybe not."

"Well, you're not entirely wrong," he said keenly, "as I am trying to impress you."

She gaped at him a moment, hardly believing the words.

"But, I am not lying about the constellations," he chuckled, "I have told you accurately."

A sideways grin tugged at her lips. "Well, then, I guess I'll blindly trust the expert astronomer here."

His grin turned boyish, and he let out a small laugh, the expression making her heart skip in surprise. "I have now only named three constellations, Aria. This does not make me an expert."

Biting her lip to hide her blush, she looked away, her heart racing. *Why had he looked so cute just now? As if we were two teens who had snuck out after dark to spite our parents.* "Protest if you want, Sovereign, but you sound like a professional sky enthusiast— otherwise known as an astronomer."

Rylik noted the pink tint at her cheeks and the tremor in her voice, smiling to himself as he looked away again. "Fine, you caught me. I have tracked the stars nightly for ages and I keep a small book where I scrawl the stars into place on the pages." He closed his eyes, allowing the moment to settle. "And I have a trove of various maps and books that I keep hidden, detailing every mystery of the sky inside them."

Aria stared at him with a dubious grin. "I don't believe that."

He rolled his shoulders slightly, the corners of his mouth lifting.

Chortling softly to herself, she looked away again. "Expert or not, I've enjoyed learning about these few. Maybe we can come out here at night a little more often and you can show me the rest that you can name."

A soft smile graced Rylik's lips as he turned his head, hoping she wouldn't see the genuine warmth in his expression. "I wouldn't mind it."

As she gazed up at the vast canopy of stars stretching endlessly above them, she felt herself relax. For a fleeting moment, she wasn't a healer bound by duty, and he wasn't the Sovereign cloaked in authority. Here, beneath the gentle glow of starlight, they were simply two souls who had stumbled upon an unspoken understanding. The night enveloped them in its quiet grace, and for once, his usual impenetrable guard seemed to waver. She sensed it in the way his voice softened when he named the constellations, in the rare calm that settled over his sharp features. He would never admit to the tenuous thread of camaraderie forming between them, but she felt it, tender and undeniable, like the faintest whisper of wind stirring the trees.

Eventually, the tranquil spell began to break as the chill of the night deepened. Reluctantly, they retraced their steps through the dimly lit corridors, his measured pace never faltering as he guided her back to her room. Their words grew playful, a gentle exchange of teasing remarks that echoed softly in the stillness, a delicate dance that felt almost normal.

When they reached the door to her suite, she hesitated for a moment, her gaze pouring over him as if trying to memorize this version of him—unguarded, almost human. The thought made her heart pine in ways she couldn't quite name, as though this fragile truce between them might vanish in the morning sun.

Once inside, she felt an unexpected pang of sadness as her eyes fell upon her bed. She hardly wanted the night to end, reluctant to let go of the fleeting sense of peace they'd found beneath the stars. Turning toward him, her voice was soft, almost anxious. "What made you like stargazing so much?" she asked, the curiosity in her tone genuine, though tinged with a faint hope to prolong the moment just a little longer.

He followed her as she walked to the fireplace, his steps slow, eyes fixed on her as she gracefully settled onto a plush green-cushioned sofa. The fire in the hearth had died down to a dull red glow within the embers, but it still held heat. She patted the seat beside her, and without hesitation, he sat down, his presence filling the space with quiet authority.

"I've always found the stars quite compelling," he began, his voice low and steady, carrying the weight of a memory. "When I was young, my father used to track them. He had an atrium filled with stargazing implements, tools he used with meticulous care. His enthusiasm for the heavens was infectious. It was impossible not to love the sky as he did."

Aria's smile brightened at the image he painted, a flicker of something tender sparking in her chest. "It sounds like you two might've gotten along well," she said softly, her gaze searching his features for hints of fondness beneath his usual composure.

He shrugged, the movement purposeful and calm. "We fought often. But at night," he sighed, "nights were almost always peaceful. He would bring out his astrolabe and measure the stars, losing himself in the vastness of the sky. I think it reminded him of how small we all are. How, compared to the eternity of the heavens, so much of this world's turmoil is inconsequential."

His words hung in the air, delicate yet profound, wrapping themselves around her like the faint glow of the firelight. Aria felt a sudden stillness, moved by the unforeseen depth of his thoughts. She looked over at him, hoping to glimpse some shared acknowledgment of the gravity of his sentiment, but his gaze remained casual, as though unaware of the effect he had on her.

She offered him a small, tentative smile. "Your father seems like he was a reasonable man," she murmured, her voice carrying a hint of reverence.

Rylik nodded, his eyes drawn to the dimming coals in her hearth. "He was," he said simply, but there was a heaviness in his tone that betrayed the unshakeable remnants of the past.

Without thinking, Aria reached out, her hand resting over his with a gentleness that startled them both. Her fingers barely grazed his skin, but the touch carried an unexpected intimacy that sent her pulse fluttering wildly. "I've never lost anyone close to me, Sovereign," she admitted, her voice faint and wavering as she avoided his eyes. "So I don't think I'm the best person to offer you comfort. But if you ever need any—"

He cut her off with a quiet chuckle, the sound warm yet laced with something she couldn't quite name. His free hand patted hers lightly, as if to reassure her. "He's been gone a long time,

Aria. It hardly affects me anymore." Yet his hand didn't move away. Instead, his fingers began tracing absent patterns over her knuckles, his touch unassuming, yet tender.

Heat bloomed across Aria's cheeks, her eyes falling to the sight of his hand, so much larger and stronger than her own, enveloping hers with an ease that left her breathless. She had only meant to comfort him, a fleeting gesture to offer solace, but now her hand was firmly held in his. There was nothing overtly romantic about the touch, yet it stirred something fierce within her—a thrilling awareness of his warmth, the strength behind his gentle grip.

Her thoughts drifted as she studied his hand, noticing the contrast between their sizes, the way her slender fingers seemed almost fragile beneath his. She felt small beside him, not just in stature but in every sense of the word. His formidable presence— his power, his ability to command the shadows themselves—was both exhilarating and a little terrifying. What would it feel like to possess such strength, to wield it with the same confidence he did? The idea both intrigued and unsettled her.

As if sensing her spiraling thoughts, Rylik released her hand, his movements unhurried but purposeful, allowing her to retreat and clasp her fingers tightly in her lap. The absence of his touch left her feeling unmoored, a faint ache settling in her chest. She already missed the warmth of his palm, the steady reassurance of his presence, and she couldn't help but wonder if there was any reasonable way to feel it again.

"If your love of stars came from your father," Aria began softly, her voice tentative, "then does your love of plants come from your mother?"

Rylik's lips curved into a faint smile. "And here I thought I was the only one adept at reading people." His gaze slid to her, catching the delighted spark in her eyes at having guessed correctly.

She hesitated, her curiosity both a thrill and a danger. "Well, now I'm almost afraid to ask. Is your mother also—?" Her voice dipped, uncertain but earnest, unable to finish the question.

The shift in his expression was subtle, the slightest shadow flickering across his features. He shook his head and turned his attention to the embers dwindling in the hearth. "Thankfully, no.

She lives."

Relief flooded Aria's chest, though she wasn't sure why she felt it. After all, this was the man who had threatened her family the very night they met, his words sharp and cutting, leaving her trembling in their wake. Would he still make such threats now, after all that had passed between them? She wanted to believe it had been a scare tactic, calculated to ensure her compliance. Yet even as she wrestled with her anger over that night, she couldn't deny the quiet intrigue she felt in uncovering the softer truths he kept hidden.

"Where is she now?" Aria asked, her curiosity softening her tone.

"Far away," he replied simply. His voice carried a note of finality, but he didn't stop there. "For her safety." He shifted his gaze back to her, his murky blue eyes glinting with an edge of mischief. "You seem intent on collecting intimate details of my life. Should I be concerned you're plotting to use them against me?"

A sideways grin tugged at her lips as she shook her head. "Sovereign, you have me mistaken for someone far more nefarious. I'm a healer. I doubt I inspire much fear."

His gaze remained on hers, unreadable, probing. She felt her confidence falter under its weight, as though he could see straight through her bravado. There was no telling the kinds of people he had dealt with in his life—deceivers, traitors, manipulators. What must it feel like to always expect betrayal? Despite her reluctance to be part of this world, she found herself pitying him in ways that unsettled her. She was no longer connected to the Rebellion and she would never tell a soul any of his mysteries. Part of that was still rooted in fear, but another part seemed to be from a place in her heart she would rather not try to understand.

"I'll keep your secrets for as long as I live," she said at last, her voice steady despite the nervous flutter in her chest.

His smirk returned, sharp and familiar. "Indeed, you will."

Before she could process his meaning, he leaned closer, the warmth of his breath brushing against her skin. His face hovered inches from hers, his voice low and silken as he murmured, "Because you cannot afford to fail me."

Aria's heart seized in her throat, choking her in an instant. Was it another threat? It wasn't laced with the same venom as his words on the night they met, yet it carried the same unyielding gravity, a quiet reminder of the power he held over her. Her eyes lifted to his, uncertain and searching, meeting a gaze that was deep and stormy, impossible to read.

He was still the villain of her story, wasn't he? No amount of stargazing, teasing, or fleeting moments of camaraderie could erase that truth.

"Do you always resort to fear?" she asked, her voice calm despite the tremor of defiance beneath it.

His brows drew together faintly, a flicker of something unreadable crossing his features. "Often, yes," he admitted without hesitation.

"There are other ways to earn loyalty, Sovereign," she replied, the words leaving her lips before she could reconsider. She doubted he needed her to tell him that. He likely knew every method for gaining someone's submission, every thread that could bind a person to his will.

He smiled, still hovering distressingly close, his breath a whisper against her skin. "And what other ways are there?"

Her throat felt tight, but she forced her voice to steady. "Some people give their loyalty freely, out of love and trust." The words sounded resolute in her mind but faltered slightly as they left her lips.

He leaned in, narrowing the fragile space between them. "Oh? And do you *love* and *trust* me, Pyra?" The mockery in his tone was unmistakable.

Aria's fingers curled tightly into the fabric of her skirt, grounding her against the intensity of his presence. "Perhaps I'd be so inclined if you spent less of your time trying to instill fear in me," she countered, though she prayed her voice carried the strength she intended.

His smirk deepened, a slow, devilish thing, as his fingers brushed lightly against her cheek. The touch was unexpected, startling her into stillness. "You really expect me to believe that you would ever love me?"

She hadn't expected the question, so blunt, so charged. Her

cheeks betrayed her, flushing with a heat she couldn't contain. He noticed—it was impossible to miss the flicker of amusement lighting his eyes like embers.

"Everyone is capable of being loved," she managed, though her voice faltered under the weight of his gaze. "I'm sure I," The words lodged in her throat, leaving her to scrape together her composure. "I could love you, I'm sure—if you stopped trying to scare me."

"What kind of love?" His voice was quiet now, intimate in its softness, as though the two of them were the only people in existence. His fingers toyed with the loose strands of her hair, brushing them behind her ear with an agonizing tenderness. His palm grazed her cheek, teasing, as though testing the fragility of her resolve. "I'm not very interested in platonic love, after all. If I'm going to be loved by someone like you," His eyes flicked to her lips, lingering there for a fraction too long. "Then I want an all-consuming love. I want you to need me more than the air you breathe."

Her heart forgot how to beat, stuttering into silence before roaring back to life with a vengeance. His thumb trailed along her lower lip, a languid, calculated motion that sent her pulse into chaos. His gaze roved over her, dissecting her reactions, searching for the cracks in her composure.

"I—I can't guarantee what kind of love would develop in the absence of fear, Sovereign," she stammered, hating how breathless her voice had become.

He clicked his tongue, a low, chiding sound. "Tsk. I'm going to need a guarantee, I think." His tone was teasing, but his expression was sharp, deadly serious.

The tension snapped her into motion, her body reacting before her mind could catch up. She pulled back from him, regret flooding her almost immediately as his touch left her skin. Rising to her feet, she gripped the folds of her skirt tightly in her hands, hoping the gesture might steady her. "It's late. Perhaps you should—" Her voice wavered, trembling with nervous energy she couldn't suppress.

Rylik rose slowly, his presence consuming the space between them as he loomed over her. His frame was solid, imposing, yet it drew her in, an intoxicating mixture of fear and fascination. He was foreboding, immovable—a force of nature. She wanted to touch him, to see if he felt as unyielding and solid as he seemed. The thought sent a flush rushing to her cheeks, and she turned abruptly and headed for her vanity.

"I should probably get undressed for the evening," she blurted, her words tumbling over themselves. "And you ought not to be here for that." She glanced up at her reflection, only to see his shadow behind her. Gasping, she spun around, her backside hitting the vanity with a soft thud.

"How do you move so damn fast?" she demanded, her voice caught somewhere between a gasp and a whisper. Her hand shot up to his chest instinctively, a futile effort to create space between them. The armor on his chest was cool as steel beneath her trembling palm. Her fingertips tingled as her heart thundered against her ribs, aching in every beat.

His lips curled into a wry smile, his satisfaction evident. "Would you like to see?"

Before she could respond, his arm snaked around her waist, pulling her flush against him. The heat of his body consumed her, the contact electric and overwhelming. She gasped, the sound soft and unbidden, as his hold tightened, anchoring her against him.

Suddenly, shadows surged around them, swallowing the room in a swirling void of dark clouds. The world around her twisted and folded, the colors of the suite bleeding into muted chaos. The ground beneath her feet shifted disorientingly, and then, just as swiftly, the shadows receded.

They were standing in the courtyard outside the ballroom— the very place she'd first kissed him.

Aria blinked against the sudden shift, her pulse hammering as realization struck. He could move between places in the blink of an eye? The distance from her suite to the courtyard spanned the entire breadth of the castle. The Sovereign wielded such terrifying power, and it was laughable—pathetic, even—that she had ever entertained the notion of evading him.

His hands remained pressed firmly against her back, holding her close as though he were indifferent to her racing thoughts.

She didn't dare push him away—not when her body betrayed her and craved the contact. He *was* as solid as she imagined. And worse, she wanted to melt into him, to let herself dissolve into his strength. She didn't want to question it.

"The night you kissed me," he murmured, his voice slipping through the cracks in her resolve like smoke. "What were you feeling then?"

The words struck like a burning ember. Her chest tightened. "Please." She forced a laugh, though it sounded thin, even to her. "I've already told you—I did it to make Leon jealous. It was foolish. Inappropriate."

He tilted his head slightly, a mocking smile tugging at the corners of his lips. "Yes, that's the excuse you gave me," he said, cutting through her deflection with ease. "But that's not the real reason, is it?"

Her heart thudded painfully as his words settled in the air, leaving her nowhere to retreat. She didn't want to face this, least of all in *his* presence. The Rebellion, her reasons, the unbearable truths—everything tangled in a web too dangerous to untangle here. "What do you want me to say, Sovereign?" she asked, her voice trembling.

His laugh was a low, teasing growl that seemed to darken the very shadows around them. "The truth would be a good place to start." His eyes gleamed, holding her captive. "I did suspect that you were connected to the feeble escape attempt that occurred that night. However," he seemed to be reliving a memory he savored, which only made her body quiver against his own. "That same night you dreamt of me, did you not?"

The ground beneath her seemed to tilt as the meaning of his words took root. He knew. Somehow, he knew. Was it not enough that he stalked her days? He now somehow had access to her dreams?! How was that possible? Embarrassment rose like a flood, staining her cheeks as she remembered that dream, of the way his hands had roamed over every inch of her and claimed her body, and how she had given it to him so willingly.

"I heard you in your suite that night," he said, his voice maddeningly soft. "Calling for me."

Aria's stomach dropped. Memories of that evening rushed

back: the heady haze of too much wine, the heat pooling in her body as her mind conjured forbidden fantasies, the betrayal of her own hands drifting lower, seeking him even in her solitude. The humiliation of the moment swept over her in heavy waves and she hoped for the ground to open up and let her hide inside. No wonder he had been so smug and so confident that morning. He had been so effortlessly convinced that she had given him a lie because he knew better.

He smiled, a predator savoring his prey. "I don't make a habit of stalking helpless women as they sleep, of course," he said gently. "I heard you call out to me, realized you were dreaming, and I left you alone."

Her entire body flushed with mortification. She couldn't bring herself to meet his gaze, afraid of what else he might have seen — or guessed. She hoped, frantically, that a mere longing dream was all he had noticed that night. She hoped he hadn't approached her bed, seen her enraptured in her own lewd fantasy.

"I know you want me, Pyra," he murmured, his hands sliding lower to cradle her hips, pulling her impossibly closer. His breath fanned against her ear. "But I can understand if you refuse to admit it to yourself."

Her teeth clenched, forcing herself to steel against the pull of his voice. He was everything she should resist. And yet, she stilled against him.

"Falling for me is likely a low point for you, is it not?" His tone was taunting, his words needling into her like a challenge.

Her head snapped up, fire lighting in her gaze. "I have not fallen for you, Sovereign," she said, her voice sharp. "One brief moment of desire does not equate to love."

His smirk deepened, cruelly amused. "So you admit it. You desire me?"

She couldn't hide under his scrutiny, and she knew there was enough moonlight to reveal every treacherous trace of passion in her stare. Suddenly, the rise and fall of her own chest felt heavier, more laborious. Her throat was tight and she wasn't sure words would even form if she tried to speak. His icy gaze drank in her expression, and under the twinkling night sky, she felt every thought, every vulnerability laid bare.

"I do not have much experience in love, but in the absence of it," he admitted, his voice turning quieter, dangerously intimate. "I have found that desire still makes for good company."

Her hand itched to slap him, her body torn between indignation and the gnawing ache to pull him closer. He was maddeningly handsome, more so than she'd ever allowed herself to admit. The cruel curve of his lips, the glacial blue of his eyes—everything about him called to the parts of her she wanted to ignore.

And he seemed to know it. His lips pulled into a victorious smile, his chin lifting smugly as if to prove her hesitation. Then, without warning, he pressed her body into his, firm and adamant.

The shadows rose again, swirling like living things. The ground shifted beneath her feet, and the world spun into darkness. When the shadows cleared, they were back in her suite.

For a moment, he waited there, his warmth seeping into her skin as if he'd branded her. When he finally stepped back, her knees nearly buckled from the absence of his touch. She stumbled a few paces away, one hand rising to cool her cheek.

"Thank you for a pleasant evening," he said, his voice tinged with dry amusement. The dangerous edge in his demeanor had softened, replaced with a casual elegance as he turned toward the adjoining door. "I'll see you in the morning. Good night, Aria."

She could only nod, watching helplessly as he exited with the smooth confidence of a man who *knew* she wouldn't stop thinking about him.

And he was right.

She was grateful for the distance, because she had been mere moments away from absolutely collapsing in on herself. She wasn't sure what she would have done in his arms, but she was fairly certain she would have felt a clawing guilt by the morning.

Guilt from what? She had to wonder. Perhaps it was merely guilt for falling prey to the Sovereign, a known enforcer of the crown; a deadly and malicious killer capable of destroying everything in her path. Such danger should be a deterrent, yet she craved the protection he could provide, knowing that he wouldn't harm her. And if she played his game right, she could have more than what she bargained for. It was dangerous, the line she was flirting with. She dared herself to cross it, to see what it might be like to know the Sovereign more fully. It was a sinful thought.

But she wouldn't feel guilt for kissing him again. She knew how those lips felt on her own, and she thought about them often. More often than she cared to admit. She thought about all the places she'd like to feel that soft caress of his. She thought of all the other ways he would like to feel him.

Her body was flushed, a dull numbing heat radiating through her as she fought to calm herself. She needed to cool down, to take a walk, to forget everything she had felt just now with him. But there was nowhere to go, and all she could do was pace. If she drew bath water, he would hear it. God forbid he enter the bathing room again, too, because he might see more than just her nakedness. She couldn't afford to let him catch her in any more fantasies. She wouldn't be able to live it down. She wanted him, and he knew it.

It was wrong. It was foolish. It was sinful.

Tonight, when sleep claimed her, she knew her dreams would be his. And she wouldn't dare try to resist.

CHAPTER 20

RYLIK

After enjoying a quiet cup of tea and tending to the small budding plants in his window sill planter, Rylik felt a subtle sense of contentment settle within him. The gentle morning sunlight filtered through the room, casting a soft light that seemed to echo his anticipation for the day ahead.

Another week had passed, and each morning, Rylik found himself eagerly awaiting his time with Aria. After the night they'd shared beneath the stars, restraining himself around her had become nearly impossible. Constantly, it felt as though he were at war with himself, torn between the urge to pull her into a shadowed corridor and claim the very breath from her lips.

It seemed she, too, was struggling to maintain her composure. He often caught her gazing at him, her touch resting just a heartbeat longer than necessary when she tended to his blight. She was stubborn, he thought with a quiet pride, taking pleasure in watching her wrestle with the growing awareness in her heart. She couldn't possibly believe he was blind to the way her affections had shifted, not after he'd laid bare her vulnerabilities beneath the moonlit sky. He'd nearly kissed her then—had wanted to.

But there was a deeper part of him that craved to see her act first, just as she had at the ball. He wanted to see that same

196

desperate hunger in her eyes again. If she would make the first move, he would savor every moment that followed, knowing she had surrendered, with no resistance left to hold her back.

With a measured breath, he rose and made his way toward Aria's suite, guided by the thought of her bringing a warm exhilaration to his otherwise tranquil mood.

It wasn't long before the door to her suite creaked open, the faint sound of his footsteps approaching her bed. Rylik strode in, his movements purposeful, adjusting the sleeves of his tunic as he neared her. His eyes fell on her still form, noting the state of her disheveled appearance—the gown loosely draped over her, the corset half-laced, giving way to the soft rise and fall of her chest as she slept.

Rylik was certain he had heard her moving around earlier. Had she given up dressing herself and simply fallen back asleep? He allowed his gaze to settle on her, azure eyes tracing the soft curls of her red hair, the pale pink of her cheeks, and her long black lashes resting against her skin.

A slow smirk crossed his lips as he again found himself wrestling with the urge to reach out and touch her. The impulse was overpowering this time, his hands desperate with the desire to possess. He gave in briefly, his fingertips brushing against a strand of her hair, letting it coil around his fingers. He couldn't help but wonder how lovely her fiery hair might look curling and resting against the silken sheets of his own bed.

His thoughts darkened as memories of the ball flooded his mind—their kiss in the courtyard, and the way her soft body had felt pressed against his. He imagined what it would've been like to push her into the shadows, flattening her back against the stone wall of the courtyard, and to hear her shallow gasps of pleasure in his ear.

Swallowing hard, Rylik released the strand of hair, his fingers curving into a fist as if to sever the dangerous connection he'd momentarily forged between his lust and reality. He took in a steadying breath as he stepped back and leaned against the wall, folding his arms across his chest. He felt his agitation rising despite himself as his eyes roved freely over her. He took in every curve of her, admiring the silhouette of her slim waist and the fullness of her hips. He let his eyelids fall shut again, his fingertips digging into his arms with failing restraint. *This is truly pitiful. I'm pathetic. I should've already awakened her by now.*

A slow, heavy breath escaped his lips. He let his eyes flutter open again, this time settling over her bosom threatening to spill from her half-laced corset. Tugging at the corner of his lip, he shut his eyes tightly, trying to quell his irritation as he rested his head back on the wall. *By the gods, Aria. I have more self-control than this. I know I have.* His vexation grew, fueled by the undeniable attraction that surged within him.

With a frustrated sigh, he turned sharply on his heel, walking to the edge of the room and pulling the adjoining door open. With more force than necessary, he shut it again, the sound loud enough to rouse her from sleep.

Aria shot upright, startled by the sudden noise. Her wide eyes darted toward Rylik, who stood a few paces away in front of the closed door, his arms still crossed, his expression unreadable. "Sovereign?"

"Morning." His tone was calm, though his gaze flickered briefly to her half-laced corset before meeting her eyes once more.

Aria flushed, quickly turning her back to him as she finished tying the laces. "I thought you were going to be here sooner, like yesterday," she said, half-accusingly, as she turned back to face him—only to find him standing much closer than before, causing her to jump in surprise.

"I thought you would already be dressed," he said with a raised brow. "Though, I'm pleased to see I was wrong."

Aria's cheeks flushed as if on cue. "I started to, but, I was tired and must've stopped midway." She was still fumbling with her gown. "Last night I was up late, puzzling over this potion and trying to think of what might work best in it." She quickly hiked up her skirt, pulling her boots on, revealing a brief flash of her thigh in the process.

Rylik's jaw tightened, and he looked away, staring intently out the window as he bit the inside of his lip, willing his lurid thoughts to calm. "If you need help with the potion, I'd be happy to discuss it with you," He said, hoping his voice sounded calm and collected.

"Oh, that's alright. I know you're busy, and I think I've got it figured out anyway." Finished lacing her boots, Aria stood, brushing her skirt down with a satisfied sigh. "So, are you escorting me to the apothecary today? No guards this morning?"

"Yes, I'll be escorting you," Rylik replied, his voice strained as he forced a casual smile. "But, I also wanted to let you know that this afternoon you'll need to be in your suite for a fitting." He strode past her quickly, his cape swishing behind him as he made for the door.

"A fitting? I thought you were joking about getting me a new wardrobe," Aria chuckled, brushing past him to grab a ribbon hanging by the door.

The scent of jasmine and vanilla clung to her hair, invading his senses as she passed, her body barely grazing his. He closed his eyes briefly, groaning inwardly. "Will it be like this all day?" He murmured softer than a whisper.

"What?" Aria asked, glancing over her shoulder as she finished tying her hair, unaware of his torment.

He opened his eyes, his gaze hardening as he turned to the door, gripping the handle tightly. "Nothing," he muttered, pushing the door open. "Let's go."

* * *

Hours later, Rylik stood among carnage, caught in the uneasy duality of longing for Aria's presence and relishing the solitude. Her absence offered him a reprieve from the tension she stirred within him—a necessary distraction, given the task at hand.

The chamber was stifling, steeped in the metallic tang of blood and the oppressive silence of death. Afternoon light seeped through tall, arched windows draped in heavy velvet, spilling jagged reflections across the polished marble floor. The walls, adorned with ornate tapestries and gold-framed portraits, now bore streaks of crimson where the blood had splattered.

He knelt, wiping the blade of his dagger with a silk handkerchief until its surface gleamed once more. With casual indifference, he dropped the bloodied cloth beside a lifeless body sprawled at his feet. His sharp gaze landed on a crumpled piece of parchment pinned beneath the dead man's hand.

Rylik leaned forward, retrieving the paper with an almost lazy efficiency. It wasn't important—at least, not to him—but Kaldros had demanded it. The king's obsession with this particular lead amused Rylik, considering he had already intercepted the original weeks ago. This decoy letter now carried little more than the amorous ramblings of a man to his mistress.

A faint sigh escaped him as he stepped over another corpse. He presented the folded parchment to Kaldros, who was lounging against the edge of a mahogany table. The king, dressed in opulent robes lined with fur, took the paper with a flick of his wrist. His jeweled fingers unfurled the sheet, scanning it briefly before crumpling it into a ball and discarding it onto the floor.

"This wasn't exactly the lead I was hoping for," Kaldros muttered, his tone heavy with disdain as he folded his arms across his chest. His dark emerald eyes swept over the remnants of the slaughter without a trace of remorse.

Rylik turned, letting his attention sweep over the room, pausing briefly as he took it in. The scene of chaos was carefully calculated—a tapestry of death executed with precision. His expression remained neutral, save for a flicker of amusement in his eyes.

"Take heart, your Majesty," Rylik said, glancing back at the king. His voice was smooth, almost detached, as if the scene around them were merely a passing inconvenience. "It means there's a grieving concubine somewhere who might appreciate a new suitor."

Kaldros chuckled despite his irritation, the sound echoing through the bloodstained chamber. "It's a dead end, Sovereign," he said, his voice tightening with frustration. "I grow tired of this spy slipping through my grasp."

"As do I," Rylik replied evenly, falling into step behind the king as he turned toward the door. His footfalls were silent against the marble, a shadow in the king's wake.

Kaldros sighed, his mood shifting as he strode through the corridor, the hem of his regal robes trailing behind him. "I think I'll console myself with Radonya," he said absently, his tone lightening at the mention of her name. "She is lovely, and I haven't had a woman's company since night before last."

Rylik suppressed the urge to roll his eyes. "An excellent choice," he replied with practiced indifference, his tone betraying neither scorn nor approval.

"You are excused, Sovereign," Kaldros said with a dismissive wave of his hand as they reached a fork in the corridor. Without waiting for a reply, the king veered off toward his chambers, leaving Rylik alone in the dimly lit hallway.

Rylik watched him disappear, then turned away, his boots clicking softly against the stone floor as he headed in the opposite direction. At last, he could attend to a task more deserving of his attention. The hunt for the spy buried within the king's inner circle had grown tedious, but it was vital Rylik uncovered the traitor before Kaldros did. His focus settled on Eldric—a man whose fractured mind held answers yet untouched. Though the poor soul had been enchanted to silence, Rylik had a plan to coax the truth from him.

The air grew heavier as he descended the winding staircase to the dungeons, the stone walls closing in, cold and damp. A faint torchlight flickered against the curved corridor, throwing jagged shadows across the slimy bricks. The rank stench of decay struck him first—rotting flesh, sour sweat, and the acrid sting of filth that clung to the underbelly of the castle. Beyond it came the muted sounds of agony: chains rattling, low moans of despair, and the occasional scream that pierced the oppressive silence.

Rylik's expression remained impassive, his strides steady and purposeful. The dim corridor opened into the dungeon proper, a grim gallery of despair. Prisoners cowered in their cells, their skeletal faces illuminated by the sporadic flicker of lanterns. Many shrank from the bars as he passed, their eyes wide with terror, their trembling hands clutching at the rags they wore. Fear was a language Rylik understood intimately, and he wielded it here with every deliberate step.

At the far end of the corridor, a guard slouched outside Eldric's cell, half-dozing on a creaky wooden stool. At the sound of Rylik's approach, the man snapped to attention, his lethargy vanishing like mist under sunlight.

Rylik's gaze swept over the guard with cool detachment.

Without a word, he set a pouch of gold and a small sapphire vial on the stool. The torchlight caught the glint of the bottle's contents, making it seem almost alive in its translucent glow. The guard glanced down, his brows knitting briefly before he looked back up at Rylik. A single, sharp nod passed between them—an unspoken agreement sealed.

Satisfied, Rylik turned on his heel and strode back toward the staircase. The prisoners whispered among themselves as his shadow receded, their murmurs blending with the rustle of chains and quiet sobs. He did not spare them a glance.

Eldric had once been an invaluable asset to the crown, a wellspring of secrets about the Rebellion and its architects. But someone had intervened, twisting his mind with enchantments that even the king's cruelest tortures could not undo. Kaldros, predictable as ever, had failed to see what Rylik had uncovered in mere moments of observation: magic had been used against Eldric, and magic would be required to set him free.

Rylik had secured a vial of potion potent enough to unravel even the most impenetrable illusion magic. Once Eldric consumed it, the haze clouding his mind would dissipate, restoring clarity to his thoughts. The guard, persuaded by the glint of coin, had been instructed to free Eldric from his cell at the appointed time. Rylik anticipated the escape would unfold smoothly, giving Eldric just enough freedom to plot his vengeance. Inevitably, the man would seek out the one who had twisted his mind, driven by a need to set things right. Rylik, ever watchful, would be there to witness the reckoning—and, in doing so, uncover the elusive spy embedded within the king's court.

On the night of the ball, someone had orchestrated an attempt to free Eldric. Perhaps it was the very spy who had poisoned his mind, though Rylik could not be certain. When he arrived on the scene, only nameless faces greeted him—faces that swiftly met their end. The men he dispatched were untrained, mere commoners swept into a futile cause and ensnared by a clumsily devised escape plan. He felt a flicker of pity for them, though it paled in comparison to the frustration he bore for failing to catch the true mastermind. This elusive spy had woven an insidious web, making himself nearly untouchable. Any captured rebel questioned about the leader carried a mind curiously barren of memories, as though the very name had been erased from their thoughts.

Emerging from the dungeon, Rylik inhaled deeply, shedding the stench of misery that clung to him like a shroud. The cool air of the upper corridors was sharp and bracing, a reminder of his purpose. Soon, he knew the man responsible would reveal himself. Rylik had already narrowed the possibilities to three: Lord Izram, Lord Thomas, and Lord Orren. Though his instincts leaned heavily in one direction, he knew better than to act prematurely. Patience would see the truth unravel in time, and when it did, he would be ready.

The sapphire-hued tonic held a dual purpose: it would not only shatter the illusions clouding Eldric's mind but also tether him to Rylik in a way the man would never suspect. Once consumed, the potion would grant Rylik glimpses of Eldric's vision, revealing fragments of his surroundings and movements at will. It was only a matter of time before the spy emerged from the shadows, and when he did, Rylik intended to be there to witness the life drain from his eyes.

It wasn't loyalty to Kaldros that drove him. Far from it. The king's throne had to remain unchallenged—at least for now. The Rebellion threatened to topple the fragile balance of power, and Rylik had no intention of letting chaos rob him of his ultimate prize. The enemies of the crown would have to be excised—root and stem—until the serpent that threatened the kingdom lay with its head severed. Only then could Rylik seize the crown for himself.

The throne would be his, not because of bloodlines or destiny, but because he had earned it in the shadows, built it atop the graves of those foolish enough to stand in his way.

CHAPTER 21

ARIA

Aria strode briskly down the palace corridors, flanked by her guardsmen as a guide led them toward the chambers of a high-ranking nobleman. She recalled her earlier work with Maven when an urgent healing request had come in from the servant of a certain lord. She hadn't been given a name, but she knew anyone requiring her services would be part of the king's inner circle, and denying such a person could be tantamount to denying the king himself. *I don't want to offend him and attract the king's scrutiny,* she thought, a twinge of anxiety forming in her stomach.

The guide slowed to a stop and opened the door to the lord's suite, allowing Aria to step through the threshold as her guards stationed themselves on either side of the entrance.

As she entered the room, her eyes fell upon a man seated by the window, adjusting his tunic. His red hair was pulled back, beard neatly maintained, revealing a stern expression that matched his athletic build. He looked over at her, beckoning her with a finger. "Aria, come closer."

*Wait. Isn't that **Orren**?*

She struggled to reconcile the man before her with the image of Orren she had encountered once before, who had urged her to align herself with the Rebellion. He looked far more regal than he had when she had met him that night in his cloak. She absently moved toward him, unsure of what would require the two of them to meet like this. She couldn't help but worry that there was a more sinister reason for their meeting than a simple healing.

"I have a wound on my forearm," he said, holding out his arm and turning it over to present it for her inspection.

As she examined the injury, she was surprised that he would choose to have it tended by her. The wound wasn't serious; it would likely heal on its own in a week or so. Perhaps he was concerned about the scarring. With a nervous exhale, she summoned her yellow-golden magic, weaving it around the wound until it was resolved in a matter of moments.

"Will there be anything else, Lord Orren?" she asked, pulling her hand back to glance up at him.

He squeezed and flexed the muscles in his forearm, testing its motility. "Yes, there is one other matter." His intense eyes narrowed as he regarded her carefully. "I was informed that you are no longer fulfilling your service to the Rebellion."

Aria felt the color drain from her face, her heart skipping a beat as she processed his words.

"Why?" he pressed, his voice low and intense.

The walls of the once spacious room now seemed to close in on her as Aria took a step back, the fear constricting in her chest. Her pulse quickened, each heartbeat echoing in her ears. *I don't want to discuss this with him. Not here. Not where Rylik could be anywhere, listening, pressing his ear to these very walls.* The shadows seemed to stretch ominously, as if watching, waiting for what might unfold.

"Do not leave until I have dismissed you, Aria." His voice cut through the air like a sharpened blade, cold and authoritative. His now-healed hand reached out abruptly, grasping her wrist with harsh fingers. The suddenness of it stole her breath, and the weight of his grip felt suffocating, as if chains had locked her in place. His touch was unyielding, tightening just enough to remind her of his control, but not yet enough to hurt.

Her heart hammered, and she fought the instinct to wrench herself free, her mind racing as she gauged the strength in his grip. Could she break away? His eyes bore into hers, daring her to try.

"It doesn't need to concern me," she whispered, her voice barely steady, each word a tremor of defiance. "I didn't swear my fealty to this cause. I didn't even want to do this." A jolt ran through her as his grip tightened just a fraction more, her pulse now thudding against his hand. "It was calloused of you to coerce me into it. I'm not ready to die for just any reason," she said, the tremble in her voice now undeniable, the strength of his grip like an iron vice.

He sighed, pulling her closer, his grip tightening just enough to force her to meet his gaze. His expression darkened, a heavy weight settling over them, the air thick with unspoken menace. "If it were so easy for someone to abandon their mission, I'm certain we all would," he said, his voice a low, threatening murmur that made her blood run cold. "But one cannot so easily vow service to the cause and then arbitrarily change their mind."

Each word felt like a hammer striking the air between them, the gravity of his tone pressing down on her, suffocating. She could feel her pulse quicken, her heart pounding in her chest like a warning drum.

"If you truly think you can escape your obligation, Aria, then you will find that there are worse things to fear." His words slithered around her, coiling tighter and tighter, a silent grip that threatened to suffocate.

"Worse things?" she echoed, her voice barely more than a whisper. She wanted to back away, to escape the growing darkness in his eyes, but his hold kept her rooted in place, a prisoner to the storm brewing in his gaze.

He leaned in closer, his breath hot against her skin, his amber eyes glinting with a cold malice that sent shivers down her spine. "If you turn your back on this Rebellion, I will ensure you are revealed as a traitor to the king," he whispered, his tone so soft, yet dripping with venom. "Your family will be lucky if all they suffer is execution."

The words hit her like a blow, her knees nearly buckling beneath her. "Wh—why? How could you—?!" she stammered, her voice trembling, each syllable soaked in terror. Her mind raced, the weight of the threat sinking deep into her bones.

He released her wrist, but the chill of his touch remained, a phantom sensation that refused to leave. "I could ask the same question of you," he said viciously. "The Rebellion does not stand for defectors. You either die loyal to the cause, or you die a traitor. You are not allowed to simply quit."

"Please," she begged desperately, "my parents, they don't deserve this. They don't deserve to die for this—"

"Then fulfill your obligation to the Rebellion," he interrupted. "If you are an ally, then you will have my protection."

Aria clenched her teeth, smoothing her wrist where he had gripped her too tightly. She hated herself for trembling in his presence, unable to regain her composure or settle her frantic nerves. *Blackmail. That's what this is. He is ensuring my alliance by threatening my family. I was a fool to think I could ever be let off so easily, when the stakes of this game were so high from the start.*

"Do you stand with me? Or are you a traitor?" he demanded, his stare unwavering and piercing, as if he could see straight through her.

Aria felt her heart race as she matched his gaze, though a tremor of fear was evident in her voice. "I will stand with you." It's not like she had a choice otherwise. She fought to keep her hands from trembling, acutely aware of the danger he posed.

"Good." His lips twisted into a smile that didn't reach his eyes, and his shoulders eased slightly, but the threat still hung heavy in the air. "You will continue to report to Leon. If you provide no helpful information to him, I will assume you are loyal to the crown, and I will reveal your betrayal to the king. Is that clear?"

Her slow nod came with a surge of anger simmering just beneath the surface, but it was overshadowed by an even more potent fear that churned in her stomach.

"I expect you to find the Sovereign's weaknesses, whatever they may be, or for you to *become* his weakness." His expression hardened, a sharp intensity darkening his features as he leaned in slightly. "He is a young man, susceptible, perhaps, to" he scanned her over, adding, "a young woman such as yourself."

Aria shifted uneasily under his gaze, trying to regain some semblance of her former composure, but failing.

"He moved you into his adjoining suite moments after meeting you. He wants you close to him. You will use his growing infatuation with you to our advantage."

She felt a surge of tension at his words, struggling to appear firm. "I will do what I can," she managed, her voice low.

"Do not turn him away. If he wants you—in *any* capacity— you will comply." His eyes were steady and calculating.

Aria was indignant at the insinuation. "I—I think you are mistaken. The Sovereign is not the sort of man to let down his guard for a woman. Whatever you think I may be capable of—"

"You are far more capable of being his downfall than you realize, Aria," he interrupted harshly. "Play your role, and we will bring him and this cursed monarchy down."

Aria lowered her gaze to the floor, a tempest of ire roiling within her. She felt too angry to speak, yet the fear that coursed through her veins rooted her in place, making retreat feel impossible. Her heart raced as she shifted her hands behind her back, attempting to smooth the skin of her wrist where he had gripped her with such force. A cold dread washed over her as she imagined the bruises that would soon surface there, a physical reminder of his power over her. The weight of her emotions swirled in her chest, leaving her breathless and conflicted, torn between her simmering anger and the palpable terror of his presence.

"We will not have many future meetings together, Aria," he said, his tone final. "But you will continue to use Leon as your point of contact. If I issue a direct order through him to give to you, I expect you to comply. Do you understand?"

She nodded, jaw tight.

"Good." He waved her off dismissively. "Now go."

Aria turned and left the room, seething with a mix of anger and fear. Outside the door, she saw her guards just down the hall, chatting with a maidservant in a flirtatious manner.

The guards caught sight of her and abandoned the woman, approaching her in haste.

"My apologies, Lady Aria. I didn't realize your healing with the lord would be over so quickly. Are you ready to return to the apothecary?"

Aria gave a silent nod and turned to lead the way down the hall. The guards trailed behind, their armor clinking softly with each step. Her expression remained neutral, though inside her mind swirled with thoughts she didn't dare voice. Without realizing it, her steps quickened, as if some unseen force were driving her forward. The soft padding of her shoes against the stone floor echoed through the otherwise silent corridor, a subtle contrast to the heavier footfalls of the guards who followed her.

They moved through the sunlit halls, the warm light streaming through the tall windows, illuminating the polished stone floors and filling the space with a soft, golden glow. Aria's gaze remained fixed ahead, but her heart thudded in her chest, each step pulling her farther from her resolve. Her breaths became shallower as they neared the arched doors leading outside.

As they crossed the threshold and stepped into the open air of the outer bailey, Aria felt the cool breeze sweep against her skin, a fleeting reminder of freedom she wasn't sure she'd ever taste again.

I'm trapped. Forced to play along with this cursed game, she thought, her heart tightening as she moved. If there was a way out, it would only be to escape. *But I'd never outrun the Sovereign. And even if I did, I'd never save my parents from their fate. How in the world am I supposed to do this?* An angry tear escaped down her cheek, but she quickly wiped it away, grateful that the guards walking behind her likely hadn't noticed. *I don't want to do this.*

"Lady Aria," one of the guards called from behind, "could you slow down? It's a little hard to keep pace with you without jogging."

Startled, Aria slowed her pace, her breath catching as her heart pounded in her chest. She hadn't even realized how fast she had been walking, the frantic energy propelling her forward without thought. Her mind raced, acknowledging what her body had instinctively known: she was desperate to run, to escape. Every step had been a silent cry for freedom. She stopped abruptly, her feet planted firmly on the stone pathway as her gaze locked onto the distant road stretching away from the palace grounds. The road was vast and seemingly endless, its promise of escape whispering to her like a distant call. *Could I?* she wondered, her thoughts spinning wildly. The weight of her situation pressed down on her as she hesitated, torn between obligation and the deep-rooted need to flee.

Her body moved before her mind had fully caught up, feet instinctively turning toward the road, drawn by the faint glimmer of hope it represented.

If I went into hiding, maybe I could get away with it.

Her thoughts spiraled as she pictured slipping away unnoticed, blending into the masses in some distant town where no one would know her name, where the looming shadow of the Sovereign's control couldn't reach her, nor the sharp eyes of Orren or the grasp of the Rebellion. The weight of his threat pressed down on her like an iron collar, his cold words echoing in her mind: *"If you turn your back on this Rebellion, I will ensure you are revealed as a traitor."*

With each step pulling her closer to the capital in the distance, reality clawed at the edges of her thoughts. *Could I really escape?* She felt a pang of dread as the gravity of her impulsive desire sank in. Even if she could outrun the palace guards, even if she somehow slipped through the city unnoticed, she knew that running wouldn't guarantee her parents' safety. No matter how fast or far she ran, they would be left behind to pay the price.

"Lady Aria?" the guard interrupted again, his voice fraught with concern. "The apothecary is in the other direction."

Aria felt herself hesitate, torn between her instincts and reason. "Right. You're right," she conceded, though her gaze remained fixed on the road ahead. Desperation weighed on her, urging her to find a way, any way, down that path. "I need something from town," she added quickly. "Can we get a ride?"

The guard hesitated, exchanging a glance with his fellow before looking back at her. "We would need permission from the Sovereign for that, my lady."

Aria's heart sank as the weight of his words hit her, the panic rising swiftly. Her eyes flicked away from the road, a grim realization settling in. "Of course," she murmured, voice tight. *What am I thinking?* Her mind raced. *I can't run. The Sovereign has already made it clear how he feels about my thoughts of escaping. He'd lock me up in retaliation.* Despite knowing the danger, her gaze remained on the road.

But, that's only if he catches me. And while he may excel in murder, and cross large, cavernous distances in an instant, he might not be a

good tracker. I can lay low. I could stay hidden. I could sneak my parents
out of the kingdom, ensure us all some safety on some boat out of here.

Time stretched as she continued forward, torn between impulse and reason. She could feel her body picking up speed again, driven by the sudden surge of desperation.

"Lady Aria!" The guards' voices were now stern, their tone firm as they realized her intent. "You are not allowed to leave palace grounds without express permission! Cease immediately, or we will be forced to detain you!"

Without thinking, Aria broke into a mad sprint, Orren's threats echoing in her mind, her parents' faces flashing before her eyes. *I have to get them out. I have to!* Panic fueled her legs, pushing her faster, her heart pounding as the urgency to flee consumed her. The road ahead seemed like her only chance, her only way to outrun the danger tightening its grip around her.

The guards' shouts blurred in her ears, drowned out by the relentless thudding of her feet against the stone road. Her breath came in ragged gasps, chest tightening as the city in the distance remained frustratingly far. No matter how fast she ran, it felt like the distance between her and freedom only stretched farther, mocking her desperation.

Suddenly, a gloved hand clamped around her arm and yanked her to the ground. She let out a sharp yelp, pain shooting through her body as she landed hard. Her eyes darted upward to find her guards towering over her, their expressions breathless and exasperated.

"What are you doing, Lady Aria? Are you mad?" one of them demanded, his grip tightening as he hoisted her roughly to her feet. "You can't just take off in a sprint and disregard orders. We will have to tell the Sovereign about this."

Aria's heart dropped, her panic swelling. "Don't! Please. I beg you, don't say anything," she pleaded, pulling her arm away from his grasp, her voice trembling.

The guard's brows furrowed, his gaze steady. "My lady, we don't report to you. We report to him. Anything you do, or anything that is done to you, is his business."

She flinched as he reached for her again, shrinking back. "Please," she whispered, her voice fragile. "I'll walk back. I won't run."

For a moment, he eyed her warily, his posture tense, but then he relented, stepping back and allowing her to walk ahead of him.

I have to think of something, she thought desperately, trying to calm her racing mind. The Sovereign won't be pleased to hear about this. *Maybe I can convince him it was just a misunderstanding, that I needed exercise and the guards overreacted.* She groaned internally. *Not even I believe that excuse.*

By the time they reached the outer bailey again, Aria could feel the eyes of the other guardsmen watching her, judging her. She averted her gaze, her muscles fatigued, her heart heavy with the weight of her impulsiveness. *How could I have thought I could get away? I would have left such an obvious trail.* Anxiety bubbled inside her as she neared the apothecary, her steps growing heavier with each passing moment.

As one guard stood post outside, the other left to presumably relay the details of her attempted escape to the Sovereign. Inside, Aria glanced down at her wrist, her skin red where Orren's fingers had dug into her earlier. *If I am going to run, it needs to be calculated,* she reasoned. *First, I need to secure my parents' safety. Get them on a boat out of here. Then, I can focus on my own escape.* She sighed, knowing it would take time. *Maybe by then, I'll have earned the Sovereign's trust.* The thought trailed off as the weight of her earlier actions sank in, leaving her feeling more trapped than ever.

* * *

It was several hours later when Aria had finished her shift at the apothecary with Maven when she was reminded by guardsmen that she had a meeting with a tailor from the capital. As she walked back to her suite, the halls of the palace grew increasingly oppressive. The usual echoes of noise and conversation were absent, replaced by an unsettling silence that amplified her growing anxiety. *What will he say?* Each step seemed heavier than the last, the weight of the day pressing down on her shoulders as she recalled her earlier failed attempt to flee the kingdom. She braced herself for the inevitable confrontation that was sure to come this evening, acutely aware that the Sovereign would be upset about her haphazard choices.

When she finally reached her door, she paused, resting her hand against the cool wood. She took a deep breath, trying to steady herself. A clothing fitting would be a welcome distraction, a simple challenge compared to what she had faced earlier. Yet, the anticipation of the Sovereign's return loomed over her like a storm cloud, darkening her thoughts. She couldn't shake the worry that had settled deep within her, and she felt her heart race at the thought of facing him again.

The weight of her parents' safety pressed heavily on her chest, reminding her of everything at stake. With a sigh, she finally pushed the door open, stepping into her room and hoping to lose herself in the world of fabric and thread that awaited her, if only to momentarily escape the complexities of her reality and the Sovereign's inevitable ire.

The soft click of the door closing behind her sent a chill down her spine. Aria turned to see Rylik standing there, his cold, observant eyes locked onto her. Startled, she involuntarily jumped, her heart racing. "Sovereign, hello."

He prowled toward her, an unsettling intensity in his gaze that sent shivers down her spine. "Are you so very unhappy, Aria?"

Feeling a wave of discomfort wash over her, Aria instinctively took a step back, her pulse quickening. "I—I'm not unhappy. I just, uh," she stuttered, "I was wanting exercise?" The words fell from her lips like fragile leaves in the wind.

"Exercise?" Rylik's tone was steeped in skepticism, his eyes raking over her figure with a predatory hunger. "Just decided to spontaneously go for a run? Right after asking for a ride into town for unspecified reasons?"

Aria stammered, heat creeping to her cheeks. "It was a beautiful day, and I—"

"That's the best you have?" He interrupted, a dark smirk curving his lips, the corners of his mouth twisting in a way that made her heart race. "If I didn't know any better, I'd say you were trying to run away. Which is folly, of course, because the attempt is so sloppy and desperate that even a child would conceive of it."

Insulted yet painfully aware of the truth in his words, Aria struggled to respond. "It's not what you think."

"Well, what is it, then?" Rylik advanced toward her, the air around them thickening with tension as he closed the distance between them.

Instinctively, Aria raised her hand, attempting to create a barrier, but he moved with a predator's grace, eyes narrowing as they fell upon her wrist. He grasped her hand, pulling her closer, his touch both firm and electrifying as he examined the red stripes marking her skin. "Did your guards do this?"

Aria furrowed her brows, shaking her head, the heat of his presence overwhelming. "No, of course not."

His gaze sharpened, an unsettling shift making him seem more menacing, and yet, there was an undeniable magnetism that drew her in. "Who did?"

Her heart thundered in her chest, each beat a reminder of her perilous position. *Damn. I should have covered it.* She desperately averted her gaze, unable to meet the intensity of his stare. "No—nobody."

Rylik's amusement twisted into something darker, his voice low and ominous as it closed in around her like a suffocating shadow. "Protecting your assailant will do you no favors, Pyra. Who did this to you?"

Aria tried to pull her hand back, but his grip was unwavering, a mixture of tenderness and control that made her head spin. "I did it. I gripped my hand for too long. I bruise easily."

He closed his eyes, exhaling with mild annoyance before releasing her hand. "You are a terrible liar, dear."

"Is this interrogation going to take much longer?" she asked faintly. "I was told that the tailor you invited would be here soon. Assuming you're not absolutely livid with me, of course, and haven't canceled that invitation altogether." She avoided his piercing eyes, focusing instead on a nearby vase.

Rylik remained casual, composed, folding his hands behind his back, his chest broad and relaxed. "The tailor will be here within the hour, I assure you. And as for my 'interrogation', yes, you can consider it over. Since you will not tell me what happened, I will use the other methods I have available to me."

Tension coiled in her belly as she met his gaze. "*Other* methods?"

He offered a wry grin, the corners of his mouth curling ominously. "I won't be torturing you. But, I can't say the same for your assailant."

Hesitation gripped her. "I don't think it would be wise to—"

Rylik's brow arched, his head tilting slightly, as if challenging her to finish her thought. "Oh? Aria, no amount of protest from you will change my course of action. But, please, think nothing of it." His smile remained, haunting yet charming. "Enjoy your time with the tailor. I'll see you again this evening." With that, he turned to leave, closing the door softly behind him.

CHAPTER 22

RYLIK

Night had settled over the kingdom of Ravenhelm, casting a deep shade of indigo across the land. Rylik slouched in front of his fireplace, the flickering flames illuminating his features and creating an ever-shifting tapestry of light and darkness as he sharpened a dagger, its blade glinting with fiery reflections. The rhythmic scraping of steel against stone filled the silence, but his mind was far from calm. Anger boiled within him as he thought of the marks on Aria's wrist.

Lord Orren Soltren.

He forced himself to focus on the dagger, making long, coarse scrapes along the sharpened edge. He was the last person Aria spoke with before she tried to run toward the capital. It didn't surprise him that the noble would touch a woman like her without regard to her own well-being. However, he didn't understand why he would handle her so coarsely. As he examined the dagger, his brow furrowed with annoyance, a thought crossed his mind. Perhaps, like the king, he has an interest in her. If he was too forward, she may have tried to resist him.

Lowering the blade to sharpen it further, he mused, *I could kill him tonight. It would be cathartic.* His eyes remained fixed on the task, but a sigh escaped his lips. *But then, I'd have to answer to the king as to why I murdered one of his favorites. And it's not time for that. Not yet. There is an order to these things.*

Setting the whetstone down on the table, he allowed his gaze to drift beyond the knife, now captivated by the flames of his hearth. He listened to the crackling sounds as though they might drown out his thoughts. Still, his treatment of her could not go without consequence. He sat upright, resting his elbows on his knees, leaning in closer to the fire as he spun the blade in his hands, watching the light reflect off its polished surface. *I'll have his manor in Eldvane burned to the ground by tomorrow evening.* Standing upright, he sheathed the dagger and rolled his neck side to side, trying to ease the tension that had built there.

He's rather fond of that manor, as I recall. Has a fair amount of money tied up in the place. It should make for a rather disappointing night for him. A slight, satisfied grin crept onto his face. Hurting him financially will have to do for now. *And perhaps,* his thoughts flickered to the adjoining suite where Aria was. *Perhaps, eventually, Aria will tell me herself what he did to unnerve her so.*

He remembered observing her earlier that morning while she slept, the way his thoughts had turned dark and sordid without restraint. *I have thought about this woman nearly the entire day. It's pitiful, really.*

Rylik ran his fingers through his hair in agitation, feeling a strange mix of frustration and longing. *I know it's only because of the relief she brings me when she heals the blight. If she were not so valuable, I would not be so fixated on her. And if she were not so beautiful, I would likely be able to hold a conversation with her without imagining her unraveling, desperate, and desirous underneath me.* He swallowed hard, his mouth parched as he stared intently at her door.

Groaning to himself, he moved to the windowsill, where plants were beginning to flower in the planter box, crisply illuminated by the moonlight. He hardened his stare at the delicate flora. The memory of her lips on his own haunted his dreams relentlessly. He was becoming too obsessed with her. He lightly touched the small green leaves, pondering his predicament.

She was his prisoner for life. She was too valuable to be allowed to slip away. Just as he feared, her betrayal might come at the expense of her own helplessness, driven away from him due to fear. He needed to find a way to convince her to trust in his protection more than she might fear her enemies.

Just then, the door to the adjoining suite opened. Rylik glanced over his shoulder, his chest tightening as he saw Aria standing sheepishly in the doorway.

"Good evening, Sovereign," she said, her voice soft and uncertain. "The tailor left a while ago, but you weren't in your room when I came to visit you earlier for the blight healing. Are you ready now?" She avoided his eyes, uncertain if the memory of her half-hearted attempt to flee earlier still plagued his thoughts.

Rylik studied her, his admiration for her loose, wild hair curling around her face blooming like the fire crackling in his hearth. He approached her with a casual grace, a need rising within him. "I have grown much colder in your absence. So, please," He reached for her hand, lifting it to his chest, pressing her warm fingertips against his cool skin. "Soothe me, Pyra."

Blushing quietly, Aria's eyes gleamed golden as her magic surged through him, filling him with heat and comfort that spread through every part of him.

Rylik breathed steadily, savoring the warm relief coursing through him as Aria's magic enveloped him, wrapping him in a cocoon of comfort. The heat radiating from her touch chased away the chill that had settled in his bones. *I wish that this could last. I wish that she would still be here in the morning, pressed close to me just like this.* The closeness between them felt like a fleeting solace amidst the chaos of his responsibilities, a rare moment of peace he yearned to prolong.

As Aria continued to pour her magic into him, Rylik's thoughts turned cold with the reminder that this moment was an illusion. He felt remorse twist in his chest, knowing that soon enough, she would pull away, and the world would intrude once more. The warmth of her presence was a temporary balm, and he silently mourned the inevitable return to emptiness.

As the magical light faded from her hand, her eyes returned to their usual hue. She looked down at his hand still pinned over hers, the firmness of his grip a mix of desperation and tenderness.

"Sovereign, my hand." She met his gaze, a flicker of speculation in her wide eyes.

His lips pressed together, stifling the words threatening to escape. *Stay.* His eyes nearly pleaded, and an inner voice urged him on. *Force her to stay.* He tightened his fingers around hers, feeling the size difference; his hand dwarfed her delicate one. *She can't deny me. If I say she can't leave, then she has to obey that command.*

"Aria," he began, his voice low, but she lifted her other hand to gently pry his grip from hers.

That simple action jolted him from his reveries. He spotted the red mark on her wrist, a remnant of Orren's rough handling, and reluctantly released her hand, turning his gaze aside to avoid the sight of her bruising.

"I wanted to apologize for my actions earlier today," she said, her voice barely above a whisper. "I still don't wish to discuss anything with you, but it was wrong of me to sabotage my guards and run off toward the city. It was desperate and stupid, and I'm sorry you had to be informed of it." She stood awkwardly, her eyes averted, murmuring so quietly he could scarcely hear her.

"I do hope whatever caused you to feel so anxious has now been abated," Rylik replied, his hands securing behind his back to resist the urge to reach for her.

"I'm fine, I suppose." Her tone was begrudging, as though she fought to convince herself of the truth.

"Excellent." He cleared his throat, adopting a more casual air. "How was your visit with the tailor?"

"It went well." A slight blush crept into her cheeks. "She showed me so many beautiful day gowns, nightgowns, ball gowns, and," She hesitated, her voice softening, "other items."

"And you selected a good amount, I assume?" he asked, his interest piqued.

"I was informed that my benefactor had already pre-purchased an enormous amount of clothing for me." She eyed him carefully. "It was merely up to me to select colors and styles. And so I did." A small sigh escaped her lips, tinged with embarrassment.

Rylik's lips curved into a pleased smirk. "That is wonderful to hear. I look forward to seeing your new wardrobe."

"And I can't persuade you to spend your gold elsewhere from

now on? I believe I'm now so far indebted to you that I will never be able to repay you." There was a slight exasperation in her voice.

"I will spend my gold however I please," he replied, a playful tone underlying his words.

"So be it." She shrugged dismissively, then offered a small sigh and a half-smile. "Thank you, Sovereign. Unwise purchase or not, I have to respect the generosity of your actions."

"Is it generosity?" he teased, a glimmer of mischief in his eyes. "Or do I just want to see you in one of your new corsets?"

She gave him a gentle shove of teasing annoyance. "Oh, be serious. You're never going to see that."

He smiled coyly back at her, a challenge evident in his gaze.

"I should be off to bed, I think. Now that your blight is settled for the evening." She glanced at her door with casual anticipation.

Rylik watched her, his familiar longing resurfacing, his hand gripping his own wrist tightly behind his back as he forced a mask of calm over his features. "You could stay." The words slipped out before he could stop himself.

Turning her head to him, she wore an innocent, inquisitive expression. "Stay? You're suggesting I stay here in your room, Sovereign? For how long? Surely not all night." She chuckled softly, but the lightness of her tone belied a flicker of uncertainty.

He maintained his stern facade, letting the quiet draw out far longer than necessary.

Her hand, which had been so eager to heal him, curled against the fabric of her skirt, squeezing it tightly. "If you're going to recommend I stay a while, then I'm going to need some supper." She offered a small attempt at levity.

"I can arrange that. What would you like?" Rylik asked, intrigued by the prospect of keeping her close a little longer.

"It's a nice night. Perhaps you might show me some stars, and I could enjoy them on your balcony while eating whatever leftovers there are in the kitchen." She glanced toward the balcony doors, her eyes alight with hope.

He smiled, relishing her request. "I will have the kitchen make your preference. What do you want?"

"The kitchen staff have completed their workday. I need

nothing from the chef. I will be perfectly satisfied with bread, dried meats, fruits, cheese, things like that."

"As you wish." He gave a brief nod, satisfaction blooming within him at the thought of her staying.

* * *

Rylik and Aria were seated on his stone balcony, the moon and stars high above illuminating the night sky. Two flickering torchlights framed the doorway, casting a faint warm hue over the scene. A spread of fruits, meats and cheese lay on a small table between the two chairs, the assorted bounty now half-eaten. Beside it, a half-full bottle of wine sat alongside two empty glasses, their bases stained with the remnants of the rich red liquid.

"The longer we talk like this, Sovereign, the more I am quite convinced that you abandoned a career path in astronomy. And perhaps also in botany." Aria giggled, a light and bubbly sound that echoed into the cool air. "I'm not saying you're wasting your talents as the Sovereign, but if we had met in another life, and these were your only passions," Her voice trailed off, embarrassment coloring her cheeks.

Rylik, wearing a sly smile, leaned back in his chair, his gaze resting on her. "Is *that* the kind of man you would see yourself with in this 'other life', dear?"

Aria's face reddened further, the wine clearly having loosened her tongue. "I have had too much to drink. I'm saying nonsensical things. Please excuse whatever comes out of my mouth next."

He found her flustered demeanor charming. "I think I rather like the sound of your other life for me. I'd get to enjoy gardening during the day and stargazing at night, and apparently I'd have a beautiful, fiery little wife to come home to every night."

Aria turned her attention to him, a teasing glint in her eye as she scoffed, picking up a piece of bread spread with grape jam. "Are you sure you're not also drunk, Sovereign?"

"It would take more than a quarter of that bottle to make me lose my inhibitions," Rylik replied, gesturing toward the wine.

"How much would it take?" she asked, curiosity dancing

across her features as she took a bite.

"Are you trying to get me drunk?" he teased, raising an eyebrow.

"No, I just have to wonder how much wine would make you sound just as stupid as I do right now." She poured herself more wine, glancing at him to see if he wanted more.

He nodded, a small smile playing at his lips as she filled his glass. "I think it has been a long time since I was last out of my mind with liquor," he said, pausing to swirl the wine in his glass, a distant look crossing his face. "That night," he murmured with a sigh, "It was cheap booze. As much as I could afford to drown everything out." The memory clung to him, vivid and relentless: the day his father died, when he stumbled into the nearest tavern and drank until the pain dissolved into a hollow numbness.

Aria watched him intently as she sipped her drink. "That was definitely much more than one bottle. So, I'm not sure exactly how much it would take, Pyra." He eyed her, amusement dancing in his gaze. "If you'd like to get me drunk, you may pass out before you ever see it."

She finished her wine and set the glass down beside his. "I should slow down."

"Perhaps," he replied, eyes flickering with mischief. "But maybe you have some feelings you'd like to drown out yourself?"

Aria sighed, looking out over the meadows and gardens. "I have plenty, yes. I'd be lying if I said I didn't dream of my life before this one. Sure, it wasn't fancy. I lived poor. But I had certain liberties I enjoyed, and I engaged with people I very much liked to be with."

"Well, that does sound peaceful." He reached for the bottle of Merlot, deliberate as he poured more into her glass. "Tell me about it, if you don't mind."

She absently reached for her glass, taking a sip. "My parents never wanted me to use my healing magic for monetary gain. I don't fault them for it, as I agree with their sentiments, but, God, would it have killed them to accept donations? We were so very poor. Oftentimes I had to pick up odd jobs on top of regular daily household chores to help them make ends meet. I can't tell if I'm more disappointed in them for not trying to use the resources they had available to them, or if I'm more disappointed in my village for not recognizing we needed help and trying to offer some."

"And that's what you want to return to?" Rylik asked, composed as ever.

"No. Yes?" She chuckled, "I'd like that life again, but maybe working less hard, less often. Definitely with more money."

"That does sound nice," he agreed. "Enjoying the benefits of a quiet village life, but with the money of a nobleman. Certainly sounds more tempting than being resigned to a palace surrounded by the members of the court and their seedy intentions."

Scoffing, she took another drink. "Seedy is putting it lightly." She held out her glass to him, anticipation in her gaze.

He poured the last of the bottle into her cup, setting the empty bottle back down on the table. "You sound as if you're referring to someone in particular?" he asked, amusement lacing his voice. "I do hope it's not me."

"You know, all things considered," She lifted her glass to her lips, "You're not so bad, Sovereign."

"I'm pleased that I am not considered to be one of the seedy people you deign to contend with," he said with a subtle smile.

"There are worse people." She sighed, sipping from her glass.

He was poised to strike as he mused, "Like Lord Orren?"

Aria paused, glancing at him with hesitation before lifting her glass again, as if to create a barrier between them. "Yeah. Like Lord Orren." Her gaze drifted away, staring out across the meadow.

"You are not required to administer healing services to him, Aria." Rylik watched her carefully, his tone firm. "You're not required to provide any service to someone who is not a Shadow Knight or his majesty himself."

"I'll keep that in mind." She drank a little more, her eyes downcast at her half-filled glass. "I would prefer to never deal with him again. I would prefer to have him thrown from a balcony."

He couldn't hide his smirk of approval. "I have heard he is quite the brute. I don't blame you for your sentiments."

"Please don't tell him I said that. I don't need him targeting me any more than he already is," she said with a meager attempt at a laugh, clearly strained with worry.

"Targeting is an interesting choice of words." He scrutinized her thoughtfully, observing as the last of the red liquid slipped down her throat.

"He wants me to play the role of some cheap consort, but I refuse," she grumbled indignantly.

Rylik's fingers tensed slightly against the arm of his chair, his eyes cool and composed.

"He wants me to do a lot of things. And I don't think that I can." She sighed, slouching back into her chair, her glass empty beside her.

"What sort of things?" he asked, appearing impassive, though his jaw tightened slightly.

She gazed up at the stars, a dreamy look in her eyes. "It's so beautiful up there."

"You don't have to do anything he tells you to do, Aria." He focused intently on her, his tone steady and resolute. "You are not beholden to him."

She huffed softly, a hint of defiance in her tone. "I respond when I'm threatened. I'm not a master of shadows like you, Sovereign. And even if I were, I couldn't save myself from the situation I'm in."

"He threatened you?" Rylik leaned forward slightly, concern edging his voice.

"Could you imagine how fantastic it would be if I could just shadow here and there like you do?" She wiggled her fingers, mimicking his shadow magic. "I'd be at my parent's house in a flash. I'd put them in a boat, sail them off to sea." A distant look filled her eyes. "And I'd follow them. With my shadow magic, of course." She gave him a smug, drunken grin.

"You're worried about your parents' safety?" He inquired.

"Always." She groaned, playing with a few curling strands of her hair thoughtfully.

"I can ensure their protection. So long as you keep my secret, I would be more than happy to offer guardianship in exchange." He attempted to meet her eyes, but her gaze was steadily becoming more muddled.

"Oh, please." She let out a contemptuous breath. "You threatened my parents the first night I met you. What makes you think I could trust you to protect them?"

"We are building trust, Aria," he tinged his voice with insincere warmth. "While I can be your greatest enemy, I can also be your greatest asset, if you can trust in my abilities."

"Asset is a funny word." She mused, giggling softly.

"Perhaps you should retire for the evening." He stood, a soft smile on his face. "It's after midnight, I'm certain."

"But I'm not tired." Her eyes were half-lidded, gazing lazily up at him. "You're so tall."

"Please," He held out a hand to her. "Allow me to escort you to your bed."

Aria took his hand, standing with his aid, a little unsteady as she stumbled into his chest. "Walk much, Aria?" she teased herself, tittering quietly.

Rylik regarded Aria with a mix of concern and amusement. "I fear I may have allowed you to drink too much." He twisted his lips into a sideways downturned expression. "You're going to require observation. Do you drink often?" He guided her back into his room, nearing the edge of his bed.

"No," she replied, her voice slightly slurred. "I really only just started drinking this year. The night I learned I'd become the king's imperial healer. That's the first night I ever had liquor at all." She chuckled, but her laughter was cut short as she lost her balance.

Rylik secured her more closely, hoisting her into his arms. "Then I definitely allowed you too much." With a sigh, he laid her down gently onto his bed.

Aria's cheeks flushed, a happy expression lighting her face. "Your bed is so soft."

He looked down at her, a pitying smile gracing his lips. "Indeed, it is." He adjusted her position so she lay comfortably on her side. "Try to lie like this, won't you?"

"I like your room," she said, her eyes wandering around, tired yet peaceful. "It's really beautiful. And so large."

Rylik took a long inhale and exhaled slowly, nodding in agreement. "Yes, it is a nice room."

Aria snickered softly to herself. "Ugh, look at me. I'm doing exactly what he wanted, aren't I?"

"Exactly what who wanted?" Rylik asked, sitting down beside her, moving a few strands of hair from her face with careful tenderness.

"Lord Orren," she scowled at the name. "I'm behaving like some consort right now, aren't I? Laying in the Sovereign's bed."

Rylik raised an eyebrow, curiosity piqued. "He wants you to become his consort? Or mine?"

She chortled, her eyelids fluttering as if they were too heavy to keep open.

Rylik leaned closer, tapping her cheek lightly with his hand to rouse her. "Aria, whose consort are you to become?"

Struggling to focus on his face, she settled her gaze on his lips instead. Reaching up, she softly traced his lower lip with her thumb. "I cannot stop thinking about our kiss."

His eyes widened slightly, captivated by her admission.

"It wouldn't be so terrible, you know, becoming your consort," she murmured, lowering her hand as she blinked slowly. "Because," Her voice trailed off, her head slackening against the pillow.

"Because?" he pressed, watching her closely. He reached for her face, but her steady breathing indicated she was unresponsive. Furrowing his brows, he observed the rise and fall of her chest. She was already fast asleep. Still, his hand remained cupped against her cheek, unwilling to relent.

He leaned closer, their faces mere inches apart, the soft warmth of her exhale brushing against his skin. His attention was drawn to her parted lips, soft and inviting, their allure almost impossible to resist. Every muscle in his body tensed, warring against the desire to close the distance between them, to capture that kiss he had craved since the night of the ball.

But she was asleep, unaware of the storm she stirred within him, her expression so peaceful, so innocent, and so vulnerable in this moment. His fingers swept across her jawline, yearning to trace the contours of her lips, to feel her respond to him once more. But as the seconds dragged on, a flood of restraint washed over him, reminding him that this wasn't the time, that she wasn't his to take—at least, not like this. With a heavy sigh, he forced himself to pull away, the tension between what he wanted and what was right hanging in the air like a tether he couldn't fully sever.

Sighing, he pulled back entirely, rising to his feet. *I need to find my composure.* He looked back at her, admiring the way her red hair spilled across his pillow, her small curving body relaxed against the sheets. *I've wanted to see her in my bed for some time now, but it's bittersweet. Had I not gotten overzealous in my attempts to extract information from her on Orren, I might've had her a little more awake.*

With a heavy sigh, he stepped away from the bed and walked over to the fireplace, sinking into his chair.

However, if she hadn't gotten drunk, there's no way she would've agreed to enter my bed. He smirked to himself. *Though it is pleasing to hear her admit she wouldn't mind being my consort, and that kissing me is something she can't—or won't—forget.*

He stared into the hearth, thoughts drifting back to the balcony as Aria briefly admitted what he knew was the truth: Orren being a brute towards her and making menacing threats.

Whether he wants her for his own romantic affairs or not, he is wanting her to play a role she would rather not. And threatening her, and her family—while it's certainly something I've done—it now fills me with a certain rage to know that he has made such an intimidation against her. He rubbed his eyes wearily. He would make arrangements to secure the safety of her parents in the morning. By nightfall, Orren's manor would be ash. And perhaps the brute would rethink his involvement with the healer.

He stood, glancing back at the bed, his eyes drawn to Aria's peaceful sleeping form, her red hair spilling in waves across his pillow. A quiet delight flickered in his chest, the sight stirring something deeper than mere affection. She looked so small and serene against his sheets, and the thought of her lying in his bed, her body nestled against his, had haunted him for longer than he cared to admit. *If I were to sleep there tonight, I'm fairly certain I would be too tempted to do the things I only dream about with her,* he mused to himself darkly.

He swallowed hard, trying to push the thought away, forcing

his legs to carry him across the room. He turned, his eyes tearing away from her as he approached his sofa instead. *She may admit her feelings of romance while drunk, but I'm quite certain she will feel less inclined to do so by morning,* he reasoned with himself, though a small, wicked part of him reveled in the idea of seeing her embarrassment come daylight. The flush on her cheeks when she realized where she had spent the night, and with whom—well, it would be a sight to enjoy. A sly grin curled his lips as he lowered himself onto the couch, knowing full well that the temptation to join her would only make the night much, much longer.

CHAPTER 23

ARIA

The morning light stretched across Ravenhelm, slowly filtering through the tall windows of Rylik's suite. Golden rays cast a soft glow over the room, illuminating the intricate details of the chamber. In the center of it all, Aria lay sprawled across his luxurious bed, her body tangled in the silk sheets, her tousled hair fanning out wildly like a crown of chaos.

Gradually, Aria's eyelids fluttered open. She blinked groggily, her eyes adjusting to the unfamiliar canopy above her. *Where am I?* The realization crept in slowly, and as her vision cleared, panic settled in. This wasn't her bed. This wasn't even her room. Her pulse surged, and in a blur of action, she sprang upright, her heart pounding.

The sudden motion brought a fierce wave of nausea, dizziness, and a throbbing ache to her temples. She staggered off balance, her hand flying to her head as she stumbled forward.

Before she hit the ground, strong arms caught her.

"Good morning, Aria," Rylik's voice was smooth, almost teasing, but the sound of it made her heart race further. He gently pulled her up, steadying her as she blinked dazedly, still trying to make sense of what was happening.

"Sovereign?" she groaned, trying to focus on him through

the unruly strands of hair that had fallen across her face. His low chuckle rumbled in her ear, the warmth of his breath grazing her neck as he guided her back toward the bed.

"Here," he said, securing a glass of bluish-green liquid in her hand. "Drink."

Aria glanced down at the liquid, confused. "What is this?"

"A hangover cure," he replied easily. "A special concoction from the Potion Master that I always keep on hand, just in case."

"Just in case?" she echoed doubtfully, still eyeing the strange aquamarine color. Tentatively, she brought the glass to her lips and sipped. To her surprise, it tasted pleasant—refreshing, even. Within moments, the pain in her head faded, and the nausea vanished entirely.

She stared at him, incredulous. "This is amazing!"

Rylik smiled, taking the now-empty glass from her. "It's more costly than a prized aged wine, so hardly worth the trade-off, but yes, it's fairly miraculous."

Aria shifted uneasily, pieces of fragmented memories from the night before slowly surfacing. She remembered the stargazing, the charcuterie board they had shared, but beyond that, everything was a blur. She glanced at him, then down at the bed, and a realization struck her like a tidal wave. Her heart sank.

"I slept in your bed," she whispered, panic beginning to flood her again. She bolted upright, stepping away from him. "How much did I drink?!"

Rylik shrugged nonchalantly. "Enough to warrant me carrying you to bed to sleep."

Her face flushed with embarrassment, anger bubbling beneath the surface. "Why your bed?!" she demanded, heat rising in her cheeks. "Did we—did you—?" She couldn't even finish the question, the mortification too great.

He stood leisurely, setting the glass down on the bedside table before taking a step toward her. "Are you asking me if I took you to bed," he said slowly, his voice dropping lower as he closed the distance between them, "and then had my way with you?"

Aria swallowed, her heart pounding violently in her chest. She couldn't form a coherent response, caught between embarrassment, curiosity, and a sudden tension she couldn't deny.

Rylik watched her, savoring her discomfort, before letting out a sigh. "Tempting as it was, no. I did not," he said, his voice carrying a note of restraint. "I do have standards, after all, when I intend to bed a woman."

She hesitated, still unable to resist the pull of curiosity. "And those standards are?" The question left her lips before she could stop it, her desire to know overpowering her sense of decorum.

His smile widened, a dark gleam in his eyes. "I want a woman to be fully aware of every kiss, every touch." His fingertips grazed her arm gently, sending a shiver down her spine, adding, "every breathless moan." He watched with satisfaction as her gaze darted away, her lips pressing together in nervous silence.

"I want her passion to be uninhibited," he continued, his voice growing more intimate, "not because liquor has loosened her restraints, but rather because she cannot contain herself any longer." His hand traveled upward, fingers brushing the wild strands of her hair as if imagining the very scene he painted with his words. "Then, and only then, would I allow such an indulgence."

Aria stood frozen, her pulse thrumming wildly in her ears. She swallowed thickly, torn between the simmering tension and her desperate urge to retreat from him. She took a step back, her hair slipping from his fingers as she tried to gather her composure.

"Yes, well, I suppose I didn't quite meet that expectation of yours," she muttered, though her heart still raced. "Gratefully. So, I'll just thank you for taking care of me, then. I doubt I've ever been so drunk before. It's quite an embarrassment." She rubbed the back of her neck awkwardly. "I'm sure I was burdensome, so thank you."

Rylik, ever composed, drew his hands behind his back, the faintest hint of amusement still playing at the corners of his mouth. "It was no trouble at all."

She bit her lip, still chewing on her thoughts, before nervously meeting his gaze once more. "What happened? Did we just talk until I passed out?" Her heart skipped a beat, dread creeping in. *Oh gods, I hope I didn't say anything about the Rebellion.*

He held her gaze steadily, his keen eyes catching every flicker of emotion. "We discussed the stars, you said you wanted to be my wife, and then you became quite tired, so I carried you to bed."

Aria's eyes widened, her cheeks burning with embarrassment. "I—I said what now?!"

Rylik's grin widened slowly, relishing her reaction. "You may have also mentioned that you wanted to kiss me."

Her mind reeled. "I—!? There's no way that I—!" *But I do. I do want to kiss him.* She bit her lip harder, trying to suppress any further incriminating thoughts.

Rylik raised an eyebrow, clearly enjoying her flustered state. "Hm, maybe I'm misquoting you," he teased, crossing one arm over his chest while his other hand massaged his chin in mock deliberation. "Let's see now. I'd just laid you in bed, and you grabbed my face, touched my lips—"

Aria frantically waved her hands, her embarrassment peaking. "Please! Don't go on! I don't think I want to know what incredibly foolish things I did."

Rylik barely stifled his laugh, using his hand in a useless attempt to mask the smile that tugged at his lips.

"Please, just forget all of it," she clamored, waving her hands as if to erase the memory. "Forget everything! That—that was drunken nonsense. I can be respectable. I will be far more composed around you, Sovereign."

His amusement deepened, delighted by her futile defenses. "Oh, there's no need for that. I think I might prefer you a little less 'composed,' as you call it."

"Regardless," Aria's voice sharpened, trying to regain her footing as she took a step back, "I will—" Her back hit the wall behind her, stopping her in her tracks. "—behave."

Rylik's eyes glittered with amusement as he closed the distance between them, a ravenous glint in his icy blue gaze. He leaned forward, the air around them quivering with tension as he pressed his palm flat against the wall beside her head, creating an intimate barrier that closed off the world outside. Aria's heart raced, each beat echoing in the silence between them.

As he leaned closer, the fabric of his tunic brushed against her, the faint scent of firewood clinging to him mingling with the fresh morning air. It was a smell that ignited something deep within her, stirring her senses. His voice was a low, taunting whisper, "If last night was you misbehaving, then I would endeavor to see much more of that in the future."

The dominance of his posture sent a thrill through her, igniting a flutter of excitement deep within. Aria felt like a moth drawn to a flame, dangerously close to getting burned. She could feel the heat radiating from his body, mingling with her own as the space between them shrank. Her pulse quickened, each thump a reminder of the desire curling in her stomach, demanding to be acknowledged. A memory flickered in her mind—her thumb grazing his lower lip the night before, the softness of his skin beneath her touch—leaving her breathless.

Her eyes drifted back to his mouth, a hunger stirring inside her that she couldn't ignore. *What would it feel like to kiss him again?* The thought was intoxicating, overwhelming, but a voice inside her screamed to stop.

Desperately, she pressed her palm against his chest, a small attempt to create distance, yet her hesitation hung in the air, like a spark waiting to ignite. She felt his heartbeat beneath her hand, strong and steady, and as his expression softened, even if just slightly, her resolve faltered. Time seemed to stretch, the world around them fading into a blur as her hand remained against his chest, tracing the outline of his collarbone with her fingertips, savoring the warmth of his body.

Then, without warning, a soft golden glow emanated from her, warmth flooding through her fingertips, pressing through his tunic and into his skin. Her magic surged, igniting the cold blood in his veins with a comforting heat that breathed life into him. She could see the moment he surrendered to her touch, the tension in his body easing as he exhaled a slow breath, eyes fluttering closed.

For a heartbeat, Aria simply watched him, captivated by the way his face softened with relief, a subtle vulnerability flickering in the depths of his gaze. It was a side of him she hadn't seen before, raw and unguarded, and it made her heart swell. But as the magic ebbed away, the golden light fading as quickly as it had come, she reluctantly let her hand fall back to her side, the warmth of his body leaving an imprint on her skin.

Opening his eyes, Rylik regarded her with a new warmth. "Kind of you, Pyra, to provide your services so soon after last night. To what do I owe the favor?"

Aria slid away from him, desperate for space, fighting the temptation to kiss him and lose herself in him entirely. "Think of it as a peace offering for my behavior last night. I'll try to be more dignified moving forward." But even as she said it, she knew it wasn't true. *I healed him because he looked as if he needed it. As if he were thirsty from days in drought, and I held the only vase of water.*

She turned her back to him, hoping to conceal the whirlwind of emotions churning inside her.

And I have no intention of being more 'dignified,' do I? Her thoughts darkened, remembering Orren's chilling words. *"Do not turn him away. If he wants you—in any capacity—you will comply."*

She stayed in the Sovereign's room last night because he had wanted her to. And she thoroughly enjoyed herself, as much as she hated to admit it. Orren intended for her to become the Sovereign's weakness. And while it wouldn't be hard to lose herself in his arms, she dreaded to think what Orren would do if the Sovereign truly began to care for her. She doubted such a thing was possible, but she couldn't stop herself from worrying. Both Orren and the Sovereign were dangerous men. She was in way over her head and her body wouldn't comply with reason.

Behind her, she felt the light touch of Rylik's hand on the small of her back. "You've become quieter this morning, dear. Have I teased you too much?" His voice was soft, but a hint of concern laced through the amusement.

Aria turned her face slightly, just enough to ensure he wouldn't see the flush rising to her cheeks. "I'll be fine. We should probably get started on the day, though."

Rylik withdrew his hand, satisfied. "I suppose so." His smile remained, and though she tried to mask her expression, he could still see the cracks in her resolve. "If I don't see you again before this evening, I hope you have a pleasant day."

"Thank you, and you too, Sovereign." She hurried to the door leading to her adjoining suite, her thoughts tangled. Maybe a bath would wash away the feelings of dread, betrayal, and the undeniable pull she felt toward him. But she knew better than to believe it would be that easy.

* * *

Aria steadied herself as she crushed a delicate mix of herbs into the stone mortar, each movement of her hand purposeful and careful. The soft crunch of dried petals and rare roots filled the apothecary, mingling with the faint, heady aroma of calming flora. Powdered moonroot, sunblossom leaves, and a pinch of starwort—each ingredient possessing ancient healing properties, some enchanted, some fiercely rare. She ground them together until they were a fine, fragrant dust, ready to be blended.

With one hand, she reached for a small vial of luminous water, its liquid shifting with faint, ethereal glints of silver and gold. This was Water of the Elderglow, rumored to heal the deepest wounds, not just of the body but of the spirit. She tipped the vial, watching as the water poured into the mortar, merging with the crushed herbs to form a shimmering elixir. Its surface glistened faintly as she worked, the mixture thickening under the steady motion of her whisk. Satisfied, she laid the utensil aside and reached for the blade.

With a sharp inhale, she pressed the knife to the tip of her finger, wincing as a crimson bead swelled against her skin. Setting the blade down, she dipped a clean finger into the potion and then brought it to her lips. The sweetness of the tonic unfolded across her tongue, spreading warmth through her like sunlight piercing through clouds.

She exhaled softly, her gaze drawn to the self-inflicted wound as it knitted itself back together before her eyes. The flesh fused seamlessly, leaving behind no scar, no trace of imperfection. Testing the spot with her thumb, she marveled at the smoothness, a triumphant smile tugging at her lips.

It worked. She had actually done it. Not only had she crafted a powerful healing elixir, but it had managed to heal *her* as well. Ever since she had gained her miraculous ability to heal others, her magic had stubbornly refused to work on herself. Conventional remedies were fine for minor injuries, but if she ever faced something truly life-threatening, it would have been the end of her. Now, staring at her unblemished finger, she smiled. Relief washed over her as she carefully poured the tonic into a glass bottle, sealing it with a cork and an iron determination.

Her plan was far from complete, she knew that. There was no clear path to escape Orren yet, nor any safeguard in place to protect her parents from his threats. Involving the Sovereign was entirely out of the question. She could almost picture it now: Rylik seated by the fireplace, his piercing gaze fixed on her as she sat beside him. She would open with a polite question about his evening before confessing that she was a member of the Rebellion seeking his protection.

The image played out vividly in her mind. He would laugh—a cold, derisive sound—and then drag her straight to the king. Her parents would hang by morning, and she would waste away in the depths of a dungeon, surviving on scraps until death finally claimed her.

She stared at the glowing vial, her emotions a tangled mix of anticipation and unease. Could she really trust the Sovereign? Perhaps he wouldn't be so cruel if he discovered the truth—but then again, how could he not view it as a betrayal? Whatever fragile trust existed between them would surely shatter. He was as much a danger as the king, and imagining he would make an exception for her was a fantasy she couldn't afford.

Yet, against her better judgment, she felt a pang of sympathy for him. She shouldn't—she knew that. But the thought of abandoning him to suffer his blight without recourse troubled her. This potion, she hoped, would provide him with the relief he needed once she was safely away. Perhaps it could serve as a surrogate for her care, a small act of mercy in her absence. Anything, surely, had to be better than what he had relied on before.

Aria picked up a scrap of parchment, her pen moving in quick, precise strokes as she listed the ingredients and instructions for the elixir. It would suffice. Rylik's extensive knowledge of botany would guide him, enabling him to recreate the potion if needed. She had enchanted a sunblossom tree in the apothecary herb garden, ensuring it would soon mature and bear its distinctive red leaves. Those leaves, dried and crushed with the other ingredients, would provide him with the means to craft the elixir whenever he required it.

She wrapped the note around the bottle with a length of twine, her fingers swiftly tying the knot as her gaze briefly passed over the neat script of her words. Timing would be everything. Giving it to him now would only arouse suspicion—accurately so—that she was planning to leave. She couldn't afford his distrust, not when her exit strategy was still so precariously incomplete.

And then there was the danger of what the elixir represented. If anyone discovered she had successfully created it, she could lose whatever leverage her healing gift afforded her. The potion, after all, was a pale but sufficient mimicry of her power, imbued with her magic through the enchanted tree. While it wouldn't heal as instantly as her touch, its capabilities could render her somewhat obsolete. Worse, if she became too great a liability to the crown, they might force her to enchant a grove of such trees— before marching her to her execution.

Sighing, Aria placed the vial of healing potion into her satchel on the desk, her gaze drifting toward the window. Outside, Maven was still tending the herb garden, her movements brisk and practiced. Aria watched for a moment, her shoulders growing heavy with an inexplicable sadness. Maven had mentioned earlier that things were improving with Leon, reassuring her that her worries were unfounded. It hadn't surprised Aria; Leon's infatuation with Maven was obvious.

Maven had also said Leon wanted to speak with her, to clear the air. Aria had no desire for such a conversation but had lied nonetheless, offering Maven a smile and empty assurances. Their working relationship wasn't something she could afford to tarnish—not over Leon, no matter how much she despised him now.

Her eyes fell to the satchel, where a folded note peeked out—a message delivered to her about an hour earlier. The handwriting was unmistakable, scrawled in Leon's familiar, hurried script:

Library, 6 pm.

She knew precisely what it meant, and it wasn't for clearing the air. Even so, she would go. For now, she remained ensnared, a pawn in a game she couldn't escape and could never win.

CHAPTER 24

ARIA

It was several hours later when Aria found herself in the castle library, tucked away in the dusty recesses where few ventured. Her guards stood watch outside, but within the shadows of towering shelves, she felt concealed yet anxious.

Feigning interest, she picked up a tattered book, its pages yellowed with age. She was prepared to look the part if anyone questioned her.

As if summoned by her thoughts, Leon rounded the corner of the stacks, stepping just behind her. His back was to her, and he appeared to search for a book among the shelves. "Don't turn around," he cautioned in a low voice.

Rigid and reluctant, Aria held the book closer, forcing herself to study its spine.

"I was told you might have information for me," he continued, a hint of urgency threading through his tone.

Gritting her teeth, she recalled Orren's warning: if she failed to provide information, he would assume her loyalty lay with the crown, marking her as a traitor to the Rebellion. "Right. Kaelith, one of the Shadow Knights, sustained an injury recently. While I was healing him, I noticed papers on his desk pertaining to a shipment arriving this weekend. It's a large shipment of weapons and enchanted artifacts, likely useful for the Rebellion. The ship is due to arrive in two days, probably by nightfall." Her lips twisted in disdain. "Hopefully that's enough to satisfy Orren's interests."

Leon set a book back into the shelf before him, exhaling softly. "That will suffice, yes. How are you doing? Are you well?"

"Don't pretend like you care." She glared at the book in her hands, irritation bubbling beneath the surface.

"I do care about you, Aria," he insisted, glancing over her shoulder before forcing his eyes to the shelves, tracing a finger along the spines of the books.

"If you gave a damn about me at all, you'd tell Orren to leave me the hell alone." Her grip tightened on the book, the edges digging into her palms.

His hand paused over a title, a quiet desperation evident in his eyes. "I don't fault him. He stands for a just cause. I'm glad you are standing with us again, even if you're a little resistant right now."

Aria bit her tongue so hard she worried it might bleed, then shoved the book roughly back onto the shelf. "Will there be anything else, Leon?" she asked, gritting her teeth.

Leon swallowed, hesitating. "No. But—"

Walking swiftly away from the stacks, Aria couldn't bring herself to care about the end of whatever sentence was supposed to come tumbling out of his mouth.

Suddenly, she came to a halt. A familiar red-haired man stood at a table, stroking his beard as he examined a few books.

Orren casually turned his attention in her direction, a subtle threat lurking in his stare.

Feeling her heart sink, Aria turned and walked back toward Leon, begrudgingly picking up another book. "Why is he here?" she asked, her tone tense as she directed her words to Leon, who stood just behind her.

"He doesn't trust you, Aria." Leon attempted to infuse kindness into his voice, but frustration edged through. "If you hadn't shown up today, he was going to assume you defected. Can you blame him?"

"I told you what information I have. I don't need to be judged by him on my way out." She eyed Orren through the gaps in the shelves.

"He also wanted me to ask how things were proceeding with the Sovereign." Leon's unease was palpable, his agitation mounting.

Aria felt anger flare inside her. "What does he care to know?"

"Are you appeasing the Sovereign? Are you giving him what he wants? Does he seem to be interested in your advances?" Each question dripped with increasing agitation, as if he loathed the topic.

"Yes, I'm playing a harlot and doing well," she mused sardonically. "Perhaps soon I'll be the mother to his children. Maybe then Orren can use my child as fodder for the Rebellion. Would that satisfy him?"

"Please." Leon's tone was clipped, annoyance thick in the air. "Keep your voice down. I know you don't want to play this role, but you're doing it in service to the cause."

Aria was rife with spite. "Oh, good. I'll keep that in mind while I'm pinned to the Sovereign's mattress as he—"

He grabbed her arm harshly, turning her to face him, his gaze piercing down at her. "Please, for the love of God, hold your tongue. You're a lady."

Aria met his venomous stare with equal intensity. "No, I am not. You and Orren are seeing to that."

Leon barely contained the anger contorting his features and released his grip on her arm. "I didn't want this for you."

"Then you should've punched Orren squarely between the eyes when he first suggested it. You have only yourself to blame for how everything will surely end. And I hope it haunts you." Her voice was cold, menacing.

Seething, Leon could do nothing but clench his jaw in response.

"I assume you have all the information you now need. Good day." She turned swiftly, striding out of the library without once glancing in Orren's direction, joining the company of her two guardsmen without notice.

Aria was outside before she realized it, storming across the garden walkway, her thoughts a cacophony of resentment as she replayed her heated argument with Leon.

The memory of Orren's threat flashed again in her mind—his firm grip on her wrist, the cold edge in his voice as he said what would become of her family should she fail him. She shuddered, tension seizing her shoulders once more. *Eventually, I'll run out of information to give to the Rebellion, and I can't risk revealing the Sovereign's weaknesses. I can't be used as a pawn in their twisted political games.*

"Is everything alright, Lady Aria?" one of the guards behind her asked, his concern tugging her from her thoughts. She realized only then that she had stopped walking.

"I'm," She clenched her fist tightly, fingers digging into the fabric of her skirt, avoiding the gaze of her guardsman. "I'm fine." She resumed walking, her expression hardening. *I need to start making my plans now. I can't just sit here waiting for everything to unravel. If I can outmaneuver Orren and the Sovereign, my family will be safe. But it has to be flawless—calculated. There's no room for error.*

* * *

The night had settled softly over the palace, draping the world in shades of deep blue and silver. Moonlight filtered through the tall windows, illuminating Rylik's suite with a gentle glow, while the flickering torches along the walls cast dancing shadows. The hearth crackled quietly, adding warmth to the otherwise calm and cozy atmosphere.

As Aria walked slowly around the room, her fingers brushed the surface of the delicate flowering plants perched on the windowsill. She leaned in closer, smiling pleasantly as she noted their steady growth. Turning her gaze away, she wandered over to Rylik's cabinets, her curiosity piqued. A row of various potions caught her eye, neatly lined up, each one hinting at mysteries yet to be discovered. Among them, she recognized a few whimsical ones from the *Alchemical Wonders* shop in town—potions Rylik had described as being procured by paying a small boy to fetch them for him.

Her fingers hesitated above a particularly striking white potion before settling on a red one. Memories of the shop rushed back, and with an absent-mindedness, she reached for the alluring red vial.

"Pyra," a deep voice interrupted, smooth yet commanding, as black shadow magic snaked around her wrist, halting her movement. Rylik's hand gripped her own, his broad chest solid against her back, his breath hot against her neck, carrying a warning that sent a shiver down her spine. "What are you doing?"

Aria gasped, surprise jolting through her as she stumbled backward into him, feeling the unyielding wall of his body.

He chuckled softly, turning her to face him, his eyes glinting with amusement as he secured her other hand, studying her intently. "Were you wanting to drink another potion?"

Heat rushed to her cheeks at the closeness, the familiar woodsy scent of him enveloping her senses, transporting her back to that morning when he had her pinned against the wall. She forced air into her lungs, stammering, "I—I wouldn't mind it. However, that red potion. Why do you have it?"

Rylik's gaze sharpened, a sly smile playing on his lips. "You recognize it?"

"It looks like a love potion." She hesitated, the implications of her words hanging in the air like a heavy fog. "That is what it is, isn't it?"

He laughed, a low sound that sent a wave of exhilaration coursing through her. "My, how observant you are." His gaze roamed over her as his hand drifted to lightly graze her waist. "Now, what would the Sovereign want with a love potion, I wonder?" His voice dipped, enticing and dark. "Perhaps I have someone I wouldn't mind having entirely bent to my will, bound to me, desperate to serve my every desire." His eyes flicked to her lips, the temptation palpable as he lingered in the moment. "Willing to satisfy me in every way, as often and as passionately as I would require it."

Aria swallowed hard, her heart thumping erratically. "You wouldn't do anything like that, would you, Sovereign?"

"Oh, wouldn't I?" His smile was dark and daunting, sending ripples of nervous excitement coursing through her.

Rylik drew near, their faces barely inches apart, his breath brushing against hers. The world around them faded, leaving only the two of them in this taut stillness.

Aria's lids fell softly over her eyes, her body instinctively leaning toward him, nearly giving in to her impulses.

Just as she felt she might drown in the moment, he pulled back, deftly snatching a potion from the shelf behind her. With a soft laugh, he presented a golden-liquid potion into her palm. "You may be an astute healer, Aria, but you are no alchemist. That red potion is not a love potion. But, I can see why you might've thought so."

Embarrassment washed over her, realizing how close she had come to abandoning all rationale. "If it isn't a love potion, then what is it?" she asked, glancing at him from the corner of her eye, her curiosity piqued despite her flustered state.

Rylik raised a finger to his lips in a playful shushing manner. "It's a secret," he said, his voice a teasing whisper that only served to increase her nervousness.

Anxiously, she contemplated, thinking perhaps it would be better to not pry further.

"Care to drink the one you have in your hand?" he asked, gesturing to the vial she held.

Aria looked down at the gilded tonic glinting in the firelight, her curiosity getting the better of her. "Sure, I suppose so." She uncorked the potion, eyeing him cautiously. "What does it do?"

Rylik leaned back casually, his hands tucked behind his back. "It's meant to give you pleasant dreams. Don't worry, though. It isn't a sleeping potion. But, whenever you do fall asleep tonight, you can expect to sleep well."

"Well, I could use some sweet dreams." She shrugged nonchalantly, then drank down the liquid, unaware of the sly glint in his eyes.

"Whoa there," he cautioned with mock seriousness, his voice casually impassive. "You only need a little of it."

She pulled the vial away from her mouth, half of it already consumed. "It tastes sweet." A smile danced on her lips as she admired the vial before handing it back to him. "Like honey almost."

Rylik accepted the vial gingerly and tucked it into his pocket, "Because it's so costly, the children of noblemen usually only place one or two drops on their tongue each night to ensure a good sleep."

"Oh, I didn't know that I wasn't supposed to drink the entire thing." Humiliation crept into her cheeks.

"Don't feel embarrassed," he replied with a kind, roguish smile. "I probably should've told you first."

"Well, thank you for the tonic," she wiggled her fingers playfully, her anticipation bubbling over. "I'm ready to heal you and get to bed. Apparently, I have a good night ahead of me."

"Indeed, you do." Rylik opened his tunic just enough to expose his chest, awaiting her touch.

"How are my healings leaving you?" she asked, her palm pressing gently against his warm skin. "Are they lasting you long enough? Are they losing effect?"

Rylik inhaled deeply, savoring the warmth radiating from her. "I'm glad you asked. I think we should have two of these a day. I have not yet begun to feel that dreaded cold today, likely due to your unexpected gift this morning."

Her heart soared at the praise as she looked into his eyes, a radiant glow emanating from her being. "I don't mind if we do this in the mornings, too. I'm pleased that you've fared so well today." She closed her eyes, a serene sense of contentment washing over her as she poured her warmth and energy into him. The connection between them was otherworldly, her magic flowing like a golden river, wrapping them both in its embrace. It was a moment of quiet intimacy, something she found herself growing more and more comfortable with—until she felt his touch.

Rylik's hands, slow and deliberate, lifted from his sides, their fingers grazing over her back before settling firmly between her shoulder blades. His touch was light but grounding, a silent reassurance as his grip gently tightened, drawing her body closer to his. The movement was subtle, but the intent behind it was unmistakable.

Aria's gaze flickered open, the proximity of him overwhelming her like a tidal wave. *Is the Sovereign hugging me?!* she thought in disbelief, her mind scrambling to make sense of the unexpected tenderness. The heat of a blush spread rapidly across her face, her cheeks flushed a deep red as she risked a glance up. His eyes were closed, his expression peaceful—almost defenseless—as though savoring the closeness they now shared. Her pulse quickened, a chaotic drumbeat in her chest, as if her heart could no longer keep up with the conflicting emotions swirling within her.

His arms still encircled her, protective and steadfast, as if he were shielding them both from a storm neither could see but both could feel. Aria's face burned like fire, her skin tingling from where his hands rested against her back. She was breathless, caught between the desire to stay in his arms and the anxious flutter of wondering when—if—he would let her go.

Rylik's eyes opened slowly, his gaze dropping to meet hers. The frazzled expression on her face made the corners of his lips twitch, amusement flickering in his eyes. A slow, knowing smile spread across his face, not unkind but teasing in a way that made her heart stutter. He held the moment for a beat longer, letting the intimate atmosphere between them repose, before his grip on her softened. With a gentle release, he stepped back, putting space between them once more, though the warmth remained.

Aria hesitated for a moment, almost missing his touch as she bit the interior of her lip. Lowering her head, she stepped back from him, letting out a shaky breath instead of words.

Rylik's gaze was satisfied as he looked her over, something mischievous in his eyes. "Have a good night, Aria. Sleep well."

She nodded, unable to form any coherent response as her heart pounded in her ears. With a light wave, she scurried from the room, her last reserve of energy propelling her through the door.

* * *

A little while later, Aria nestled into her bed, wrapped in the soft embrace of her new nightgown, one of many the Sovereign had gifted her. The sheets felt luxurious against her skin, their warmth inviting her to relax. As she settled in, a blush crept across her cheeks, igniting a fond recollection of the tender embrace she had shared with Rylik not that long ago. Pulling the covers over her eyes, she tried to hide her face from his memory.

If I am to have such good dreams tonight, I wonder if I'll be dreaming about that hug again. Because, god knows I can't afford to keep getting closer to him like this. Not when I still have to abandon him. A bittersweet smile spread across her lips as she surrendered to the comfort of her bed, her eyes fluttering closed, cocooned in the sheets.

CHAPTER 25

RYLIK

Rylik chuckled to himself after the door to their suite had closed behind Aria, leaving him alone with the echoes of their shared moment. *Had I known her reaction would be so delightful from a mere hug, I'd have done it sooner. God knows I've wanted to. And so much more.* A sigh escaped his lips as he turned away from the door, his thoughts still on the warmth of her presence, and approached his bed.

He reached into his pocket, pulling out the small vial he had slipped away earlier. The golden liquid shimmered enticingly in the firelight that danced around his room. Rylik mused to himself as he removed the cork and drank the last of the potion. *The Dream Weaver. Quite the little potion. While it is true that some privileged children use drops at night for sweet dreams, men have long since used it for other purposes as well.* A satisfied smile crept across his face as he set the empty vial down on his desk with a soft clink. *To see into another person's dreams, to view their innermost desires and secrets. It's been a tool of information gathering for longer than I've been alive.*

As he began undressing, the silence of the room enveloped him. He removed his boots and armor with ease, his movements fluid and practiced. *I almost feel a little guilty at how naively she fell for such a snare.* He gently eased into his mattress, a sly smirk playing on his lips as he closed his eyes. *Almost.*

A few moments passed in the quiet as Rylik lay in the darkness of his room, the stillness enveloping him like a thick fog as he prepared for the familiar ritual. He closed his eyes, exhaling slowly to center himself, allowing the stasis to seep into his bones. In the void behind his eyelids, shadows coiled and twisted, but he remained undeterred, for he knew the way through the murky depths of his own mind. With practiced ease, he reached within, searching for the magical golden thread that would lead him to Aria's consciousness.

It was there, faint at first, like a glimmer of sunlight breaking through an overcast sky. Rylik latched onto it, feeling its warmth pulse beneath his fingertips, a beacon in the darkness. As he followed the thread, the surroundings began to shift, colors blooming around him like wildflowers after a long winter. The deeper he delved, the more vibrant the hues became—fiery reds and deep blues intermingling in a dance of emotion, hinting at the complexities of her inner world.

Yet his approach was methodical, each pull of the thread leading him closer to her thoughts, to her dreams, where he would tread softly like a predator on the hunt. The excitement hummed beneath his calm exterior; he was not here for wonder, but for insight. He envisioned the labyrinth of her psyche ahead, a territory he was eager to explore, confident in his ability to navigate its twists and turns. As the last remnants of darkness faded, he braced himself for the intricate tapestry of her mind, ready to uncover its secrets.

Her dreamscape unfurled in a flourish of vibrant flowers, a kaleidoscope of colors stretching as far as her eyes could see. The meadow she'd conjured was alive with hues he had never imagined, the air sweet with their fragrance. He watched, invisible to her for now, not far from Aria's turned back. She looked up in amazement at the sky, painted a deep blue and punctuated by fluffy white clouds. As she turned aside, her heart swelled at the sight of her parents standing just a short distance away, their farmhouse and the village she had grown up in glowing softly behind them.

They beckoned her forward, their smiles wide and welcoming.

Overcome with apparent joy, she ran toward them, wrapping her arms around them in an embrace that felt like home, savoring their familiar scent and the gentle strokes of their hands through her hair.

Suddenly, the scene shifted and Rylik found himself standing in a crowd amidst a bustling plaza. Aria was in the middle of the square far in front of him, adorned in a stunning dress that shimmered in the sunlight. Minstrels played a jaunty tune as the townspeople around her began to dance in unison.

As the music swelled around her, wrapping her in a warm embrace of sound, Aria swayed in Leon's arms. The vibrant colors of the flowers and banners in the plaza danced with the melody of the singers, each note stirring the petals into a delicate ballet, while the minstrels played in harmony, their instruments echoing the ethereal tune.

Yet, a short distance away, concealed among the throng, Rylik remained like a shadow, his customary black attire contrasting sharply with the brilliance around him. His arms were folded across his chest, but the tension in his posture spoke of an inner struggle. Though it was only a dream, the sight of Leon's arms around her made his chest burn with frustration and jealousy. He stiffened, his arms dropping to his sides as a scowl crossed his face, shadowing his features. Tension coiled within him like a serpent, ready to strike as he prepared to approach them. The joyous melody resonating in the plaza now felt like a distant memory, eclipsed by the storm brewing in his heart.

Aria suddenly stopped dancing with Leon, her expression turning severe when she noticed his attention waning. Behind her, she could see Maven approaching, wearing a luxurious dress. Her brows furrowed together as she pushed back from him forcefully.

"I don't care what you do with your life, Leontias," she said with a tremble in her tone. "But, I do care that you tricked me into what I did with my own."

"What do you mean? You wanted this as much as I do," he said, his expression becoming stern.

"Why?" she asked, voice breaking as her eyes filled with sadness. "Why, after all these years, do you still not know me?

How can you look at me and think you know what I want? You were all I wanted for so long."

Leon was silent as he observed her, the music around them fading into a hush.

"It's fine that you love her. I don't care," she said, a tear slipping down her cheek. "But, I don't want anything to do with you anymore. You don't even value my life. That much is evident." She waved a hand through his body like the apparition he was, watching him vanish like glitter into the wind.

Rylik stood just before her, appearing as though he were formed entirely from the darkness, his pensive eyes scanning her face.

She stood still in the moonlit square, captivated by his approach. "Sovereign?"

"Hello, Pyra." A subtle smirk played on his lips as he took in her exquisite appearance, the elegant dress still clinging to her form.

"I cannot keep consoling myself with you here in dreams," she murmured in embarrassment, turning away from him. "Night after night of this is becoming torture when I awaken. Please, Sovereign, just go before I lose my self restraint—"

Before Aria could finish her words, Orren materialized behind her like a dark specter, his presence suffocating the air around them. He lunged forward, grabbing her with an iron grip, wrenching her further away from Rylik in one swift, brutal motion. Rylik's sharp, cold eyes widened in disbelief, his breath hitching at the sight of Orren—a looming shadow—holding a struggling Aria in his grasp, her terror evident.

"Fulfill your duty, Aria." Orren's voice was a low growl, fierce and unbending. His eyes blazed with a ruthless intensity as he squeezed her arm painfully, eliciting a whimper from her lips.

"Stop!" Aria trembled, her voice cracking as she pleaded with him, every fiber of her being screaming for escape. She was helpless, caught in a web of fear and despair, the threat of violence hanging heavily in the air like a storm cloud.

In a flash of raw, unrestrained rage, Rylik's shadow magic flared to life, dark tendrils swirling around him like a tempest. With a furious determination, he unleashed his power, expelling the image of Orren from view. The world around them warped and twisted, the very essence of reality bending to his will.

In an instant, Rylik pulled her swiftly into his arms, the heat of his body a stark contrast to the cold dread that had surrounded them moments before. His heart raced as he scanned the plaza, his instincts on high alert for any further disturbances. The air bristled with tension, every shadow lurking in the corners seeming to pulse with potential danger. The urgent need to protect Aria surged within him, igniting a fierce determination to shield her from the darkness that threatened to consume them both.

As Aria embraced him, a warm, golden light sparked between them, casting a radiant glow that banished the darkness surrounding their world. It was as if the very essence of hope had ignited, illuminating their hearts and binding them together in that fleeting moment. Rylik was taken aback by the intensity of her gesture, the way she clung to him as though he were her lifeline, a refuge from the chaos that lurked just beyond their shared warmth.

The scene shifted once more, transforming into a stately vessel adrift on the moonlit sea, its silhouette outlined in silver by the glow of the crescent moon. The ship swayed with a tranquil rhythm, its towering masts reaching toward the heavens, sails hanging like ghostly whispers in the night. Above, the sky unfurled as a vast, celestial canvas, spangled with stars that gleamed like scattered diamonds cast across an infinite expanse. A large, silvery moon hung low, casting a soft, ethereal glow over the caravel, while delicate lanterns flickered to life around them, their gentle light dancing in the cool breeze like fireflies at dusk. Her dream world felt truly enchanted, suspended in time as if to hold this moment sacred.

Rylik glanced around, memories washing over him like the waves lapping against the hull. He remembered how Aria had, in a moment of intoxicated whimsy, spoken of her desire to put her parents on a boat and sail away into the horizon, leaving behind all worries and fears. It was a longing for freedom that now felt painfully close. With a tenderness that belied his usual stoicism, he pulled back gently, his fingers brushing through her hair, savoring the silken strands that flowed like moonlight itself. "Are you running away, Aria?" he asked, his voice low and soft, as if afraid to disturb the fragile magic surrounding them.

"I have to," she replied, her gaze piercing through the surface of his calm facade, sadness flickering in her eyes like dew on morning grass. "Otherwise, they won't be safe. I won't be safe." The weight of her words hung heavy in the air, her vulnerability laid bare before him, drawing forth a fierce protectiveness within his chest.

"I will ensure your safety, and that of your parents," he said, his voice firm and unwavering, a promise that echoed against the soft lull of the waves.

But Aria tensed, a bitter edge creeping into her voice as she looked up at him, her expression a blend of longing and disbelief. "You are surely a dream, not the real Sovereign. He would never say such words." With a determined shake of her head, she pulled away from him, turning on her heel, the gleaming lanterns peppering shadows that danced like fleeting memories between them.

Rylik's voice carried a subtle undercurrent of sympathy as he reached out for her arm. "Don't be so certain of that. If you keep my secret, dear, and heal my blight, I would give you almost anything you desire."

A soft laugh escaped Aria's lips, but it was tinged with bitterness as she shook her head. "I'm your prisoner," she scowled, each word tainted with a mixture of hurt and defiance. "I know what we have is transactional. It's in your best interests to ensure that I'm at least somewhat happy here. It's easier that way. I'm easier to manipulate." Her voice rose, likely fueled by the injustice of her real world situation, and the air around them simmered with her growing frustration.

Rylik smiled knowingly, but it only served to stoke the flames of her anger. "You are more cunning than I give you credit for," he replied, his tone calm, as if he were discussing a mere game of strategy rather than the emotional battlefield they occupied. *I'm so tired of playing this game*, she thought, her voice echoing around him amidst her ethereal world, unaware that he could hear her. *I'm so tired of these smothering feelings of being trapped.* The injustice burned inside her, a raging fire fueled by helplessness and fury.

"You don't deny it, then?" She whirled to face him, her cold scowl transforming into a fierce glare that could cut through stone. Her heart raced, pounding like war drums in her chest. "You only want what serves to benefit you." The accusation rolled off her tongue like poison, her hands curling into fists at her sides as she fought to keep her composure. "Well, I can do that too."

Rylik raised an eyebrow, intrigue dancing in his darkened eyes. "And what is that—"

Before Rylik could finish his thought, Aria surged forward like a tempest, her hand cupping the side of his face as she pressed her lips against his in a deep, fervent kiss that ignited the air between them. *I can be selfish too,* her thoughts echoed around them as her tongue sought his own. *All I have is this moment, and there is nothing to hold me back from it. Until I awaken, I will find solace in a fantasy of my own making.*

For a heartbeat, Rylik was frozen, astonished by her boldness. But that astonishment quickly melted into a warmth that spread through him like wildfire, consuming every ounce of restraint. His eyes softened as he kissed her back, surrendering to the moment. The world around them faded into a blur of colors and sounds, reduced to the singularity of their connection. He backed her against the cabin wall of the ship, the rough wood pressing against her back, a harmonizing divergence to the feverish intensity of their embrace. He squeezed her waist, reveling in the depth and pleasure of their union, each heartbeat echoing like a drum in the stillness of the night.

Aria moaned softly into his mouth, the sound reverberating in his chest, sending shivers down his spine. Her body responded eagerly, igniting a fierce desire within him as she pulled at the fabric of his sleeves, desperate for him to come closer. Every second spent wrapped in his arms ignited an urgency that coursed through her veins, a fire that threatened to consume her whole.

Rylik returned her affections with an intensity born of desperation, pouring every unspoken desire and longing into the kiss, drowning in the fervor of their connection. His hands roamed her body as if memorizing every curve, every contour, savoring the taste of her passion as it mingled with the salt of the sea air. Each breath she took was shaky, fueled by a longing so profound it left her breathless, as if the very essence of her soul were laid bare before him.

With frantic urgency, he yanked at the laces at the back of her bodice, the constricting fabric tearing in a chaotic rush, giving way like a suffocating weight, leaving her gasping for breath as she moaned again in ecstasy.

Rylik swallowed hard, suddenly aware of the reality of their situation, the intensity of what he was doing, despite her believing it to be a dream. "I think that it is time for you to wake up, Little Pyra." His voice was thick with unfulfilled desire, a low rumble that sent a thrill through her.

"I'm not ready. We've barely begun." She pulled him in close again, her lips brushing against his in a plaintive plea for more, igniting a spark that threatened to blaze out of control.

His lips hovered over hers, a tantalizing breath apart, and he growled softly in frustration, wishing to remain lost in this intoxicating moment with her, and consequences be damned. But duty clawed at him, pulling him back even as his heart ached to stay.

In that brief, electric pause, everything hung in the balance—a fragile thread woven of desire and desperation, and he sliced through it, jarring himself back into his waking reality.

CHAPTER 26

RYLIK

The morning light cut through the window, piercing Rylik's eyes as they snapped open, his breath caught in his throat. He bolted upright, the wild thrum of his heart pounding so fiercely he thought it might tear through his chest. His tunic clung haphazardly to his broad, muscular frame, the fabric twisted, mirroring the chaos in his mind. His hair was a disheveled mess, falling in unruly waves around his face, but he barely noticed. All he could focus on was the lingering heat on his lips, the vivid memory of her kiss, searing and reckless, and the effect it now had between his legs.

He raised a hand to his mouth, his fingers brushing over his lips as if to remind himself that it had been a dream. But gods, it had felt so real. Her desperation. Her fire. The way she had sought to claim him with no hesitation, no fear. He inhaled sharply, a quivering breath escaping him as he sank into the guilty pleasure of it all. *I am going to hell*, he thought bitterly, savoring the memory like a forbidden indulgence.

His gaze drifted to the adjoining suite door, and in that instant, his entire body tightened with need. His hands, restless at his sides, yearned to touch her, to hold her, to confirm what the dream had ignited. Without thinking, he moved toward the door, every step filled with the weight of his desires pulling him closer. His hand hovered over the handle, his mind and heart warring. *What am I doing?* His chest tightened, breath ragged. *Taking what is mine, right? She wanted it.* His pulse thundered in his ears, and his fingers brushed the cold brass, the temptation of it nearly undoing him.

He clenched his jaw as the fire of his desire warred against his reason. The heat from her dream-kiss still simmered through his veins, clouding his judgment. His fingers curled tighter around the handle, his knuckles white. *She didn't want to stop. She wanted me.* The weight of those thoughts was intoxicating, pulling him deeper into the abyss. *She would've given herself over to me entirely. She was practically begging me to finish what she started. And I should've.*

With a low, guttural sound, he wrenched the door open and stepped into the bathing room. The cold marble floor beneath his bare feet barely registered as he moved swiftly, his entire being drawn to her. The stillness of the room around him was in stark contrast to the storm raging within him—desire clashing with self-restraint, lust fighting against conscience.

He halted at the threshold of her suite, standing at a razor's edge of reason and madness. His hand lifted, unsteady as it reached for the handle. His heart pounded, each beat a painful reminder of what lay just beyond that door. *Move your damn hand, Rylik.* The thought echoed in his mind, but his body felt frozen, caught in the undertow of his own desires. *Enter that suite and make her beg for more.* His breath came in short, labored bursts as he fought himself. The weight of his emotions was suffocating, as if the air itself conspired against him.

With a frustrated growl, he let his hand fall, defeated. He spun away from the door, his pulse still throbbing in his ears as he stormed back into his own room. His steps were harsh, uneven, every inch of him strung tight and rigid with pent-up frustration. Reaching the chair, he gripped the back of it, his knuckles whitening as he squeezed. His eyes screwed shut as he fought to steady his breathing, his chest heaving as he forced himself to let go. *I need a long soak in a cold lake. What the hell is wrong with me?* The thought was bitter, edged with guilt.

Staggering over to the armoire, he yanked it open, hoping that the mindless act of dressing himself would somehow pull him back from the brink. He knew he was in trouble—knew that today would be anything but easy with her. It would undoubtedly drive him mad to be in the same room with her, knowing what lay just beneath her chaste exterior—the desperate woman that wished to be stripped bare beneath him. Moistening his lips with his tongue, he let a heavy sigh escape him. Today would be a torment, and he would somehow have to find his composure before he completely unraveled in her presence.

* * *

The daylight poured into the grand dining hall, casting a soft glow over the king as he leisurely buttered his bread, humming a jaunty tune in time with the clatter of cutlery. He was clearly thrilled about the upcoming Summit of Realms starting at dusk that evening. The king was apathetic to Rylik's familiar presence, his mind focused on the pleasures of the day ahead.

Rylik stood nearby, his eyes unfocused, thoughts pulled toward Aria. He had almost sought her out this morning, for healing, but ultimately resisted. The memory of last night's dream—so vivid, so powerful—hung over him like a storm cloud, threatening to break his resolve.

His fingers dug into the armor on his forearms, hands clasped behind his back, tense.

Somehow, the thought of being alone with her so soon after that dream sends me into a mad panic, he thought, eyes moving restlessly across the room, *If she even looks at me this morning, I'll be too tempted to drag her to my bed and lose the last of my self-restraint. No, as much as I'd love to feel the soothing touch of her healing, I'll have to forego it for now. At least until I've cooled off.*

His train of thought was abruptly cut short by the distant sound of angry shouting. Rylik's head snapped up, eyes locking onto the large double doors of the hall as the sound grew louder. His body shifted, taking a few steps closer to the king, his face now set in steely resolve. The door was thrown open with force, and in stormed Lord Orren, his face a mask of fury, a crumpled piece of parchment gripped tightly in his hand.

Orren barely spared Rylik a glance, bowing swiftly to the king.

"Ah, good morning, Orren!" The king greeted him with a broad grin, still cheerful as ever.

"My king, please forgive the intrusion." Orren's voice was tight with anger, and he lifted the crumpled parchment in his hand. "I've just received word." He slammed the paper down onto the table in front of the king, his face barely containing his rage. "My manor! It has been burned to the ground, your majesty. An act of arson—of treason!"

The king's brow raised, but the concern on his face was mild at best as he set down his butter knife and took a bite of his roll. "Oh, that is unfortunate," he muttered, mouth full, hardly affected by the news. "Which one was it?" he asked, licking honey from his fingertips.

Rylik fought the urge to laugh at the king's indifference. *I'm already feeling much better*, he thought, satisfaction curling through him. His shoulders loosened, and his earlier tension melted into calm, dark amusement. Orren's manor had been his target, and the sight of the man so livid was sweeter than any morning diversion. Orren's manor in Eldvane had of course been his doing—his plan executed perfectly and entirely untraceable back to him.

Orren, clearly barely containing himself, seethed. "The manor in Eldvane, Sire. I have yet to identify the culprit behind the attack. But I suspect it has something to do with the Rebellion. It's no secret that someone like myself, so close to your inner circle, would be targeted."

The king continued chewing, scanning around his plate observantly as he replied with a sigh, "Yes, that does sound serious, old friend." He spied a napkin and used it to dry his fingers. "But I do think you'll feel better tonight at the Summit. There will be beautiful women and the finest ale. It will lift your spirits."

Orren's red-bearded face flared with barely-suppressed fury. "Respectfully, your majesty, I doubt my wrath will be abated until I've found the one responsible. Might I request a few of your men to aid in the interrogations?"

The king waved a hand dismissively, his voice bored. "Yes, yes. Take what men you need. But you will be at the Summit."

Orren stiffly bowed his head. "Yes, your grace."

"Be excused," the king added, his eyes now drawn to a pastry dish just past his own plate.

Orren turned on his heel, leaving the room in a huff. Rylik felt the weight on his chest lighten with satisfaction. The sight of Orren so incensed by his ruined estate filled him with quiet amusement, his shoulders fully relaxing. *Ah, if it might only stay this way for a few moments longer, that I could truly savor it. I feel like I can breathe again.*

The king beckoned him closer with a buttery finger. Rylik smoothly approached, leaning down to listen.

"Sovereign, I've been thinking," the king began, a mischievous glint in his eye. "The imperial healer — Aria — I think I'd like her at my side tonight."

Rylik's gaze darkened slightly, though he kept his expression neutral.

"I know the Summit is mainly for people to bestow their gifts upon me, but it would be a nice display to present Aria and her healing gifts tonight," the king continued, reclining in his chair, a scheming look in his green eyes. "Perhaps she can heal a few people and maybe garner even more gifts. Wouldn't that be impressive?"

Rylik didn't need to mull it over. It couldn't be allowed to happen, yet it looked as if Kaldros had already made up his mind. Annoyance mounted into his chest, wondering just how much this might test his already waning patience with the man.

The king licked his lips as if tasting some savory idea. "See to it that the healer is beside me tonight. And have her adorn herself, won't you? I want all to know the prize I have in my possession."

Rylik's pulse quickened, fury simmering under his calm exterior. His voice, though level, was laced with warning. "I would be more than happy to arrange that, your majesty. However, I trust you haven't forgotten about her curse."

The king dismissed the thought with a wave of his hand. "Yes, yes, I know. A man can still dream, can't he?"

The word 'dream' clawed at Rylik's composure, dragging him

back into his own recent reveries—of Aria, her lips against his in the vivid dream that tormented him. He could almost feel the way her tongue had moved against his own, her insatiable, lurid hunger threatening to consume him whole. His eyes snapped back open, forcing the memory down as he briefly shifted his attention to the sharp knife resting on the napkin beside the king's plate. He kept his hands restrained behind him, fighting the urge to lift the blade to the king's throat. "Dream, yes, but withholding oneself from temptation may present its own challenges." His words were wanton, cold. "I speak only out of concern for you, your majesty."

The king grumbled, clearly annoyed. "If I'm truly bothered, I'll summon a concubine."

Rylik inclined his head. "Very well, your excellency."

A sly smile danced across the king's lips as he stroked his beard in thought. "I want her in red and gold. I want her draped in finery. I want her radiant so that all that may look upon her will know that this priceless asset is my plaything."

Rylik's jaw tightened, his chest heaving with barely-contained rage. His breath shallowed as he gave a passive nod. "As you desire."

The king, lost in his own salacious fantasies, dismissed him with a wave. "Good. See to it that she's prepared to my liking. You're dismissed."

Bowing at the waist, Rylik vanished from the room in a swirling cloud of black mist, reappearing in the empty corridor outside. His cape caught the tendrils of his shadow magic as it faded into the cold air. His steps quickened, boots pounding against the stone floor, each step carrying the weight of his fury.

If he were not such a formidable opponent, I would have slit his throat there at the dinner table.

The king's disgusting words echoed in his mind, fueling the fire that churned within him. The thought of the king, eyes leering, demanding that Aria dress in something meant to feed his desires churned Rylik's stomach with a white-hot fury. Rylik's jaw clenched tighter as he stormed down the hall, his fists curling into tight balls at his sides, his boots pounding against the cold stone floor with each heavy step.

He has been worse than a blight upon my life—the very source of agony—and now he wishes to toy with his new "plaything," does he?

The torches on the walls flickered as he passed, the shadows around him writhing, thickening with his anger, responding to the tempest within him. The castle's air grew colder, oppressive, bending beneath the weight of his power—unleashed in subtle, dangerous waves.

The urge to strike, to kill, surged within him. But he forced it down. *Soon. I will savor his last dying gasps as I watch the light leave his eyes, my blade running hot with his vile blood.* Rylik vowed silently, his icy eyes flickering with lethal intent. *His time will come.*

CHAPTER 27

ARIA

Daylight flooded Aria's room, illuminating the soft blush on her cheeks as she lay staring up at the ceiling, lost in the remnants of her vivid dream. Memories of kissing the Sovereign flickered through her mind, the way he had torn her bodice in a moment of passion, igniting a longing that swelled in her heart with agonizing pleasure. She smoothed a hand across her chest, attempting to stifle the frantic pounding of her heart. A small whimper escaped her lips as she closed her eyes, surrendering to the intoxicating recollection. *I am a filthy little thing.*

Groaning softly, she rolled over onto her stomach, burying her face into her pillows, the silk and cotton muffling the sounds of her disgraceful hunger. Time slipped away as she lost herself in the warm embrace of her bedding. Eventually, the need for air tugged at her, and she flopped onto her back, opening her chest to the sunlight streaming in.

Aria's eyes fluttered weakly, her resolve fading with each passing moment. *Where is my focus? I'm supposed to run away, to develop my convoluted escape plans. I'm deluding myself.* She winced, squeezing her eyes shut against the grief that threatened to consume her. *The Sovereign will never be on that boat with me, much less anywhere else, seizing me, claiming me.* Blushing at the audacity of her own thoughts, she dragged a hand across her face in distress. *Get it together, Aria! The best you will ever have is that dream. And that sinfully delicious golden potion.* She bit her lip, her curiosity piqued. *I wonder, if I would've drunk the entire bottle, would I have been able to see things to their end?*

A yearning squirm coursed through her body, her loins tender and saturated, a shameful testament to the craving she had just indulged in. She felt needy, languishing in her bed alone, and covered her lips to stifle a moan at the memory of his tongue against her own. *I should ask him if he has any more of it. Or perhaps I could use some of my gold to purchase some on a trip into the capital. I know after I've escaped I'll want the comfort of a good dream, since I can never have the real thing.*

With determination igniting within her, she edged over the side of the bed, anticipation swirling in her chest as she prepared for a hot bath to soothe her nerves and mounting desires. She would have to deal with the shame of her predicament later. For now, all she needed was the memory of his body pressed against hers, his fingertips burning against her skin. A fantasy was all she could afford of him, so she would not deny herself that.

* * *

Several hours later, after her day had already begun, Aria now found herself back in her own suite. She let out a slow, steady breath, as she gazed into her reflection in the mirror. *Today hasn't gone at all how I thought it might.* She traced the gilded embroidery running along the bodice of her ornate red dress, her fingertips brushing the intricate golden vines and floral patterns that spread like creeping tendrils. She had intended to visit the Sovereign's chambers to heal his blight. Yet when she'd arrived that morning, he was already gone, perhaps off to some shadowy errand she hadn't been told about.

By the time she'd reached the apothecary to fetch herbs and tinctures for her morning tasks, one of the guardsmen—one she didn't recognize—had intercepted her, informing her with stiff formality that she was needed back at the palace. There was to be a fitting, no explanation offered. She'd thought perhaps it was another gown for an evening feast, something simple and appropriate, but when she'd seen the yards of crimson fabric draped over the seamstress' arm, her stomach had churned.

Why this? Why now? Her thoughts had been scattered ever since, even as maids fussed over her in her chambers, weaving intricate braids into her hair, pinning jeweled clips into place as though she were a royal herself. Hours had passed in a blur until she found herself standing before this reflection—transformed into something entirely different, someone entirely different.

The opulent scarlet gown she wore shimmered softly in the afternoon daylight, its sumptuous fabric whispering of luxury with every ripple. Intricate golden embroidery swirled across the bodice and cascaded down the voluminous skirt, resembling vines of molten gold in an eternal dance. The craftsmanship was beyond anything she had ever imagined, and as she admired the sweetheart neckline and puffed sleeves, she felt a reverence in how the dress hugged her curves. The gown flared dramatically at the hips and flowed into a grand, sweeping train, its weight grounding her—perhaps an omen of what lay ahead.

Moving closer to the mirror, Aria ran her fingers over the embroidered vines climbing from her waist to her shoulders, the gold glinting and flashing sparkles of light along her reflection.

She hadn't expected to wear anything so grand, so regal. And now, she had been told, she would sit beside the king at the annual Summit of Realms.

The thought made her stomach twist once again, though this time it was pure discomfort. *I hate him.* The words echoed in her mind as she glanced at her reflection one last time, knowing full well she could not refuse the command. She had no choice, no say in the matter. He hadn't even exchanged a word with her to this point, much less even spared a passing glance in her direction. Yet, now, he was making her into a prize he could display at his side? Why? And yet, despite the growing knot of dread in her chest, she forced herself to remain composed.

Her eyes flicked toward the door as it creaked open, the faint sound breaking her concentration on her thoughts. A sharp rush of cold air slipped into the room, but it did nothing to quell the heat now rising within her. Rylik entered, cloaked in his signature black attire, the long cape trailing behind him like shadows come to life. His obsidian armor, threaded with silver, caught the light just enough to hint at the deadly power concealed beneath his poised exterior.

The moment he crossed the threshold, the atmosphere shifted, the air thickening with something unspoken, magnetic. His gaze locked onto her, a searing, intense stare that seemed to strip her bare, laying her soul open to him. He did not just look at her—he devoured her with his eyes, as if each curve, each delicate line of her form, was etched into his memory, a vision of beauty he would never allow himself to forget.

Her heart raced under the weight of his stare, every second stretching between them, fraught with unspoken desire. The room felt too small, too intimate, with him standing there like a hunter who had finally cornered his prey. His eyes darkened, a slow burn of raw hunger flickering in their depths as he closed the door behind him. The soft click reverberated like the final tether snapping between them, leaving nothing but a shared heat in the silence.

Her pulse echoed in her ears, the memory of last night's dream unfurling vividly in her mind—the feel of his hands on her skin, his mouth consuming hers with a hunger she hadn't known she could possess. Her body remembered even if her mind fought to stay grounded. Her cheeks flushed a soft shade of pink, a whisper of her inner turmoil and the forbidden desire curling deep within. But no matter how hard she tried, she couldn't look away from him. He was a living, breathing temptation, and in his gaze, she saw her undoing.

"You weren't in your room this morning," she finally managed, her voice soft but steady.

Rylik's eyes gleamed with a hungry intensity as he regarded her. "Be grateful for that." His voice was a low, dangerous purr as he took slow, deliberate steps toward her, each one steeped in dark, insatiable desire. "How did you sleep?"

Her face warmed into a deeper shade of garnet, unaware of the satisfaction his smirk held at the sight of it. "It was a good rest. I think I might like to purchase more of it. Maybe we could go into town this weekend and get some?"

He let out a soft, dark laugh, the sound laced with intent. "You wish for more?" He closed the distance, his fingers grazing her sleeve delicately. "It must've been a pleasant dream. Care to tell me what it was about?"

Aria's thoughts scattered, her focus locked on the nearness of him.

The scent of him enveloped her senses like a warm embrace—heady and rich, with deep, earthy notes of aged wood mingling with the primal allure of smoldering fire. It was the intoxicating aroma of dark forests after rain, damp bark in the air, fused with the raw, smoky heat of low-burning embers.

"I'm waiting," His voice, a low and sultry whisper, sent a shiver down to her core, "to hear what your fantasies are, Pyra." His tone was teasing and dangerous, practically stealing the air from her lungs.

She closed her eyes, stepping back in a weak attempt to create space, to breathe. "Do you," her voice was faint and winded, catching her off guard, "do you know why I'm supposed to sit beside the king today at the summit? Wearing *this*?" She gestured to herself, frustration flickering in her expression.

Rylik's gaze swept over her, a flicker of restraint passing through his eyes as he drew his hands behind his back, perhaps to keep from reaching for her. Lifting his chin, he adopted a mask of indifference. "The king wishes to show you off to his potential enemies. He intends to exploit your miraculous healing magic as a demonstration—one facet of his supreme arsenal of defense."

Her brows furrowed in confusion. "I'm going to be healing people? Then why the dress?"

Rylik inhaled deeply, as though trying to steady whatever emotion was threatening to escape him. "He wants you to look resplendent," he said, his voice tight, "no doubt as some trophy of conquest."

Aria subtly clenched her teeth, her jaw shifting as her shoulders squared up slightly. "A man like him wouldn't merely put a woman in a dress like this for something so fickle."

Rylik's smile was soft but daunting, his intrigue barely masked. "You're right. There's also the matter of his interest in you."

Disgust flashed across her face, and she stepped back as though the king himself were present in the room with her.

Subtle satisfaction crept into Rylik's expression at her clear refusal. "But, please," he said with confidence, "don't concern yourself with this. I have the matter well in hand."

"Do you?" Aria's voice was tinged with anxiety, though her expression, framed by the daylight streaming through the window, held both hope and concern.

"There is nothing His Majesty does that is unseen by me," Rylik's voice carried a dangerous certainty, his words rolling over her like the slow pull of a tide, impossible to escape. His confidence was absolute, unwavering, as he stepped toward her, the space between them shrinking with each purposeful stride. The air grew heavy with his presence, the subtle power he wielded an undeniable force that pressed in on her, daring her to resist.

"And as I've said before," His voice lowered, darkened, each word a silken thread tightening around her. He leaned in closer, his breath a faint brush against her skin, igniting a fire beneath her surface. "I will play any role necessary to ensure that you remain mine alone."

His eyes gleamed with an unspoken promise, a possessive intensity that sent a tremor coursing through her. "Because no one," he paused, the measured gravity of his words sinking into her like a slow, creeping shadow, "will take what is mine."

Her heart stilled, faltering under the burden of his vow. His words echoed in her mind, dragging her back to that night in the gardens. The memory flashed vivid and sharp—Rylik slipping in and out of shadows, his expression dark and lethal as he cut down her captors with merciless precision. He had saved her, but his protection hadn't come without cost. That night, he had made the same vow, and she'd known it wasn't to free her from the invisible chains of her fate. No, it had been a declaration—if she was to be bound to anyone, it would be to *him*.

The realization should have chilled her to her core, should have sent her recoiling from the very idea of belonging to a man as dangerous as Rylik. And yet, beneath the surface, a part of her couldn't deny the strange comfort his words stirred within her. It was an instinctual, unspoken need, an attraction to the darkness that clung to him like a second skin. She wasn't ready to admit it, not even to herself, but some deep part of her felt safer under his shadow, even if it meant stepping willingly into the fire.

"I did not come here merely to escort you, Aria." Rylik's voice was smooth, his words carrying an undercurrent of mystery as he shifted the tone between them. He took a step back, as if in mercy to her beating heart. "I've also come with a gift."

Aria blinked, caught off guard as he held out his hand. In his palm, a small potion bottle glimmered, its contents swirling in alluring patterns of black liquid laced with silver streaks. She accepted the bottle, her fingers brushing against his. "What is it?" She turned it over in her hand, watching the mesmerizing way the light caught the silver.

Rylik's shadowed smile widened, his eyes full of devilry. "It's a little something that may put your mind at ease. Let's just say it has a pleasant flavor and is a tonic meant to provide comfort." He gestured with an open hand, his expression soft but unreadable. "Seeing as you are feeling quite uneasy at the day ahead, I can assure you that this little wonder will come in rather useful to negate those feelings. Please, drink."

Aria glanced between him and the bottle, her suspicion flickering briefly in her gaze. *What is he really offering me?* But something in his demeanor—a gentleness amid the enigma—prompted her to trust him. After all, he hadn't given her an unsafe potion yet. She uncorked the bottle and tipped it back, drinking its contents in one fluid motion.

Licking her lips, she blinked in surprise. "That's really delicious." Her smile blossomed, eyes wide with a mix of delight and wonder. "Thank you. I can't tell if I feel better or if I simply just like the taste."

Rylik's smile sharpened, though his tone remained velvety smooth as he extended his hand toward her. "Good, I'm glad you like it. Now, if you would please come along with me, I'll escort you to the summit."

Aria hesitated for just a heartbeat, but the pull of his presence, the strange and growing sense of comfort, beckoned her forward. With newfound resolve, she placed her hand in his, the warmth of his touch strangely reassuring.

* * *

The click of Aria's heels on the polished marble floor echoed softly through the corridor as Rylik escorted her toward the grand foyer. Her stomach twisted in uneasy knots, the silk of her crimson gown feeling heavier with every step closer to the throne room. She glanced at Rylik, his profile composed and unreadable, as always. His long strides set an even pace, but she struggled to match it, her nerves making her movements feel clumsy.

"What exactly is the Summit of Realms?" she asked, her voice low but firm enough to break the silence.

Rylik turned his head slightly, a faint glimmer of amusement lighting his icy blue eyes, though his lips remained in their ever-knowing smirk. "It's a gathering of the king's chosen dignitaries and noblemen," he explained, his tone smooth and unhurried. "They present their tributes—gifts, wealth, resources—and report on their lands, each vying for favor. In truth, it's less about governance and more about feeding the king's ego. Forced praise, lavish offerings, all designed to affirm his supreme authority."

Aria tightened her grip on the fabric of her dress, not soothed by the explanation. "And the king enjoys this sort of display?"

Rylik's smirk deepened. "Enjoy is too modest a word. He revels in it."

Before she could press further, they reached the towering double doors leading into the foyer. Two guards stepped forward, pushing the doors open with a heavy groan that gave way to a cacophony of music and laughter.

The grand foyer unfolded before her in an opulent display of power and wealth. Sunlight spilled through tall arched windows, casting golden streams across intricately carved stone walls and sprawling tapestries depicting the kingdom's victories. Gilded chandeliers hung above, their candlelight mingling with the natural glow to bathe the room in warm brilliance. A group of musicians played a lively tune in one corner, their melodies competing with the hum of conversation and the clinking of goblets.

Noblemen and women adorned in their finery lounged on

A WICKED GAME

plush chairs or stood in clusters, drinking and talking animatedly. Among them were a few breathtakingly beautiful companions draped in jewels and fine silks, their laughter high and bright as they entertained their patrons. The air was thick with the mingling scents of wine, perfume, and roasted meats, a haze of indulgence and power.

But the room's focus shifted as Aria stepped inside. Heads turned, voices quieted, and eyes were drawn to her striking beauty and the regal red of her dress. Aria felt the weight of their gazes, her cheeks warming despite her best efforts to appear composed.

Her attention moved to the raised dais at the far end of the room, where King Kaldros sat like a beast in its lair. The throne dwarfed even his large, muscular frame, but he seemed entirely at ease, his broad chest on full display beneath his open surcoat, a thick dark beard framing a mouth twisted in smug satisfaction. Beside him, a smaller but equally ornate chair waited—her chair.

The king's dark eyes locked on her, and her stomach churned at the unabashed way he looked her over, his covetous gaze dragging over every inch of her as though she were another item to be added to his collection. He didn't bother hiding his interest, his lips curving into a smirk that made her want to turn and run.

Rylik moved forward, his poise unshaken, and Aria forced herself to follow. He seemed to glide rather than walk, his long cape sweeping behind him with every step. Though his expression was as composed as ever, she sensed a storm beneath the surface, a tightly wound tension in the way he held his shoulders and the harshness in his eyes.

As they approached the dais, Kaldros was still watching them with a leer that sent unease coursing through Aria's veins. She had never been this close to him before, never seen him in such detail. The sight made her stomach turn. His presence was imposing, even as he sat upon his grandiose throne. Subtle scars marked his skin, hints of battles fought long ago. Though easily twenty years her senior, he radiated vitality, his thick, powerful frame barely concealed beneath his rich attire.

The King's gaze slid over her, lewd and calculating, as if undressing her with every glance. A sickening wave of disgust rose within her. His smile was lecherous as he spoke. "Lady Aria, at long last, we meet."

Rylik's hand touched lightly on her upper back, his breath ghosting her ear. "Bow," he whispered, the command firm but soft enough not to draw attention.

Aria's jaw tightened, but she obeyed, lowering herself in reverence despite the reluctance gnawing at her insides. The king's eyes gleamed with barely concealed pleasure at her submission, his gaze fixed on her bowed figure as though savoring the moment.

Rylik stood stiffly beside her, his annoyance concealed, though his eyes never left the King's face. He was watching, waiting, his displeasure a quiet storm beneath the surface.

When Aria straightened, she avoided looking at the King directly, careful not to let the revulsion show on her face. She swallowed hard as she stood before him, every instinct screaming at her to turn away.

Kaldros gestured leisurely to the chair beside his throne. "Please, do be seated," he said with a sly smile.

Rylik led her to the smaller chair beside the king's throne, his hand gesturing subtly for her to sit. Aria crossed to the chair, her movements precise, but her discomfort was plain. She could feel the King's gaze on her with every step she took. She sat down with a graceful but uneasy movement, her back rigid against the plush chair beside his grand throne. His eyes remained fixed on her, as though savoring her unease, and she found herself gripping the arms of the chair to keep from fidgeting.

Her gaze drifted across the gathering before her, unease prickling at the back of her neck. Though she sat there in the seat of honor, an unwanted guest amidst a show of vanity and groveling, her discomfort only grew with each passing second. The heaviness of eyes upon her felt unbearable—hungry, covetous stares—and though she looked away, she could still feel their attention like a caress she didn't want.

Rylik stepped behind the king, his place marked just between the two chairs, where his shadow loomed quietly like a predator waiting for its moment. From this angle, she couldn't see him fully, but she could feel his presence—calm, composed, yet unnervingly watchful.

The music faded slightly as the king raised a hand, signaling for the room's attention. Aria's pulse quickened as the murmur of voices settled, all eyes turning toward the dais. Whatever words Kaldros had planned, she already knew they wouldn't ease the dread twisting in her gut.

He rose from his throne with a languorous air, every motion evoking the quiet dominance of a hunter on the prowl. His broad frame seemed even more imposing as he stood, the thick fur-lined cloak draped over his shoulders adding to his regal yet barbaric air. A goblet of wine dangled from one massive hand, and the faint smirk on his face suggested he was more entertained than solemn. The room, buzzing with conversation and the harmonious strains of lute and harp, quieted as he raised his hand for silence.

"My friends," Kaldros began, his voice deep and carrying effortlessly through the vast space. He opened his arms, as if the entirety of the opulent foyer was his to offer. "It pleases me greatly to welcome you all here tonight. The Summit of Realms is a tradition older than any of us—a time to reaffirm the strength of our alliances, to exchange gifts and wisdom, and most importantly, to remind us all who holds the reins of this great kingdom."

A ripple of polite laughter coursed through the nobles. Kaldros chuckled, lifting his goblet in a mock toast before taking a long, exaggerated drink.

"Of course," he continued, swiping a hand across his beard, "it is also a time for celebration. We are not here merely for politics, but for pleasure. So, eat, drink, enjoy yourselves. Share your tributes and flatteries, and I promise to reward your loyalty in kind."

His words hung in the air for a moment before the crowd erupted into cheers and applause. Aria forced a smile, folding her hands tightly in her lap as the room came alive again. The musicians resumed their lively tune, and the hum of conversation swelled once more. Servants flitted through the crowd with trays of wine and delicacies, while noblemen leaned closer to their companions, laughing and whispering as if the weight of the king's speech had lifted any pretense of solemnity.

Aria stole a glance at Kaldros, who had resumed his seat with a satisfied sigh. He slouched back into his throne, gesturing lazily for more wine as his concubine leaned in to whisper something in his ear. The king laughed, his gaze flicking momentarily to Aria, and her stomach tightened when she realized he was once again appraising her with unabashed interest. She dropped her eyes to her lap, willing herself not to fidget under the weight of his attention.

The minutes stretched into what felt like hours. Aria remained poised, though the ache of holding her posture grew more pronounced. Around her, the festivities unfolded in vibrant splendor: nobles gossiping and jesting, the delicate strains of music weaving through the air, the soft clink of goblets and laughter punctuating the opulent haze of candlelight.

Every so often, she would glance at Rylik. He hadn't moved from his position behind the king, a silent figure shrouded in his usual composed detachment. His piercing eyes swept the room with careful precision, though he did not focus on her.

The crowd ebbed and flowed, nobles filtering toward the king in ones and twos to offer gifts and praises. Lavish treasures — golden trinkets, rare gemstones, bolts of fine silk — were presented, each more grandiose than the last, while Kaldros accepted them with a smirk and half-hearted nod.

As the night wore on, Aria's tension began to build. The king had yet to call on her, yet she knew it was coming. She could feel it in the way he occasionally cast a lurid glance in her direction, like a cat watching its prey before pouncing. Her pulse raced as she wondered what he would say, what he would ask of her.

The music slowed, signaling a shift in the evening's pace. Kaldros leaned forward, resting his forearms on his knees as he surveyed the room with a wolfish grin. His goblet, now nearly empty, was set aside as he raised his voice once more.

"My friends," he called out, silencing the room yet again. "Before we lose ourselves entirely in the pleasures of the night, I have something rather special to share with you all."

Aria stiffened, her hands gripping the edge of her seat. She cast one more glance at Rylik, hoping for some unspoken reassurance, but his expression remained as stone.

"Tonight," the king continued, "you will witness a gift unlike any I have ever received. A miracle, some might call it." His gaze settled on Aria, and the smile that followed was as cold as it was greedy.

The room leaned forward in unison, eager to see what spectacle the king had planned. And though she couldn't yet see what lay ahead, Aria knew she was about to be thrust into the center of it all.

CHAPTER 28

ARIA

The king's voice rang out in the grand and glittering foyer, commanding and smooth as he addressed the assembled nobles. "Trust and loyalty," he began, his gaze sweeping over the crowd, "are the foundations upon which a realm is built. Without them, we are nothing. And fealty," he emphasized the word, his voice lowering, "is everything." His eyes gleamed with a dark purpose as he looked over the nobles, who all nodded enthusiastically, murmuring their approval. Aria felt the weight of their sycophantic praise hang in the air like a heavy fog.

But the king's tone suddenly shifted, as if the very atmosphere thickened with his malevolent presence. "Lord Izram," he said, and his voice sliced through the room, cutting like a blade. His gaze fixed on the nobleman. "Step forward."

A hushed murmur spread through the crowd as Izram, who had been quietly observing, rose with a hesitancy in his movements, a mixture of fear and anticipation. His eyes darted nervously between the king and the nobles around him, the weight of everyone's attention pressing down on him like a vice. Slowly, he moved toward the throne, each step careful, as if the floor beneath him might suddenly give way.

The king's expression softened slightly, just enough to put a false warmth into his words. "I have a very special reward for you, my lord," he said, his tone dripping with feigned affection. The crowd shifted, eager to see what was to come. But there was an underlying edge to the king's words that made Aria's pulse quicken.

Izram, still unaware of what was coming, smiled cautiously, a look of excitement crossing his face. He took another step forward, waiting for the king's next command. But the king's eyes never left him, his smile now gone, replaced with something much darker.

"Sovereign," the king's voice cut through the tension. The single word, spoken like a death sentence, sent a shiver down Aria's spine. "Step forward."

Rylik moved with his usual precision, his expression unreadable, but there was an unmistakable sharpness to his movements. As he approached, Aria's eyes flickered between him and Kaldros, sensing the stillness in the air, the unnatural calm before the storm. She could feel her heart hammering in her chest. Rylik stood behind the king, poised and silent, as if waiting for a signal.

The king's voice broke the silence, smooth and effortless. "Your reward, Lord Izram," he said, his gaze never leaving the trembling man, "is long overdue."

Without warning, Rylik's blade flashed, and with a sickening thud, it sank into Lord Izram's side.

The room seemed to hold its breath, the suddenness of the action stunning everyone into silence. Aria flinched instinctively, her hand flying to her mouth to stifle a gasp. Izram crumpled, falling to the ground in a heap, his blood staining the floor in an instant.

The noise of the room—the murmurs, the gasps—faded into a hollow, eerie quiet. The only sound was the sickening rhythm of Izram's ragged breaths and the sharp scrape of boots across stone. Aria couldn't bear to look at him, her stomach churning. She turned her head, but she could feel the room's gaze burning into her, as if the entire crowd was waiting for her to react. The king, however, remained unfazed, his eyes cold, scanning the crowd as though nothing out of the ordinary had happened.

Izram's voice broke through the silence, weak and tremulous. "Please—please, Your Majesty," he begged, his hands clutching at the cold stone floor, his body writhing in pain. "I swear, I—I didn't mean to—"

The king's voice cut him off with an icy finality. "Lord Izram," he said, his tone filled with a cruel mockery, "you've betrayed me. Your ledgers were lies. Your debts, much greater than you've admitted. You owed me far more than you ever paid." A slow, calculated smile curled on his lips as he continued, "And you dared think you could escape this?"

Izram was gasping now, struggling to hold onto life, but he could barely keep himself upright. His eyes rolled with terror as he reached out toward Rylik's boots, his trembling hands brushing against the cold leather. "Please! I'll pay. I'll make it right. Just let me live. I—I beg you!"

The king's gaze was dark and disinterested, as though Izram's pleas were a mere distraction. He turned his attention back to the room, his voice a mock-thoughtful hum as he spoke, "You want mercy, Izram?"

The room fell into an uneasy stillness, the air thick with anticipation. The king stood slowly and stretched out his hand toward Aria. "Healer, show them," he said, his voice a cruel whisper. "Show them your magic."

Aria's breath caught in her throat. The king's words were not an invitation—they were an order. She knew what was expected of her, but the very idea made her stomach churn. She had never been asked to heal in such a way, to be put on display like some trained animal. The eyes of every noble were on her now, their gazes full of expectations she could not escape.

Her legs moved as though they were not her own. Reluctantly, she stood, Rylik's shadow looming over her as he stepped aside to allow her space. She walked toward the broken man on the floor, his labored breath rattling in his chest as his fingers clutched at the stone. She could feel his bloodstained touch, still wet, as she knelt before him.

The golden warmth of her magic flared to life in her hands as she pressed them against his wounds. Light spilled from her palms, and the room was momentarily bathed in the soft glow. Slowly, cautiously, Izram's breathing began to even out. The jagged wounds in his side began to knit together, the blood ceasing to pour from him. The healing was swift, almost effortless, and for a moment, there was peace.

Izram's eyes fluttered open, and a look of shock spread across his face as he gasped in relief. "I—I feel better." His voice cracked, barely a whisper, as he looked up at her with wide, grateful eyes.

The room was filled with stunned silence, every eye trained on the miraculous display. Aria's heart beat faster, but before she could withdraw her hands, the king's voice rang out, sharp and cold, slicing through the wonder of the moment.

"Thank you, my dear." With a flick of his wrist, the king reversed time.

The magic unraveled in an instant. The golden glow flickered, and in its place, the wounds that had been healed reopened with a sickening rush of blood. The jagged edges of the wound tore open once more, and the blood poured from Izram's body in a torrent. His scream echoed through the room, raw and desperate as he writhed in agony.

Aria recoiled, a sudden tension gripping her as she turned away. Her hands trembled, the horrific reversal of the healing gnawing at her. She could still hear the sickening sound of the blood flowing once more, feel the weight of the king's cruel amusement pressing down on her. She had no idea that this was the power he possessed, and now she was certain no one would be capable of killing him.

Kaldros, his face filled with twisted satisfaction, continued his cruel game. Time bent and snapped, and with each reversal, Izram's pain deepened, his cries growing weaker as he gasped for breath. It was as though the king enjoyed watching the man suffer, prolonging his agony as if it were some form of entertainment.

Aria closed her eyes, unable to bear the sight. Her heart pounded, her stomach churning, but the king's voice cut through her shock, as casually as if he were issuing a command for the evening's entertainment.

"Sovereign," he said, his tone bored, "finish it."

And with that, the final blow was inevitable.

The room was silent, every noble too afraid to speak. The

weight of fear hung heavy in the air as Rylik stepped forward, and in one swift motion, swept his blade harshly across the man's throat.

The silence that followed his execution was a suffocating shroud, laden with a grim sense of finality. Lord Izram's body collapsed in a graceless heap, his once pleading form now rendered a motionless shell. A crimson tide crept outward, its dark sheen glinting faintly under the light, spilling across the marble like an ominous shadow that seemed to taint not just the floor, but the very air around it. The stain spread slowly, deliberate and inescapable, a silent testament to the violent act now etched into the room's memory.

Rylik remained unmoved, his face impassive as he wiped his blade clean, the movement methodical, almost practiced. His expression was cold, unreadable—nothing about him seemed disturbed.

The room was frozen, the weight of the murder settling over the crowd like a leaden cloak. Not a single person dared to speak, their breaths held, their eyes wide with fear. The flickering candlelight cast long, trembling shadows across their faces, their terror reflected in their wide eyes. A few of the women looked away, though none dared to make a sound.

"Remove him," the king ordered, his voice casual, almost disinterested. His gaze never left the scene, as though he were giving no more thought to the dead man than he would a fly on his sleeve. The guards moved quickly, but their hesitation was clear—slow to approach, unsure of whether to touch the corpse of the man who had just been sacrificed to the king's whim.

As they dragged the body away, the king clapped his hands together, the sound sharp in the otherwise hushed room. "Let us continue, my friends," he declared, his voice carrying with unnerving ease, like a tyrant's command. His eyes scanned the room, daring anyone to defy him. The nobles, still shell-shocked, exchanged nervous glances. Slowly, almost imperceptibly, they began to shift, resuming their conversations, but the forced laughter and strained pleasantries were more hollow than before. They had no choice but to comply, the weight of the king's authority pressing down on them like a vice.

The musicians began to play once more, their instruments trembling in their hands, the once lively notes now stiff, the melody lacking any real joy. The king's eyes never left the crowd, savoring the fear, his lips curling slightly in satisfaction. He turned to Rylik, his voice lowering, a private exchange meant only for the two of them.

Rylik stepped forward, his posture still elegant, but his mind was elsewhere. The king's words were indistinct, too soft for anyone else to hear, but Rylik nodded slightly, acknowledging whatever directive had been given. Without another word, the king waved him off, his dismissal almost lazy.

Rylik's figure seemed to shimmer for a moment before the shadows seemed to claim him. With a flick of his wrist, the air around him rippled like ink bleeding into water. In the blink of an eye, he was gone—swallowed up by the darkness, vanishing like a phantom.

The king's gaze shifted to Aria next. His eyes, gleaming with amusement, locked onto hers. She felt a shiver run down her spine under the weight of his look. There was something in his eyes—something sinister and yet strangely intrigued.

"Are you feeling well, my dear?" The king's voice was soft, teasing almost, as though the slaughter moments before were merely an afterthought.

Aria's throat tightened, her voice catching as she shook her head, her nerves frayed, her stomach twisting. "No," she whispered, her voice barely above a breath. She couldn't shake the feeling of unease settling deep in her chest. She longed to be away from this place, away from the king, from the blood, away from the oppressive weight of his presence.

The king observed her for a moment longer, as though savoring the discomfort that radiated off her. Then he smiled, a slow, calculating curve of his lips. "You look distressed. Perhaps you need some rest."

Aria's heart skipped in her chest. He was offering her a reprieve, but she couldn't shake the gnawing feeling that he had something else in mind. He extended his hand toward her, and she hesitated, her eyes flickering toward the door. A guard, perhaps? She was accustomed to being escorted by one, not the king himself. But something in the way he regarded her told her that he wasn't offering her solace, but something else—something far more unsettling.

Her hand trembled as she placed it in his, the king's touch cold and firm, his fingers brushing hers with a tenderness that made her skin crawl. He didn't speak, but he led her through the corridors, the silence between them thick with tension.

Aria's mind raced. Why was he escorting her? Why not a guard? Did he mean to be alone with her? The thought made her skin prickle, a wave of dread washing over her as she fought to regain composure.

What did he want from her? What was his plan? Her thoughts spiraled, each more fearful than the last. The further they walked down the halls, the more she felt the sense of being led into something she couldn't control. A tightening in her chest, a sickening twist in her stomach—each step seemed to bring her closer to the unknown, to a fate she couldn't yet see, but feared deeply.

The corridors seemed endless, stretching before her like a maze of uncertainty. And all the while, the king remained beside her, his presence suffocating, his every step calculated. The walk felt longer than it should have, each footfall heavy with anticipation, the silence between them suffocating. By the time they reached the towering double doors ahead, her pulse was nearly deafening in her ears.

When the doors opened, her heart lodged sharply in her throat. She froze in place, her body refusing to move, though her mind screamed for her to turn and run. This wasn't just any room. It was the king's.

Stunned, Aria forced herself inside, though her feet felt like lead, her eyes skimming over the grand opulence of the chamber. The deep crimson drapes, the ornate furniture—it all blurred together, though one thing stood out in sharp, terrifying clarity: the massive, luxurious bed that dominated the room. Her gaze clung to it unwillingly, fear spiraling tighter in her chest. Each passing second felt like a countdown to something inevitable. Something she could no longer escape.

"Please, make yourself comfortable," the king's voice came

low from behind her. His gloved hand grazed softly along the nape of her neck, sending chills down her spine.

Startled, she moved away from him, spinning around to face him. His eyes were full of desire, his fingers loosening the belt that held his sword and dagger.

Her heart thundered in her chest. "I—I thought you were offering me an opportunity to rest, your majesty. As I'm not feeling well. Wouldn't it be better if I lay in my own bed?"

The king unbuckled his belt, letting the sword and dagger clatter to the marble floor, then removed his gloves. "It matters not to me which bed we lay in, my dear. But since we're already here," He walked toward her, peeling off his outer robe and hanging it over a chair, cuffing up the sleeves of his tunic. "We might as well make the most of it."

Aria's eyes widened, taking in his broad, muscular frame stretching the fabric of his tunic. He was strong—far stronger than she could ever hope to resist. Anxiety crawled through her, making her nauseous. "I—I'm sorry, your grace," she stammered, her voice barely holding steady. "Are you suggesting that we—you and I—are to—?"

She couldn't finish the sentence, too terrified to give voice to what she already knew. He wanted to bed her. *Where is the Sovereign? Where is my damn shadow when I need him?!*

The king chuckled, pulling at the hem of his tunic and approaching her with slow, deliberate steps. "Yes, dear girl. I have been wanting this for quite some time." His eyes roved over her body, hungry and dark. "And despite the rumors of your dread curse, I find myself insatiable."

Her brows furrowed. "My dread curse?"

"Surely you don't pretend to be unaware of it?" The king's eyes glinted with amusement and a hint of cynicism. "Your lovers were rather scarred. Unless, of course, it is some elaborate charade." His hand shot out, grabbing her waist, pulling her against him as he breathed in the scent of her neck. "And let us hope it is, because I will not be satisfied until I have had you."

Fear hit Aria like a tidal wave, and she recoiled instinctively, pushing against him with trembling hands. But his grip was immoveable, as solid as stone. Panic surged through her veins, her heart hammering so violently she thought it might tear from her chest. He leaned in closer, his lips brushing her skin in a sickeningly gentle trail down her neck to her collarbone, his touch cold and voracious.

"Are you nervous, healer?" he whispered, his voice low and mocking, savoring the shiver of fear that rippled through her. His breath was hot against her skin, his words a sinister caress.

Her mind spiraled into chaos, each thought more frantic than the last. *I can't move—I can't breathe.* Her chest tightened as waves of panic flooded her senses, and she knew—resistance could mean pain. Or *worse.* He was the king. Brutal, unrelenting. And she could hardly forget what he had done to that nobleman in the foyer. Her fate would be no better if she resisted him. There was no escape from him, no reasoning with someone who took what he wanted without hesitation. Her limbs felt heavy, paralyzed by the weight of her fear, her every muscle tensed as if she could break free—but she knew it was futile.

A soft, terrified whimper escaped her lips as her body betrayed her, frozen in his iron hold, her terror growing by the second as his presence consumed her.

The king laughed, the sound low and sinister, his lips trailing up her neck as the thick scent of ale filled the air between them. "Yes, I will savor you for hours." His hand tangled in her hair, pulling the adornments loose, letting the wild curls spill down her back.

Suddenly, his body stiffened. He opened his eyes, only to recoil in horror. He shoved her away with a force that sent her sprawling onto the bed.

Aria yelped as she hit the mattress, watching in confusion as the king wiped at his mouth, his eyes wide and dazed. The whites of his eyes had turned a deep, unnatural obsidian, threaded with silver streaks, moving like smoke. It looked the same as the potion she had taken earlier from Rylik.

The king swatted at the air as if fighting off invisible wraiths. "D—Demon!?" he shouted, his voice trembling with fear.

Aria's heart pounded. She didn't understand what was happening, but she wasn't about to stay and find out. Scrambling to her feet, she fled from the room, her breath ragged as she raced down the hall. Whatever the black potion had done, it had driven the king to madness—but she wasn't sticking around to let him recover and try again.

She sprinted down the dim hallway, her heart pounding in her chest as the urgency of escape surged through her. The image of the king's terrified eyes flashed in her mind, a look so deeply unsettling it spurred her legs to move faster. She had to get out of this kingdom—sooner, rather than later.

As she turned a sharp corner, she collided heavily with something solid, dark, and unyielding. A fresh wave of fear surged through her, but steady hands quickly reassured her. Rylik stood before her, his form cloaked in shadows. Without a word, he pulled her into his magic, and together, they disappeared into the inky darkness, reappearing moments later in his bedroom.

Still caught in the panicked haze of her escape, Aria struggled, her body instinctively resisting his touch. Her mind spun, but she froze at the soft sound of his voice.

"Shh, it's over, Pyra. You're safe now."

The warmth in his tone broke through her fear, and her hands, once clenched in his, went limp. She stared at him in shock, her lips trembling. "Sovereign?"

CHAPTER 29

RYLIK

Rylik's gaze softened as he took her in—Aria's once immaculate hair now a wild mess of curls, her dress askew, and her eyes shimmering with the last remnants of fear. Rage knotted tightly in his chest, but he suppressed it, knowing that unleashing it would only unsettle her further. Instead, he gently pulled her to him, cradling her trembling body against his. Her small frame shook with quiet sobs, but he held her close, reverent in his touch, allowing her to find solace in his embrace.

He had known this moment would come. The king, always reckless in his desires, wouldn't be able to resist the temptation of having Aria for himself, especially after having her dressed up as though she were some concubine. Rylik had foreseen the danger, using the earlier hours of the morning to acquire a specific tonic from a lesser-known apothecary in the capital.

The black and silver potion, which he had given Aria under the guise of calming her nerves, had a much darker purpose. The Nightmare Elixir, once ingested, bound itself to the drinker's essence, forming a protective aura. It lay dormant until someone with hostile intent made contact—then, it would stir, latching onto the offender's mind and conjuring their deepest fears into vivid, paralyzing visions.

Only those with ill will would be affected, and it would leave others entirely unscathed. Unfortunately it loses its potency and usefulness after the first perceived enemy, but he knew it would still prove necessary for Aria's protection from the king's advances.

With this Nightmare Elixir, the king would suffer a little while longer, perhaps until morning—if Rylik did nothing to stop it—before the visions would subside and allow him to rest again. He smiled at the thought of the king undergoing prolonged torture, a small price to pay for trying to take what wasn't his.

Rylik wanted to kill him. It would be so easy right now. The man was undoubtedly in a frenzied state of panic and would be unable to properly use his magic. But the time was not yet ripe for such a confrontation. Patience, he reminded himself. When the time came, he would face the king in combat—steel to steel, eyes locked—and then he would drive the blade through his blackened heart.

For now, his focus was on Aria.

She pulled back from him, still trembling slightly, and hastily wiped at the tears staining her cheeks, a flush of embarrassment creeping over her face. "I'm sorry," she whispered, her voice small.

"Don't be," Rylik said, his tone gentle but firm. He offered her a small smile, brushing a stray curl from her face. "If anything, I should be the one to apologize."

Her brows knit in confusion, but before she could ask, he continued. "I won't be able to stay with you here. There are pressing matters that require my attention. But I will return." He reached up, his fingers lightly brushing the side of her face in reassurance. "In the meantime," his voice hardened, warning clear in his gaze as he placed a firm hand on her shoulder. "Do not leave this room."

Aria swallowed, her fear bubbling up again. "Why not?"

"I'll be back before nightfall," Rylik said simply, his form dissolving into a swirl of smoke, leaving her standing in the quiet of his suite. The crackling of the fire in the hearth was the only sound that remained, filling the space with an unsettling stillness.

* * *

Rylik stood in the heart of the forest, the sky overhead a tempestuous black, laden with rain. The storm had reached its full fury, and he melted into the shadows, feeling the pulse of magic coursing through him. He retrieved a bottle of glowing red elixir from his pocket and, with a swift motion, downed half of it in one gulp. As he stowed the half-empty vial back, his eyes shifted, awash in an ominous red haze not unlike the luminous potion, scanning the darkened woods that surrounded him.

After carrying out the king's order to kill Lord Izram, Rylik had been tasked with locating another missing noble: Lord Thomas. Thomas's absence from the grim spectacle had not gone unnoticed, and Rylik suspected the man might also be due for one of the king's "rewards." The king had an uncanny ability to root out disloyalty—a talent that made it no small feat for Rylik to have remained beyond suspicion all these years.

It hadn't taken long to find Thomas through the Veil. The man had been attempting to flee, his efforts both futile and clumsy. Perhaps he'd realized the king was onto him, and desperation had driven him into rash action. Rylik caught up to him easily, cornering him in a narrow alleyway. Thomas had barely managed to stammer a plea before Rylik silenced him with a sharp blow to the ribs—a wound designed to disable, not to kill. The king wanted him alive, whether for questioning or, more likely, for the slow torment he so relished. Rylik delivered the writhing nobleman back to the palace without ceremony, his duty executed with cold efficiency.

His thoughts flickered to another figure—Eldric, the very reason he had been drawn to this forest this evening. Through the sapphire elixir's magic coursing in his veins, faint glimpses began to sharpen in his mind: a dense woodline, the thundering of hooves, and Eldric's silhouette cutting through the trees.

The confrontation was inevitable. Rylik would finally see the traitor—the leader of the Rebellion—before the night was over. And when that moment came, one of them would not live to see the dawn.

His eyes darted around, observing the unfolding spectacle as everything proceeded according to his designs. Even with the king's lecherous advances on Aria, things had mostly gone how he anticipated they would. The Nightmare Elixir he'd given Aria would leave her tired and disoriented, and she would need rest in their time apart. If she stayed in his room like an obedient little captive, the night would pass without incident.

But, he knew better than to trust her to do that. She was desperate for an escape from the palace, and knowing that he was preoccupied with other matters would only fuel her more to try brazen actions. He couldn't blame her, especially given the way the king had no doubt treated her before the effects of the Nightmare Elixir had taken place.

Smoky black tendrils of magic seeped from him in barely restrained fury. Rylik closed his eyes, forcing himself to calm. Focus was essential now; he needed to remain sharp to accomplish the myriad tasks that awaited him this evening.

As he steadied himself, a cloaked figure emerged a short distance away. *Right on time.* Rylik vanished fully into the shadows, hovering like an unseen wraith as Eldric glanced around him, fear etched into his features, clutching his cloak tightly.

Another cloaked figure flickered into existence, a small glimmer of blue magic that barely registered in the dim light. Had he not consumed the Clarifying Tonic, Rylik might have missed it entirely. As he had long suspected, the spy in the king's court had to be a skilled illusionist to make it this far without attracting the king's notice. Operating in plain sight was something this noble would rarely, if ever, consider. Rylik moved undetected, drawing closer until he caught sight of Orren's familiar red beard peeking from beneath the hood. A smirk crept across his lips at the confirmation of his suspicions. *Fantastic.*

"I need out," Eldric implored, desperation seeping into his voice.

"There is no way 'out,' Eldric," Orren growled, grabbing Eldric roughly by the front of his tunic and pulling him close.

"Please," Eldric stammered, fear lacing his tone. "I'm putting myself at risk just to meet you here today. I've been the king's damn puppet for a year now, barely feeding him usable information to evade death, and now I—"

Before he could finish, Orren drew a dagger from within his cloak and plunged it deep into Eldric's abdomen. Rylik watched unflinchingly as shock and horror washed over Eldric's face.

"You served your purpose," Orren said, his voice a menacing whisper. "And in many ways, you have cost me too much." He twisted the knife, savoring Eldric's anguished cry. "I thank you for playing your role in the cause. But I agree, it is time that you left."

With a swift yank, Orren withdrew the blade from Eldric's body, leaving him to crumple to the forest floor, sputtering blood and gagging, unable to utter a single word. In a flicker of blue magic, Orren vanished, gone as quickly as he had come, leaving Eldric lifeless in a sanguine halo of his own blood upon the damp earth. Rylik stood, his eyes cold, grateful for the confirmation of the spy and already plotting the ways he would decimate Orren and his bothersome Rebellion. But, for now, there was still the matter of dealing with the king. He would need to paint the story for him before anyone else did.

* * *

The rain smattered against the windows of the king's chamber, each droplet a stark reflection of the storm raging inside. The room was illuminated by flickering torchlight and candles, emitting a warm glow that sharply contrasted with the chaos of the night. On the floor, the king thrashed against invisible foes, a pitiful sight in his mussed and torn tunic, his pants in disarray—far from the fearsome ruler he usually portrayed.

Rylik stood over him smugly, aware of the blade sheathed at his side, imagining how satisfying it would feel to drive it into the man's withered heart. He sighed, breaking the heavy silence. "Your majesty?"

The king convulsed, his eyes wide with terror as he caught sight of Rylik. "Back!! Back, you beast!!"

A cool smile crept onto Rylik's lips. He wondered how horrifying he must appear in the king's distorted vision. With a steadying breath, he masked his amusement, allowing his expression to settle into neutrality. He pulled out his Clarifying

Tonic, the remaining red liquid shimmering in the dim light. Using his shadows, he restrained the king effortlessly, pinning him to the floor with silky black tendrils of mist. Ignoring the king's cries of panic, Rylik knelt beside him, forcing his mouth open and dumping some of the tonic down his throat, clamping it shut to ensure he swallowed.

Moments passed, and the black and silver mist in the king's eyes began to fade, gradually restoring his normal state, briefly flashing red as the tonic took full effect.

The king looked up at Rylik in shock. "Sovereign?"

"Your majesty," Rylik replied, masking his dissatisfaction at the relief now etched on the king's face. It displeased him that he had been the one to provide comfort at all. He withdrew his shadows, allowing the king to stand.

"Where is the woman? The healer?" the king demanded, glancing around the chamber as though expecting her to materialize from the shadows.

"Not well, your majesty. It seems she has taken ill, but I'm sure she will be fine by morning." Rylik watched the king approach his bed, a look of dread crossing his features as if reliving the final moments before the nightmares had overtaken him. "I did not realize you were in here, writhing under the Dread Curse, until I found the healer stumbling through the hallways."

The king's eyes narrowed, fear flashing across his face. "The Dread Curse, of course!"

"She told me she was too afraid to caution you, knowing she had no control over the curse. She didn't want to reject her king." Rylik spoke with conviction, spinning an effortless lie as he placed his hands behind his back.

The king nodded, as if understanding her plight. "Perhaps that was why she was so fearful."

Rylik's gaze sharpened with malice, though he remained restrained. "Just now, what did you give me? You were able to recover me from the curse." The urgency in his voice heightened as he turned to face Rylik.

"It took time to acquire, but I procured a potion that might alleviate the symptoms of your Dread Curse. Though, I must know," Rylik's eyes bore into the king, his expression stern. "Did you take her to bed? Will you be forever cursed to relive these nightmares every night, your grace?" His voice dripped with grim foreboding, ensuring the king would be rightfully fearful of ever fulfilling his unsavory desires against Aria.

The king swallowed hard, shuddering as he recalled the gallows that had haunted him for hours. "No. No, I did not."

Rylik's shoulders visibly relaxed, a sense of relief washing over him that he didn't hide. "Good. I'm pleased to hear you have been spared a lifetime of agony, your majesty. I doubt the potency of that tonic would provide you any relief at all had you finished your intentions with her."

A slow, cautious smile crept across the king's face. "I pity the man who would ever seek to take her from me. She will be their ruin."

"Indeed, your majesty," Rylik replied, amusement simmering just beneath the surface. "She is your healer of miraculous ability, a fortification of your defenses. You can surely covet such a gift, regarding her as such. And yes, any man seeking her harm will surely meet their downfall. Let us be grateful, then, that you are fully aware of the formidable force you now possess."

The king nodded firmly. "And you say she is unwell, Sovereign?"

"Yes, surely a side effect from her unfortunate curse that ails her so. But she will recover by morning, she assures me. She wanted me to relay her deepest apologies to you, Sire. So long as the lady remains celibate, she will stay in fine health, and so will you." Rylik's voice was confident, laced with double meanings, certain that the king could never discern the subtleties in his tone.

The king gave a brief, shuddering nod, shaking his head to recollect himself. "Right. Now, Thomas. Did you apprehend him?"

"Swiftly, Sire. He is in a cell downstairs, awaiting you." Rylik offered a respectful nod.

A slow smile spread across the king's face. "Good. Excellent. Perhaps dealing with him will be a fine distraction. I'll head down there. You're excused for the night."

Rylik raised an eyebrow, eyeing the king's disheveled appearance. "You may want to be dressed first, your majesty."

"Ah, yes," he muttered as he examined himself, then waved him off absently.

Turning away, Rylik allowed a smirk to slip onto his lips at the successful execution of his deception. He felt confident that the temptation the king felt toward Aria had been fully extinguished—finally. The man was an insatiable lecher, but Rylik hoped the hours spent crying on the floor would ensure he would never attempt this again. Because if there were ever a next time, he would not be able to keep his blade sheathed any longer.

With that thought in mind, he exited the door, leaving the king to gather himself.

CHAPTER 30

ARIA

Aria staggered down the dimly lit corridors of the palace, her worn brown cloak hanging from her like a shroud. Fatigue ate away at her, every step a battle as disorientation swept over her in relentless waves. The stone walls offered her only fleeting support, her fingertips brushing against the cool surface in a feeble attempt to stay upright. The usual palace guards were nowhere to be seen, likely drawn away by their duties at the Summit of Realms. It was her only chance to escape, and she clung to that hope with desperation, though her body seemed to betray her at every turn.

The thought of seeking the Sovereign's protection flickered in her mind, but was quickly snuffed out. His threats still echoed, dark and unforgiving, making it clear that he was no less dangerous than Orren. The fear of what he could do to her parents if she revealed his secrets haunted her, as her legs buckled momentarily. She pressed her back against the wall, struggling to keep the hallway from spinning. Each breath came heavier, slower, her thoughts muddled.

I can't trust him, she reminded herself, shaking her head as if to clear the fog that was settling in. *He's part of this world. Just as much as Orren. And the way he so easily executed Izram at the king's order—the way he so easily cuts down anyone in his path—should not be so easily overlooked.*

Her thoughts turned to her parents. What if they couldn't escape? What if they fell under Orren's cruelty because of her reckless decisions? The weight of her helplessness seemed to crush her all at once. She had no plan, no way to rescue them. And now, she was losing herself to this strange, overpowering fatigue.

With a groan, she turned to glance behind her. The Sovereign's room loomed just a few paces away, still taunting her with its closeness. She had barely managed to put any distance between herself and that suite. Frustration and panic warred within her as her vision blurred, the edges of her sight darkening.

The hallway tilted violently, and her knees gave way. She grasped at the wall, but her fingers slid uselessly down its smooth surface. The world spun as she crashed to the floor, her body crumpling into the cold stone beneath her. There was no pain, only a distant awareness that her body had hit the ground. Her head struck the edge of a tapestry, but even that was muted, the once-vivid colors swirling into indistinct shapes.

With a soft, helpless moan, her vision faded completely. Darkness claimed her, and the palace walls vanished into silence.

* * *

The soft flicker of candlelight stirred Aria from sleep, its warm glow dancing across the walls of her suite and coaxing her from the depths of a dreamless sleep.

"Oh, good. I was worried I had wasted my time sticking around," came a voice, tinged with irritation.

Aria didn't move immediately, her body sluggish and heavy, but her eyes darted to find the source of the voice. Seated in her chair by the vanity, Thorian stared back at her, elbows resting on his knees, his expression mildly agitated.

"Can you move at all?"

"Thorian?" Aria asked, her voice thick with sleep as she struggled to sit up, her body unwilling to cooperate.

He sighed, leaning back in the chair, his dismay evident. "Well, that's unfortunate."

"I'm sorry," she mumbled, her thoughts a muddled haze, weariness still pulling at her eyelids. "I don't know what's wrong with me, but thank you, if you found me? I was on my way back to my room, I think." She remembered exactly what she had been doing, of course. She was trying to escape. And something in his eyes told her he knew it too.

Thorian shifted in his seat, his russet-colored eyes catching the flicker of candlelight. He studied her, his gaze sharp and probing, much like Maven's—his cousin. She could almost see him piecing together her thoughts from the tension in her expression. "Do you want to leave?" he asked, his question cutting through her fog with startling directness.

Aria pushed herself up on her elbows, her body sluggish but her mind suddenly alert. "Leave?" She needed clarity—this felt like a trap.

Thorian glanced toward the door, as if ensuring they were still alone, before standing and approaching her. "Do you want to leave Ravenhelm?" he clarified, striding closer with intent.

Her heart leapt as he neared, but her muscles failed her, and she slumped back onto the bed. The mattress felt soft yet stifling, and frustration built as her body refused to cooperate in this crucial moment. "I do," she admitted, her voice barely a whisper.

Thorian knelt down in front of her, their eyes now level. "I could get you out," he murmured, his voice as quiet as hers. "We'll just have to do it my way. I'll need you to do what I say. Everything that I say."

She searched his face, trying to gauge his sincerity, feeling the weight of his offer press down on her. "Why?" she asked, her voice filled with wariness. "What do you get out of this?"

His eyes flicked to the side again, still affirming that the room was clear before he continued, "I have someone that needs access to your gifts. He's a good man, but he's becoming desperate." He swallowed to remove the tremor caught in his throat. "Without my approval he sent mercenaries to retrieve you."

The memory of the night she was attacked by rogues resurfaced sharply, and her body shuddered at the realization. She suddenly felt vulnerable, alone with him in her room, his words unraveling her defenses.

"I'm sorry for the fear they caused you," he said, his voice softening with regret. "It was reckless of him, but desperate men make desperate choices. He's dying, Aria. He needs you."

That line—she'd heard it so many times before. Desperation clung to her everywhere she went. As word spread of the miracles she could perform, she had become increasingly coveted. She didn't need to be coveted by yet another powerful man.

Sensing her reluctance, Thorian leaned in slightly. "He won't harm you. He can offer you protection, a place to live, coin. He's not as wealthy as the king, but he would give you something far more valuable—freedom."

Aria hesitated, uncertain. Could she trust him? "It's not just me I'm worried about," she said, her voice quiet but firm. "I have my parents to think of."

Thorian nodded, his tone resolute. "My general will take care of them as well. Whatever you need, we'll make sure they're safe."

She studied his eyes for what felt like an eternity, her mind racing. Was he genuine? Or was this a trap, another lie cloaked in promises of safety? Doubt lingered in her mind, but beneath it, there was a flicker of hope. Could this be her chance?

The door creaked open, and Thorian shot to his feet, swiftly adopting an impassive stance, his hands folding low in front of him. His face was unreadable, but the tension in the air sharpened as a shadow fell across the room.

Rylik entered with an ominous presence, his gaze sliding from Thorian to Aria sprawled across the bed. His jaw clenched, and a cold, joyless smile twisted at the corner of his lips as he carefully sealed the door with slow precision. "Thorian," he greeted smoothly, advancing toward them. "I see you've been keeping our healer company."

Thorian stiffened, his posture rigid. "I found her passed out in the corridor, Sovereign."

Rylik's eyes flicked to Aria, noting the guilt that darkened her features as she avoided his gaze. A smirk played on his lips before he turned back to Thorian. "You're excused."

Without hesitation, Thorian inclined his head and left the room in silence, the soft sound of the door latching behind him.

The room felt smaller, the air heavier as Rylik stood, his focus now entirely on Aria.

Dread pooled in her stomach, the weight of her body pinning her to the bed as her thoughts raced. Would he ask why she had left his chambers? Would he know she had tried—yet again—to escape? Had he overheard Thorian's offer?

"How are you feeling?" His voice was unexpectedly gentle, catching her off guard.

She blinked, trying to sit up but finding her strength still lacking. "Weak," she admitted. "That potion you gave me. It, um," Her words trailed off, unable to shape the confusion swirling in her mind. How could she even begin to ask about the strange, unsettling way the king had been both obsessed with and terrified of her, as if driven mad?

Rylik's expression remained calm, his voice as cool as ever. "It was a precaution to protect you. I didn't want to concern you unnecessarily." His tone allowed for no opposition, a finality that closed the subject. "The potion's power drains the drinker's energy if its effects are triggered. It's temporary, I assure you. You'll be fine by morning, You just need your rest."

Aria's thoughts were muddled, but a flicker of frustration broke through. "Why didn't you tell me the king was interested in me?" she asked, her voice quiet but filled with unease.

Rylik sighed, stepping closer to her. "Like I said, I couldn't be sure if he ever intended to act upon his desires."

"But I would've preferred to know," she pressed, managing to push herself up slightly. The effort left her breathless, but she didn't back down. "I don't like being kept in the dark."

"I'll make an effort to keep you more informed," he replied smoothly, though she suspected he wasn't entirely sincere.

Her frown deepened as she met his eyes. "I am grateful, Sovereign. Please don't misunderstand. I was afraid, and that potion was a well-timed defense. However, what will happen to him? And by extension, what will now happen to me as a result?"

"Nothing," Rylik said dismissively. "As I said, I had the matter well in hand. And I can promise you, his majesty will never touch you again—not without swift repayment. You will instead be revered by him. You needn't worry."

"Revered?" Her confusion was evident. "But why?"

A soft, almost amused laugh escaped him as he glanced aside. "He believes you suffer from a curse that only harms those who seek to take you to bed."

Aria's eyebrows shot up. "What? How could he think that?"

Rylik's gaze returned to her, his amusement evident.

"Because, he's a superstitious man who believes in rumors. I have no control over his biases, and I have little interest in encouraging him to believe otherwise. Do you?"

She shook her head, baffled but unwilling to challenge the misconception. Better that the king believed such nonsense than for her to face his advances again.

Rylik's lips curled into a smile as he folded his hands behind his back. "Get some rest, Aria. You certainly need it."

She watched him as he turned to leave, heading for the door at the far end of the room. "Wait," she called out, her voice softer now. "Your blight, Sovereign."

He paused, glancing over his shoulder with his hand on the handle of the door. "Rest. You're in no state to help me tonight."

The room felt hollow after he left, the sound of the door shutting reverberating like an endless echo through the silence. Aria's heart twisted painfully in her chest. Why did it ache now? He hadn't even pressed her about her escape attempt, though she knew he must have realized it was the only reason she'd been in the hallway when Thorian found her. And yet, despite everything, why had she felt the urge to heal him—one of the very men she had been trying to run from? Why did she find herself starting to care for him?

Gritting her teeth at her own dual-mindedness, she murmured under her breath, "he is your enemy, Aria." Her fingers dug into the soft fabric of her bedspread, hating the way the words sounded on her tongue.

He didn't *feel* like an enemy these days. She recalled when he had held her trembling body not long ago in his room, when she had been so terrified of the King trying to force her. His hands had been so soft on her face, grazing through the strands of her hair with a certain gentleness that she didn't know he possessed. And it had been because of him that she wasn't in the King's bed tonight. If he had not intervened on her behalf, she would've been his latest conquest. Aria swallowed down a hard lump of air.

No one in her life had ever, *ever* been such a sentinel for her like he was. Sure, her parents had been proper guardians. But, beyond that, had she not lived a life as the subject of exploitation? Perhaps he was exploiting her too, no different in his ambitions than anyone else. But he shouldn't have to care how she feels, or whose bed she ends up in.

A low groan escaped her lips as she pulled herself upright, leaning against the bedpost for support. He cared about her, didn't he? Her gaze drifted to the adjoining suite door. She gripped the post and, with a surge of effort, pushed herself to her feet, her legs wobbling beneath her as she steadied her weight. If he didn't care, he wouldn't have given her that potion. He wouldn't have held her as she cried. He wouldn't have done likely half the things he'd done for her by now.

Unsteadily, she found herself drawn to the door, crossing the cold marble floor with purpose. She wasn't blind to his ulterior motives, but people had always used her without a second thought to her wants or needs. And flawed though he was, Rylik seemed to care—at least in some way—about her happiness. Her hand closed over the handle, pulled the door open as she willed her body to find its strength again.

Her mind replayed the dream she'd had last night, when Rylik hadn't denied manipulating her. Even though it hadn't really been him in the dream, she knew there was truth in it. But did it matter? If he was manipulating her, she hardly cared anymore. She liked the way he sought to make her smile. She was so content, even, that she had allowed herself to kiss him in her reveries.

Aria moved through the bathing room, her steps gaining purpose. Opening the door to his suite, she scanned the dimly lit space until her eyes fell on him.

Rylik slumped in his chair by the fire, his figure shrouded in shadows that danced across his features, revealing a coldness that made her heart ache. A rush of warmth surged within her at the sight, urging her forward, but fatigue clawed at her limbs, dulling her senses. As she stumbled forward, Rylik's eyes flicked open, instinctively locking onto her approaching figure. He barely had time to register her unsteady gait before she fell into his lap, but his arms shot out, catching her with ease.

"Aria?" he asked, his voice smooth and melodic, breaking the stillness of the room.

She smiled weakly, her hand sliding up to his chest, fingers slipping through the laces of his shirt until her palm lay flat against his cool skin. Summoning her magic, she sent warmth into him, a gentle fire spreading through his body like the first light of dawn chasing away shadows. She heard the quiet exhale he let out, felt the tension slowly melt from his muscles, like ice giving way to the warmth of spring.

She liked this. She liked the way he seemed to thaw beneath her touch, the way his cold exterior gave way to something softer. She savored the way he leaned into her touch, as if seeking refuge from the chill that had long plagued him. In that heartbeat, their worlds intertwined, and she wondered if she could be the one to keep him warm, to be the flame that dispelled the darkness surrounding him.

Her head rested against his shoulder, her grin faint but content as the glow of her magic faded. He smelled of firewood and earth, the scent wrapping around her like a forest after rain. Her fingertips brushed his chest, feeling the steady, rhythmic beat of his heart beneath her hand.

"Pyra," His breath was warm against her cheek, and though she barely registered the word, she was dimly aware of his hands tightening around her, possessive yet protective.

As the warmth of his body seeped into her, Aria's chin dipped lower, her body surrendering once more to the darkness that beckoned her into sleep.

CHAPTER 31

RYLIK

Rylik closed his eyes, a long, unsteady breath escaping his lips as he tightened his hold on Aria's delicate form draped across his lap. *The gods are testing me*, he thought, his heart beginning to race with a mixture of frustration and desire. Why had she come to him after he'd told her to rest? Was it truly so important to her that she heal his blight? Since when had she begun to care? And why did that thought send a swell of emotion into his chest?

His gaze softened as he looked down at her, the firelight casting her face in a golden glow. Slowly, his hand moved to her cheek, his fingertips grazing her skin with a tenderness he hadn't realized he possessed. His chest soared with warmth and something dangerously close to affection. He swallowed, thankful for the darkness and seclusion, only his hearth bearing witness to the frightening realization that crept below the surface: he *cared* for her. The truth of it hit him like a blade slipping between ribs, sharp and undeniable. He kept his eyes on her lips, parted slightly in the peaceful haze of sleep.

Memories of the night before surged back, burning through his restraint. Though a dream, she had still kissed him with such a reckless disregard for the consequences. She had been greedy, selfish even, when she had claimed his mouth with her own. The way she had enveloped him, taken him ravenously without fear or repercussion—it had ignited something in him. His thumb brushed over her lower lip, tracing its curve with excruciating slowness. His body tensed, heat unfurling low within him, a need he had long since tried to suppress roaring to life.

He wanted to claim her as fiercely and selfishly as she had done with him. Because, there were consequences to her actions, after all. The hunger in his chest deepened, burning through him, pulling him dangerously close to the edge. A shuddering, agonized breath fell from his throat as he pressed his forehead against her own, his lips grazing her cheek with a featherlight touch. The softness of it made his chest ache. What was happening to him?

He had gone through the events of the night unshaken. It had been an evening of bloodshed and bedlam, all of it like second nature to him after years of war. He'd even known she would try to escape again tonight. It hadn't angered him, only saddened him in a distant way. She feared the king. She feared her future here. He could hardly fault her for that.

But when he'd seen Thorian standing in her room, his eyes on her while she lay defenseless in her bed, Rylik had felt a primal rage rise from within, one that was becoming harder to contain of late. That fury had simmered beneath the surface all day, ever since the king had forced her into that dress, molded to her curves with perfect precision, crimson and exquisite. His eyes traced the rich fabric now, fingers following the same path as they slid down her cheek, along the curve of her neck, and across the supple skin of her chest. His eyes flicked down to the plunging neckline where the luxurious material teased at what was below.

Stop, he commanded himself, but his fingers twitched in defiance. He groaned, a low, husky sound vibrating from deep within his chest. He didn't want to stop. He wanted to wake her, to hear her whisper his name in the quiet dark, to pull the fabric from her delicate skin. He wanted to lay her bare in his lap, feeling her breathing labored against his neck, unable to hardly speak between the gasps of pleasure that trembled through her at his touch. He needed to hear how that would sound. He needed to feel her. *All* of her. He wanted to know what it felt like for her to want him as he wanted her—to need him with the same reckless abandon she had shown before.

His breath grew ragged as the fire within him flared brighter. *Reckless*, he scolded himself, his body taut with restraint. But the need was intoxicating, dangerous, a force pulling him deeper into her orbit. *You're being reckless*, his mind echoed, but he no longer cared.

Rylik shot to his feet, fury igniting in his eyes, yet his movements remained careful as Aria slept soundly in his arms, cradled against his chest. Rylik strode across the room, each step over the cold stone floor an ache in his chest, the weight of Aria in his arms both a comfort and a torment. With a slow, reluctant motion, he laid her down on his bed, his jaw clenched as if releasing her from his hold brought him a pain he couldn't escape.

He gazed down at her, his eyes following the graceful lines of her face, each quiet breath she took only heightening the storm of conflict raging inside him. The pull to stay beside her, to hold her again, to lose himself in the feeling of her warmth was maddening. Yet equally fierce was the urge to walk away, to put as much distance as possible between them before he did something irrevocable. His hands tensed at his sides, anger simmering just beneath his skin, not at her, but at himself for feeling this restraint at all. Women had never posed this problem before. They'd come to him willingly, eagerly, with no need for hesitation or second thoughts. But she wasn't like the others. She was practically untouched, innocent in ways he'd long forgotten existed, fragile in body and heart, and there was something almost sacred about her presence in his bed.

She deserved reverence, a carefulness he was unaccustomed to giving, and it tore at him. How could he possibly show restraint when everything in him screamed to take her, to claim her fully as his? His hand hovered near her cheek, inches away from the smooth skin he ached to feel again. The struggle within him felt unbearable, as desire warred with the reverence she unknowingly commanded. It infuriated him, this weakness, this hesitation. Since when did guilt have a place in his thoughts? He was Rylik,

Sovereign to the king, and yet here he stood, paralyzed by a need to protect her from himself.

Taking a long, unsteady breath, Rylik finally tore himself away, the ache of longing twisting inside him like a blade. He returned to his chair by the fire, collapsing into it with a profane curse, reaching for a bottle of wine to steady his hands. The rich, dark liquid filled his glass, but even as he sipped, the relentless yearning persisted, pulsing like a constant reminder of what he wanted but couldn't have. It would be a long night. The thought of her lying just a few feet away was enough to set his teeth on edge, the battle within him far from over.

* * *

The morning air hung heavy with the essence of a torrential downpour, each droplet transformed into glistening jewels upon the earth. Soft light filtered through the windows of Rylik's chamber, illuminating the room in a gentle, dew-laden glow that felt both soothing and inviting. The sweet aroma of freshly baked bread wafted through the air like a warm embrace, a stark yet comforting contrast to the coolness outside.

Rylik heard Aria stirring behind him slowly, and a part of him was thankful that she was awake now, if for no other reason than to put up a strong defense to his desires. After a long moment, he heard the sheets of the bed rustle under her. His ears pricked at the sound of soft footsteps drawing near, the gentle rustle of fabric announcing Aria's approach. He shifted slightly in his chair, anticipation twisting in him like a tightening spring as he heard her emerge from the shadows.

With her nearness, his gaze settled on her in the soft morning light, the deep red of her dress stark against the pale glow, still conforming to her curves with an almost ethereal grace. Her wild, curly hair tumbled in disarray, framing her face like a fiery halo, each strand catching the light as if it were alive. He maintained a passive expression, concealing the tumult of emotions brewing within him, but the sight of her—beautiful yet undone—stirred something deep and unnameable, an ache that whispered just beneath the surface.

He breathed out a soft huff of air as he placed a partially eaten sweet roll into the parchment paper on the small table beside him.

"Good morning, Pyra," Rylik greeted with calm authority. He gestured to a basket sitting in front of the hearth. "I had breakfast brought here from the capital. Help yourself."

Belly rumbling as if on cue, embarrassment colored Aria's cheeks.

Rylik covered his mouth to hide a grin, pretending to find something of interest in the papers he held.

"Thank you, Sovereign," Aria replied, sitting down in the chair between him and the small table. She reached for a sweet roll, biting into it eagerly. After a day of meager sustenance, the roll probably tasted divine. She had hardly eaten at all yesterday, and he was pleased to see her now satisfying her hunger. She polished off the first one in a few bites, quickly picking up another with enthusiasm.

Rylik watched her with a pleased expression. "I thought we might visit the capital today if you're up to it. I have a few things I need to get while we're there, and you could tag along."

Eyes lighting up, she nodded fervently. "Yes, I would love to go with you."

Rylik felt a surge of satisfaction at her answer, a small smile creeping onto his lips as he took a hearty bite of his pastry, the buttery layers crumbling delicately in his mouth while the sweet flavors danced on his tongue.

However, as Aria glanced down at herself, seeing the red dress still clinging to her frame, her expression seemed to twist into something else. He supposed she might've suddenly remembered yesterday's events with some amount of discomfort. That is one of the reasons he would have to take her into town. He needed to make sure that she smiled today, many times over.

"Now that you're awake, I wanted to take a moment to thank you for last night's unexpected healing," he said coolly, catching the look of surprise in her eyes. It was almost as if she thought she'd dreamed it. He smothered the desire to chuckle. "I didn't want to cause you any further strain on your body, but I'm glad that the decision you made led to you falling asleep in my arms." He could hardly stop himself from the desire to tease her.

Her freckled cheeks pinkened as she looked down at her lap, drawing a hand up to her lips. "I probably should've been a little less impulsive. I didn't realize just how weary I was. I shouldn't have—"

"It is your impulsivity that I find myself craving so much recently, Pyra." He cut her off, not wanting to hear a half-hearted apology of something that had brought him unspeakable satisfaction. "So, please, be *reckless*," he urged, a mischievous smolder in his eyes as he added, "so long as that recklessness leads you into my arms."

She lowered her hand to her chest, seemingly trying to still her drumming pulse. He loved that mere words were enough to affect the rhythm of her heart. The effortless ease in which he strung words together to coax and tease such a response would likely be the driving force of his actions today. He smiled at the many, many opportunities that he would seize in order to pull out every vulnerable expression into those lovely yellow eyes of hers.

"Can we visit the potion shop?" she asked shyly, her voice quiet with what he could only assume was thinly veiled shame.

Damn it all, she wanted to dream of him again. Now it was his turn for his heart to race. *Damn.* He felt a familiar tightness in his trousers and he readjusted himself in his chair. Setting his jaw, he swallowed down the compulsion to act on his base instincts.

"Yes," he answered her with an unintentional tightness in his throat that he struggled to hide. Drawing in a steadying breath, he finished more firmly, "Yes, we can go anywhere you'd like to, Aria."

Aria's thighs subtly pulled together and she let out a soft breathy smile, looking into his fireplace.

Gods, he groaned inwardly. She *wanted* him. His teeth were tensed so tightly together that he thought he might grind them into dust.

Lightly licking the sugary glaze from her lips in thought, she smoothed her hands down her dress and inquired, "Is that where you purchased the golden potion?" She had meant to sound innocent, he was certain, but he knew it was anything but. "The potion for sweet dreams, I mean." She looked at him, a certain brightness in her eyes at the prospect of securing another fantasy for herself.

He was going to combust. Closing his eyes with barely masked agony, he inclined his head to her. "That is where I purchased it, yes," his reply was gracious, betraying none of the turmoil brewing low and heady within him.

Her eyes flicked briefly to the adjoining suite door after his confirmation, palms again sliding down her dress in an impatient gesture. She squirmed slightly in her seat. "Are we leaving immediately? Do I have time for a bath?"

Rylik crumpled the parchment paper that had held his roll, tossing it into the fire. *Naughty little Pyra,* he thought with an aggravating inhale. She wanted to relieve the pressure budding between her legs, he could see it as plainly as he could feel the same provocation within himself. "How long do you need?" A coy smile played on his lips as he met her eyes, wanting to see how she crafted her response.

Aria's cheeks flushed as looked away from his stare. "Um, probably not too long, I suppose. I can be quick."

An image of her in his bath assaulted his senses as he unwillingly pictured her exhaling a satiated breath, her fingers low and pressed against herself under the water. If she needed to be satisfied, there was no need to do it quickly. If it were up to him, he would draw it out into an eternity, savoring every frantic moan she made. He clenched his eyes shut as if he could banish the thought.

"Alright." Rylik stood, the sudden movement exposing his nerves as he slipped on his cloak with more speed than he intended. "I have a few things I'll need to arrange, so please get ready at your leisure. We will need to leave before noon to make the most of the day. Excuse me." He turned away, careful not to look back at her. If he did, he would undoubtedly take away her reasons for wanting a bath at all.

CHAPTER 32

ARIA

The wooden sign of *Alchemical Wonders* creaked softly in the morning breeze as Aria approached, its familiar scent of herbs and potions welcoming her. Rylik had kept his promise, escorting her into town for errands that he claimed needed his attention. As they reached the potion shop, he paused, his shadowed eyes softening as he gestured toward the entrance. "You're welcome to browse here while I tend to another matter," he said, his voice low but warm. Before she could ask what business called him away, he was already moving further down the street, disappearing into the bustling crowd.

Left to her own devices, Aria hesitated for a moment before stepping inside. The shop's fogged windows distorted the vibrant colors within, giving the impression of a swirling, magical storm trapped inside. As she pushed open the creaking wooden door, a symphony of clinking glass, the soft rustle of dried herbs, and a faint, metallic hum greeted her. The air carried a heady mix of lavender, crushed mint, and a sharper, undefinable tang that made her chest tighten slightly. Shelves climbed the walls, stacked with countless vials of strange hues, powders in tightly sealed jars, and peculiar trinkets whose purposes she could only guess at. A copper cauldron bubbled quietly in the corner, adding a faint, rhythmic sound to the room.

The old potion master appeared from behind a curtain, his wiry gray hair more disheveled than she remembered, his spectacles perched precariously on his nose. His sharp eyes softened the moment he saw her.

"Ah, Lady Aria," he said, wiping his hands on his apron. "Back so soon? What brings you to my humble establishment today?"

Aria smiled warmly. "Hello again, sir. I was wondering if you might have some golden dreaming potion?" She hesitated, then clarified, "I don't know the name of it, but Sovereign bought it here. I'd like to purchase one vial, please."

His eyes gleamed with recognition. "Dream Weaver is the potion you must be referring to. Let me fetch it for you." He shuffled toward a high shelf, pulling out a wooden stool to reach a series of small, gilded bottles that caught the light like miniature suns. He plucked one of them from his collection, humming softly to himself.

"These are the finest Dream Weaver potions I've crafted this season," he said, carefully handing her the bottle she requested.

"Thank you," she said gratefully as she admired the shimmering liquid within the bottle. The potion master turned to her, his demeanor radiating kindness.

"And how have you been, my dear? Palace life treating you well?"

She sighed, her fingers tightening around the vial. "It's been complicated," she admitted softly. "Rough, even. But that's palace life, I suppose." She would spare him the unsavory details of her horrific dealings with the king. He likely could assume as much anyway.

The old man chuckled knowingly. "Indeed, the castle of Ravenhelm has a way of testing even the strongest of souls."

Aria hesitated before glancing down at the counter. "Since I'm here, I have been so curious. You see, upon our first meeting, you gave me a potion. You called it the Potion of Reflection. But, it wasn't, was it?"

The potion master's laughter bubbled forth, warm and mischievous. "Caught me, have you?" He leaned on the counter, lowering his voice as though sharing a great secret. "You're right, my dear. That potion was something far more intriguing—a mind-reading elixir."

While the confirmation brought her some comfort, it didn't quell her inquisitiveness entirely. "I gathered as much, but why?"

"Well," he began, his grin unfaltering. "I suppose I thought it might be illuminating for you to see what lurked behind the Sovereign's stoic mask. Did it not prove enlightening?"

She crossed her arms, torn between indignation and curiosity. "Why the secrecy? Why do this at all?"

"If I'd told you what the elixir did, the Sovereign would have found out, and my game would have been spoiled," he chuckled softly. "I'm an old man, and I've lived a long time. After a while, I grow accustomed to seeing the same faces pass through my door, day in and day out, year after year. But now and then, someone enters my shop who catches my interest." He seemed lost in thought, his gaze distant as he recalled something from long ago. "The first time I met the Sovereign, I knew immediately he was someone worth watching."

His eyes slid over to her, as though reading her with a practiced eye, his gaze observant on her face. "You know of his blight, do you not?" he asked, a sobering edge to his tone that seemed to cool the air between them.

Aria hesitated, a knot tightening in her chest. That blight was her darkest secret, one she would take to her grave. To her surprise, he smiled gently, turning his eyes away with a shrug.

"He knows I know. For years, I provided him with a tonic to ease his suffering, but it seems he's found a better remedy." He didn't need to look at her to know they both understood exactly who he meant. "It's important that you know this. His soul is not as shadowed as the magic he wields. He's a good man, though perhaps too guarded. I suspect he needs someone like you to heal the wounds he's kept hidden."

Aria blinked, his words striking a chord deep within her. "I'm not sure I know what you mean, Sir."

The potion master smiled knowingly. "Healing comes in many forms, child. Magic is but one of them. You may find you have other gifts far more powerful than you realize—gifts that can heal even the heart itself."

A gentle comfort filled her chest, a spark of hope that settled into quiet determination. If it was love he was referring to, she could certainly feel a similar emotion blossoming within her like a flourishing garden.

The potion master clapped his hands together. "Now then, what are you planning to use the Dream Weaver for? Want to spy on your looming shadow?"

She frowned, confused by the question. "I just wanted sweet dreams. What do you mean?"

The old man's face lit with surprise, followed by an amused chuckle. "Ah, I see! You didn't know. The Dream Weaver is no ordinary sleeping draught. It's meant to connect two dreamers. Two people share the same bottle, and their dreams intertwine."

A rush of panic swept through Aria, her thoughts tumbling over one another. *Two people? Shared dreams?* A memory surfaced: the vivid dream she had shared with Rylik. The kiss on the boat. Her heart leapt and then plummeted as realization struck. *He was there. He kissed me back.*

Heat flooded her cheeks as she tried to suppress the flurry of emotions rising within her. Anger at the deception, confusion over what it meant, and an undeniable thrill that sent her pulse racing.

"Use it wisely, my dear," the old man said with a wink.

Aria managed a weak smile, clutching the bottle to her chest. "Thank you. For everything."

After paying him, she stepped outside, the fresh air washing over her like a balm, though it did little to soothe the tempest raging inside her. She spotted Rylik standing a short distance away, speaking to a man in hushed tones. When his gaze lifted and found hers, a smile spread across his lips, and her heart betrayed her by fluttering wildly.

She swallowed hard, gripping the bag tighter. She desperately wanted to feel anger upon seeing him, especially knowing now that he had tricked her that night with the Dream Weaver potion, but instead she felt ravenous.

Rylik tucked something small and black into his pocket and the man he'd been speaking to turned and left him. He approached Aria with a keen expression, gaze dropping down to her bag in hand. "Everything go well? Got your golden potions?"

She gave a subtle nod, a dark thread of mischief weaving its way through her thoughts. He was so smug—and annoyingly justified in it. She wanted revenge, some delicious, harmless form of payback. "I got enough to share," she said, carefully lacing her tone with innocence. "If you wanted to share it like last time, to repay you for the portion I drank, I'd be happy to do that."

His smile turned wry, his gaze flicking briefly to the potion shop behind her before settling back on her with a taunting glint. He cocked his head slightly, studying her with infuriating leisure. "I suppose I could do with a good dream tonight," he said, his voice low and edged with a teasing intent that made her wonder what, precisely, was going through his mind at that moment.

A flicker of giddiness sparked in her chest, though she quickly averted her gaze, her cheeks warming at the idea of her own clever retribution. "Very well. What's next for us in the capital today, Sovereign?" she asked, feigning composure.

Rylik clasped his hands neatly behind his back and glanced toward the far end of the bustling plaza. "The corsetière is expecting you. We ought not to keep her waiting. Come," he said smoothly, turning on his heel with impeccable poise, leaving her to grapple with the rush of heat flooding her face.

"Sovereign!" she exclaimed, darting after him and catching at his arm in a desperate bid to halt him. "We are *not* going to do that!"

Without missing a step, he grasped her hand and tucked it neatly into the crook of his arm, his movements fluid and inexorable. "You have an appointment. It would be rude not to show up," he replied, his tone maddeningly composed. With a dismissive pat to her hand, he trivialized her protest entirely, leaving her with no choice but to match his stride.

Aria kept begrudgingly close to Rylik as they weaved through the throng, her cheeks still warm with apprehension.

"Do we *really* have to do this?" she asked, her voice barely above the din.

Rylik cast her a sidelong glance, his lips curving into a subtle, amused smile. "We do. You need proper attire for upcoming occasions, and the corsetière comes highly recommended."

Her blush deepened as she tugged on his arm to convey her resistance. "It's not the *corsets* that bother me—it's the thought of you being there."

"Should I leave, then?" he teased, his tone smooth as silk. "Or perhaps you'd prefer me to supervise?"

Aria's sputtered protest drew a low chuckle from him. "Relax," he added, his voice lowering just enough to soothe her nerves, though his teasing glint remained. "You're welcome to peruse without me for now. I have another matter to attend to, but I'll return before you're done."

They reached the shop, its modest exterior hiding an air of exclusivity. The sign above the door read *Silk and Sable Corsetry* in elegant gold lettering. Aria hesitated as Rylik held the door open for her, his expression unreadable except for the faintest trace of mischief in his gaze.

Inside, the world transformed. The interior was warm and opulent, lit by a dozen candelabras whose soft glow reflected off gilded mirrors and rich velvet drapes. Mannequins adorned with intricately designed corsets and gowns stood like silent guardians, each piece more exquisite than the last. Rows of fine silks and lace spilled from shelves, their delicate patterns practically begging to be touched. The air was perfumed with the subtle scent of rosewater and something faintly musky, lending the space an intimate charm.

"Welcome," came a velvety voice, drawing Aria's attention to a statuesque woman gliding toward them. The shopkeeper was elegance personified, her silver hair swept into a chignon and her gown tailored to perfection. Her sharp eyes softened as she took in Aria, a gracious smile spreading across her lips. "My, what a lovely figure you have."

Aria's blush reignited, and she opened her mouth to respond, but the woman's gaze flicked to Rylik. "And such fine taste in companions. You do know how to choose well, my lord."

Rylik's amusement deepened, though he responded with a slight bow of his head. "I've been told that before."

"Come, my dear," the shopkeeper said, taking Aria's arm and leading her toward the back of the shop. "We'll find something perfect for you."

Aria shot Rylik a flustered look over her shoulder, but he simply offered a serene smile before stepping away, leaving her to her fate.

The fitting room was an intimate sanctuary draped in soft fabrics and lit by the flicker of candles. The shopkeeper guided Aria through a whirlwind of laces, ribbons, and silks, her hands deft and practiced as she adjusted each corset. Time passed in a blur as Aria tried on various styles—dainty white corsets with delicate embroidery, deep crimson ones that made her cheeks heat, and shimmering gold designs that clung to her curves in ways she didn't dare acknowledge.

The shopkeeper hummed approvingly at Aria's choices, particularly a sleek black corset with a sweetheart neckline. "This one suits you perfectly, my dear," she remarked. "It's bold, but not overstated. Just enough to make any man lose his breath."

Aria bit her lip, staring at the mirror. Her reflection didn't look like her—it looked confident. Maybe even alluring. But before she could overthink it, the door creaked open.

"Pyra."

The low cadence of his voice struck her like a spark to dry kindling. She whirled around, clutching the edge of the fitting screen as if it might shield her.

Rylik stood at the doorframe, one shoulder leaning lazily against the carved wood. His gaze was unhurried, dragging from the smooth curve of her waist to the delicate slope of her shoulders, finally meeting her wide, flustered eyes.

"You look," He paused, the words hanging in the charged air between them. A faint smile ghosted his lips. "Incredible."

Aria fumbled, crossing her arms over her chest as if she could block his view. "Sovereign! What are you doing in here?"

"Admiring." He stepped further into the room, the door clicking shut behind him. "Black suits you."

"Have some decency!" she snapped, her voice higher than she meant.

Rylik stopped in front of her, his smirk deepening into something undeniably wicked. "Decency?" he repeated with mock thoughtfulness. "Whatever gave you the impression that I was a man of decency?"

She drew in a shallow breath as he reached out—not to touch her but to adjust a loose ribbon at her shoulder, the back of his fingers brushing her skin with maddening softness.

"I must admit," he began, his voice so low it seemed to curl around her. "I do like seeing you like this, wearing my color, a piece of me—and on you, it feels like a promise, like you're already wrapped in something that belongs to me. In a way, it's like a brand, a mark that you're mine, whether you admit it or not."

Her cheeks burned, her eyes glancing nervously in the direction of the shopkeeper. "Sovereign, I'll remind you that we are not, in fact, alone in here," she whispered, her voice trembling as she gripped the skirt at her sides.

Rylik's gaze flicked to the shopkeeper, his expression cool but expectant. Without a word, the older woman straightened, her practiced hands pausing over a folded ribbon. She gave a polite, knowing smile and murmured something about tidying up the counter before excusing herself from the room.

The faint echo of her footsteps disappeared beyond the door, leaving the quiet stillness of the room to stretch like a held breath.

Rylik leaned closer, his voice dropping as he said, "It's just you and I now, as you desired."

Aria's pulse quickened, and without thinking, she took a half step back. She fought to find her voice, her words faltering as she managed, "That wasn't what I meant for you to do."

"Oh? Didn't you?" His lips curved in that infuriating, knowing way, his dark eyes dancing with mischief. "Because from where I stand, it looked as though you were inviting this very moment, eager to be alone with me, like *this*."

"I wasn't," she replied, her voice unsteady. "I'm not in the mood for your teasing, Sovereign."

His gaze deepened, predatory, as if he could see straight through her. A slow, hungry smile spread across his face. "Then what are you in the mood for, Aria?"

The room seemed to shrink around them, thick with an intimacy that pressed on her chest. The flickering candlelight painted the space in soft, trembling shadows, their warm, intoxicating scent drifting through the air like a whispered secret. His presence surrounded her, each breath she took tangled with the weight of his gaze—those deep, icy eyes pulling her in, clouding her every thought. Slowly, he stepped forward, closing the distance between them with an intentional slowness that made her pulse race. His hands, warm and firm, settled on her shoulders, guiding her gently to face the mirror as he stood close behind, his body a heat that radiated against her skin.

He leaned in, his breath warm against the back of her neck, his voice a low whisper. "You tell me, little Pyra," His body pressed possessively against hers, a subtle yet undeniable force that framed her smaller figure with his. "Because when you look like this, can you even begin to understand the power you have over me right now?"

CHAPTER 33

RYLIK

Rylik was aware of the temptation he was inviting in this moment, hidden away inside this back room with Aria, but he didn't care. In this secluded space, he was alone with his most prized possession, and he planned to toy with her until she melted beneath his touch, her resistance slipping away as he molded her to his will.

She swallowed hard, her throat dry, struggling to process the intent of his question. "Power?"

"Mmm." He hummed in contemplation, trailing his fingers lazily up her bare arm, letting the lightest touch linger. "You could command kingdoms dressed like this. Men would go to war just to catch a glimpse of you."

"You're being ridiculous," she muttered, her voice trembling ever so slightly.

"Am I?" he replied, his voice an edge of velvet. He lifted her chin with a soft touch, forcing her gaze to the mirror. "Look at yourself."

Her reflection caught his eyes—bright, challenging, defiant—and he reveled in the way her expression softened under his scrutiny. His voice dropped lower, heavier with intent. "Every line, every curve—it's like temptation itself was made flesh."

She broke his gaze, shifting her attention to the mirror, though it wasn't the corset she focused on. It was him, watching her — aware of every tiny movement she made. He saw her eyes track the way his hand settled possessively at her waist, the subtle pressure of his touch pulling her nearer. He moved his hand to span a wider portion of her body, pressing her firmly against him. He felt the small hitch in her breath, the quick rise of her chest, and he savored the dark satisfaction of her reaction.

"I appreciate your compliments, Sovereign," she muttered, forcing composure into her voice — and failing spectacularly. "But, don't you think this little tease of yours is over with? You should go."

He chuckled, the sound rich and deep. "No, I wouldn't dream of leaving." His voice dipped to a near whisper, "and you're the one teasing *me*, Pyra. Can you not see that?"

"I—I'm not—" she started, but the words failed her as he leaned closer, his lips hovering near her ear.

"And what a lovely tease you are," he murmured, the words leaving a soft challenge between them.

He pressed a soft, almost imperceptible kiss to the curve of her neck, savoring the way her body shivered in response, the faintest moan escaping her lips. In this small, shared space, they were both testing the limits of their restraint. She wanted him — he could feel it. And though he longed for her just as fiercely, there was still the matter of the morning's bath, where her thoughts would have been consumed by him, yet her hands would have only touched herself. The memory stayed with him, unresolved, begging a thorough punishment.

How much longer would this dance continue, he wondered. How much longer would they both teeter on the edge of temptation, exchanging subtle provocations and feigned indifference, before she finally shattered? When would all her carefully constructed defenses crumble, her excuses evaporating into nothing as the tension between them finally snapped — leaving only soft, breathless gasps and discarded fabric at their feet?

"You're the one who showed up to a fitting you weren't invited to," she retorted, her attempt at firmness undermined by the way her knees weakened beneath her. "I am no tease. I had no intention of ensnaring you in any of this. I'll remind you that it was *your* idea to even come here—"

"It is customary," he interrupted, his voice smooth and unwavering, "for lords to stay with their ladies while they try on their various little satin slips and bodices." His grin spread wider, and he met her gaze in the mirror, his presence closing in on her like a tangible force. "I very much want to see you in more delicate, lace-trimmed undergarments."

"The corsets are not for *you*," she snipped, though her trembling voice betrayed her bravado.

"Oh, yes they are." He smirked, reaching down to gently pluck a stray ribbon from her skirt, his knuckles brushing her hip. "And I will see you in every last one, rest assured." He smiled again, his eyes steady on hers with a hint of seductive warning, "Wholly savoring every moment you are dressed in them, and every moment that you are *not*."

The gravity of his words struck her, their significance settling heavily in her chest. He searched her eyes, finding only traces of yearning, and it caused an unexpected pang in his chest. A familiar and unnecessary tightness strained against the fabric of his trousers and he pulled back from her before she might notice.

"Consider this a mercy, Pyra," he said, his voice smooth as silk. "Because next time I have you alone in something like *this*, I may not be so composed."

Rylik could feel the heat of her gaze as he turned, walking toward the door with a measured, effortless stride. He paused at the threshold, glancing over his shoulder, letting his eyes settle on her for a moment longer, savoring the effect he had left behind.

"I look forward to the rest of the collection," he said, the low, sultry edge in his tone making her stomach flutter against her will. "I'll be waiting outside."

The door clicked shut behind him, leaving Aria alone to process the whirlwind of emotions he'd just dragged her through.

Rylik leaned casually against the wall outside the fitting room, a quiet observer, his senses sharpened as he listened to the soft murmur of voices within.

"Let's get you settled and on your way."

The shopkeeper's tone was soft and unhurried, but he caught the edge of amusement in her words, the knowing laugh she gave as Aria protested.

"Are you packaging *all* of them, Madame?"

"Yes, of course," he could hear the shopkeeper explain confidently, "And I'll need the one you're wearing, too, assuming you are leaving in the same wardrobe you arrived with?"

He smirked to himself, enjoying the slow burn of tension building inside the room, though his attention was fixed entirely on the woman who had no idea he was waiting just outside.

"Of course I'll be wearing what I came in," he listened to Aria's aggravation. "There's not a single thing I've bought here today that I should be wearing out in a public setting, however, I couldn't possibly purchase all of them—"

"Your lord already purchased your selections," the shopkeeper keenly interrupted her, clarifying, "every last one."

"What?!"

He could hear her exasperated voice, tinged with a mix of indignation and something else, the familiar fire of defiance that only seemed to stoke the flames of his amusement. He could picture her now—flushed cheeks, lips pressed tight in frustration, still wrapped in those delicate fabrics.

A small chuckle escaped him as the conversation turned to his purchases. So, she didn't realize just how thoroughly he had planned this little excursion. The idea of her trying to wriggle out of it, of her huffing and blushing at the idea of owning and wearing his selections, was too satisfying. He leaned in closer, his ear at the door.

"He said you'd make good use of them," the shopkeeper continued, her tone conspiratorial. "And I told him he must insist on a private show later. He seemed to agree."

"A private show!?"

His smile deepened—this was exactly the kind of reaction he'd been hoping for. He had her, and she didn't even realize it yet.

After a little while of grumbling and rustling of fabric, enough time passed for Aria to have changed back into her prior drab yellow gown she had been wearing before the fitting. The shopkeeper would be sending the corsets to the palace within the hour, and a small part of him hoped he might catch her in one later that evening.

As the door clicked open, he straightened, turning to face Aria as she emerged, her cheeks still flushed with that perfect combination of indignation and embarrassment. His smile curled as he took in the sight of her, his eyes tracing her figure, already yearning for the way the corset had so enticingly accentuated her curves.

"Ready?" he asked, his voice a low, smooth drawl that he knew sent a ripple of warmth through her. He saw the way her eyes flashed with a mixture of fury and something more dangerous—a little storm waiting to break free.

She nodded stiffly, and they fell into stride together. As they made their way through the plaza, he could practically hear the whirlwind of thoughts racing through her mind. And, damn him, he enjoyed every minute of it.

Upon reaching the bakery, they stepped inside and the scent of freshly baked bread and spiced pastries wrapped around them like a comforting embrace. While Rylik exchanged coins for a parcel of honeyed rolls, he noticed Aria waiting by the display, the simple act of choosing a treat loosening the tension in her shoulders. After a while, they emerged back onto the sunlit streets and her expression had softened, her hands clutching the warm paper-wrapped goods.

The air was sweet with the mingling aromas of fresh bread and blooming flowers from nearby window boxes. Laughter and cheerful chatter floated through the plaza, punctuated by the occasional clatter of hooves against the stones. Aria was practically radiant, her vibrant hair catching the light as she turned her gaze toward the square, where the soft strains of music drifted over the city's gentle bustle.

It seemed the visit to the bakery had cooled her ire. Though he'd relished her earlier embarrassment, he'd hoped she might calm her nerves enough to enjoy the rest of their time in town. After enduring a horrible evening in the king's company yesterday, she needed this—and, for once, he was happy to provide it.

The joyous strains of music rising from the plaza's core seemed to reach out, encircling them in their bright, irresistible pull. Already talking excitedly, she pointed down the street, her eyes sparkling with anticipation, as if sheer will might quicken their pace. Rylik smiled, letting her infectious enthusiasm wash over him, but even in that moment of shared delight, his thoughts drifted elsewhere—toward his earlier purchase with the silversmith and his other errands within the town.

Alastair, one of his Shadow Knights, had been dispatched to check on Aria's parents. Rylik needed to be certain they were safe, especially with Orren's threats still hanging in the air. Alastair's report was reassuring: they remained unharmed, occupied with the usual homestead tasks. Still, Rylik had instructed him to leave a small pouch of coin behind. He knew their poverty too well—Aria's modest earnings were hardly enough to support them. The king's pitiful salary for her was an insult, a hollow gesture meant to feign goodwill. But Rylik understood the game. A healer who felt appreciated, even if grudgingly, was far more useful than a resentful captive.

Rylik had also been watching Thorian closely ever since the botched abduction. It surprised him that Thorian hadn't yet made another attempt, but he doubted the man had given up— more likely, he was lurking in the shadows, waiting for the right moment to strike. And if the other night had proven anything, it was that he wouldn't hesitate to slip into her chambers. He had wanted to ask her what was discussed between them, but knew better than to ask her outright. She would only lie, and he would need to circumvent that. His preferred methods of coaxing information from her—like strong merlot and perhaps the Dream Weaver potion—were far more enjoyable than torture.

He smirked, toying with the idea of a truth elixir instead. From the playful glint in her eyes earlier, when she'd teasingly suggested sharing the potion with him later, it was clear she now understood its true purpose. The potion master must have let the secret slip—and the thought thrilled him. The idea that she would dare try toying with him sparked a wicked amusement. Yet, tonight, he wasn't in the mood for simple games. If she wanted to play with him, she would soon find that his intentions with her teetered on the edge of forbidden temptation.

They reached the square, where the crowd thinned slightly

as they moved toward the stage. He watched her, entranced by the performers, her gaze filled with a wonder that pleased him. His thoughts wandered, shifting to his other tasks—particularly the report from another of his spies, who had brought news of his mother. As expected, she was in her usual health, though her letter had been filled with sharp words, scolding him for sending yet another spy in his place. She'd threatened to visit him in person if it happened again—an empty threat, perhaps, but one he knew better than to ignore.

She missed him, and the feeling was undeniably mutual, yet with everything at the castle reaching its tipping point, he couldn't afford to visit her just yet. She lived two days' journey from the palace, tucked away in a secluded region, surrounded by security, ample coin, and a life of quiet contentment. The king had taken so much from her when he executed her husband— Rylik's father—years ago, and Rylik had vowed to keep her safe, far from the reach of the crown. She needed to remain unknown, shielded from any further disruption.

She was a spry, stubborn woman, yet even she understood the necessity of remaining hidden for her own safety, lest the king seek further retribution for the so-called treason of her late husband. The king had no knowledge of Rylik's true identity— how could he? Rylik had been little more than a boy, barely seventeen, when his father was executed for a crime he hadn't committed. After their family's disgrace, Rylik had taken his mother far from the reach of the crown, vowing to restore his father's honor, no matter the cost.

He had dedicated himself to his training, and over the years, his diligence earned him the king's notice and, eventually, his favor. His final, decisive act to prove himself came at a brutal cost— the Frostwraith Blight, a wound that would never fully heal. The war had ended in victory, both for him and, by extension, for the king. In the aftermath, he had been offered the position he'd long coveted: The Sovereign. No other role within the palace could grant him such proximity to the king, nor the political power to learn every secret of the court and exploit every weakness. Since his arrival, he had been a quiet poison within the castle, methodically weaving his influence, cultivating a future court of his own. One day, very soon, not only would the Rebellion be crushed, but the king's tyranny would fall with it. A new king would rise—one far better than the last. An ominous grin curved his lips at the thought.

His eyes settled gently over Aria's red hair, shining like burnished copper under the noonday sun. He mused to himself that his mother and Aria might get along well—if he dared to allow it. Once he was king, he could return his mother to their former estate, or even bring her into the palace, should she wish it. Of course, she would likely be insufferable, eager to meet the woman he would have to make his consort. His gaze shifted to Aria, an expression of brazen intent crossing his features. He couldn't help but wonder how she might react when he sat upon the throne and made her an offer of courtship—an offer that would bind her to him in ways she could never have anticipated.

Aria's attention drifted to the side, and her expression changed. Curious, Rylik followed her gaze and found the familiar, broad-shouldered figure of the Corporal standing outside a shop with his arms folded across his chest. Leontias, he thought with a bored sneer. Maybe he was off duty for the day, but his nearness to Aria felt like an intrusion. When Rylik looked back at her, he saw her already trying to turn away. He reached out, catching her shoulder.

"What's wrong?" he asked smoothly, as though he hadn't noticed the unease that Leon's presence had stirred in her.

She shifted under his touch but didn't pull away. "It's stupid. Nothing, really," she sighed. "I just don't want Leon and I to have to talk. I'm afraid he'll want to, and I don't."

Her words wavered on the edge of uncertainty, and Rylik noted the restless flicker in her gaze. Was it simply the weight of unrequited feelings, or was there something darker lurking beneath the surface—perhaps a dangling thread connected to the Rebellion? His eyes darted back to Leon, irritation flaring within him like a freshly stoked fire.

"Sovereign?" Aria's voice, soft yet tinged with unease, pulled him from his thoughts. "My shoulder?"

The realization that his grip had tightened somewhat around her sent a surge of surprise through him. He reluctantly released her, but the resistance felt like a silent war waging within him. "Sorry," he murmured, his voice low and nearly swallowed by the city's clamor.

A hint of possessiveness filled the space between them, an unspoken promise that he would not easily let her go. Adopting a sly tone, he let a playful smirk dance across his lips, attempting to weave levity into the tension. "Why so averse to him now? After all, it wasn't long ago that you claimed to have kissed me in order to make him jealous." The sarcasm dripped gently from his words, and he found himself yearning for the warmth of her smile in response. "So, what's changed, Aria?"

She smiled, much to his satisfaction, and replied, "I've begun to see him in a different light, if you must know." She sighed, glancing reluctantly in Leon's direction, though she remained close to Rylik, half-hidden behind him as though he were a shield. "I think he and I want different things. I've wasted enough years pretending otherwise."

Rylik savored the nearness of her body next to his own, her fingers absently settling against the chest plate of his armor. When had their closeness evolved into this tangled intimacy, where merely standing together felt both exhilarating and dangerously familiar? Did she even realize the effect she had on him, or was she blissfully oblivious to the tempest of longing raging inside him? He inhaled deeply, trying to tame the wild emotions clawing at his resolve, before his voice slipped into a low, probing tone, "What was it that drew you to him in the first place?"

Aria didn't look up at him, her eyes fixed on Leon as though she were watching a memory more than a person. "He was an orphan when my parents took him in. He was fifteen, I think, which would've made me thirteen. But we'd known each other for years before then. He always saw me as a little sister, I think, something annoying he tolerated. But he wasn't unkind." She smiled, though the smile was faint, tinged with a sadness that seemed to settle deep into her expression.

Rylik doubted any kindness from Leon could be worth a smile, but he nodded to show he was listening.

"We were close, once." She shifted a little nearer to him, as if unconsciously seeking his presence. "He was protective of me, always showing he cared by looking out for me. I never had to worry about being bullied or mistreated, because he was always there, making sure I was alright." Her tone held an edge of bitterness, as though the years since had chipped away at the comfort she once found in Leon's presence. Rylik could easily imagine why—joining the Rebellion, Leon had likely left her safety far behind.

"As he got older, he earned favor with the Valenforth family," she continued, her voice tinged with something bittersweet, as though each word was another step down a road she'd already walked a thousand times in her mind. "It wasn't long before he started training for the king's army. That was around the time my healing powers awakened, and we just grew apart." Her voice softened, faltering as if the weight of old memories bore down upon it, unearthing fragments of dreams that hadn't quite come true. "He was," she hesitated, eyes drifting somewhere far away, as though searching for the right word among the pieces of her past. "He was busy."

Rylik's eyes held on her, tracing the sadness she wore so softly. He felt the familiar rise of envy and anger at Leon—he'd been so blind, so careless, not to have seen her transformation, not to have claimed the treasure she so openly offered. Gently, he reached out, running his hand along her arm, fingers grazing her skin with slow, measured possession. "Well," he murmured, letting his voice settle low and smooth, "then he was unwise, if he was too busy to see you becoming a lady right before his eyes."

He was delighted to see the familiar warm blush of color flood her cheeks at his compliment. Her eyes flickered up to meet his, caught between shyness and the thrill of being seen in a way she hadn't expected. Rylik's hand remained, his touch barely moving but unmistakable, grounding her there with him. He wanted to erase every careless word, every indifferent glance Leon had ever given her, and replace them with his own—a look that claimed, a touch that promised.

She seemed to realize that her fingers were still tracing his armored chest plate, and she pulled her hand back, taking a small step away. The moment her touch slipped away, a deep, possessive yearning stirred within him—he ached to pull her back, to feel her warmth pressed close, to make her understand she belonged here, with him. But he reined it in, letting the desire simmer beneath his control.

"It's in the past now, anyway," she said, as if to brush away the weight of old feelings. "We're just too different, he and I, and there's no need for me to—" Her voice trailed off, faltering as she stared ahead.

Rylik followed her gaze back to Leon, who now had company—Maven had stepped out of the shop he had been waiting by. Leon's face transformed, a wide, unguarded smile breaking across his features as he offered Maven his arm. She took it easily, the two of them slipping into the crowd, conversing as though lost in their own world. Leon was clearly enamored, his manner soft, attentive—traits Rylik had never seen him show to Aria.

Rylik looked back at Aria, a pang of anger simmering beneath the faint sorrow in her expression. Leon's laughter with Maven was an affront—a reminder that the Corporal had never given Aria the attention she deserved, had never seen her the way she needed to be seen. He felt jealousy twist in his chest, dark and consuming, tempered only by his determination to claim what Leon had so carelessly disregarded. She deserved more, far more than to be discarded like some passing fancy. Rylik would be the one to erase that pain, to draw from her the devotion she had wasted on others.

Yet even as he imagined it, he felt a wary caution, a whispered warning at the edges of his thoughts. There was danger in wanting her like this, in letting his desire become tangled with possessiveness. But he wouldn't yield to doubt. If it meant defying whatever weak attachments still tethered her to others, he would do it. He would make her see that it was he, and no one else, who could fill the ache in her heart. She would be his to protect, to hold, to make her smile—and one day, he would be the only one she thought of, the only one who mattered.

CHAPTER 34

ARIA

The rest of the day had slipped by far too quickly for Aria's liking once she and Rylik returned to the castle from the capital. She'd spent a few hours in the apothecary, her mind drifting through the motions as the afternoon waned, and now, in the evening, she found herself at the door to the Sovereign's room. She hesitated there, feeling an inexplicable pull to simply turn back, retreat to her own quarters where she might find the solitude she craved. But she pushed open the door, and a comforting warmth met her, the familiar scent of burning wood winding through the room. The fire crackled softly in the hearth, the quiet murmur of flames the only sound in the stillness.

Rylik sat in his usual high-backed chair near the fire, the warm glow accentuating the sharp contours of his face as he took a slow sip of wine. The glass caught the firelight, gleaming a deep crimson. At her arrival, his gaze lifted, sharp and intent, and a faint smile curved his lips. "Aria," he drawled, his voice slipping through the quiet room, "I was beginning to wonder when you'd finally arrive."

"I lost track of time, wrapping things up with Maven," she explained, hoping to leave it at that. Her time in the apothecary had been laced with discomfort, but she couldn't place the blame on Maven, and she couldn't resent Leon for choosing someone else. If anything, her frustration was reserved for herself.

Her gaze drifted to the chair beside his, separated by a small wooden table, yet she hesitated. Despite the warmth she'd come to find in his company each evening, tonight she simply wanted to retreat to her room, let her pride nurse its bruises, and hope morning might feel different. She knew she couldn't sulk forever, but she figured one evening of it wouldn't hurt.

Rylik studied her quietly, his intense gaze following her as she wandered to the fireplace, remaining on her feet instead of sitting beside him. "Something troubling you?" he asked, his voice breaking through her thoughts.

"Nothing of consequence." Her response was low, edged with a quiet frustration she couldn't shake. She kept replaying the look she'd seen in Leon's eyes as he'd smiled at Maven—the look she'd once longed for herself. Why was it so difficult to let go?

Rylik placed his glass down carefully, his attention on her unwavering. "If it's enough to put a shadow over your evening, then perhaps it's worth mentioning. I'm here, if you'd like to talk."

A faint smile tugged at her lips, though it barely masked the ache beneath. "Some things are better left unspoken, Sovereign. I think you, of all people, understand that." She glanced at him, her tone playful yet subtly evasive.

"I do," he said, tracing the base of his wine glass as the firelight glinted against the dark red wine. "But, even so, I did appreciate what you shared with me earlier. Your past with Corporal Valenforth." His gaze lifted, catching the sadness in her expression. He knew the reason behind it, yet he was giving her an opening, inviting her to speak further.

She tried for a smile but couldn't keep the hurt from her voice. "Honestly, the little I shared of Leon today is more attention than he deserves, Sovereign." Turning her eyes away, she focused on the firelight flickering in the hearth. "This childish hurt will fade. There was never any real hope for something between us. He was never going to see me the way I wanted him to. And honestly, I would be unhappy if he did. I don't want him anymore. But, I still feel indignant somehow."

Rylik's smirk darkened, and he reached into his pocket. "Perhaps he isn't worth your time, but these feelings, they're worth something." With a flicker of movement, he caught her attention, his hand lifting to reveal something glinting in the firelight—a pendant, delicate and glowing softly, as though it held a hidden light within. It was set in a small black box inlaid with a smooth satin interior. She tensed as he plucked it from the box and held it out, the silvery stone pulsing faintly like something alive.

"That is beautiful," she murmured, awe in her voice.

"It's yours, if you want it," he said, his voice quiet but rich with depth, sending a shiver through her.

She blinked, both surprised and deeply moved. "I—I couldn't possibly." Her eyes were drawn to the pendant, the soft light within pulling her closer, as though it spoke to her in a language only she could comprehend.

"It's called a Lyrica Pendant," he explained, his gaze intent on hers. "A song is woven into the stone. It's meant to soothe, if your heart is open enough to hear it." He tilted his head, watching her closely, as if daring her to try.

Her heart softened at his words. He'd known how shaken she'd been by seeing Leon with Maven and had thought to offer her something precious, a gift to ease her troubled spirit.

Rylik rose from his chair and crossed the short distance between them, the firelight painting his features in shifting shadows and amber highlights. Her pulse quickened, and when he moved to drape the chain around her neck, her skin tingled where his fingers brushed. She held her breath as he fastened it, his touch lingering just a moment longer than necessary, a deliberate claim that made her feel both exposed and safe, in a strange, electric way.

"Do you hear it?" he murmured, his voice brushing against her cheek, his breath warm.

Closing her eyes, she let the pendant's warmth seep into her, listening beyond the crackling of the fire. And then, faint as a whisper, a melody began to fill her senses, stirring something gentle and joyful within, as if it were sweeping away the shadows of her day. "Yes," she whispered, her heart lifting as the song filled a quiet emptiness she hadn't realized was there.

When she opened her eyes, he had moved in front of her, watching her with an expression she couldn't quite decipher, as if he were savoring her reaction yet holding back his own emotions. "Good," he murmured, his hand moving to rest against the pendant, his fingers grazing her skin. "Wear it often." His voice held a dangerous edge, though his touch remained gentle. "As often as you need to lift your spirits, Pyra."

Her hand instinctively covered his, the metal of the pendant cool beneath her fingertips, but his hand—steady, possessive— was warm. She couldn't ignore the effect his touch had on her, nor the closeness that somehow felt more intimate than words could convey. His gaze dropped to her lips, and her pulse fluttered, the world around them shrinking to this moment, this breath between them.

Soft embers snapped and whispered in the hearth, a quiet rhythm Aria only half-registered, her mind swirling elsewhere. She wondered what it would feel like to kiss him again, if the thought had crossed his mind, too. Was it the lightness in her chest now, the enchantment of the pendant's gentle lullaby, or simply the way he looked at her, unblinking and intense? Lowering her hand from his, she took a cautious step back, trying to distance herself from the rush of her thoughts.

"Sovereign," she began, her voice soft. "Thank you. You didn't have to—"

"You're welcome," he interrupted, clasping his hands behind his back. His expression was calm, though something deeper simmered beneath it. "It's late. Perhaps you'd like to retire for the evening?"

She gave a slow nod, even though part of her ached to stay. It was for the best she went to her room, lest she stay any longer and find her lips seeking his in some moment of longing she knew she should keep buried. "I'll just heal your Blight," she said, hesitantly closing the distance she'd created. Her hand slipped beneath his loosened tunic, her fingertips brushing against the warm skin of his chest. The sensation felt almost forbidden, a touch that carried far more than healing in its intent. Summoning her magic, she focused on the pulsing warmth of her power, watching as a golden light unfurled from her palm and seeped into him, its radiance pooling like sunlight into shadow.

She felt his heartbeat steady, sensed the quiet release of tension in his muscles. When she looked up, her eyes glowed with the intensity of her gift, like molten gold, while he had closed his own, seeming to bask in a rare, unfettered peace. How she wished she could prolong that for him, to see him like this always—unguarded, unburdened.

As she allowed herself to sink into the warmth between them, the pendant at her chest hummed softly, its melody weaving a delicate whisper in her ears. A strange comfort washed over her, a quiet joy that made the world's worries feel distant and inconsequential. For a fleeting moment, everything hushed—a silence so profound it felt almost eternal, as if time itself had paused.

Then, without warning, a tear slipped down her cheek, catching the light of her healing glow and breaking it into a fragile, golden prism.

Rylik's ice-blue eyes opened slowly, his gaze sharpening as it settled on her face. The golden light beneath her palm faltered, and she blinked as the healing warmth faded, leaving only the soft flicker of firelight to bridge the space between them.

His hand lifted, his fingers brushing her cheek with surprising tenderness as he wiped away the tear she hadn't realized she'd shed. "Aria?" he murmured, his voice low, almost hesitant.

She blinked, startled at the emotions suddenly breaking through. "I don't know why I—" She shook her head, laughing softly, though her voice trembled.

Rylik's hand was suddenly at the back of her head, his fingers tracing a delicate line through her hair as he pulled her to his chest. She let herself melt into his warmth, feeling the steady beat of his heart beneath her ear, her pulse matching its rhythm. In this strange, forbidden moment, she felt sheltered, as if here, in his arms, nothing could touch her.

Yet it felt impossible, even dangerous. They were so close, sharing a kind of intimacy that went beyond what either had acknowledged aloud. She could hear the soft thumping pulse in her ear, her face nestled against his chest.

She was safe here, in a way she had never been before. But,

that couldn't be right. He had never promised her more than his protection as an asset. He shouldn't care to provide her any comforts, but here he was, reacting to foolish and insignificant tears in her eyes. Why was she crying? Was it sadness because of Leon? No. No, it was something else entirely. It was happiness.

She let herself hold him, slipping her hands beneath his cloak, pressing against the fabric of his tunic as if to preserve this closeness forever. Why was it so comforting to be held by him? Why did it make her heart swell with joy and longing? She should still fear him, shouldn't she? But, she knew he was just a man. He was a man with a weakness that she had discovered, and his fear of losing her remedy to that weakness had caused him to be cold and fierce. But, over time, she had chipped away at that facade, hadn't she? She hadn't intended to have such an effect, but that is what happened. Cold and cruel he may still be, but with her— *with her*—he was everything that Leon wasn't.

Aria squeezed him tight, breathing in the earthen scent of him as if to carve the memory in stone. She never wanted to leave this moment, but even she knew that all perfect things had to end eventually.

Rylik's hand stilled against her back as if sensing her inner turmoil. Slowly, she drew away, dabbing at her damp eyes, cheeks flushed with embarrassment.

"There's a festival tomorrow night, in the square," he began, a small, knowing smile crossing his face, perhaps sensing she wasn't ready to discuss what had just happened. "Have you heard of it?"

Aria dried her eyes and nodded, her voice still a bit unsteady. "The Festival of the Sun and Stars, right?" Aria had heard about that Festival her entire life. It was held every year in the capital, a celebration of the delicate balance between day and night. During the day, the streets would be alive with a sunlit parade, dancers and musicians filling every corner with color and sound. By nightfall, the city transformed into something almost ethereal—a starlit ball, where nobles and commoners alike danced under shimmering lights.

Lanterns were released into the sky like drifting stars, carrying whispered wishes and hopes aloft. She knew of the fireworks that painted the dark in brilliant bursts, the bustling night market, and the dawn vigil meant to honor both the sun's rise and the enduring mystery of the stars. Though she'd never seen it herself, the festival had always felt like a dream just beyond her reach, a place where magic, music, and possibility seemed endless.

"I'd like to take you," he said, and her head snapped up, meeting his gaze. A smile played on his lips. "What do you think?"

Aria felt her cheeks flush, her heart pounding at the thought of experiencing the capital on such a night. "I," she stammered, unable to suppress her joy. "I'd love to go."

He seemed pleased with her answer and gave a small nod. "Wonderful. It should be an unforgettable night."

Her smile grew as her chest filled with pride. "Thank you, Sovereign."

"Think nothing of it," he replied smoothly, his gaze unwavering. "I'll have the tailor prepare something radiant for you to wear. Since there will be dancing, after all—primarily with *me*."

Without thinking, Aria threw her arms around him, her smile hidden as she pressed her face to his chest. She felt his hands stroke her hair gently, a comfort she hadn't expected but deeply needed. She pulled back with a sigh, looking up at him. "Thank you, truly, Sovereign."

He inclined his head, his eyes soft. She took a step back, trying to rein in the emotions that threatened to spill over. She needed to leave before her gratitude, or the thrill coursing through her, made her do something reckless. "Goodnight," she whispered, turning quickly and leaving the room.

She was practically floating, gliding across the bathing room floor in a dreamy daze. Tonight, instead of brooding alone in her room, she would sink into her sheets with thoughts of the Festival of Sun and Stars, dancing and laughing well into the evening. Her fingers grazed over her Lyrica pendant and she caught a glimpse of herself in the mirror by the door.

Despite the redness of her tear-streaked cheeks, the delight on her face was unmistakable. She beamed at herself, though couldn't help but to laugh at her own disarray. She sorely needed a bath, she surmised, and unclasped the pendant from around her neck, as she stepped through the doorway into her room. She set the necklace down on her vanity and reached for her robe, but as she looked up, her heart froze. There, standing by her bed, was Lord Orren, inspecting her room as if he belonged there. He turned slowly, his gaze settling on her with a cold, almost clinical curiosity. Her pulse surged, her body instinctively moving for her own door.

"Stay where you are, Aria," he ordered, his voice calm but sharp, each syllable a chain keeping her rooted in place.

CHAPTER 35

ARIA

She felt her heart drop, her stomach twisting with fear. "Why are you in my room?" she asked, voice barely steady, her mind racing with escape routes. He was close enough to reach her if she dared to run again, and his presence filled the small space, stifling any illusions of safety.

"I'm here to check on your progress," he replied with a detached authority, almost bored. "Leon tells me you're becoming hostile toward him."

Aria's eyes widened, indignation flashing through her fear. "Hostile—?!"

Orren's gaze was steady, unnerving. "I don't care how you act, as long as you're serving the cause. And it seems you're doing quite well in your objective." His eyes flickered toward the adjoining suite door, and then back to her. "The maids inform me you've spent at least a few nights in the Sovereign's bed."

A chill ran through her. Yes, it was true—but not in the way he was implying.

"Is he pleased with you?" Orren asked, his gaze sweeping over her, probing for any weakness, any sign she might slip.

Aria shifted, feeling exposed under his scrutiny. "I wouldn't know."

"Oh, wouldn't you?" He took a step forward, each footfall loud as it echoed on the marble floor. "You just came from his chambers, did you not?"

"Yes, but—" She tried to explain, but he cut her off with a dismissive wave of his hand.

"A woman knows when she can bend a man's will, whether or not he's aware of it." He was just an arm's length away now, his dark eyes boring into hers as she took a reflexive step back, her backside brushing up against the wooden edge of her vanity. "Can you bend his will yet, or no?"

Every instinct screamed at her to run, to escape his oppressive presence. "I have no sway over him, Lord Orren," she said, forcing her voice to remain even.

"Give it time, then." His eyes flicked to the pendant resting on the vanity's table behind her, the one Rylik had given her. "A gift?" he mused darkly. "That's good. Jewelry is a significant gesture—a sign that you're being accepted as his consort."

Aria swallowed, throat tight with the unsettling truth of his words. She should have felt flattered, but Orren's presence made every thought twist into dread.

"Do you have nothing else to wear?" he asked, his gaze sliding down the soft, modest yellow fabric with clear disdain. "Perhaps if you wore something a little more like what you'd worn yesterday, you'd have more sway with the Sovereign. That is hardly a dress to make a man yield."

Memories of the red dress flashed in her mind, the vulnerable moments it had accompanied. She looked away, a sick feeling twisting in her stomach, aware that there was nowhere left to retreat to.

Orren's eyes followed her every move, his voice soft but biting. "What happened with the king?" he pressed, stepping forward to close the distance. "Whatever it was, he clearly no longer wants you."

She forced herself to meet his gaze, shock and fear mingling at his knowledge of the king's rejection. "Wh—why does that matter to you?"

"Perhaps," he replied coldly, his gaze sharpening with a sinister edge, "I should have arranged for you to entertain only one of them. Maybe the king was disgusted, knowing you've also shared the Sovereign's bed."

Aria went rigid, the implication slicing through her. Was Orren behind the king's sudden interest in her? Her mind raced, heart thrashing as she stared at him, struggling to comprehend the cruelty woven into his words. She opened her mouth to respond, to defend herself, but no words came. She felt trapped, the walls of her room closing in as Orren's eyes never left her, dissecting her every reaction.

"I thought you might ensnare both," he sneered, as if it were obvious, as if she were nothing more than a pawn to him. "But even whores have preferences." His tone was so sharp, so cold, each word like a slap. "It didn't take much to put the idea in the king's mind. After he saw you at the ball, he was practically salivating."

Aria's lips pressed into a thin line, her jaw tight as she forced herself to stay composed. She wanted to scream, to strike him, but her voice came out in a low, controlled hiss. "You encouraged the king's interest in me?"

"Yes," he replied, a hint of disappointment clouding his features. "But it seems he'd rather you remain untouched by any other man." His dismissive tone, as if she had no autonomy, made her skin crawl. "No matter. I have plans for him, and I'll settle for the Sovereign falling to your charms."

Aria's pulse quickened, each word adding a fresh wave of fear and disgust. "What exactly was I supposed to do here? Be a bedmate for powerful men?" She kept her voice low, desperate not to let it carry, terrified Rylik might hear. The truth of her connection to Orren's Rebellion would destroy everything.

Orren's smile was cool, patronizing. "You were brought here as a healer, of course. But when I saw how the Sovereign looked at you, well, it was too perfect. Even the king had noticed you, so it took only a nudge to let the idea simmer." He waved his hand, as if brushing off a trivial inconvenience.

The revelation left her numb, her mind reeling, her throat dry. He was using her as a weapon, something disposable.

"I have known the Sovereign for some time now, and I have never seen him become so attached to a female before." A predatory smile crept onto his face. "I have no doubt that you will be his undoing. Soon, the Rebellion will strike."

Her heart skidded. "Strike?" she managed, voice barely above a whisper.

"Yes," he confirmed, his tone as dark as his gaze. "You'll be used as bait." He let his eyes drift over her, coldly assessing. "You may be somewhat injured in the trap, but you are a healer. You'll undo any lasting damage."

"I can't heal myself," she replied, her voice steady despite her racing pulse. "Why am I going to be injured? What are you getting at?"

Orren's eyes gleamed with a twisted curiosity. "You can't heal yourself? All that power and you cannot use it to help yourself?" he mused, almost to himself.

Aria's eyes narrowed. "I suppose we all have our own vulnerabilities, Orren. So, if I am to be injured, I hope you understand whatever my threshold is."

He sighed, glancing aside. "You are valuable. I will tell my men to be careful with you. I won't make any promises."

"What are you intending to—"

"You're not the one who's meant to die, Aria." He leaned in, his words invading her like poison. "The Sovereign will follow a blood trail until he finds you, and then I will kill him."

Her vision swam, her heart battering her ribs as she processed his intent. Orren wanted Rylik dead, wanted her to lure him into a fatal trap. The thought of Rylik—steady, strong, invincible Rylik—falling because of her made her insides twist painfully. Orren would turn Rylik's attachment to her into a weapon, exploiting his care to lead him straight to his death. He was right: attachment was a weakness.

"When?" she asked, afraid to know the answer.

He was detached, somewhat amused as he replied, "You'll know."

He wasn't going to tell her. And why would he? It would only give her time to run and hide from him. But, perhaps tonight she still had a chance to avoid it.

"Play your part well, Aria. Give him whatever he wants. Satisfy him." Orren took a step forward, and she felt knees waver as she steadied herself on the ledge of the vanity. His voice dropped to a whisper. "Make him trust you completely."

She doubted he would be able to survive such a trap. He was powerful, but she was a weak point in his armor. She could see it. If Orren knew just how much, he would act right this moment.

He cast one last, chilling look at her, his gaze holding a hint of dark amusement, before he stepped back. He disappeared in a flash of cold blue light, and she was left in the eerie silence, her heart pounding.

Thorian. His name surfaced in her mind like a lifeline. *I need Thorian.* He'd offered her a way out, and she needed one now more than ever. If she stayed, Rylik would be left to suffer at her own expense. She would slip him the potion she had created to help his Frostwraith Blight, knowing that her absence wouldn't have to be a death sentence on its own. With her gone, it would give Rylik the clarity and strength to remain unstoppable.

Her pulse steadied as she made up her mind. She would find Thorian, secure safety for her parents and herself, and she would get out.

Aria stepped out of her suite, the cool hallway air brushing against her skin as her eyes scanned the dimly lit corridor. A lone guard stood at his post, his expression stiff but alert. She approached him, her footsteps light against the stone floor.

"Excuse me," she said softly, though her voice carried an edge of urgency. The guard turned to her, his posture straightening as she continued. "I need you to send a message to Thorian. Tell him," she hesitated, "tell him that I have thought about the remedy he needs. I expect to speak with him in the morning."

The guard hesitated for only a moment, his gaze flickering with curiosity before he nodded. "As you wish, my lady." With a brief bow, he strode off into the shadows, his boots echoing faintly as they receded into silence.

She turned quickly, re-entering her suite and shutting the door hurriedly behind her. Alone again, she released a shaky breath and moved toward her vanity. She caught her reflection in the polished glass—her face pale, her expression drawn—and began to undo the clasps of her dress. The fabric slid from her shoulders and crumpled at her feet, leaving her in a thin, gauzy nightgown.

She crossed the room, picking up her pendant from where it rested on the table. Its soothing weight pressed against her palm as she walked to her bed, the soft glow of the fire casting flickering shadows across the chamber.

Sliding beneath the covers, she slipped the pendant over her head, the chain cool against her neck. Her fingers rested on the charm, her chest tightening as a deep sadness took hold. Leaving Rylik would be like tearing away a piece of herself, but she couldn't let Orren use her as bait against him. Not after everything.

She stared at the ceiling, her thoughts twisting into knots as she imagined all the ways this could go wrong. The escape, the healing, the plan itself—it all felt so fragile, so dangerously close to shattering.

Her eyelids grew heavy, but the unease in her chest refused to fade. As she drifted closer toward sleep, a whisper of fear coiled deep within her, its cold tendrils wrapping around her heart. The future loomed ahead, uncertain and perilous, and for a moment, she wondered if she would even live to see it unfold.

CHAPTER 36

RYLIK

Rylik gripped the edge of his balcony, knuckles white, as if by sheer force he could shatter the stone beneath his fingers. The night stretched around him, vast and indifferent, its silence only sharpening the heavy beat of his heart—a relentless rhythm that seemed intent on tearing through his ribs. The cool air brushed against his flushed skin, a faint attempt at quelling the fire she'd left simmering beneath his flesh.

Her touch lingered, imprinted there, a delicate ache he couldn't banish, and it burned with a fervor he struggled to comprehend. He could still feel the whisper of her fingers threading through the laces of his tunic, tracing a path along his chest, their warmth settling in a place just over his heart. The memory was both torment and solace, a fleeting touch that felt branded upon his skin, and as he breathed the chilled night air, he knew that no amount of distance or darkness would dim that mark.

She had wanted him. He could feel it in the wild beat of her heart, thrumming against his own, and in the way her arms had wrapped around him, desperate and trembling. Her touch had carried an urgency that left him raw, igniting a need that echoed through him even now. Slowly, he opened his cold blue eyes, letting them drift across the shadowed meadow stretching beyond the balcony, where only the distant, restless chirping of crickets disturbed the silence. He took a slow, steady breath, letting it fill his lungs and release in a futile attempt to clear his mind. He wouldn't step back into those chambers until he could be certain—absolutely certain—that he could resist the pull of her presence waiting within that suite.

His intentions for her tonight had been simple—first, to present her with the Lyrica Pendant, and second, to invite her to the Festival of the Sun and Stars. He knew these gestures would lift her spirits; she had been unusually distant since encountering the Corporal in town. Yet somehow, the evening had taken an unexpected turn, slipping from his control, leaving him in a haze of emotions he couldn't fully name. He dwelled on the uncertainty, unsure if what had unfolded would ultimately lead them to something greater—or to something far more precarious.

Rylik had tried to send her away after that embrace. He hadn't meant to hold her so close; it had been a reflex, an unstoppable urge at the sight of her tears—an offense to him that he felt bound to remedy. It had torn at something deep within, compelling him to shield her from any echo of sadness. He'd wanted only to bring her peace, to place a simple gift in her hands and watch her eyes brighten with gratitude. Yet, as he let her go, he felt a raw ache, a pull that loomed painfully in the space between them.

And then she had hugged him in return, and in that moment, he was undone. The way she pressed herself against him, her touch both urgent and vulnerable, had left him defenseless. He felt her longing, a yearning she hadn't shown before, and it both comforted and shook him. When had she become so at ease with him? When had she begun to crave his touch, as though he were the very solace she sought?

He had wanted to seize her wrist before she could slip away, to draw her back into his embrace and weave his fingers through her hair, feeling the silken strands slip through his grasp like whispered secrets. He craved the taste of her, the heat of her body melding with his in a fevered dance, each heartbeat an urgent plea for more.

More than anything, he yearned to ignite the passion she so fiercely denied, to awaken the fire that simmered just beneath her surface. He could sense her desire in her fingertips, in the way they had grazed along his chest, a tantalizing trail of longing that beckoned him closer. She had stood before him, open and unguarded, practically his for the taking, a tempting prize wrapped in vulnerability. Yet, an invisible barrier held him back. Why hadn't he taken what was so clearly within reach?

He closed his eyes again, taking a deep breath as he fought to steady the chaos within him. He wasn't ready to enter his suite yet. A muffled curse escaped his lips, laced with regret for the decision to place her so tantalizingly close. He hadn't anticipated the exquisite agony of her proximity, how every heartbeat echoed the truth of his desire. She was so very near. Too near.

If she wants me, he reasoned with himself, *then why am I denying her? Why am I denying myself?* The idea of surrendering to the moment pulled at him, promising a much-needed release for both of them, an escape from the tension that hung thick in the air between them. They would each stand to benefit. The only risk would be in her own feelings. This would undoubtedly tether her to him in ways she could never break. He wanted that. *But, that isn't the only risk, is it?* He knew the answer to his own question. At this stage, it was more than simply a carnal desire.

He wanted more than just her body. He wanted everything. His need for her was all-consuming, and he understood why. Sex had always been a thrilling but efficient transaction, something that sated him physically but remained devoid of anything else meaningful. With Aria, he knew that this would be a possession of her body and soul.

He yearned for her, not just to take her, but to savor every moment—each kiss, each whispered word—slowly and deeply, as if imprinting her essence onto his very being. The thought of losing himself in her was intoxicating, a sweet poison that threatened to engulf him. Yet, therein lay the danger. He craved to claim her, to possess every part of her, and in turn, he longed for her to lay claim to him, to bind him with a connection that could rival the stars themselves. But he understood the peril of such a bond; it was a tether that would entwine their fates, a chain that not even he could easily break.

Rylik swallowed hard, his body taut and raw with a hunger

he could not satiate. Would he have to spend the entire night out here? Was his resolve so pitifully weak that he couldn't even step inside? With a groan, he hung his head, his wavy, tousled locks falling around his face like a shroud, masking his turmoil. But then, a glimmer of red light caught his attention. He glanced down at the ring on his left hand, a new purchase, bought as a set alongside the Lyrica pendant. The silver stone set in the obsidian band was gleaming a vivid garnet in the moonlight, casting an ominous glow that set his pulse racing.

The pendant, he reminded himself, had a dual purpose. It was forged by a master jeweler, enchanted to forge a link in the steel between this ring—the *Sentinel band*—and the necklace he had given Aria. While the pendant was meant to bring her peace, it also held another kind of magic—one that spoke of protection. He could feel the urgency coursing through him as he recalled its purpose; the pendant reacted to Aria's moods, and his ring was the conduit of that emotion. It conveyed two signals: sadness and *fear*.

In a flash, he shadowed away from his balcony, reappearing in Aria's room with a suddenness that made his heart race. The silence enveloped him like a fog, and the air felt heavy with tension. He scanned the room slowly, every instinct on high alert as he searched for signs of danger. The space was eerily still, with embers in the hearth slowly settling, their gentle crackles the only sound breaking the heavy silence. The faint scent of lavender mixed with the warmth of the fire's fading heat. The curtains hung motionless, untouched by any breeze, while her belongings lay meticulously arranged, undisturbed as though frozen in time.

He stepped cautiously, his boots echoing softly against the solid marble floors, each step reverberating like a distant warning bell. His gaze fell to her bed, where he vanished into wisps of shadow before reappearing at her bedside. There, Aria lay, her wild curls spilling over the pillow, her face obscured in the dim light. She seemed peaceful, but the knowledge of the ominous glow on his ring sent a chill down his spine.

Concern etched across his brow, Rylik reached to brush aside the stray strands from her face. She flinched slightly, her eyes flickering open with a wary surprise as she took in his form looming over her.

"Sovereign?" she gasped, pushing herself upright and instinctively leaning away. "Wh—what are you doing in my room?" In her startled state, she hadn't noticed her nightgown slipping askew, one shoulder bared, the gown pooling unevenly along her frame.

He pulled his hand back, his gaze briefly dropping to the bedspread as he swallowed, trying to ignore the way the delicate silk clung to her breasts, faintly translucent in the dim glow of the fading embers. "I apologize. I thought I'd heard something in your room and came to ensure you were safe."

Aria's expression shifted quickly, concern coloring her features even as she avoided his eyes. "I, um, probably just had a nightmare. I'm sorry if I disturbed you."

"Not at all," he replied, shaking his head. "I was only resting by the fire." He took a step back, distancing himself from the tantalizing view of her barely-concealed form. "Though, I am sorry to hear about the nightmare. Did you not take some of that golden potion?" He asked this lightly, a hint of mischief lacing his tone as he tried to gauge her reaction.

Her cheeks flushed a familiar shade of pink, one he had come to relish. "I should have, but no," she murmured, glancing down, suddenly aware of her exposed shoulder and the flimsy fabric of her gown. Hastily, she pulled the blanket up to cover herself, her blush deepening.

He offered a slight smile, letting out a quiet breath of relief. So it was only a nightmare after all. A brief blessing, perhaps, to see her like this rather than imagining it alone on his balcony. But now, he had to leave before the pull of her presence took hold.

If I stay in here with her any longer, I might—

His thoughts trailed away as he caught the red shine of his ring. Glancing back, he noted the furrow of her brow, the shadow of apprehension still persisting in her gaze. She was still afraid. Was she afraid of *him*?

He turned back fully, sweeping his gaze over the room one last time, searching for any signs of intrusion. *No, she couldn't be in fear of him, but perhaps something else.* Though, nothing was amiss. The only source of unease lay in her own expression, as if she were keeping something from him. His gaze fixed on her with quiet scrutiny as he closed the distance in steady, confident strides.

"Sovereign?" she asked softly, pressing back into her pillows as if trying to create distance, as if she truly had any hope to hide from him.

He paused, the silence heavy, before his words broke through. "Why are you afraid, Aria?" His voice was low, but insistent. "Is it really only a nightmare that plagues you?"

"It was deeply unsettling, I assure you. But I am confident that with enough rest, I'll get over it." Her voice held a practiced calm, but Rylik sensed the edge of false sincerity woven in her tone.

Without hesitation, he tugged the blanket from her grip, and she gasped softly, the delicate nightgown clinging to her frame in elegant disarray. He skimmed over her, searching intently for any hint of bruising or harm, finding only the smooth, untouched expanse of her skin. His chest tightened, and he fought to anchor himself, his gaze unable to resist tracing the fine lines of her gossamer nightgown stretched and creased around her curves.

She attempted uselessly to cover herself, eyes wide with indignation. "What do you think you are doing!?"

He concealed his desire beneath a faint, playful grin. "I'm only admiring what my coin bought. It does look good on you." His words held an edge, one he couldn't keep from surfacing.

"Sovereign, this is—this is entirely inappropriate!" she managed, cheeks flushed, struggling to hold onto her resolve.

"Inappropriate?" His voice dropped as he leaned in closer, bracing himself with one hand on the mattress, the other against the headboard behind her. "Are you sure you want to lecture me on what's inappropriate, Pyra?" His gaze poured over her, savoring the telltale tremor in her breaths. "Tell me, then—how exactly is me seeing you like this," he let his gaze drift slowly over her, letting her feel the weight of his intent, "inappropriate?"

The ring on his hand dulled back to silver, and relief tempered his desire. Yet, her gaze remained, flickering to his mouth, and he felt a jolt of triumph at her thinly veiled longing. He smirked, thinking to himself how easy it would be to enter her bed, pull that gauzy material up to her thighs, and spread her open for him. He wanted to, his mind was practically screaming at him to act. His fingers curled tighter around the headboard, hidden from Aria's view as she continued to gaze intently into his face.

Whatever had frightened her seemed to vanish in the quiet exchange between them, leaving him with no excuse to stay, to keep testing both their wills. Because that's what this was, wasn't it? A slow torture he inflicted on himself, feeding the need that always surged to life around her, daring him to see how close he could get before the boundaries blurred beyond reason.

His teeth pressed into the inside of his lip as he willed his pulse to settle, taking a steadying breath as he eased back. It was time to let the distance return—to retreat to his own quarters and keep himself far from her bed. Any more of this, and he would put much more than her chastity at risk, stirring a storm he wasn't prepared to face within either of them.

"Goodnight, Aria," he muttered, his voice rough as he turned away, forcing his feet to carry him out of the room. With every step, he felt the weight of what could have been, a flame he couldn't quench but dared not ignite.

CHAPTER 37

ARIA

The apothecary had a hushed, sacred quality to it that morning, as if the shelves of carefully curated potions and powders were guardians of secrets too delicate for the outside world. Aria stood just inside the doorway, her expression calm and carefully measured. She'd spent the early hours keeping her demeanor as normal as possible under Rylik's watchful gaze. If he suspected anything was amiss, he hadn't shown it, and for that, she was grateful.

Her eyes quickly fell upon Thorian, already waiting for her. He stood near the far wall, his broad frame stiff with purpose. Maven was there as well, though she had retreated to her shelves of herbs and tinctures the moment Aria arrived, her back turned as she muttered something to herself. The tension in the room was palpable, and it only heightened as Aria closed the door behind her.

"You're certain?" Thorian's tone was controlled yet firm, his eyes fixed on hers with unwavering intensity. "The message you sent—does it mean you're ready to move forward?"

Aria swallowed the knot forming in her throat and nodded. "Yes. I'll go along with your plan."

His expression didn't change, but there was a hint of something in his eyes—satisfaction, perhaps, or grim determination. "Good," he said quietly. "Your best chance to escape will be tonight, during the Festival of the Sun and Stars."

Aria froze, her stomach tightening. She'd suspected he might suggest the festival, but hearing it confirmed sent a jolt of unease through her.

"The Sovereign plans to take you there," Thorian continued. "A public event like this will give us the cover we need. All you have to do is stay close and follow my lead."

She nodded again, her voice barely above a whisper. "I understand."

From behind, Maven whirled around, her jaw tightening with unspoken tension. "This is madness," she muttered, striding forward with a vial in hand. "But if you're determined to go through with it, I won't have you getting caught and executed on my conscience." She extended the vial to Aria, her expression grim.

"What is this?" Aria asked, taking the delicate glass bottle. The contents inside shimmered faintly, almost like liquid moonlight.

"Invisibility potion," Maven said briskly. "It will last for five minutes—no more, no less. You'll need to use it wisely. Move quickly and then find somewhere to hide as soon as it wears off." She hesitated, then added, "I don't support any of this, but I won't stand by and watch you fail either."

"Thank you, Maven," Aria said softly, touched by her reluctant kindness. She knew that invisibility potion was hard to come by, as it was a difficult potion to make, and even more difficult to procure illegally.

Maven shook her head, her brows furrowed. "Don't thank me. Just don't get yourself in trouble."

Thorian stepped closer, his presence steady and commanding. "It will work," he said, his tone reassuring. "As long as you stay with me, you'll be fine."

Maven shot him a wary look, her disapproval evident. "You'd better hope so. This is a dangerous game you're playing, and she's the one who'll pay the price if it goes wrong."

"I won't let that happen," Thorian said firmly, again steering his attention to her. "So long as she does exactly what I say."

Aria glanced toward Maven, noting the crease of worry still etched between her brows. "Maven, is your only concern that I'll get caught? Or is there something else you're not saying?"

Maven exhaled heavily, her hand rising to rub the back of her neck in a gesture that spoke of unease. "If you're asking about the man you're going to meet, I trust him. The general is a good person, but there's no realistic way for you to evade the Sovereign, let alone the crown."

"She will be fine, cousin," Thorian interjected, his hand coming to rest on Maven's back in an attempt at reassurance.

Despite his confidence, Aria couldn't suppress the flutter of anxiety building in her chest. She clutched her skirt under her palm, her mind racing with possibilities—both of success and failure.

As the conversation lulled and Thorian departed, her thoughts turned to Rylik, her heart tightening at the mere thought of leaving him. The weight of it pressed down on her chest, smothering her. She didn't want to leave him—she *couldn't*—but she knew there was no other choice. If she stayed, Orren would use her against him, and that was a fate she could never allow him to endure. But the thought of walking away, of tearing herself from his side, felt like a betrayal that cut deeper than anything she'd ever known.

He had been kind and protective, watching over her when she was at her weakest, holding her when she needed him most. He didn't deserve this—this *abandonment*. The elixir she had prepared for him felt like a cruel joke now, a hollow gesture that could never replace the one thing he truly needed from her: her healing, her presence. She would no longer be able to soothe his pain with her touch, and he would never be able forgive her for such a trespass. The thought of no longer resting in his embrace, of not feeling the steady warmth of his arms around her, was unbearable.

Tonight, everything would change. She would make the hardest choice of her life, all for a chance at his protection, and yet every inch of her screamed that it wasn't enough. She only hoped it wouldn't come at too high a cost—too high for *him*, too high for her.

By the time she reached Rylik's suite, her hands were

trembling, but she let out a quiet sigh of relief to find it empty. With a shaky breath, she withdrew the healing potion she had created a few days before, plucking it from her purse and set it carefully in his cabinet. He likely wouldn't reach for his elixirs tonight, so perhaps this would remain hidden, at least until she was far beyond his reach. She had written him a letter, an attempt to explain it all—her regret, her apology, Orren, her ties to the Rebellion—and she crossed the floor, her movements swift yet careful, slipping the envelope into the top drawer of his desk.

Her eyes hovered there briefly, catching on the signet ring she'd only glimpsed once before, its crest bearing twin swords crossed within a crescent moon. She ran her fingers over the smooth metal, tracing the emblem, as if trying to memorize the insignia. It felt like a parting touch, a keepsake of him. Taking a slow breath, she pocketed the ring and gently closed the drawer. A memento, she reasoned, though she knew he would hate her for this theft, too. It meant so much to him. It represented so much. Perhaps that's the very reason she wanted to take it—to have something so intimately connected to him. He was already going to hate her after this, anyway. She should have something of his to cherish.

With her emotions teetering between grief and purpose, she left his room, her heart thudding heavily in her chest, almost as if he were lurking nearby, waiting to catch her in the act of leaving him behind.

Back in her suite, her eyes were drawn to a gown placed with care upon her bed, and her steps slowed. The dress was beautiful, almost painfully so—a deep sapphire blue, as if dyed from dusk itself, the fabric shimmering in the light. Tiny crystals adorned the bodice, scattering like stars across the night sky, while intricate silver threads traced delicate patterns along the neckline and hem, capturing the grace of an evening breeze. The sweetheart neckline was cut just daringly enough, likely to reveal an expanse of chest she would only barely be comfortable with. He had chosen it for her, and the thought brought a tender ache to her chest, for she knew she wouldn't wear it by his side as he intended.

But she had to follow through. Sentiment couldn't hold her

back now. It was risky to wait for Orren to act. She had told herself she wouldn't mourn her departure, that her last evening would be spent with him as freely as possible. Tonight, when she rode under the starlit sky, she would allow herself the heartache she'd been holding back, let the night witness her resentment as she rode into the unknown. Thorian had assured her a safe path to the general's manor, far from Rylik's reach. The general could protect her, and she had to believe that Rylik would not be able to follow.

With the threat of Orren and the Rebellion looming so close, she could never be certain. Rylik's power was formidable—she had felt it, and she dreaded finding out just how far he would go. But her distance from him would keep him safe, and that thought offered her a small measure of solace. Perhaps, one day, when the shadow of the crown no longer haunted them and the Rebellion was done, they might find their way back to each other. And maybe they might see where this unlikely entanglement would've led.

Her fingers brushed a stray tear from her cheek. There was no time for regret, not now. She needed to focus. She'd save her tears for the road. Tonight, she would put on that dress, dance with the Sovereign, and enjoy the most perfect night in the plaza until it was time. She picked up the gown, pressing it gently against her frame, breathing in slowly. She would survive tonight, without breaking, and leave Rylik with the memory of her song. Then, she would slip away, her heart tethered to a feeling she could never fully let go of.

* * *

Stepping into the capital plaza, Aria's chest tightened as her eyes drank in the sparkling panorama. Lanterns were strung from every archway and building edge, glowing orbs shining a warm, golden light that mirrored the sinking sun. Beneath them, crowds wove together in joyous celebration, their colorful garments swirling like flowers in a summer field. There was laughter and music everywhere, and the air held an earthy blend of roasted almonds, spiced wine, and fresh-cut flowers. Every corner seemed alive with beauty, and Aria marveled at how the festival had brought the city to life.

Beside her, Rylik led her through the bustling streets, pointing out the different stalls and events, his voice low and gentle in her ear. His hand rested gingerly on her back, guiding her as he showed her the sunlit parade winding through the streets, the performers spinning in dazzling costumes of gold and white. People paused in their merrymaking to bow respectfully as they passed, casting glances her way, drawn in by the dress he had chosen for her. The gown sparkled under the lights, and Aria felt a strange mix of pride and sadness wearing it for him, knowing it was the last time they'd share an evening like this. But in Rylik's presence, with his steady warmth at her side, she allowed herself to bask in the fleeting moments.

As they wandered through the bustling plaza, Rylik purchased a few fresh cakes for Aria to sample, their delicate sweetness melting on her tongue with every bite. She couldn't help but beam at him, declaring them the best she'd ever tasted. He only smirked at her enthusiasm, brushing off her protests when she fussed that he was spending far too much on her. In turn, she bought a few simple trinkets with her own coin, insisting it was only fair. As they meandered back toward the heart of the festivities, the first lilting notes of a waltz began to drift across the square.

Rylik turned to her with a coy smile. "Would you care to share a dance with me?"

She flashed him a brilliant smile. "Of course."

As Aria accepted Rylik's hand, he pulled her into the dance with surprising grace, the music swirling around them as they began to move in time with the rhythm. She was caught off guard by how natural it felt, their steps meshing as if they'd practiced together for years. It hadn't been that long ago when they had danced under the glittering chandeliers of the royal ballroom, when he had held her like this for the first time. It felt like an eternity ago, slipping from her even as she fought to hold onto this very moment in time with him.

"Where did you learn to dance, Sovereign?" she asked, struggling to anchor herself in the present. She wasn't gone yet—her hands still rested in his, a lifeline she wasn't ready to let go of.

Rylik's lips curled into a slow, almost knowing smile. "I was a nobleman once, before I became the Sovereign. I had my fair share of lessons in dancing."

Aria's attention remained on him, a teasing gleam lighting her expression. "You're incredibly skilled, you know. I was never taught the proper steps."

He leaned in just a little closer, his voice dropping to a more intimate tone. "Well, you're doing wonderfully," he said, his gaze softening as he studied her with genuine admiration. "And even if you weren't, I'd gladly lie and tell you that you were."

She tilted her head, a skeptical smile tugging at her lips. "And how am I supposed to know you're not lying right now?"

He chuckled softly, a spark of mischief dancing in his ice-blue eyes. "You don't," he replied simply, his voice low and filled with intrigue.

Aria laughed softly, the sound light and carefree, but her mind was racing. She found herself wanting to cling to the moment, to ignore the tension building in the pit of her stomach. She shifted slightly in his arms, trying to ignore the growing weight of the evening.

"Are you alright?" Rylik asked gently, his voice softer than before, his gaze searching her face. "You seemed a little quiet this morning."

She blinked, taken off guard by his attentiveness. "Oh. I was just nervous, I think. I've been so excited to come here tonight." She gave him a bright smile, hoping it would mask the tightness in her chest. "Thank you for bringing me. It's more magical than I could've ever dreamed."

Rylik raised an eyebrow, as though considering her words carefully, before his lips twisted into a faint but skeptical smile. "Is that so?" He spun her gently, their steps precise as the song began winding to its conclusion.

She swallowed, knowing the evening's enchantment was about to end. Thorian's warning echoed in her mind—one dance. Then, she'd have to go. "I truly am grateful," she murmured, her voice almost a whisper now, fraught with emotion. "Tonight has been everything I could've hoped for."

The final notes of the waltz drifted through the air, and with a reluctant but graceful bow, Rylik brought the dance to an end. He took a step back, his eyes resting on her with quiet intensity. "I'll fetch us a drink," he said, his tone warmer than it had been before. "Wait here."

Aria nodded, her heart pounding as she watched him walk away. She didn't wait long before she reached into her pocket and pulled out the small vial Maven had given her. The weight of it in her hand felt surreal, like a step she couldn't undo. With a glance over her shoulder, she uncorked the vial and swallowed the contents in a single, swift motion. Almost immediately, the world around her seemed to blur, the colors shifting as she faded from view.

Gone.

She stood there for a moment, feeling both invisible and oddly free. As Rylik returned with drinks in hand, she slipped silently away into the crowd, the final notes of the song still ringing in her ears.

CHAPTER 38

RYLIK

Rylik strolled away from the street vendor, honey-gold meads in hand, his posture relaxed as he surveyed the lively scene of the plaza. He allowed himself a brief moment of ease, watching festival-goers dance and laugh, the warmth of the evening air and the sounds of music soothing his senses. His gaze drifted across the crowd, searching for the elegant blue of Aria's dress. But as his eyes landed on the spot where she had been standing just moments before, the calm he'd been holding onto slipped away. A weight settled in his chest, and an unsettling chill ran up his spine, causing him to pause abruptly.

Where is she?

His steps quickened, just slightly, as the crowd moved around him. He deftly sidestepped a pair of dancers, his eyes scanning the sea of people with practiced precision. The music, once full of life, now felt hollow, a distant echo beneath the tension tightening around him. He slowed to a stop, taking a measured look around, assessing the faces and the shifting bodies. His gaze sharpened as he swept through the crowd, searching with a focused intensity, though the apprehension tightening in his chest betrayed none of his outward calm. The festival's hum—laughter, chatter, and the rhythm of feet—swirled around him, but a shadow of dread crept into the corners of his mind.

Since last night when the stone had flashed red—a warning he had not been able to dismiss—there had been no further incidents today. Aria had quickly thrown herself into her work, diligently crafting potions with Maven, as if to keep her mind occupied and suppress the eager anticipation building for the evening's festivities.

Rylik's eyes flickered across the sea of people, his growing concern sharpening his focus. He tracked every movement, his instincts honed and alert to any sign of her. The lively music reverberated through the air, but Rylik felt a disconnect, the joyous noise fading into a muffled backdrop to his mounting anxiety. Without thinking, his hands jerked, and the mead sloshed over the edge of the cups before they clattered to the cobblestones, the sharp sound cutting through the din like a warning.

Where the hell is she?

The urgency surged within him, his steps quickening, every passing moment adding to the suffocating weight of something being horribly wrong. He scanned the bustling streets, searching for the glimmer of her fiery red hair, the way it would catch the lantern light, drawing the eye amidst the growing shadows of night. But the more he looked, the more a chilling realization set in—she was gone. A cold darkness settled over him, deeper than the night itself.

His body moved before he could think, spinning on his heel and pushing through the crowds of people with force, ignoring the surprised gasps and protests that followed in his wake. Each shove heightened his agitation, a seething fury boiling beneath the surface. They were needlessly in his way, adding to the heavily thrumming pulse building in his ears as he cursed himself for letting her out of his sight. He shouldn't have turned his back to her. He had become too lax with her of late, complacent even. Careless.

Who would've taken her? Would she have left of her own accord? The ring on his finger glowed with an ominous blue, a sign of her sorrow that he had been unable to quell. She likely couldn't have accomplished such a vanishing act in her own. His fingers clenched into fists at his sides, shadows beginning to unfurl from within. Someone else had ensured her successful disappearance. And now that someone would *die* for it.

His dark mist coiled around him, his eyes gleaming with a haunting silver light. Like a smothering fog, shadows poured out from him, spreading across the plaza and draping everything in pitch-black darkness. As the eerie fog enveloped the square, gasps rippled through the crowd, followed by screams of terror and confusion echoing into the night. The distant music stuttered to a halt, panic igniting like wildfire, the vibrant atmosphere morphing into chaos. Rylik remained still, the storm of emotions raging within him as he pierced the Veil and honed in on the movement to his right—a shimmering yellow orb of light, barely visible, fading fast down a narrow alleyway.

His chest clenched with fierce intensity at the sight, recognizing the signature of her aura immediately.

"Mmm, there you are, Pyra," he purred, his tone dark and sinuous. The low timbre seemed to cling to the shadows as if summoning them to life. The seething ire beneath his tone smoldered, dark and unrestrained, until his form dissolved into black smoke, vanishing in an instant only to reappear down the narrow alleyway.

Another sphere of light flickered just ahead, only to sputter out like a dying ember as he approached, his presence pressing down on the air itself. He moved with an ominous grace, a shadow in motion, his black boots striking the cobblestones in measured, unhurried steps, each one a chilling echo that reverberated through the silence. She thought she could escape him. *Foolish girl.* There was no escape from him. There would never be another chance after this, not ever again. There would be no further, needless self-restraint. She belonged to him, and he would lay his claim.

His pace was deliberate — hunting, savoring each second as he closed the distance. Moonlight filtered weakly through the high, crumbling walls, casting everything in shades of silver and shadow.

Ahead, Aria ran, the last traces of invisibility making her appear as though she were an apparition. Her black cloak billowed around her, her breath coming in rapid, desperate gasps that filled the tight space, blending with the uneven beat of her hurried steps. The red glow of his Sentinel band was a mere echo of the trepidation in her form. He stretched his fingers, already aching to grasp her, to force her into submission. But he wanted to prolong her agony a few moments more, to relish it. She had tried to flee, and now the cost would be more than she could ever hope to repay.

Her figure was nearly swallowed by the darkness, but he could make out the frantic sway of her hair as she moved, her every footfall tinged with the unmistakable urgency of fear. A thin glint of moonlight caught the edge of her face as she glanced back, her wide eyes searching the shadows.

But he was already there.

The dark thrill in him sharpened as he listened to her ragged breaths, felt the frantic beat of her footsteps against the alley floor. The sound of her retreat was a fleeting, frantic symphony, an ill-fated melody disrupted by his own relentless pursuit. He let her footsteps get louder, just as she thought she might gain speed. Just as she thought she might escape.

In a single fluid motion, he closed the remaining distance, his fingers curling around her shoulder like an iron vise. With effortless strength, he jerked her back, the suddenness disorienting her as he spun her to face him. Her back hit the cold, unyielding stone of the wall behind her, and he watched, entranced, as her eyes widened with a blend of defiance and fear.

She tried to turn her face away, but he was already leaning in, his gaze devouring every subtle shift in her expression, the crimson glow of his ring casting an eerie warmth across her features. "Running from me?" he murmured, his voice low, laced with dark amusement. His fingers tightened on her shoulder, his other hand pressing against the wall beside her, caging her in. The alley seemed to close in, the walls shrinking, trapping them in their own private world of shadows.

"Where is your accomplice?" His voice slithered out in a dark, velvet hiss, barely containing the rage simmering just beneath his composed surface.

Aria gasped, breath trembling, her eyes wide and desperate. "S—Sovereign—" she stammered, her chest rising and falling in frantic rhythm as fear overtook her.

"Where," he repeated coldly, "is he?"

Her throat tightened visibly as she swallowed, her silence betraying her nerves. "He—he must've seen you coming. He's gone."

The answer only fueled the fire in his eyes, his lips twisting into a dangerous smile. "I'll have my shadows find him, then," he murmured, each word carrying a quiet fury. "And I'll cut out his tongue so he can no longer use it to persuade you to run." He began to turn away, but her fingers grasped at his arm, clinging to him in desperation.

"Don't go!" Her voice cracked, raw with fear and urgency. "Please, it's not what you think!"

Rylik's gaze dropped to her hand, his jaw taut as he met her eyes, his patience thin. "Oh?" he drawled with cold amusement. "Then by all means—enlighten me." He pushed her back firmly against the wall, his hand sliding from her shoulder to press against her collarbone, a possessive hold that forced her to face him. "Because from where I stand, it appears nothing short of a pathetic escape, plotted by a traitor." His tone dripped with venom, his words wrapping around her like a tightening vice.

Aria's voice wavered as she fought to hold steady. "I—I went along with it only to protect you, Sovereign," she whispered, the truth spilling out in a single desperate breath.

A flicker of uncertainty crossed his gaze, a hint of curiosity breaking through the ice. Save him? His confusion was evident, because she was quick to continue in earnest.

"Lord Orren plans to use me," she said hurriedly, her words spilling over themselves. "To use me to draw you into a trap and kill you!" Her eyes shone with pleading as she continued, her voice barely above a whisper. "Please, I beg you, don't tell the king. Don't let Orren know I said this."

His gaze sharpened, his hand resting steadily against her, feeling the frantic beat of her heart under his fingers. His voice turned quiet, commanding. "Speak plainly, Aria."

She swallowed again, her resolve faltering before she forced herself to continue. "I—I'm part of the Rebellion," she confessed, each word pained as if she had a blade drawn against her throat.

Her eyes flicked to the ground in regret. "I never wanted this, but I had no choice."

For a moment, his expression twisted into something close to sardonic pleasure. His lips pulled into a dark smirk as he watched her, savoring the confusion that spread across her face when she met his gaze again.

"You," she murmured, her words catching in her throat, "you knew, didn't you?"

A low chuckle rolled from him, rich and sinister, reverberating through the space between them as he leaned in close. "Oh, Pyra," he taunted, his fingers trailing slowly along her skin, brushing through her tangled red hair in a touch that was both gentle and possessive. "Of course I knew."

He watched the way her eyes widened in disbelief, relishing the satisfaction that pulsed through him like a drug. The uncertainty in her gaze fueled his darker instincts, igniting a fire he was all too eager to fan.

"How long have you known?" she asked, her voice barely a whisper, trembling with both fear and the weight of revelation.

Rylik leaned in, his breath warm against the delicate shell of her ear, his words a gentle caress laced with a predatory sweetness. "From before you first entered my bedchamber." He inhaled deeply, the intoxicating scent of her skin driving him wild, stirring a ravenous hunger that gnawed at his insides. "If you hadn't discovered my blight, I might have delivered you to the king that very night, out of *loyalty*, perhaps." His tone was dripping with mockery at the word. He had no loyalty to the king beyond what served his own interests. "But I knew that would be a poor decision. I realized it the moment I first laid eyes on you, when you knelt before me by the fire, it was then I decided you were *mine*."

Aria inhaled sharply, a shaky breath escaping her as her instincts kicked in. She reached up, her hand instinctively pushing against his chest as if to create even the slightest distance. "You cannot *own* me, Sovereign."

His breathy laugh washed over her neck, warm and taunting. "Oh, but I can do whatever I wish." His fingertips reveled in the silken strands of her hair, pulling her head back slightly to tilt her

362

chin upward, to hear her gasp like a sweet reward. "I could kiss you right here in this dark alley, feel every part of you trembling beneath my touch, long into the night." His voice dropped to a husky whisper, each word dripping with intent, "I am grievously upset that you dared to run from me, Pyra. I did tell you before, didn't I?" His fingers tightened subtly at her throat, just enough to invoke fear, not to harm. "That if you tried to leave, I'd put you in shackles." A faint gulp moved down her throat as his touch relaxed, trailing his fingers down to her racing heart, savoring the frantic rhythm beneath his palm.

"I wasn't running away from you," she managed, her voice quivering. "I was running away from Orren."

At the mention of Orren, his expression hardened like stone, the name leaving a bitter taste on his tongue. "Right. You said he has plans to kill me? To use you against me?"

"Yes," she replied, struggling to keep her voice steady as the shadows danced around them.

A cruel smirk stretched across his lips as he surveyed her under the silver moonlight. "You should have come to me with this information. I would have soothed your fears."

"I didn't want to risk you finding out that I was part of the Rebellion," she confessed, anxiety lacing her words, "though I see now that concern was pointless."

Genuine pity flickered within him, a rare crack in his guarded facade. She was a pawn ensnared in a game far beyond her grasp, yet somehow—despite everything—she mattered to him more than he could rationalize. His heart twisted with a painful ache, his blight sharpening at the thought of her naive willingness to leave him suffering alone. She had no idea what she truly meant to him—nor did he, entirely. That ignorance stung; she had been ready to abandon him, as if her presence were anything less than essential. His grip on her tightened, a subtle warning that he would not be so easily discarded.

His lips twisted into a sneer, masking the surge of emotion clawing at him. "You were still going to leave me, knowing about my blight, knowing what it might do to—"

"I left you a potion," she interrupted, pain shadowing her features. "I worked tirelessly on it, and I left you instructions.

You don't need me, Sovereign. This potion can sustain you, it can—"

He silenced her with a feral kiss, his lips crashing down on hers with a possessive force that laid bare the words he couldn't speak. The world around them dissolved, leaving only the two of them caught in a tempest of yearning and despair. He groaned into her mouth, wrapping his arms around her waist and pressing her body against his with a raw urgency. She responded, softening under his touch, her tongue dancing with his own in a fervent, desperate longing that matched the wild storm brewing within him.

The world outside faded away, leaving only the heat of their bodies and the dizzying thrill of the moment. She melted against him, surrendering to his touch as if they were two lost souls finding solace in the chaos of the night.

He parted his lips from her own, whispering, "I do *need* you, Pyra." His tone was low, raspy, thick with greed and desire. "I want you." Every singular word was an effort, an admission of guilt as he exposed his weak, pitiful reliance on her.

Aria's lips were reddened from the kiss, parted just lightly as her eyes dimmed to a heady longing. "Because of my healing?"

He understood the question. He knew what she was hoping to ascertain. "It's not only that," he said passively, his thumb gliding over her lower lip as he watched her eyes darken with anticipation for more of him. "I'm afraid it's become much more than that," he let his hand trail across her cheek and find the tendrils of her hair again, his lips hovering close to her own. "I do not mean to offend you when I say that your potion simply will not do. What I want from you far exceeds a mere healing. What I want," he lingered, watching her eyes flutter shut, "is to own you, to dominate you, to *claim* you."

Aria's stifled gasp betrayed her soft carnality. He smirked. She was *enjoying* this.

"Is that what you want?" He teased against her lips, "do you want to be dominated? To be claimed by me?"

She said nothing, only pulled lightly at his waist, delicate fingers seemingly desperate to break through his armor. He felt his body tighten with an oppressive need, a barely contained urge to show her exactly what it would mean to be dominated by him. *But, not here. Not in this dirty alleyway, and certainly not with her treacherous accomplice Thorian making his escape at this very moment,* he thought as he turned his head to the side.

In an unexpected rush, her hand found its way to his cheek, and with a swift motion, she drew him back to her. Her lips brushed softly against his, a tentative plea that stirred something primal within him, igniting an insatiable hunger. He growled, a deep sound rumbling in his chest as he surrendered to the moment, losing the last remnants of his sensibility. Without hesitation, he seized her, one hand circling her waist while the other tangled in her hair, pulling her closer as if to fuse their very beings. The kiss deepened, transforming into a slow, intoxicating dance of desire, each movement stirring a whirlwind of pleasure that coursed through them both, drawing them deeper into a world where nothing else mattered but this connection.

He *wanted* her. He craved this. And if her wandering, eager tongue was any indication, she did too. The skirts of her dress bunched against his palm as he lifted them, burning to touch the smooth bare skin of her thighs. His pants were strained as he pressed against her, their tongues entwining with an unspoken urgency. He could imagine her softness, the embrace he might feel around his length if he entertained the provocation.

But this was not how he wanted her. Not like this, not here. He groaned, muscles taut with restraint, and released her skirts, his lips finally breaking from hers. "Pyra," he rumbled, his voice laced with a dark, raw desire he struggled to suppress.

"Please, don't stop," she whispered, her voice trembling with need as she clung to him, her lips trailing desperate, feverish kisses down his neck.

A fierce strain tightened his throat as he swallowed, his pulse thundering beneath her touch. "Pyra," he said again, this time sharper, the tone a clear warning.

She seemed to sense the dangerous edge in his voice, her kisses slowing and then halting. With a flicker of guilt, her gaze softened as she pulled back, her lips parted, breathing heavily. "I—I'm sorry," she whispered, almost breathless. "I don't know what came over me."

His hand closed around her arm, firm but restrained, his touch a barely controlled promise. "You *will* be sorry," he murmured, voice low and jagged, "for what you've stirred in me. I will ruin you." It was a warning he meant to chill her, to push her away, to shake her from whatever reckless force had awakened between them. His dark imaginings, his need, twisted inside him, urging him to claim her in ways that would leave no question of his power over her.

But instead of shrinking back, her gaze darkened with a gleam of wicked intent. Her lips curved ever so slightly as her teeth grazed her lower lip, mirroring his forbidden hunger, almost daring him to act on the words he'd spoken.

Gods, she will be the death of me. Unable to resist, he pulled her close again, her body molding against him, a deep, shuddering groan slipping from his chest. "Don't let go," he growled, his voice drenched with command and hunger as his shadows unfurled around them, engulfing them both as they vanished from the alley.

CHAPTER 39

ARIA

The dark, swirling shadows that had thundered around them began to slow, ebbing like a retreating storm, until the faint, familiar scent of the Sovereign's chambers—the mingling of aged parchment, leather, and faint smoke—was the first thing Aria sensed as the magic finally stilled. They had traversed a multitude of spaces, Rylik's power leaping through each in swift succession, every shift seamless and precise, until at last, they materialized here.

The room held its silence, save for the rhythmic crackle of flames licking the hearth. The silence swallowed them as she looked up at Rylik, heart stumbling with the significance of his presence. Her body remained against his, and in that fragile clarity of the moment, the gravity of her actions crashed over her: she had kissed him. She had done so deeply and unapologetically. The fantasies she had just had of him had resulted in an ache between her legs, a craving that could only be satisfied if she invited him in.

That strong, roaring desire surged within her once more, tugging her toward him even as she fought to cling to reason. Her stare locked with his, those piercing blue eyes ablaze with the same obsession she felt, a thrilling confirmation that sent a shiver down her spine. Every instinct urged her to break away, to flee to the safety of her chambers and bolt the door behind her. But she knew it would do nothing to keep him at bay—not now, not after she had been so desperate in that shadowed alley. He had been right: she had awakened something dangerous within him, and he seemed determined to unravel her entirely. The thought sent a wave of molten heat pooling deep within, a yearning she couldn't ignore.

Stop this madness, Aria, she begged herself. But she knew she couldn't, not when she'd dreamt of a night like this more times than she dared admit. Her fingertips trailed over the intricate designs etched into his armor, savoring the cool metal and the strength beneath it. She wanted to shed it from him, to strip him of every weight, every wall that kept them apart. Her heart pounded violently in her ribcage, imagining the expanse of him, the way his hard muscles might feel as she grazed her hand over them. She longed to touch every part of him to know fully his bare form, to take in the majesty of it.

For the better part of two weeks, she had convinced herself that this was beyond her reach—a wistful thought destined to live only in her dreams. Yet no fantasy could have prepared her for the reality of him, the way his presence enveloped her, his body towering over hers with such intensity. In his grasp, she felt small, fragile, and captivated by a closeness she'd never dared hope to feel.

Rylik inhaled slowly, a forced calm overtaking him as he said, "You should return to your suite, Aria. It's been a long night. And I have a hunt to tend to."

Aria blinked up at him, her heart hammering at the very idea of him pursuing Thorian. She knew he would find him—of that, she had no doubt. But Thorian didn't deserve death for his actions. His intentions were noble. She clenched her grip around Rylik's strong arm, a silent, urgent plea. "No, I've told you. It isn't what you think. He has good intentions—"

"His intentions," Rylik cut in, a biting tone in his voice as his hand clamped around her waist, drawing her backward until her spine met the sturdy post of his bed, "nearly took you from me." His gaze roamed over her, admiring her face illuminated in the glow of the firelight. "And for that betrayal," he murmured, fingers slipping through the curls of her hair, watching as its silken red caught the light, "he will pay."

A spark of both fear and delight rippled through her at his touch, at the heat radiating from his form as he held her close. "You could stay," she ventured lightly, her voice barely a whisper, as if fearing the consequences of the suggestion. And she was right to tread carefully, for at her words, he emitted a low, dangerous growl, pushing her backward onto the bed with a restrained fervor. Her back now flat against the blanket under her, she barely had any time to react.

He moved over her in an instant, his presence enveloping her as he blocked out the glow of the fire, casting her in his shadow. His powerful arms braced on either side of her, milling into the mattress as he leaned in, watching her unwaveringly as though he regarded her as prey caught in his snare. She quivered under his scrutiny, her hand instinctively reaching up to his collarbone, just above the cold armor, as if to push it aside—to remove any barrier that separated them, that kept from her what she could feel wholly, without restraint.

He smirked down at her, his fingers moving effortlessly to unclasp his cape, letting it fall in a dark ripple to the floor. Piece by piece, he shed his armor, revealing the simple black linen of his tunic, the pale expanse of his skin peeking through the loosened laces. Aria's hands were already there, her fingertips hot against his chest as she fumbled with the ties. She molded herself to him, trailing fevered kisses along his neck, every tender press a wordless plea for more.

Rylik's hand grabbed the hem of her skirts, slowly pulling them up as his fingertips teased her naked thighs. Ecstasy rippled through her body at the touch, instinctively feeling her hips pull in his direction. "Careful," A faint warmth traced her neck, carrying a passive hint of caution. "This will not be as you may have imagined it," he murmured, an enticing note of amusement in his voice, even as she continued to nestle fervent kisses along his nape, each touch a blaze against his skin. "As you have practiced alone in your bed, and in my bath."

Aria released a tenuous moan, too consumed in the moment to

feel any shame that he knew. *Of course*, he knew. He had sensed her feelings for him long before she ever acknowledged them to herself. A darker, insidious part of her wondered if he had heard her hushed sounds of bliss, and if he had liked it. She felt the slow, teasing glide of his fingers tracing up the inside of her thigh, each impassioned touch sparking a thrill of anticipation, building a pleasure that had yet to fully unfold. Her hand drifted down to his, guiding his wrist with a subtle invitation, urging his touch to deepen. She *needed* it. She needed *him*.

Rylik chuckled, a deep, low sound that made her stir with heat. "Aria," he murmured, brushing against her cheek with a feather light kiss. "Do you have any idea of the agony you've put me through?" he asked, feeling her faint, pleading tug on his wrist. Yet he held firm, feasting on the sweet impatience that simmered between them. "You have indulged in your fantasies of me while I have been left to suffer in my restraint," he murmured, his lips tracing a slow, smooth line along her jaw.

She tugged at his hand once more, only to feel his gentle resistance. He smiled, watching her eyes open, teeming with a silent plea. "Do you know how I've wanted to interject, knowing that you were pleasuring yourself at my expense?" He shifted her grip on his wrist, taking control of her hand with soothing authority, gracefully moving her fingers low against herself. His gaze held hers solidly as he added, "I want to watch the very moment you tip over the edge of ecstasy."

Aria's throat constricted with memory, with an eagerness to feel *more*—to feel *him*. No amount of personal release could ever subdue the ache she had, pining for the fullness of him. Words deserted her, leaving just a faint, unsteady sigh in the space between them. She felt him press her, a familiar sensation, now intertwined with the forbidden thrill of his large hand guiding her own in something that had always been hers alone. She felt intoxicated by the touch, unable to look away from him while his fingers overlapped her own, dipping low and warm, trespassing her with sweet, unforgivable rapture.

His blue eyes locked onto her, delighting in the vulnerable way her expression succumbed to her salacity. Her mind was nearly blank, overtaken by a pull too powerful to keep restrained beneath him. She was slick, and every knot of pleasure along her form was tense and greedy. She knew he was savoring the sight, the feel of her, reveling in the knowledge that she was wholly at his mercy and unabashedly impetuous.

Rylik clicked his tongue softly in a taunt, "My little Pyra, you are so *very* enjoyable to watch." He pushed in deeply, firmly as he spoke, his fingers gliding past her own with invasive gentleness. He watched even as her eyes fluttered shut, as her hips bucked against the tantalizing pressure. Once more, his hazy, ominous laugh reverberated through her, stirring her senses as she whimpered in elation. She scarcely minded that he was teasing, that he was relishing her predicament at his leisure.

"P—please—!" Her voice was little more than a whimper, a pained plea on her tongue, swallowed by the heat that thrummed between them.

"Please?" He asked slowly, seductively, eyes roving over her. A playful, mocking smile curled at the corners of his mouth, prompting her to speak. But, before she could utter another syllable, he drew his shimmering fingers up toward a small swathe of nerves, provoking a moan from her as he kneaded over it.

Aria felt a rush of warmth flooding low and deep within her. She pulsed against him, her slippery fingertips wrapping over his wrist once more, angling him without contrition. "Please!" She begged, her throat dry and constrained, her hand leaving his own to reach for his waist.

He huffed a small laugh, his tone teasing as he chided her, "Oh, you need more, do you?"

A flicker of euphoria swept over her as her palm brushed over the expanse of him, solid and strained against the seam of his pants. She wanted to feel the fullness of him, the way he might satiate her more deeply than she could ever hope to know. "Yes!" A strained sound escaped her, "Please, Sovereign, I—!"

Rylik claimed her mouth, his tongue mirroring the grace of his own fingers against her, the shared heat between them making her body burn with lust.

She struggled to catch herself, every sound slipping out as a hushed gasp, "Please!"

He kissed her again, deeply, groaning against her mouth as her hand fumbled against his seam.

"Please, Sovereign—!" Again she pleaded, feeling the buckle loosen, the breadth of him free from its bounds.

He silenced her with another kiss as her fingers wrapped around his length, a rush of arousal unfurling low with a growl in his throat. He cursed under his breath as her soft fingers moved in languid strokes, pulling on him as if she might anchor him to her. "Pyra," he warned her, "I intend to make this last a long, long time." His lips swept over her cheek as his fingers continued to trace gentle circles against her. "I intend to watch you writhe in pleasure many times over."

"Yes," a delicate moan escaped her, "just, please—I need you inside of me. Please—!" She felt her hips lift absently toward him, her hand tense and impatient against his steely column, urging him nearer.

He mocked her with that derisive laugh, seizing his fingers more deeply past her barriers, feeling her tremble against him. "Not yet." He teased her neck, drawing out the exquisite bliss of her heightened senses. She was consumed by desperation, as if she might cease to exist without his touch, without every part of him. Her fingers clasped around him like a lifeline, imagining the bliss of taking him in fully. It was sinful, primal, wicked, and she had long since abandoned the question of why she craved it. All she knew was that without him, she might diminish into nothingness.

"Sovereign—!" She lamented weakly, her heart pounding in her chest as he toyed with her nerves. She was saturated, wrestling against a volatile mix of anguish and passion, her frustration simmering at his distance.

"Yes?" He replied, tone sultry and threaded with opulent provocation.

This was some kind of *torture* she had never known. He wanted her, she knew that. She could feel the evidence of it in her hand. Why was he indulging in this cruel amusement with her? Did he not crave her as desperately as she longed for him? How much more would she have to beg? That's what it was becoming—an endless cycle of pleading, while he reveled in her surrender. "I want you inside me," she said, her voice tense and resonant with impatience.

A laugh rolled through him at that, and another wave of intensity moved in her. "How brazen," he jeered, barely ignoring her next assertive tug against him. A quivering exhalation left him as she wrenched against him, a little more persistently than before. "I just want to see your face, dear, when you lose what is left of your composure." He smirked at her wryly. "And maybe, if I feel so inclined, I might make you do it again."

Aria's lashes lowered in a delicate sweep as treacherous waves of euphoria washed over her. She was intoxicated, drunk on the sensation of him, her pulse racing with a blinding frustration at not having all of him. Emotions tangled within her, a whirlwind that blurred any sense of reality that could exist beyond this moment.

Her mouth trembled open, her voice barely a whisper. "Rylik! Please!"

His eyes shadowed with intent, a sharpened edge to them as he slowly withdrew his hand. "Say that again." His voice, low and commanding, sent a flutter of emotion through her. "Say my name *again*."

Aria was helpless under the depth of his stare, her heart racing as she peered past the disarray of his tousled hair casting shadows over those haunting, pale blue eyes. "Rylik," she said, her voice fragile, as if her very soul hung on the sound of his name.

A faint sheen gleamed on his fingertips as they lightly brushed his tongue, savoring the taste of her as though it were the finest nectar. He seemed to bask in the cautious reverence with which she spoke his name. A sinful, slow smile curled at the edges of his lips. "You will say that name," he murmured, each word weighted with an intensity that left her aflame, "All night long." His hand lowered slowly down the center of him. "You will scream that name until you are breathless, Pyra."

A shaky gasp escaped her, a tremor of fire that pulsed through her, too powerful to restrain. It was a promise—one she was determined to keep.

The quiet was suddenly shattered by a deafening, relentless banging on the Sovereign's door. The sound ripped through her, catching them both off guard. Aria's heart skipped, her chest tightening as the stillness shattered in an instant. She froze, her body alive with a thirst that now seemed impossible to quench. She had never felt more torn, her body incensed with an unfulfilled want, and yet, the intrusion—so jarring, so unforgiving—made her pulse race with anxiety. Someone was there, and by the urgency of their knocking, they would not be easily deterred.

Rylik's body stiffened on top of her, his muscles taut with barely contained fury. With a furious growl, he yanked her skirt down, his hands rough and demanding, before rising to his full height. The knocks continued, persistent and insistent, followed by frantic shouts on the other side.

"Sovereign! It's urgent! Open the door! Are you in there?!"

A savage fury twisted his features as he buttoned his pants with almost painful haste, the sound of the fastenings echoing in the room. He stormed toward the door, flinging it open with a violent growl, the tension in his frame like a beast held just at bay. "What the hell is it, Sylas?" His voice was a low, dangerous growl as he faced the man who stood frozen mid-knock, eyes flicking between Rylik's untamed appearance and the sight of Aria on his bed behind him.

Sylas's brows shot up, his attention darting from Rylik's wild state to Aria, as if she were a delicate secret he wasn't meant to witness. Rylik stepped forward, a scowl darkening his features. "Open your damn mouth, or I'll run you through. What is it?"

Sylas, still a little dumbfounded, forced himself to speak. "It's Thorian," he said. "He killed Alastair. I just found his body in his room. We need to find Thorian and figure out what's going on."

A heavy sensation filled her throat at the name Alastair. She knew of him—a Shadow Knight, one of Rylik's men. Aria had never spoken to him, but she had seen him in passing. Her hand instinctively rose to her chest, the shock sinking deep as she tried to process the horror of what Thorian had done.

Rylik glanced over his shoulder at her, his brow furrowing as he contemplated his next move. The storm of emotions swirling between them became palpable, charged with something forbidden that now felt impossibly distant.

"Go," Aria whispered, her voice trembling with reluctance,

but a muffled urgency. She couldn't stop him. He had to go. But her heart screamed for him to stay, to return to what had been stolen from them so abruptly. "You should go, Sovereign."

Rylik's jaw tightened, his face set into a hard line as he turned back to Sylas. "I'll be out shortly." He didn't wait for a reply, slamming the door shut behind him with an impact that felt final, his presence momentarily gone from the room. Aria felt the absence of him as keenly as if the very air had been stolen from her.

He crossed the room in a few long strides, gathering his armor from the floor, the heavy burden of his movements belying his internal turmoil. She reached for his cape just as he was about to do so, the rough material cool against her fingertips. She handed it to him wordlessly, her gaze downcast as she twisted her skirt anxiously in her hands. "Sovereign, I—"

Before she could finish, Rylik cupped her face in his hand with a tenderness that stole the breath from her lungs. His thumb traced her lower lip in a caress so intimate, so intense, that it left her unsteady. Then, without a word, he claimed her in a kiss that was replete with yearning, that spoke of everything unsaid, of promises left unfinished.

When he pulled back, his voice was hoarse, rife with a hypnotic intensity that seemed to settle into the very air between them. "I only want to hear my name on your lips, Aria. To everyone else, I am the Sovereign. But to you," he brushed his lips over hers again, soft but filled with an undeniable longing. "For you, I am simply Rylik."

The words burned into her like a brand, searing into her heart as she melted into his touch. She closed her eyes, wishing with every fiber of her being that the moment could stretch into eternity.

"Stay here," he whispered, his authority wrapped in a velvet tenderness. "Because I am not done with you, Pyra."

He cast one last glance before turning, fading into shadow, and leaving her in the oppressive stillness of the room. Alone. Unsatisfied. The silence around her felt deafening, and yet, nothing could erase the rising current swelling within her. The door slammed shut, the sound echoing in her chest, leaving her to mourn his absence—a loss that was unbearable, a desire that was far from sated.

CHAPTER 40

RYLIK

The moon hung low above a forest clearing, Rylik's gaze settling on a lone horse tethered to a gnarled tree. He had been mere moments away from laying claim to Aria's perfect body, and yet now, here he stood—stalking Thorian. Shadows danced along the ground, orange light flickering from the small, smoldering fire up ahead. Thorian's figure sat silhouetted against the flames, his form still, yet radiating an unsettling vigilance even in his rest.

His jaw set, Rylik stayed in the cover of darkness, his stance tense, every nerve wound tight with simmering tension. How would he kill him? Quickly? Slowly? It was challenging to decide. If he killed him off in haste, he could return to his prior interest. He smiled at the thought, but some spiteful part of him wanted Thorian to feel unspeakable pain for the agony he had caused him to experience tonight.

For weeks he had grown increasingly ravenous for his little prisoner, and now that she was finally within his grasp, he had to leave her? Perhaps it was the culmination of all of his calloused actions that had led to the miserable consequence that was this night. It was his penance, he supposed, for being such a reprobate for so long. An inaudible groan of annoyance rumbled in his chest. He should've told Sylas to go to hell, returned to his bed, and driven Aria to her peak.

Had he known that he would be interrupted before he could begin, he might've taunted her a little less. Though, he couldn't deny he loved that too, the thrill he took in watching her impatience melt into something beautifully raw and urgent. He was somewhat of a sadist, delighting in drawing out her every tremble and sigh, even at his own expense. He ran his tongue along his lower lip, savoring the thought of finally feeling her warm, swollen embrace around him.

Thorian shifted in the burnished light, the flicker of movement pulling Rylik sharply out of his reverie. In many ways, he was still in his bed, teasing his Pyra into full, decadent submission. He needed to finish his matter quickly. Though he'd tasked Sylas with her guard while he took on this hunt, he had no desire to keep them in each other's company for long. Sylas was a notorious flirt, and he'd rather not have to kill yet another of his Shadow Knights. Thorian's execution of Alastair had been bad enough. At this rate, he might be left with only one of his original knights, forcing him to endure the annoyance of recruiting replacements.

Judging by the coldness of the corpse, Thorian had murdered Alastair hours before the Festival of the Sun and Stars. Alastair had always been a private sort of man, which had always made him somewhat difficult to read. Perhaps Thorian would finally shed light on why he killed him—just before Rylik returned the favor.

With a silent resolve, he dissolved into dark wisps, reemerging just behind Thorian, blade in hand and angled against his throat.

"Good evening," Rylik greeted him in cold mockery, his voice heavy with resentment.

"To you as well, Sovereign," Thorian replied, his voice unnaturally calm despite the cool metal sharp against his neck.

Rylik sneered, pressing the tip of the dagger inward, a small bead of blood forming at the gesture. "A modicum of self-preservation would be advised, Thorian. I am about to kill you, after all."

"No, you won't," he retorted, lifting his hand to show him the small trinket he had been playing with between his fingers.

When Rylik's stare dropped to the black ring in his hand, his heart squeezed in his chest like a vice. "Where did you get that?" He couldn't help but to ask, bewildered by its appearance in his knight's grasp.

"Aria," he said coolly, "she had it in her meager belongings." He motioned toward the small bag by the fire, likely containing no more than one or two dresses from her entire wardrobe. She might have seen it as a mercy—only a few to carry away, perhaps to ease the guilt of leaving Rylik after all the coin he'd spent on her.

"I'll address her thievery later," he muttered, the thought of punishment already brewing in his mind. He fought to suppress a sadistic smirk, forcing himself to focus on the present moment.

"My mentor," Thorian began, "made the penultimate sacrifice to avenge your father's reputation, and subsequent death." He let the ring's broken silver emblem catch the light as he spoke. "He suffers not only for your father's sake, but for mine as well."

"The mentor you speak of. He is the illusive general, I take it?" Rylik inquired, hand steady, always distrusting. Thorian already knew too much about him now, and time would tell how that would result.

"Yes. General Hamish Levgard," Thorian spoke, his voice smooth but carrying the weight of long-held secrets. "Whether you recognize the name or not, he was one of the few real allies your father had."

Rylik's grip on the hilt of the knife tightened, though his eyes betrayed no emotion, only the shifting tension of unspoken thoughts. "I know the name," he murmured, the memory of a past too far gone to touch stirring inside him, "only I thought he had died."

"In some ways, he has." Thorian's tone grew colder, a bitter rancor seeping into his words. "After your father was betrayed by members of the court, they sought to kill Hamish when he uncovered it. They would've succeeded, if not for his own sharp defense. As far as they're concerned, though, Hamish is long dead."

The mention of betrayal made Rylik's stomach tighten, but he didn't move an inch. His presence loomed behind Thorian, the cold edge of the knife pressed gently against his throat, a constant reminder of the danger hanging between them. "What happened to him?" Rylik's voice was low, heavy with guarded tension, but beneath it, his curiosity cut through the night air with undeniable force.

Thorian's mouth twisted into a grim smile, his eyes glinting in the firelight. "He was poisoned, betrayed by the last ally he thought he truly had—Lord Eldric Magnace."

Rylik felt a shock ripple through him, though his expression remained unreadable.

"Though it would seem fate saw fit to reward his betrayal," Thorian continued, his voice hardening with a cold satisfaction. "His body is now a crumpled heap in the king's forest, fodder for beasts by now. I only regret that I was not the one to have had the honor."

Rylik's jaw clenched, his eyes narrowing, recalling when he'd watched Orren drive a blade through the nobleman's gut. "Hamish should've died the day he was poisoned," Thorian went on. "But he took an antitoxin in time. However, it wasn't enough. He needs a complete healing, an eradication of that bitter drug from his system entirely."

"And you think Aria can undo this, do you?" he asked, his voice dark with skepticism.

"I'm confident she can." Thorian's gaze flicked upward, his posture unflinching. "And Hamish has offered her employ within his keep as payment for the healing she would render to him."

Rylik's gaze hardened, his stance shifting ever so slightly as his grip on the dagger remained steady. "Aria is mine."

Thorian's lips twitched, but he didn't falter. The fire crackled louder, almost mocking the tension in the air. "You would withhold a healing from the man who tried to avenge your father?" His words hung heavy, the accusation sharp and unapologetic.

"I need proof of that." Rylik's voice dropped lower, his tone menacing, like a storm just waiting to break.

"His life is proof of that." Thorian's eyes narrowed slightly. "You said yourself you knew the name. He is dying slowly because he was a remnant of good in this vile world."

Rylik's pulse quickened, a flare of doubt igniting in him. He didn't want to believe it, didn't want to think that someone—

anyone—could still be innocent in a world so rife with treachery. "I wish to speak with him, then," Rylik said, his voice firm, "and if I find him even slightly distrustful, I'll finish what the poison failed to do."

Thorian's gaze softened, though it didn't reach his words. "He cared for you, Rylik. He still does, and your mother, too."

At that, Rylik's eyes wavered, a sudden vulnerability slipping through the cracks in his carefully maintained armor.

Thorian pressed on, his voice quiet but persistent. "You can ask her yourself. She receives anonymous payments in exchange for healing elixirs. He pays her handsomely, far more than the elixir is likely to cost her. This is partly in gratitude, but also to render some extra help to a woman who lost everything."

Rylik's mind raced, trying to digest the information. Why had his mother never mentioned this in any of her letters? He knew she was a medicine woman and was likely to work with people anonymously. Perhaps she never met the man face to face.

"Why has he not spoken to me directly about this?" Rylik's voice was steady, though the question itself gnawed at him.

"He had no idea you were alive. Rylik is a nickname, is it not?" Thorian's voice was softer now, the answer wrapped in quiet understanding. "He would've known you by another name. Your father's name—Rysandrian."

A flash of shock registered on Rylik's face, quickly masked by a careful stoicism. *Rysandrian.* The name of a man long dead. It was as though a piece of his past had been resurrected, an old wound reopened. Without a word, Rylik pulled the dagger away from Thorian's throat, the tension between them momentarily easing.

If I had never seen this ring tonight," Thorian said, his voice steady but laden with unspoken meaning, eyes tracking the Sovereign as he rounded slowly upon him, "I would've been equally prepared to take your life as well. But now, I can see we are similarly wounded by the crown." He let the words linger in the cold air, each one a silent testament to their shared history.

Rylik's gaze never wavered from Thorian's face, his mind still reeling from the revelation. "I killed the man who framed my father," he said, his voice heavy with conviction, "and I will soon kill the king who inspired it."

A rare moment of respect passed across Thorian's features, though it was swiftly replaced with something more calculating. "I would gladly assist you in that effort, Sovereign."

Rylik's eyes darkened, the weight of his words pressing down on him. "Kind of you, Thorian, but this is a selfish need I alone will have to satisfy."

A long silence stretched between them as they regarded one another. The fire snapped and hissed, and the air seemed to vibrate with unspoken words.

"Then, what of Hamish?" Thorian asked, his voice steady but tinged with a thread of urgency. "Will you speak with him? Would you allow Aria to administer a healing?"

Rylik's eyes narrowed, his thoughts clouded with uncertainty. "I will speak with him," he finally said, his voice quiet but resolute. "And then I will make my decision."

Thorian nodded, a flicker of relief crossing his features. He didn't dare let it rest. The moment of tension had passed, but it had shifted, becoming something far more fragile.

Rylik fixed Thorian with a solid gaze, his voice cold and cutting as he asked, "Why did you kill Alastair?"

Thorian froze, his confusion flickering into plain view. "Alastair is dead?"

The words struck like a thunderclap, sending a jolt of dread ripping through Rylik's chest. His mind raced, the pieces falling together with chilling clarity.

Sylas.

The name surged to the forefront of his thoughts, a dark certainty gripping him. Sylas had killed Alastair.

Rylik felt the familiar heat of his Sentinel Band pulse against his skin, a haunting red glow intensifying in the darkness. A sharp chill seized him as the realization hit: Aria was in danger. The glow of the ring was unmistakable, a beacon of her fear that he couldn't ignore.

Without another word, he turned, his body already dissipating into darkness.

CHAPTER 41

ARIA

Aria sat on the edge of Rylik's bed, her gaze fixed on the closed door, her mind swirling. The room was quiet, save for the faint crackle of the fire in the hearth, but her heart was anything but still. She pressed a hand to her chest, trying to steady her uneven breaths, still reeling from the charged moments they'd shared not long ago.

She couldn't shake the memory of his touch, his nearness, and the way his gaze seemed to pierce through to her very soul. Her lips tingled from the kiss they hadn't finished, and her body burned with an ache she didn't know how to soothe. She hadn't wanted him to leave, not after what they had nearly done, but he'd drawn away, his face darkening as Thorian's name surfaced — along with the revelation of Alastair's death.

There was a reason for his departure, she reminded herself. She understood. Yet doubt whispered in the back of her mind. How safe would she have been with Thorian? Would he have killed her too?

Her thoughts unraveled as the door creaked open, breaking the room's fragile stillness. Aria's head snapped up, her stomach twisting. Sylas stood in the doorway, his frame blocking the light spilling in from the hall.

"The Sovereign sent me," Sylas said, his tone clipped. "You need to come with me."

Aria rose slowly, uncertain. "What's going on? He told me to stay here."

Sylas took a step inside, his expression hardening. "There's been a development. He believes you're in danger. We need to move you somewhere safe."

Danger. Aria's mind leapt to Orren's warning, his promise to strike, surely when she least expected it. Her pulse quickened as her thoughts raced. "Did he say anything more on it?" she murmured, stepping closer, searching Sylas's face for confirmation.

Sylas's jaw tightened. "There's no time to explain. Come with me."

But something in his demeanor set her on edge. Perhaps it was the urgency of the moment, but she had never seen Sylas like this. He was always smoothly gliding into rooms and smiling a needless cheeky grin. But now, it seemed, he looked a little desperate in a way that felt uncanny. She hesitated, her gaze flicking down to the pendant at her neck—the one that Rylik had given her, glowing faintly like a comforting heartbeat. She took a step back. "If the Sovereign told me to stay, I think I'd better listen to him."

Sylas's eyes darkened, his tone sharp as a blade. "You're coming with me. Willingly, or by force."

Fear tightened around Aria, her body jerking as his hand reached for her arm. His grip was like iron, his fingers biting into her skin. "Let go!" she protested, panic blooming in her chest.

The pendant around her neck flared brighter, a soft silvery light spilling from it. Sylas's eyes narrowed, his lips curling into a sneer. "Enchanted talismans," he muttered. "Of course." Without hesitation, he ripped it from her neck and hurled it to the floor, the clink of silver against stone echoing in the room. "Can't have that giving me away so soon."

The loss of the pendant felt like a blow, a tether severed, leaving her adrift. As Sylas shifted in the momentary distraction, Aria wrenched her arm free, darting toward the door.

But she didn't make it far. His hand tangled in her hair, yanking her back with a brutal force that made her cry out. She stumbled, her balance stolen, as Sylas pulled her close. "Aw, don't be so coy now, Aria," he mocked. His face hovered near hers, a cruel smirk spreading across his lips. "If you're with the Sovereign," he drawled, "you must like it rough."

Aria struggled, terror climbing in her throat, but Sylas was too strong. Before she could summon the strength to scream, he raised his free hand, dark purple magic swirling around his fingers. The energy washed over her eyes, her vision dimming, the world dissolving into a haze.

Her knees buckled as consciousness slipped through her grasp, her last coherent thought a desperate plea for Rylik to find her. Darkness claimed her, cold and absolute.

* * *

Aria's vision swam as she forced her eyes open, the world around her shifting in and out of focus like a half-remembered dream. The dim flicker of firelight illuminated fractured shadows across towering stone columns and broken stained glass. She blinked sluggishly, her mind clawing through the haze of residual magic, trying to grasp at the threads of reality.

Muted laughter echoed from somewhere beyond her line of sight, mingling with the crackle of flames. The chill of the night air seeped through the stone floor beneath her, cutting through the muddled warmth of her sluggish body. She shifted her weight, feeling the rough scrape of rope against her wrists and the cold, hard column she was bound to.

"She's awake," a voice murmured, low and sardonic.

Her gaze darted toward the source, her surroundings sharpening into grim clarity. The vaulted ceilings of a cathedral loomed above her, its sanctity marred by desecration. A massive bonfire raged in the space where the altar should have stood, its flames licking hungrily at the air, casting cruel shadows on the faces of the men scattered throughout the room.

The Rebellion.

Aria's heart slammed against her ribs as her eyes landed on a figure striding toward her. Sylas. His expression twisted with dark amusement as he crouched in front of her, the firelight reflecting off his sharp features and lending a sinister glow to his dark eyes.

"Comfortable?" he asked, his tone laced with mockery as his gaze swept over her bound form.

Aria was angry, but the fire in her chest dimmed as a pitiful whisper escaped her lips instead of the firm demand she had intended. "Where are we?"

Sylas kept his gaze locked on her, his eyes brimming with cruelty as he answered, his tone cold and dismissive, "An old church outside of town. And the fact that the Sovereign hasn't found us yet is," he clicked his tongue against his teeth, "very disappointing." His eyes raked over her, a predator's glint sparking to life. He leaned in closer, his breath cold against her skin. "How loud can you scream?"

A shiver coiled through her, sharp and unwelcome.

"Hey," a voice called from behind her, making her flinch. Leon. "You don't need to scare her, Sylas. She's bait, nothing more. No need to treat her like an enemy."

Relief and dread warred within her as she twisted to glimpse Leon striding toward them. His expression was firm, but something about the stiffness in his jaw kept her on edge.

Sylas barely spared him a glance, his irritation palpable. "She's the Sovereign's bedmate, boy. Wake up. She's just as much an enemy to the Rebellion as he is."

Leon's eyes narrowed, sharp and unrelenting. "She's not his bedmate. You're mistaken."

Sylas barked out a laugh, sharp and cruel, as though Leon's words were the punchline of a joke. "When I found her in his chambers, she was in his bed, looking like she'd been thoroughly fu—"

Steel rasped as Leon's blade cleared its sheath in a single, fluid motion. His voice was low, deadly, a growl of barely contained rage. "Stop talking."

Sylas straightened, towering over him, his frame pulsing with a dark authority. Purple magic swirled like smoke around his fingers, casting faint, ghostly shadows on the cracked stone floor. "You really want to challenge me, Corporal?"

The tension in the air thickened, suffocating Aria as she sat frozen under Sylas's calculating gaze. Leon's hesitation was like a wound to her already frayed nerves. Every second stretched, the oppressive magic swirling around them, heavy and suffocating. Sylas's smirk deepened, cruel and knowing, his eyes flicking from Leon to Aria.

"You like the healer, hmm?" Sylas drawled, his voice dripping with malice. "And here I thought it was just Maven you wanted. Greedy of you." His words sliced through the air, each one laced with venom.

Leon's glare was cool and stoic, but the tension in his shoulders told a different story. His eyes flickered to Sylas's glowing fingers, the swirling magic crackling ominously.

Sylas's grin widened, a taunting gleam in his eyes. "Go on now, while I still feel like being merciful."

Leon's reluctance was palpable, but he begrudgingly sheathed his sword and slowly backed away, his eyes never leaving Aria or Sylas. Aria's pulse hammered in her ears, her body stiff and trembling, caught between the suffocating fear and the growing terror of what might come next. She was helpless, bound to this pillar, every instinct screaming for escape, yet knowing there was none.

Sylas bent down, his presence oppressive and cold, his palm a sickening warmth as he rested his hand on her thigh. She recoiled involuntarily, heart racing. "Alright, sweetheart," he crooned, his voice low and dangerous, "here's what I want you to do for me."

Aria's skin crawled at the way his fingers splayed, possessive and invasive. She swallowed, her throat dry as she tried to pull away, but he gently tapped her chin, forcing her gaze upward. His eyes locked onto hers with cruel amusement, savoring the fear in her gaze. "Eyes on me," he purred, dragging out the words, savoring each syllable like a feast.

Her stomach turned, panic rising like bile in her throat.

"I want you to start screaming for me," he demanded, his voice a whip. "Can you do that?"

Her blood ran cold, instinct telling her to fight, yet her body refused to respond. Sylas chuckled, the sound dark and satisfied, like a wolf savoring the chase before the kill. "The fear is good," he taunted, his voice slithering over her, "but I want you to make a *sound*." His hand tightened on her thigh, squeezing with brutal force, sending a jolt of pain through her that made her yelp uncontrollably.

Leon's grip tightened on his hilt, his eyes seething with disbelief and rage, but he stood frozen, a silent witness to the torment unfolding before him.

Aria's chest rose and fell in frantic gasps, her heart pounding, the oppressive air around her thick with fear. Her eyes burned, her body trembling with the effort to keep herself from breaking. Sylas's hand softened against her, almost tenderly, but the cold cruelty in his eyes never wavered. "Shh, now," he coaxed, a mockery of comfort. "I want you to be much louder than that. Orren tells me you can't heal yourself. So I don't intend to brutalize you. You're still valuable." His gaze tracked the tears that had begun to slip down her cheeks, and his smile deepened, sickening.

"Now," his words slid out, warm and inviting, like silk concealing a trap, "can you scream for me?"

Aria opened her mouth, but no words came—only a ragged breath, a broken exhale. Her body was paralyzed with terror, every muscle frozen in place as if the very air around her was made of stone.

Sylas's grin stretched, relishing her helplessness, and then he squeezed her thigh again. The pressure built, unbearable, and she screamed—truly screamed this time—as pain flared through her body. The sound tore from her throat, raw and uncontrollable.

Sylas's hand softened for a moment, his touch almost affectionate as he patted her. "Very good," he mused, low and pleased, his voice dripping with mockery.

He leaned in closer, his breath hot against her ear as his hand slid further up her thigh, dragging her fabric along with it. Aria's breath seized, her entire body tense with fear. "You know," Sylas's voice was a whisper now, slithering into her ear like a serpent, "after we kill the Sovereign, you're going to need a new suitor."

She shivered violently, repulsed by his proximity, but he was relentless, placing an unwanted kiss on her neck, his lips cold and intrusive.

"How about I take you to his bed tonight?" he mused darkly, sliding a calloused hand over her skin. His fingers traced the marks he had left on her, the imprints of his cruelty. An involuntary whimper escaped her lips, and another tear slipped down her cheek, her body betraying her once again.

A sharp sound rang out, the harsh scrape of metal against air, and Sylas's gaze flicked to the side, his smirk faltering for a brief moment. Leon stood there, his sword drawn, the tip cold and sharp, aimed directly at Sylas's throat.

"Get your damn hand off of her," Leon growled, his voice an icy edge of fury.

Sylas's grin returned, but it was dark and cruel. "You already have Maven, Corporal," he mocked, his voice dripping with disdain. "You try to interfere here, and I'll take both of the little whores from you."

In a flash of movement, Leon lunged forward, his blade slicing through the air, but Sylas was faster—inhumanly so. Violet wisps of magic swirled around him like smoke, blurring the space between them. In an instant, he drew his own blade, the motion so quick it left Leon no time to react.

Suddenly, a deafening scream echoed from the back of the church, chilling the air.

Black clouds of magic surged into the room, thick and oppressive, billowing like a storm made of shadows. The dark tendrils of power twisted and coiled, wrapping around each person, freezing them in place, and the room seemed to hold its breath. A tremor of panic rippled through the air, thickening the already tense atmosphere, as if the very walls of the church had begun to suffocate them all.

And then, amidst the chaos, Aria's heart stilled. She felt it—a presence cutting through the weight of the moment.

Rylik had arrived.

CHAPTER 42

RYLIK

Rylik was going to savor this slaughter. He'd known it from the moment he shadowed into his bedchamber and found Aria's Lyrica pendant discarded on the floor, the faint melody silenced as if mocking him with her absence. The rage that followed was swift and all-consuming, an inferno fueled by betrayal—his own, for trusting Sylas with her care, and Orren's, for orchestrating this trap. He had stalked to his cabinet, his movements quick and unrelenting, snatching the elixirs he would need before vanishing into the Veil. It hadn't been as quick as it should have been.

The golden yellow thread of her aura was there, faint but undeniable, weaving through the shadows like a frayed lifeline. Yet something had tampered with it, clouding its clarity and forcing him to focus harder, push deeper into the Veil to find her. Sylas's magic, no doubt—an attempt to distort her presence and buy himself more time. It wasn't enough to sever the thread completely, but it had slowed Rylik, forcing him to claw through the interference until he could finally lock onto her. When he did, he wasted no time, unraveling the distance in an instant and slipping into the darkness like a wraith on the hunt.

His chest heaved, his hands trembling with the force of his fury as the memory burned vivid in his mind—the moment he'd closed in on her, her aura flaring brighter than ever, a desperate, golden beacon against the Veil. And then, her scream. It had cut through the cathedral like a blade, raw with pain and terror, reverberating off the walls and spilling out through shattered windows into the night. The sound of it was still ringing in his ears, stoking his wrath to a fever pitch.

Rylik had shadowed into the church within moments, his fury a razor-sharp edge as his gaze locked onto the scene before him. Aria was bound to a pillar, her body trembling, tears streaking her face. Sylas's hand gripped her thigh, his lips pressed against her neck in a mockery of intimacy. A strangled cry escaped her, and the sound ignited a wildfire in Rylik's chest. His blade was in his hand before he registered the movement, but his steps faltered when Leon stepped forward, sword drawn and leveled at Sylas's throat. Fool. Leon didn't stand a chance. Sylas wasn't just a fighter; he was an archmage, a killer far beyond Leon's skill. The idiot would die within moments.

Rylik's narrowed gaze burned into the scene, his mind racing. He couldn't charge in. Sylas would sense the ripple in the Veil the moment he moved too close. He needed an opening—an instant of chaos. Cutting his eyes to the side, he spotted his first victim: a Rebellion soldier relieving himself against the church wall, oblivious to the predator in the shadows. Rylik moved without hesitation, the attack swift and brutal. He made sure the man saw him first, let him catch a glimpse of the fury in his eyes before he drove the blade into his heart. The sharp, guttural sound of the soldier's dying breath rang out, slicing through the tense air of the church. Rylik let the body fall hard against the stone floor with a resounding thud, the noise shattering the silence like a war drum. All eyes would turn to him now. Exactly as he intended.

Obsidian mists unfurled from him and poured into the church like a living tide, swallowing the flickering glow of the fire on the altar and plunging the room into impenetrable darkness. The air turned thick and stifling, pressing down on every chest, muffling breath and sound. Sylas would die tonight, and so would anyone else foolish enough to lay a hand on what was his. There would be no mercy, no second chances—only the cold certainty of death. Rylik would carve their regret into the stone of this wretched church, their blood staining the floor as a warning to anyone who thought to cross him again.

Screams sliced through the blackness, sharp and desperate, but Rylik moved like a storm, deaf to the chaos around him. He was a shadow in motion, a blur of rage and precision, every strike a heartbeat, every step an inevitability. The clash of swords echoed like thunder, steel scraping against steel with a shriek that filled the air, followed by the sickening thud of a body hitting the stone. His eyes never wavered. A man lunged at him, wild and untrained—too slow. Rylik's blade slashed through the air, and the soldier crumpled before he could even cry out, the floor swallowing him with a dull, final thump.

The air thickened with the stink of sweat, blood, and fear, mingling with the distant roar of the bonfire. Its flickering light cut through the gloom, offering only brief glimpses of the carnage unfolding. His rage was a living thing now, a fire within him that would consume everything in its path. And as the bodies piled at his feet, he felt nothing but the promise of vengeance.

Rylik's eyes glinted with dark amusement as he watched Sylas's purple magic flicker and crackle, attempting to wrestle control over the shadows that clung to every inch of the cathedral. The erratic flashes of lightning against his own black magic were almost laughable, like a desperate attempt to catch the wind in a net. He smirked, the edges of his lips curling in disdain. Sylas thought he could quench this darkness? How charming. Rylik could still slip through it, unseen, faster than the mage could even blink. It was laughable that Sylas even dared to challenge him, to believe he could control the shadows Rylik commanded. Powerful as he was, Rylik was something else entirely.

The room was thick with the acrid scent of blood and smoke as Sylas stepped forward, his voice a low drawl that cut through the chaos. "Come out, Sovereign," he called, his lips bending in a hollow semblance of a smile. "You can't hide in the shadows forever. I've seen your tricks, felt your power. But what good is it when you're nothing more than a coward lurking in the dark?"

Rylik didn't answer at first, his blade flashing in the gloom, the body of another soldier collapsing with a sickening thud. He didn't even look at Sylas's violet aura amidst the blackness, his eyes focused only on the next target. But Sylas wasn't finished.

"You think you're superior to me?" Sylas's voice grew louder, mocking. "You think your shadows will protect you? You're nothing without them. The same way you'll be nothing after I kill you!"

Rylik paused mid-strike, his eyes narrowing as he felt the flicker of Sylas's magic ripple through the air. The taunts were irrelevant, but Sylas was getting closer to locking onto him.

"You think I'm hiding, Sylas?" Rylik's voice was a low growl, a thread of menace woven through it. "I'm giving you a head start, so I can savor your death slowly. Trust me, I'll make sure it's worth the wait."

The shadows around him seemed to tighten, like an embrace, but his words hung in the air — chilling, deliberate. His next victim fell with a dull thud, and Sylas's face twitched with a menacing rage.

"Show yourself, Sovereign!" The command lashed out from his throat, harsh and demanding, echoing off the cathedral's stone walls. But instead of a response, Rylik's laughter rang out in a dark and mocking tone, a sinister harbinger of the threat that loomed in the abyss.

Sylas's eyes burned as he hunted for Rylik's unseen shadowed form in the dim light. "Aria has a pretty mouth, don't you think?" he taunted, a twisted grin crossing his lips. "I quite enjoyed making her scream." His purple magic writhed up his arm, coiling like a snake ready to strike.

He took a slow step toward the shadows where Rylik's form was barely visible, his eyes narrowing as he licked his lips. "I think I'd enjoy doing it again. Maybe tonight, in your bed, I'll make her cry out in another way altogether."

The words hung in the air like poison, meant to provoke. To tear at Rylik's control.

But before Sylas could savor the moment, the shadows in the corner of his vision moved. Rylik was upon him, a blur of rage and deadly intent. Before Sylas could even react, a blade buried itself deep into his back. He gasped, the searing pain tearing through him like fire. His magic flared, but it was too late. He staggered forward, his breath ragged.

"Unfair," he spat, his voice strained, trembling with both fury and disbelief. "I thought you had honor—!"

Rylik's voice came low and chilling as he wrenched the man's head back by his hair to whisper at his ear, "There's no honor among the wicked."

Rylik twisted the knife slowly, savoring every inch of Sylas's agonized cry. A ruthless satisfaction gleamed in his eyes at the sound, his expression calm and unshaken as he delivered retribution. "I would prefer to take my time with this, but, alas, my evening's pleasures are not quite over. Goodbye, Sylas."

Sylas choked on his breath, fear flashing in his eyes, but it was too late. Rylik had already claimed his victory.

"Rylik!"

Rylik's attention snapped to the towering cathedral doors at the far end of the room, a surge of fury flooding his veins at the echo of Aria's frightened shout. He let Sylas's lifeless body collapse to the stone floor with a savage finality. And there, in the cruel moonlight, stood Aria—vulnerable, her silhouette framed by the archway.

Orren's arm was like a steel band around her throat, choking off her scream and leaving her struggling for air. Leon lay motionless at their feet, his face pale, and blood pooling slowly from the gash in his side. His sword, discarded a few feet from his reach, was a futile reminder of the brief, desperate fight he'd put up—one he had lost while Rylik's back was turned. Orren had crushed him, and now he held Aria, a triumphant sneer on his face as he relished the moment.

"I know your weakness, Sovereign," Orren said, his voice a melodic snarl. "And once the king learns of it, you'll face the only fate befitting a traitor—death."

Rylik's muscles coiled like taut wires, his every instinct screaming for action, yet he held still. Any misstep could send Orren vanishing into the night, shattering what was perhaps a mere illusion. But, he couldn't be sure, not without his clarifying potion. He had enough left in his pocket to drink, but the time that it would take to do that would be wasted in these fragile, rapidly depleting moments. For now, all he had was his instinct to see through the lies.

"And what about you, Orren?" Rylik called out to him, fingers desperate to seize, searching for an opening in the Veil. "What will the king say when you're revealed as the leader of the Rebellion?"

Orren's laugh was a low, arrogant rumble. "He will be delighted when I tell him that *you* are the leader. I must thank you, after all, for killing so many of my men tonight. With all the more of these pathetic commoners dead, there are less to challenge me when I sit upon the throne."

Rylik's eyes flicked to Aria, struggling in Orren's grasp, her small gasps and frantic kicks pulling at his resolve. The sight burned through his chest, but he forced his voice to remain calm, almost dispassionate. "Cruel of you, Orren," Rylik mused, "You used them only to kill off your potential defectors. It's sensible, if not a little malicious."

Orren's grin gleamed in the moonlight, sharp as a dagger. "Spare me your hypocrisy. You're the very same."

"I never claimed otherwise."

There. Just a narrow opening in the Veil.

Rylik struck without hesitation, shadow-stepping through the darkness in a single, silent motion. His dagger found its mark—sharp, sure, and lethal. But instead of flesh and blood, Orren dissolved into cascading shards of sapphire light, scattering like dying stars.

Rylik froze in the empty archway, the blade trembling in his grip. Another illusion. They had escaped, and he hadn't even sensed their departure.

He heard a pained groan behind him. Odd, since he had killed everyone. He turned sharply, knife still in hand, to find a figure sprawled on the bloodied ground.

Leon. Though, it was surprising that he was still alive.

The Corporal clawed weakly at Rylik's boot, his breath coming in wet, choking gasps. Blood pooled beneath him, dark and glistening in the pale light. "T—tell her—" he rasped, his voice barely audible over the sound of his own labored breathing. "Tell Aria I'm sorry"

"Tell her yourself," Rylik muttered coldly. He kicked Leon's hand off his boot and shoved him flat against the ground with calculated indifference.

Leon let out a strangled cry, his hands clutching his side as fresh blood seeped through his fingers. He spat a curse, his body trembling against the effort to stay conscious.

Rylik sighed, annoyed. From his pocket, he pulled the golden elixir—Aria's creation. He'd spotted it earlier, tucked away behind his other tonics, its faint glow catching his eye. Without ceremony, he knelt beside Leon, seizing the man's jaw in an iron grip. "Open," he ordered, his tone sharp enough to cut. When Leon groaned in resistance, Rylik's fingers tightened mercilessly. "Swallow it, or die. Your choice."

He tipped the elixir into Leon's mouth and clamped it shut, holding it firm until the Corporal gulped down the shimmering liquid.

The transformation was instant. Golden light coursed beneath Leon's skin, trailing through his veins like molten fire, illuminating his broken body. It was an otherworldly sight, almost beautiful in its radiance. Rylik watched, a faint smirk tugging at his lips. So, she'd made this? His Aria. When had she become so skilled, so capable of crafting miracles in a bottle? Pride flickered in his chest, warm and uninhibited.

Leon gasped, his wide eyes fixed on his healed wounds as the pain ebbed from his body. "Wh—what is this?" he whispered, his voice hoarse with disbelief.

Rylik was dismissive as he stood to his feet. "A mercy. From *my* healer." He cast Leon a dark look, his shadow falling across the man's trembling form. "Do not make me regret it." With that, he vanished into the shadows, leaving Leon alone in the moonlit archway—healed, awestruck, and haunted by the Sovereign's warning.

Rylik didn't pity Leon—he rarely pitied anyone. But the man had shown unexpected courage when Sylas had tormented Aria. Leon had stood up, reckless and outmatched, to protect her. It was foolish, certainly, but in Rylik's eyes, anyone who dared to defend her—her honor, her life—deserved a debt repaid. Even if it was his only favor.

The forest loomed thick and impenetrable around him as he came to a stop, barely half a mile from the church. The shadows whispered and coiled, but their usual clarity was hindered, twisted by Orren's illusion magic. Rylik's jaw clenched. The nobleman's parlor tricks were an irritation, masking the faint traces of Aria's presence and forcing him to sift through the dark with singular focus. But Orren couldn't travel through the Veil— not like Rylik.

No, he was likely on foot, dragging her deeper into the wilderness. Aria would be resisting, no doubt, her cries silenced by force or spell. Wherever he was taking her, it wouldn't be far. Delivering her to the king, spinning lies to conceal his treachery as the Rebellion's leader, was the most likely outcome.

Rylik exhaled sharply, frustration burning through his veins. From his pocket, he retrieved another of his options—this one a small red vial. He had used it once before, and had to waste half of it on the king the night he unwittingly partook of the Nightmare elixir. There was enough to do at least this, to find Orren despite all his illusions, and to kill him. Without hesitation, Rylik uncorked it and downed the crimson liquid in one smooth motion. The bitterness stung his tongue, and he closed his eyes, letting the tonic burn its way into his blood.

Orren had said he knew of Rylik's weakness, but that could've been a bluff, or even a misunderstanding. He might assert that Aria is his weakness, which wouldn't be entirely wrong, but certainly not the complete story. Regardless, it didn't much matter now. Rylik's focus was absolute, his rage a storm unrelenting. His eyes flashed open, two haunting red orbs glinting like rubies in the moonlight. The illusion had shattered. Orren's magic dissolved like ash on the wind, and through the Veil, he saw her: Aria's glittering yellow aura, blazing bright like sunshine, a beacon pulling him forward.

They were fast approaching the king's manor in Cressmont. Rylik had been there on several occasions in the past, but the king had made no mention earlier that he intended to go there this evening. The sudden secrecy, especially for someone in his position as right hand, spoke of something darker—a betrayal carefully planned, down to the smallest detail.

With a fluid, lethal grace, he moved through the shadows, swift and silent, like vengeance given form.

CHAPTER 43

ARIA

Aria's fingers clawed at the loose dirt beneath her, lungs straining to catch the air that had just been knocked from her body. Her vision swayed as she blinked against the dizziness, the world a haze of muted colors and shifting shapes. Shadows wavered like specters on the edge of her sight, and the faint outlines of towering walls blurred into the horizon. Gradually, the scene sharpened—a sprawling manor came into view, its imposing frame silhouetted against the night sky. Her gaze dropped, focusing on the gilded edges of regal boots planted firmly in the dirt before her, their polished sheen catching the moonlight like a cruel mockery of her predicament.

"You were right, your majesty," Orren's voice came from somewhere behind her, drenched in bitterness. "I found her consorting with the Rebellion, just as you suspected."

Aria struggled to pull herself upright, but rough hands seized her arms, yanking her back down with a force that bruised. The guardsmen's grips were unyielding, their gauntlets cold against her skin as they restrained her. Her heart raced as her blurred vision sharpened, landing on Kaldros. His imposing figure stood framed in the moonlight, his presence both regal and suffocating.

The king's gaze locked onto her, piercing and calculating,

savoring every detail of her disheveled state. Dirt streaked her ivory skin, and her sapphire dress hung in tattered disgrace, speckled with blood. Her tear-reddened eyes met his, and a flicker of satisfaction played on his lips, like a conqueror admiring the spoils of victory.

He approached her slowly, his boots pressing firmly into the packed dirt, each step carrying an unspoken menace that made the air feel heavier with every stride. When he reached her, he leaned down slightly, his hand lifting her chin with a gentleness that belied the malice in his eyes. His touch was ice against her skin, his smirk deepening as he studied her trembling face.

"Where is the Sovereign?" he asked finally, his voice calm yet dripping with menace, like an adder poised to strike.

Behind her, Orren's voice broke the silence, smooth and composed. "Still alive, Your Majesty," he said, his words an elegant deceit. "I saw him rallying his forces at the Rebellion's camp. He is their leader, my king." His tone sharpened as he gestured toward Aria with disdain. "And *she* is his woman."

Kaldros's eyebrows arched with interest, and he returned his gaze to Aria. His lips parted in a mocking smile as he leaned closer, his breath hot against her ear. "Of course. He lied about you so he could have you for himself." The wicked gleam in his eye darkened as his tongue flicked out, wetting his lips as if savoring a private thought.

Aria's stomach churned, a leaden weight dropping into its depths as fear took hold. Her body trembled uncontrollably, and her mind screamed at her to run, though her limbs remained tethered to the steely grip of the guards who restrained her.

Kaldros dismissed her with a languid wave of his hand, and the guards dragged her aside like a broken doll. His focus shifted to Orren, his demeanor softening with a show of warmth. "My friend," he murmured, arms spreading wide as he stepped toward Orren, "it is rare to find loyalty in a den of vipers." He embraced the nobleman with a disarming sincerity, patting his back in camaraderie. "You've done well, Orren. Bringing me such a prize, exposing the traitors—truly, your service is invaluable."

Orren allowed a brief smile of pride, but it froze on his lips as Kaldros whispered near his ear, "And it ends here."

His blade struck with terrifying speed, piercing Orren's side before he could so much as flinch. His body jerked violently as Kaldros steadied him, whispering in a melodic tone, "Shh, now. It's done. No need to fight it."

A strangled gasp escaped Orren as he staggered, his knees buckling under him. Aria flinched, a sharp whimper emitting from her lips before she could stop it. She clenched her eyes shut, but the sound of the blade twisting in flesh reached her ears like a sickening echo, sending a tremor through her body.

"Why—?" Orren rasped, his voice strangled and weak.

Kaldros withdrew the blade with a vicious flourish, his expression devoid of pity. "You led the Rebellion," he said smoothly, as if stating a fact in court. "Did you think I wouldn't eventually find out? A public execution might have been fitting, but I preferred to handle this personally."

Orren crumpled to the ground, his hands clutching his side in a futile attempt to stop the bleeding. His breathing was shallow, ragged, his life spilling onto the floor in uneven streams.

Aria's vision wavered as she stared at the man who had dragged her through the forest mere hours ago, his voice brimming with cruel confidence as he plotted Rylik's death and his own ascension. Now, he was nothing but a broken shell, his arrogance reduced to silence as he knelt before the king he had vowed to overthrow.

She felt sick. Her chest heaved with short, frantic breaths, and her legs trembled beneath her as the weight of the moment pressed down on her like an iron vice. Escape felt impossible, a fleeting hope crushed by the sight of Kaldros standing tall and untouched, his blade gleaming crimson in the dim light.

The king turned his attention back to her, his gaze crawling over her like a deadly caress. "Take her to my chambers," he ordered the guards, his voice smooth and low, "and have the maids make her ready for my bed."

Her heart thundered in her chest, her mind screaming for an escape that didn't exist. Her lips parted, but no sound came. All she could do was meet his eyes, her silent plea swallowed by the pitiless smirk curling his lips.

The guards dragged Aria forward, her legs moving as though

each step cost her a fragment of her soul. She didn't resist; terror had numbed her body to submission. The king's presence loomed behind her like a shadow as they passed him, his cold eyes following her as she was ushered into the manor. The large oak doors groaned shut behind them, sealing her fate.

The interior of the manor was stiflingly grand, echoing the castle's opulence in a way that made Aria's stomach turn. The walls, carved from smooth gray stone, bore intricate tapestries of crimson and gold, each thread a symbol of wealth and dominion. Braziers cast flickering light over the polished floor, their glow failing to chase away the oppressive air. A sweeping staircase dominated the foyer, its balustrade adorned with gilded carvings that gleamed like distant stars. The faint scent of wax and perfume clung to the air, mingling with the more earthy traces of damp stone.

The guards steered her toward the stairs, their grip firm but not bruising—almost as if they didn't need to hurt her to keep her compliant. Her feet shuffled, half dragging, the weight of dread anchoring her steps. Memories of Orren's lifeless body sprawled in the dirt played over in her mind, sharp and unrelenting. She was walking toward the unknown, and yet the terrifying certainty of the king's intent made her feel as though she were stepping into a grave.

The stairway ascended into a darkened hallway, the air cooler, heavier. Their boots clapped against the stone floor, the sound sharp and unforgiving. Aria's gaze darted fleetingly at every door they passed, every corridor branching from the main hall—her mind cataloging routes, searching futilely for a glimmer of escape. But the windows were high and narrow, the thick walls betraying no weakness. There was no way out.

They stopped before a set of double doors carved with intricate floral patterns, as though beauty could mask the rot behind them. One guard swung them open, revealing a grand bedroom within. The room was richly adorned, almost suffocatingly so. Heavy velvet curtains of deep crimson pooled on the floor, their gold tassels catching the light of a dozen flickering candelabras. A massive bed sat at the center, draped in silken sheets the color of blood, its towering headboard carved with serpentine designs.

The air here smelled cloyingly sweet, a mix of incense and roses that turned Aria's stomach.

The guards shoved her inside, their voices hard and flat as they barked orders to the maids who awaited her.

"The king wants her ready for his pleasure," one of them said, the words cold and devoid of humanity.

The maids—a trio of silent, pale-faced women—nodded stiffly as the guards departed, the heavy doors closing with a sound that made Aria flinch. Their movements were mechanical, their eyes avoiding hers as they stripped away her ruined dress, bathed her in perfumed water, and dried her with brisk but not unkind hands. Dressed in a cream-colored gown so light it clung to her frame with unnerving delicacy, Aria sat motionless, her fiery curls falling in stark contrast against the pallor of her skin. She glanced toward the windows and doors, knowing escape was futile; no Sovereign, no Nightmare Elixir, only the king's will, leaving her entirely at its mercy.

They stepped back once their work was done, their expressions blank as they filed silently from the room. The door clicked shut, leaving her alone in the vast, suffocating space. Aria's knees threatened to give way, but she forced herself toward the gilded mirror that dominated one corner of the room. Her reflection stared back at her—a stranger. The gown, the curls, the sheen of perfume on her skin—all of it felt wrong. She looked like a doll dressed for display, stripped of her will, her voice, her dignity.

Her hands trembled as she pressed them to the edge of the vanity, her knuckles white. Memories of the Summit of Realms flooded her mind—the king's cold smile as he tortured and killed Lord Izram. Orren's gasp of betrayal as the blade was driven into his side. Both men had underestimated Kaldros and paid for it with their lives. And now, Aria stood in his gilded cage, awaiting her turn.

She stared into the mirror, her wide eyes pooling with tears before fluttering shut. There was no escape, no salvation, no hope. Only the dread of what came next.

"Pyra."

Aria's heart skipped at the familiar voice, her head snapping up to meet the reflection in the mirror. There he stood, his figure dark and commanding, inches from her turned back. Relief crashed over her like a tidal wave, stealing her breath.

"Rylik!" she gasped, spinning to face him. Tears spilled freely as she threw herself into his arms, her desperation unrestrained. Her curls swayed with the motion, catching the flicker of firelight as she clung to him, her fragile form melting into his solid embrace.

His arms wrapped around her with fierce urgency, one hand tangling in her hair while the other pressed against the small of her back, pulling her close. "I'm here," he murmured into her ear, his voice low and steady, grounding her as her world threatened to unravel. His fingers gripped the delicate fabric of her gown, anchoring her as if she might slip away.

A shuddering sob escaped her lips, muffled against his shoulder. The scent of him—wild and woodsy, tinged with the faintest trace of steel—flooded her senses, pulling her from the edge of despair. For a fleeting moment, she dared to believe he was real. Not a dream, not some cruel trick of her broken mind. Rylik was here.

"He killed Orren," she choked out, her words trembling as her tears soaked into his tunic. "And he'll want to kill you too! We have to leave—we need to go before—"

"Shh." His voice was a velvet command, silencing her panic. He pulled back just enough to frame her face with his hands, his thumbs brushing away the tracks of her tears. His gaze burned into hers, a piercing blue and steady as the earth beneath them. "Aria." Her name left his lips like a vow.

And then he kissed her.

The world seemed to halt, collapsing into the space between them as their lips met. His kiss was slow at first, a tender assurance, but it deepened as her arms tightened around his neck, fingers gripping his shoulders as though he were her lifeline. His mouth moved over hers with unyielding passion, their breaths mingling in the charged air.

Her lips parted beneath his, and his tongue swept in, coaxing a soft moan from her that vibrated between them. The kiss was heady, desperate, and impossibly sweet, a symphony of heat and longing that drowned out every fear, every shadow that had haunted her since the king's cruel decree. Time no longer mattered. Only him. Only this.

When their mouths finally broke apart, she gasped softly, her forehead resting against his. Her fingers trembled as they caressed the nape of his neck. His gaze roamed over her in the firelight, lingering on the sheer fabric that clung to her like a second skin. Hunger flickered in his eyes, raw and unguarded, yet tempered with a tenderness that made her knees weak.

"Rylik," she whispered, her voice shaky, her heart pounding against her ribs. "We have to go. Please."

He cupped her cheeks again, his touch impossibly gentle as he tilted her face to meet his. His expression was calm, unhurried, though the firelight sharpened the hard line of his jaw. "After tonight," he said, his voice a silken promise, "you'll never have to endure his presence again."

Her heart swelled as he brushed a stray tear from her cheek. There was no hesitation in his tone, no doubt. Only assurance.

"I have a plan," he continued, steady as a heartbeat. "You must trust me, Aria. Follow it exactly, and by dawn, Ravenhelm will be free of its tyrant king."

She blinked, his words sinking in like stones into a deep lake. "You—you're opposed to the crown?" Her voice trembled with disbelief.

The corner of his mouth tugged upward in a smirk, shadowed with grim satisfaction. "Few hate him more than I, dear. I assure you of that."

Her chest squeezed at the words, even as the gravity of the moment pressed down on her. She wanted to know more—needed to—but now wasn't the time. Instead, she searched his face, finding strength in the unwavering determination that shone in his eyes. "What do you need me to do?" she asked, her voice firmer now, fueled by the last shred of courage she could muster.

Their gazes locked, and in that moment, the storm of fear and uncertainty gave way to something brighter. Whatever was coming, she knew she wouldn't face it alone.

CHAPTER 44

RYLIK

The door to the king's bedchamber groaned on its hinges, breaking the heavy stillness of the room. From his hidden perch in the shadows, Rylik saw Aria look up, her gaze shifting toward the sound with quiet apprehension. She rose slowly from her seat by the fire, her movements careful and subdued. The king stepped inside, his strides measured, and let the door fall shut behind him with a muted thud, his eyes fixed on her with unnerving intensity.

Rylik had instructed her to remain cooperative and reverent, no matter the revulsion coursing through her. The king was a perceptive man—too perceptive—and he wielded fear like a weapon. He had known exactly what he was doing when he butchered Orren before her eyes, just as he had when he tortured and executed Izram. Each act was calculated, meant to strip away resistance and instill the cold certainty that defiance was futile. The king didn't care if she feigned delight in his presence as his concubines did. He thrived on the knowledge that she wanted no part of this, likely finding some perverse thrill in her quiet dread. The thought turned Rylik's stomach, his teeth grinding together as he forced a silent breath to steady the storm within him.

The chambers were deathly quiet, the only sound the faint

rustle of Aria's gown as she moved under the king's piercing gaze. Rylik remained hidden in the shadows, blending into the Veil, his eyes fastened on the king with contempt. His hand brushed the small vial tucked into his pocket — the pearlescent elixir known as *Voidbane*, his one shot at rendering the king's magic useless. It would disrupt the magic of any spellcaster nearby, severing their connection for a crucial sixty seconds, leaving them vulnerable and powerless. One minute. That was all he would have.

Aria stood before Kaldros like a lamb before the slaughter, her eyes downcast, shoulders rigid.

The king circled her slowly, like a wolf savoring his prey. "You're trembling, dear girl," the king drawled, his voice smooth and sickly sweet. "But, if you serve me well, there is no need to fear me."

She swayed slightly as she drew her arms up, unnerved by his staring at her. "What do you want with me, your majesty?" She asked, voice faltering with her nerves.

His gaze raked over her, laden with intrigue, as if all too eager to reveal his thoughts. As his hand reached to brush against her cheek, Rylik saw her flinch, a subtle but unmistakable recoil. His stomach twisted.

The king noticed her unease, his smile deepening as his hands slid into her hair, pulling her closer. "I want to make you one of my concubines," he said, his tone disturbingly casual as he toyed with her curls, his gaze fixed on the anxiety tightening her expression.

Aria's voice trembled as she spoke, a fragile wisp of sound that drew the king's full attention. "And what then? After I am to be your concubine, what will you expect of me?"

The king chuckled, a low, condescending sound. "You were drawn into this Rebellion, likely against your will. But you strike me as a clever girl—careful, even. I expect nothing less than your absolute fealty, and you will obey my every command without question or hesitation. And if you betray me," He warned, his fingers clenching into a fist in her hair, yanking her head back with a sharp tug. "You will pay in blood," he murmured, ignoring her soft whimper, forcing her chin upward to bare the vulnerable line of her neck.

Rylik's grip constricted around the hilt of his dagger, his knuckles blanching with restraint. He forced himself to focus, to let the anger fuel his clarity rather than cloud it. The king was a man consumed by his own power, blind to the shadows that crept ever closer. Rylik would be that shadow, silent and deadly.

Kaldros was reveling in her form, taking in the sight of her as if she were a feast laid bare before him, meant to be savored at his leisure. A wicked gleam lit his eyes as he pulled on her hair, dragging her with force toward his bed, the shadow of his intent looming heavy in the air. Aria stumbled to keep up, her head bowing under his grip. Tears stung her eyes, blurring her vision, as a terrified gasp broke from her trembling lips.

Rylik's eyes burned with a fierce, unrelenting fury, his jaw locking with barely restrained rage. He slipped the vial from his belt, the glass cool in his palm. He uncorked it soundlessly, his movements precise and practiced. He tipped his head back and drank, the liquid bitter as it slid down his throat. *Sixty seconds.*

With a harsh shove, Kaldros forced Aria onto the bed, his hands quickly untucking his shirt from his trousers and loosening his belt. He gripped the fabric of her nightgown, yanking it up to her thighs as he climbed onto the bed, his movements purposeful.

Rylik stepped forward, the dagger drawn. His boots made no sound against the stone floor. The king's back was to him, his attention fully consumed by the woman who had become his obsession.

Fifty seconds.

Aria's eyes flicked toward Rylik, just for an instant, a spark of recognition flashing in her gaze. She didn't react—didn't give the king any indication that his death loomed behind him. *Good girl.*

Forty-five seconds.

Rylik closed the distance in three swift strides. Kaldros never saw it coming. The blade plunged into his side with a force that sent him staggering forward, a guttural gasp escaping his lips. Aria shrieked, twisting desperately to escape him, her trembling hand flying to her lips as horror etched itself across her face. Blood bloomed crimson against the king's white tunic, dark and spreading fast.

Thirty seconds.

Kaldros jerked violently, his face contorting with rage and disbelief as his magic faltered, the crushing realization of his powerlessness dawning in his eyes. "Sovereign," he spat, his voice a venomous snarl. "What have you done?!"

"I am repaying you, *my king*," Rylik growled, his voice low and taunting as he continued, "your reward for the curse you have been upon my life." He wrenched the blade free and thrust again, this time aiming for his vile, blackened heart.

Twenty seconds.

But the king's hand shot out, faster than Rylik had anticipated. The glint of a blade caught the firelight—an ice blue dagger, its jagged edge glowing faintly with enchantment. The king drove it into Rylik's chest with a brutal, desperate force. Pain exploded through him, searing cold and piercing. He staggered, his grip on his dagger faltering.

Ten seconds.

The king let out a wet, gurgling laugh, blood spilling from his lips with every sound. "I always knew you'd betray me, just as I knew you would come here for your wench," he rasped, his voice thick and hollow. "I just didn't suspect you'd be so clever in your betrayal." His eyes glinted with ruthless gratification, even as Aria's desperate cries filled the air. "This blade should've ended you that day, both you and the duke were meant to kill each other," he sputtered, choking on his own blood. His lips curled into a venomous sneer. "But, you lived, proving yourself worthy as my Sovereign, and I kept this blade as a reassurance. And now, even as I die, I'll have the satisfaction of knowing you'll descend into the depths of hell alongside me."

Five seconds.

"No," Rylik growled, the single word a defiance against the pain that tore through him. Agony rippled through his body, but he forced himself upright, muscles trembling with the effort. His grip tightened on his own dagger, and with a final surge of will, he drove it deep into the king's chest. The monarch's laughter cut off, his body jerking once before falling still against the bloodstained mattress.

It was over.

Rylik staggered, his breath ragged and shallow as he pressed a hand to the wound in his chest. The enchanted blade remained lodged there, its cruel magic seeping through his veins like tendrils of frost, each icy pulse dragging him closer to collapse. Kaldros had kept it all these years, hoarding it in secret, waiting for this very moment. The realization stung almost as much as the wound itself. If he weren't dying, Rylik might've begrudged the king a shred of admiration for his foresight.

His knees buckled, and he sank to the floor, the world tilting violently around him. The pain from the enchanted dagger was a cold, cruel bite, lancing through his chest, the metal pulsing with every beat of his heart as if it had become a part of him. His vision blurred, his strength failing him. A bitter laugh rose in his throat, but it died on his lips, choked by the taste of blood.

So this is how it ends, he thought, his mind a quiet storm. It was fitting, in a way—*tragic*—that the life he'd fought so hard to build, the future he'd once dreamt of, would be shattered here. On the cold floor of the king's bedchamber. Another kind of death he would face alone, another battle lost, felled by the same cursed weapon as before. But this time, there would be no survival. No recourse.

There was nothing Aria could do. Not anymore. His chest tightened as the dark edges of his vision crept in, his body weakening with every breath. He could feel her—her frantic movement, her quiet desperation as she reached for him from across the bed. He wanted to reach out to her, to touch her, to tell her that it wasn't her fault. That he hadn't wanted this, hadn't wanted *her* to see him like this. But the words died before they could form. His hand trembled, fingertips grazing the floor, reaching for her as if she were the last spark of light before the void consumed him.

Stay with me, Pyra, his mind whispered, but his voice would never speak it. His body was surrendering to the darkness, and the cold was creeping over him faster than he could fight it. But still, his gaze sought her as he sank further into the abyss, her face a fading memory. A fading *dream*.

"Rylik!" Aria's voice was a lifeline, cutting through the haze of pain. She was at his side in an instant, her hands trembling as they reached for him. "Hold still!"

Aria's hands shook as they hovered over the dagger lodged in his chest, the cold metal a cruel reminder of the life slipping away from him. With a breath that trembled like the crack of dawn, she pressed her fingers against the dagger's hilt, each movement measured and desperate as she poured her healing magic into him. It surged through her, hot and brilliant, flooding into his broken body, chasing away the sharp bite of death that clung to him. His skin flinched under the intensity of it, but she pushed deeper, weaving her power into his blood, binding the shredded flesh together with each whispered command of magic.

Slowly, reverently, she drew the dagger free, the blade's unearthly chill meeting her touch as if it fought to remain, to bind him to the cold. As it slid from his chest, the icy blue sheen that had clung to it like a vengeful spirit dulled to a muted silver, and with it, the frigid aura surrounding Rylik began to dissipate. His chest, once frozen with the weight of his affliction, began to glow with an unfamiliar warmth. He gasped, the breath of a man who had been drowning and had found air once more. For the first time in a decade, he felt heat—raw and alive—blooming inside him.

The blackened remnants of the Frostwraith Blight that had defined his existence seemed to melt away beneath Aria's touch, and as the last traces of her magic flowed into him, the weight of his curse lifted. She kept her hand pressed to his chest as if afraid the warmth might vanish if she let go, her light dimming with the final flicker of power. Her fingers trembled against his skin, her face soft with the exhaustion of what she'd done.

Rylik's breath was slow, deep, each inhale feeling like the first true breath he had taken in years. He looked up at her, disbelieving, the world spinning around him as he lay on the cold stone floor. He didn't know how it was possible—how *she* had done this—but all he knew was that, for the first time in his life, he was free. The Blight was gone. The chains that had bound him to his own slow death were shattered. And she, his lovely Pyra, had delivered him from it.

His lips found hers before thought could intervene, pressing into her as though she were the very remedy his soul had craved, the antidote to every pain he had ever endured. The kiss was unyielding, an urgent melding of mouths that carried every ounce of his relief, gratitude, and longing. He held her firmly, one hand tangled in her hair, the other spanning the curve of her back, pulling her flush against him as if afraid she might vanish if he didn't anchor her to him. Her hands clutched at his shoulders, trembling at first, before gliding to cradle his face, answering his fervor with a desperation that matched his own.

She kissed him back with a tenderness that unraveled him entirely, her lips parting against his as if surrendering every fear, every doubt, to the trust she placed in him. There was no hesitation in her touch, no fragility, only the steadfastness of someone who had chosen him wholly in this moment. The heat of her mouth burned away any last cold from his chest, a warmth so vivid it felt as though it might restore parts of him long thought dead. He tilted his head, deepening the kiss, savoring the velvet glide of her tongue, the intoxicating way she seemed to give herself to him without reserve.

His breath merged with hers, their closeness obliterating the space between them, and for once, the ache in his heart wasn't one of loneliness or pain but of an overwhelming need to keep this—to keep *her*. She let out a soft, broken sigh into his mouth, a sound that sent shivers down his spine and ignited something feral within him. His fingers tightened their hold, kneading her against him, as if he could fuse them together and never face the world outside this embrace.

The kiss slowed, not from lack of desire, but from the sheer weight of their emotions. His lips brushed hers softly now, reverently, savoring her as though the moment were fragile and sacred. Her forehead rested against his as they broke for a breath, their eyes half-closed, her chest rising and falling in sync with his. The firelight bathed them in a golden glow, shadows dancing across their faces as the world around them faded into irrelevance.

"You're alive," she whispered against his lips, her voice trembling, as though saying it aloud might solidify the miracle before her. He pressed another kiss to her, softer this time, as if to reassure her—reassure *himself.*

"Thanks to you," he murmured hoarsely, his voice thick with emotion. His arms stayed wrapped around her, holding her close, unwilling to let go as he savored the warmth of her presence. "And now, let's leave this place. I'll take you out of here."

Rylik's arms tightened around Aria, his embrace both protective and possessive as shadows coiled beneath them, rising like an ominous tide. The dark mist enveloped them in an instant, swirling with an unnatural ferocity as the air seemed to shatter, bending reality itself. Together, they dissolved into the onyx haze, crossing through the veil and vanishing from the manor, leaving only the trace of smoke in their wake.

CHAPTER 45

RYLIK

The familiar scent of burning wood greeted Rylik as they materialized in his bedchambers, the tendrils of shadow reluctantly receding from where they had entwined him and Aria moments before. He exhaled a long, steady breath into her soft hair, keeping her pressed firmly against him, unwilling to let go. It was over. The chaos, the fighting, the agony that had threatened to consume them both—it was finished. And in the quiet that remained, only she mattered. Only the surge of something unspoken and undeniable between them filled the silence.

Aria shifted gently, pulling back just enough to meet his gaze. Her hands rose to cradle his face, her palms warm against his skin. She was radiant despite her weariness, her smile bright and unguarded as if the weight of the night had finally lifted. "Are you alright now?" she asked softly, her voice threading with concern.

"Never better," Rylik murmured, his eyes roaming her face as a deep, stirring need began to unfurl within him. He covered her hands with his own, lowering them slowly as he leaned closer. His lips brushed hers in a tender caress, drawing a shiver from somewhere deep within him. "But more importantly, how are you feeling?"

She tilted her head ever so slightly, returning his light kiss with a delicate press of her lips. "I'm well," she said, her voice a soft murmur, though it faltered for a moment. A faint shadow crossed her expression as she whispered, "Though I must admit, I'd like to go to bed."

A pang of disappointment passed through him, swift and sharp. But he buried it. She had every reason to feel exhausted after the night they had endured—the horrors they'd both faced. It wasn't his place to be selfish, not now. With a measured nod, he offered, "I'll escort you to your bed." He strove for neutrality, though the thought of parting from her so soon filled him with quiet dismay.

But then, she surprised him. "Why not your bed?" she asked, her tone light and seemingly innocent, though her blush betrayed her.

He froze, caught between disbelief and something far more potent. "You want to sleep in my bed?" he managed, his voice careful even as a cautious thrill sparked within his chest.

Her gaze flicked aside, her blush deepening. "Who said anything about sleeping?" she murmured, her words both shy and impossibly bold, igniting a fire within him that no shadow could extinguish.

He looked at her closely, her hair tumbling over her shoulders in a cascade of unruly red curls, each strand catching the firelight like molten copper. Her ivory skin seemed to glow, kissed by the warm flicker of the flames, a luminous pale gold that rendered her almost ethereal in the quiet of the room. She was still dressed in her silky thin nightgown, the gossamer fabric laying gently over her soft, delicate breasts. His body went taut, a desperate sort of hunger clawing within him.

As his eyes locked with hers, he found her gaze heavy with yearning, a silent invitation that sent a thrill coursing through him. Without a second thought, he acted on impulse, sweeping her off her feet with effortless strength, her small, startled yelp quickly softening into a quiet excitement.

Rylik carried her to his bed, laying her down with a blend of gentleness and urgency that left her breathless. His hands moved swiftly, stripping off his armor and letting it fall to the floor with a dull clang, followed by the blood-stained tunic he pulled over his head. The firelight bathed his bare chest, the smooth, unscarred skin where the wound had been standing as a testament to her gift. Her eyes traveled over him, lingering on the sculpted lines of his chest and the defined curve of his abdomen, her lips parting with a soft gasp of adoration. Her gaze, so openly brazen, sent a ripple of heat through him.

A smirk slowly spread across his face as he leaned in closer to her, savoring the vision of her beneath him. Her eyes were shadowed with desire, her fingertips pressed against the center of his chest before slowly trailing down. She paused at his waistband, cautiously letting her eyes flick up to his own as if in invitation. But, she didn't need to hesitate. Anything she would want, he was compelled to give to her. Anything at all, so long as it kept her here, in this bed with him, until the first light of morning.

Her fingers fumbled slightly with his clasp, a gentle blush spreading over her cheeks as she did so. She lacked experience, he presumed with quiet adoration, in the art of removing a man's trousers. Stifling a chuckle, his hand covered her own, his thumb passing over the closure and unfastening it for her. She suppressed a soft gasp, her gaze fixed as she caught her lower lip gently between her teeth.

He felt her fingers next, crossing like satin down the length of him, and with it, a deep moan unfurled from within. She smiled at that, he noticed, and it only served to make him harden more.

"Naughty little Pyra," he murmured, the taunt laced with amusement as he watched her lips curve into a pleased, knowing smile.

She was far more audacious than he'd ever given her credit for, and that realization unraveled the fragile limits of his restraint. He reminded himself that she had already abided in this fantasy countless times over the past weeks, indulging her desires while he had fought to suppress his own. If desperation hadn't already consumed him, he might have relished drawing out her torment a little longer, savoring the tension as a kind of cruel indulgence. But no—he could hold back no longer. Even the sadistic pleasure he might have taken in prolonging her anticipation couldn't withstand the raw, aching need to claim her in this moment, to close the unbearable distance between them.

He leaned close, the tip of his head brushing against her soft entrance. He slanted his lips over hers, teasing a kiss as he barely grazed her below. A whining groan left her throat at the feeling of it.

A slow smile curved his lips at the sound. She was impatient.

Perhaps there was yet some part of him that still needed to make her suffer, that needed to hear her make more of those intoxicating, needy sounds.

"Please," she murmured, her voice barely above a breath, "don't tease me like before."

His eyes smoldered with a forbidden satisfaction. "Why not?" he asked, his voice laced with mischief as he pulled back slowly, his fingers grazing her thigh, inching her dress higher.

With a languid gaze, she looked down at him, her words carrying a gentle chide. "Because I need you, Rylik."

Again, the sound of his name on her lips sent a jolt of exhilaration through him. He stiffened, desperate to bury himself in her until all she knew to do was scream that name at the peak of her ecstasy. "You need me?" he challenged, lowering his head to place a heated kiss on the exposed curve of her stomach.

He felt her quiver at the press of his lips and he smirked, trailing lower in a gentle line. His fingers curled around her soft, ample white thighs, parting them gently, wide and vulnerable, as his caress glided downward.

Aria's hand shot down to his thick raven hair, her fingers grasping the strands with an urgency. He met her eyes with playful defiance, relishing in her gasp of surprise before his eyelids fluttered shut. His tongue brushed softly against her, eliciting a sharp tug from her fingers against his mane.

Rylik chuckled, undeterred, savoring the sweetness of her as his tongue delved deeper into her succulence. If she wanted him to stop toying with her, pulling his hair was hardly the way to make him relent. If anything, the dull pain of it made him want to remain between her legs until his pristine satin sheets were drenched. He gently pressed his tongue into her, sliding up her center, his touch tender as he drew a reaction from her delicate nerves beneath the surface.

A small, faint moan escaped her as her fingers tightened in his hair, giving a soft pull. He grinned, kneading over the spot with increasing intensity. She weaved her remaining fingers through his hair, urging him closer with both hands. He groaned against her, a strained noise of longing. She wanted this now? How was he to make her suffer if he would be the first one to break?

He moved more persistently in her, trailing circles with soft, teasing flicks of his tongue. Every subtle movement he made drew out hushed gasps of frustration that shuddered through her. Her hips began to rock gently, those agile fingers of hers now threading and tugging against him.

"Please, don't make me beg," she whispered, her voice laced with a feeble, pleading whine. "I need you," she insisted.

He pulled back slightly, his lips brushing against her softness. "Oh, but I want to hear it," he mused, his tone carrying a challenge. "I *need* to hear you beg."

Aria drew in a breath, her gasp betraying an uncertain mix of astonishment and something more intimate. It was possible he had caught her off-guard, and perhaps she was too proud to grovel for her own gratification. Yet, he would savor the idea of forcing her to admit that her surrender would only bring her bliss.

"If you can do that for me," he purred mockingly as he pulled up, placing a kiss on her stomach. "Then I will gladly give you what you want." His fingers drifted lower as his kisses drifted higher. He drew her dress up over her breasts, his tongue soft against her nipples. They pebbled beneath his touch, and a dark grin curved his lips.

The hardened length of him pressed against her entrance, just lightly enough to make a frustrated whimper leave her throat.

"Beg," he reminded her, barely keeping his restraint.

She parted her lips, tasting the cool air before she moistened her throat, her voice a soft whisper, "Please."

He let out a low, husky laugh. Again, he let himself graze her, just enough to torment the both of them for a few moments longer. "Once more," he chided playfully in her ear.

Her small pale fingers dug into his bicep as she whimpered,

"Please, Rylik!"

He drank in the sound of her voice, her impatience fueling the fire of his yearning for her. Hearing her like this was a pleasure unlike anything he had ever known—a sound that ignited something primal within him. The sheer knowledge that she wanted him, entirely and without reservation, left him questioning if he could ever find the strength to resist her again. He braced himself, then claimed the space between them with a deep, satisfying thrust of his hips. The sensation of being inside of her flooded his mind, a radiant warmth that drowned out everything but the feel of her.

And, *gods.*

She felt divine.

A soft groan escaped him as he buried his face in her neck, her matching sigh wrapping around him like a melody.

"Yes," her trembling voice barely broke through the storm raging in his mind, yet it carried enough weight to pull him back to her, anchoring him in the heat of their shared longing.

He moved on pure instinct, gliding in and out of her with unspoken grace. Each silken motion was seamless, a rhythm as natural as breathing, unyielding in its gentle cadence. There was an unhurried reverence to every advance and retreat, as though each measured moment was an endless rediscovery of bliss.

Her breathing was shallow, warming his neck as she panted, "More."

It wasn't a command, nor was it truly a request, but the pull to fulfill it was irresistible. Her voice alone was enough to stir something deep within him, and his body answered without hesitation, driving forward with a strong yet achingly tender motion.

Her breath caught in her throat at the fullness of him, at the way he left no space unclaimed between them. As Rylik withdrew, a trembling inhale escaped her, only for it to falter as he pressed into her once more, stealing what little composure she could muster.

"*More,* Pyra?" he asked with a mocking tilt to his voice, fully aware that her inexperience couldn't bear more of him, yet he'd give it to her all the same. "Are you certain?"

"Yes," she said in a breathy tone, "I need—"

She choked on her words as he sank deeply into her, the expanse of him suddenly stifling any sound. A smug smile pulled at the corners of his mouth, satisfied solely by the quiet, suspended awe that came from her being completely filled by him.

"Why do you beg for more of me?" he taunted softly, pressing a tender kiss to her cheek, his voice low as he added, "When you're barely able to catch your breath?"

She released a shuddering sigh against his neck as he drew back, gasping again when he returned, her labored sounds threading through him like a silken tether, binding him closer with every moment. "I will beg for you, Rylik, " she said in a reverent whisper, her voice strained with desire, "I will do anything you desire, so long as you never stop."

He chuckled darkly, relishing the way she took him in, as though the only thing she could do was succumb, offering herself willingly to be pleasured.

And he *wanted* her pleasure. He *needed* it.

She had woven herself into the very fabric of his existence, breathing purpose and life into the darkness that had once consumed him. Freed from the affliction that had tormented him for years, he should have no further need of her touch, yet it was her touch he now craved more than ever. Not for her kindness, not for her healing, but for her, in this very moment, beneath him, where she belonged. Anything else was inconsequential.

"Faster," her quivering voice reached him, her eyelids fluttering as she struggled to lift her hands, each rhythmic shift into the mattress leaving her movements helplessly undone.

"As you desire," he grinned as he obliged her, moving his hand to brace her arms and pin them to the pillows above her head, driving into her again and again, the arch of his waist moving in fluid harmony with her own rhythm.

He let his eyes rove across her form, her gossamer dress twisted and bunched, her breasts swaying with every thrust. She was a vision of beauty, her copper curls tumbling wildly across her face as her expression teetered on the edge of reckless abandon. He watched, spellbound, a dark satisfaction curling in his chest as he took her in—*his* to dominate, and he'd make sure she understood that.

She was *his*. With every roll of his body pressing into hers, and with every soft little sound she made, she belonged to him in a bond that she could never break.

Her breaths were shorter now, ragged, as her hips matched with his. He was relentless, rapidly driving himself thoroughly into her, indulging in the feel of it. Her yellow eyes fluttered open, weak and unfocused, only to widen as a fiery blush bloomed across her cheeks. He was staring down at her, unwavering and intent, as if nothing else in the world could hold his gaze.

There was no reason for her to be shy now. Where else was he supposed to look? For weeks, his mind had been consumed by visions of her—just like this, panting and taking him deeply into herself. He refused to look away, reveling in the sight that had once been the subject of his darkest, most insatiable desires—but was now his reality, tangible and undeniable. No longer a dream to torment him, but a truth he could savor, claim, and possess. And he would savor it, again and again, for as long as she was his—and she would always be his.

Her eyes slowly traveled down his body in a centerline, resting for a moment at where she watched him connect with her own. He grinned, slowing his cadence just enough so that she would see the extent of him glistening with the evidence of her arousal. The sight seemed to invigorate her, and a warm saturation surrounded him as he again buried himself inside.

A raw, aching moan rumbled from her chest as she arched her back and spread herself more openly. It was an invitation, and one that he was all too eager to take advantage of.

Over and over, he savored the feel of her, the tight embrace of her inner walls squeezing against him. His body trembled with the effort, each movement full and deliberate, as though the strain itself was a delicious form of agony; his breath came in shallow, heated gasps, the tension in his muscles building, but the pull of her was far too consuming to resist.

He was close. And by the way she was saturated, greedily taking all of him in, he knew she was too. Her body began to shake, clamping down around him with exhilarating pressure. He exhaled a trembling note against her neck, her breathy reply lilting in the space between them. The passion in her voice overtook him as she moaned his name in his ear, his body shuddering as his seed spilled from him and filled her.

The smooth, melodic undulation of his form melding with her own was nothing short of poetry. He wouldn't relent. He couldn't. She felt like a promise fulfilled, tender and achingly perfect.

Rylik lay above her, his breath uneven as he fought to steady himself, the overwhelming presence of her soft, trembling body beneath him. Her skin, flushed and glistening, burned against his own, and her chest rose and fell with the rhythm of their shared exhaustion. She was his now, in every way that mattered, and the thought awakened something raw and unrestrained within him. His lips curved into a slow, dark smile as his fingers trailed possessively along her arm, memorizing the shape of her, the proof that she belonged to him and no other. He adored her—not with the gentle reverence of a saint, but with the fierce, all-consuming hunger of a man who had claimed what his soul had always craved. She was his salvation, his obsession, his queen—and he would never let her go.

CHAPTER 46

ARIA

The golden light of dawn spilled into Rylik's chambers, washing the stone walls and heavy curtains in warm hues. The morning sun bathed the bed, its rays catching in the tousled copper waves of Aria's hair, spread like silk over his chest. Her soft breaths fell against his skin, her body draped across his in a tangle of sheets and limbs. Beneath the delicate curve of her arm, his fingers traced absent patterns over her forearm, his other hand weaving idly through her hair.

Rylik stared down at her, captivated by the tranquility of her face. She stirred slightly, her cheek nuzzling against his chest, her lashes fluttering like hesitant wings. When her amber eyes finally opened, their gaze met his, and she smiled, a tender curve of her lips that he felt all the way to his core.

"Good morning," she murmured, her voice soft and still weighted with sleep. She tilted her chin up, brushing a featherlight kiss to his lips, and warmth flooded her cheeks as fragments of last night danced vividly in her memory. She felt the ache in her muscles and the blush that followed, but none of it overshadowed the joy simmering inside her.

He smirked lazily, his hand slipping from her arm to cradle her jaw. "You're awake." His thumb grazed her cheek, the affection

422

in his touch undeniable.

She traced her fingers over the firm expanse of his chest, marveling at the steady rhythm of his heart. He was healed—fully, completely—and for the first time since meeting him, she felt like she could finally exhale. Her voice was quiet but full of meaning as she asked, "How do you feel?"

His grin widened, wicked but genuine. "I've never felt better. Thanks to you." His hand slid lower, resting at her hip as his gaze took on a teasing edge. "Though last night might have had something to do with it."

Her blush deepened, and she let out a flustered laugh. "Oh, don't remind me. I was impossibly vulgar."

He chuckled, his voice dropping into a sensual cadence. "Vulgar?" he mused as he leaned closer, his lips brushing her ear as he murmured, "Not nearly vulgar enough, Pyra. I can show you *vulgar*."

Her eyes went wide, a shiver racing down her spine as his hand settled on the curve of her lower back. "Right now?" she whispered, her voice tinged with equal parts excitement and uncertainty. The heat rising to her cheeks betrayed her eagerness, even as she tried to suppress it.

Rylik chuckled, his grin sharp and teasing, the kind that sent shivers cascading through her. "You'd like that, wouldn't you?" he drawled, his voice smooth with wicked amusement.

Aria swallowed, her gaze softening, lids heavy with unspoken longing. "What would you do?" she asked, her words barely audible, as if she wasn't sure she could handle the answer.

His eyes gleamed, dark and hungry, tracing her every reaction with predatory satisfaction. "Oh, Aria," he murmured, his grin deepening into something mocking, almost dangerous. "It would be *indecent* for me to put to words all the ways I would have you submit to me."

A rush of heat flooded her, her pulse quickening as the tension stretched taut between them. Before she could gather herself to respond, his expression shifted, though the glimmer of wicked intent never left his eyes. He brushed a knuckle along her jaw, his voice dipping into something smoother, more restrained. "But, unfortunately, such pleasures will have to wait. I have pressing matters to attend to first, now that Kaldros is dead."

His words pulled her back to reality, cutting through the haze of bliss like a cold breeze. The warmth in her chest began to dissipate, replaced by a flicker of unease that crept up her spine. Last night hadn't been so long ago—*not long at all* since the moment he had plunged the dagger into the king's chest, an act so swift and brutal it still felt more like a nightmare than something she had witnessed. Her fingers twisted into the sheets as her expression sobered, the weight of the memory settling heavily over her.

She hesitated, unsure how to bridge the growing tension between them, before finally asking, "What happens now? What should I do?" Her voice was soft, uncertain, and the vulnerability in her tone felt jarring even to her.

Rylik's brow arched, his confidence unshaken. "We'll discuss that this evening. After my business is settled."

She swallowed, her fingers gripping the sheets tighter. "What business?"

He stood, his voice steady as he began pulling on his clothes. "I will take the throne, naturally. With the king dead, no one else is left to challenge me." He fastened his belt and slid on his armor, glancing at her with a smile that didn't waver. "It was always the plan."

Aria's heart sank. The ease with which he said it startled her. She hadn't anticipated this—not the throne, not the calculated way he spoke of it. She realized, in that moment, how little she truly knew him. While he busied himself with his preparations, she sat frozen, her mind a whirlwind of thoughts.

Had he only wanted her to heal him? Was that all she was to him—a means to an end, useful only until her purpose was served? Her gaze dropped to the sheets as insecurities clawed their way to the surface, each one sharper and louder than the last. Perhaps last night had been fleeting, a momentary indulgence that meant far more to her than it ever could to him—a sweet but hollow dream destined to dissolve in the morning light. She thought of the man she'd given herself to years ago, of how easily he had discarded her, and how cold and empty she'd felt in the days that followed. The memory resurfaced now like a fresh wound, the ache of it twisting alongside her doubt. Was Rylik the same?

She'd thought she understood him, but the truth was she knew so little. The man who had held her so tenderly last night was the same man who had driven a dagger into the king's chest with terrifying precision. He'd kept that plan hidden, along with countless others, no doubt. How could she claim to know him when he moved in shadows she couldn't penetrate, when his motives were locked behind a wall she had never been invited to climb? She had trusted him in ways that frightened her, and yet she was beginning to realize she didn't know what he truly wanted, what he truly intended—not for her, not for himself, and not for them.

The man she thought she'd begun to understand now felt cloaked in mystery, his intentions impossible to read beneath the armor of his confidence. She couldn't shake the creeping sensation that she no longer mattered, that last night had only been a step on the path to something greater—something that didn't include her. She had healed him, given him back his strength, and now, what use was she? The thought sent a chill through her, and she sank further into the bed, trying to suppress the growing ache in her chest. How could she ever be certain of her place beside a man she could never truly predict?

He finished dressing and crossed back to her, his presence commanding yet warm. Bending down, he cupped her cheek and kissed her, his lips crushing against hers in a way that sent her heart spiraling. "I'll return tonight," he promised softly. "We'll discuss everything then."

She kissed him back, savoring the connection even as her fears threatened to unravel her. When he pulled away, she already missed him, the ache of his absence settling in as the door clicked shut behind him. Alone in the sunlight-drenched room, she sank back against the pillows, uncertain of what the future held—and whether she had any place in it at all.

* * *

The apothecary brimmed with the familiar scents of herbs and tinctures, the air tinged with the earthy notes of crushed lavender and sage. Aria stood behind the counter, quietly mixing a tonic under Maven's watchful eye. Sunlight filtered through the warped glass windows, casting fragmented patterns on the stone floor.

They both knew—everyone knew—that the king was dead, yet neither of them had said a word to each other about it. While the kingdom scrambled to make sense of what came next, Aria clung futilely to the comfort of routine, though solace eluded her. It was far from an ordinary morning, and everything felt subtly out of place, as if the world itself held its breath, teetering on the edge of change.

The events of the last few days swirled in her mind like a storm cloud. Rylik was going to be king. The weight of that realization pressed on her chest, making each breath feel heavier than the last. How could things stay the same when everything in her life had already begun to shift? And yet, here she was, going through the motions of daily work, as if nothing had happened.

The chime of the apothecary door startled her from her thoughts. Before she could look up, a familiar voice rang out, breathless and urgent.

"Thank God you're all right!"

Aria barely had time to react before Leon swept across the room and enveloped her in a fierce hug. His arms were strong, his grip tighter than she remembered, and she stood frozen for a moment, her mind catching up with the sight of him.

"Leon?" she finally managed, pulling back just enough to look at him. Her eyes darted to his torso, scanning for any sign of the wound she'd seen Orren inflict on him. "The last time I saw you, you were—I thought—"

Leon's expression shifted, his usual rugged demeanor giving way to something unexpectedly tender, a rare glimmer of emotion breaking through. "You mean when Orren stabbed me?" He gave a half-smile, shaking his head. "It was your potion that saved me. The Sovereign gave it to me himself, and the moment I drank it, I suspected it was you—your magic. I just don't understand how you managed it."

Aria blinked, the weight of Leon's words sinking in slowly. Rylik had done that? For *Leon*? The thought both warmed and unsettled her, a tangle of emotions she wasn't sure how to unravel. Her fingers lightly brushed the edge of the counter, grounding herself as her voice emerged, tentative and low. "He gave it to you?" she asked, as though speaking too loud might undo the fragile truth.

Leon nodded, his features softening in a way Aria rarely saw. "He did," he said, his voice steady but warm. "It saved my life." His words held a quiet intensity that hung in the air, and Aria felt herself captivated, unable to look away. Rylik's actions puzzled her. Why would he do this for Leon?

Before she could respond, Maven bustled over from the other side of the shop, her movements brisk yet tinged with concern. "You should have said something earlier, Leon," she chided, her sharp tone undercut by the relief in her eyes. She pressed a hand to his chest, as if verifying for herself that he was truly standing before her. "I wondered why you were so late this morning."

Leon exhaled a small chuckle and reached for her hand, lowering it gently before leaning in to press a brief kiss to her temple. "I'm sorry, Maven. I'll be better about that. I promise."

Maven huffed softly, a mix of affection and exasperation crossing her face. She stepped back slightly, but her attention never strayed far from him.

Leon turned his gaze back to Aria, and his next words dropped into the room like a stone into still water. "The fight is over now," he said simply. "The king is dead after all."

The air seemed to shift. There it was—the declaration that both Aria and Maven had refused to admit out loud to each other all morning. Aria froze, her stomach twisting as her gaze darted to Maven. The healer gave a solemn nod, folding her arms over her chest in discomfort.

"The news is spreading quickly," Maven said, her lips tightening into a firm line. "And good riddance, I say."

"You're glad?" Aria asked, her voice edged with surprise, almost disbelief.

Maven's brows lifted slightly, her usual composure unshaken. "Not because I was part of the Rebellion, if that's what you're thinking," she replied, her tone matter-of-fact. "But I knew Leon was. And I've seen enough suffering under that man's rule to know he got what he deserved."

Leon sighed heavily, his shoulders slumping under the weight of unspoken guilt. "I'm not part of the Rebellion anymore," he said, his voice low and burdened. "I was lied to, Aria. Orren wasn't leading a fight for freedom—he was leading us to our graves. He used the Rebellion to root out dissenters and then had them slaughtered. Every promise he made was a lie. He didn't want justice; he wanted the throne."

Aria's body tensed, the true meaning of his words settling over her like a shadow. She frowned, her thoughts a whirlwind of disbelief and growing unease. "That can't happen now," she said, her voice trembling slightly. "Orren was murdered by the king last night."

Both Maven and Leon froze, their eyes widening in shock.

"What?" Leon breathed, his disbelief laced with apprehension.

"It's true," Aria confirmed, her voice steadier now. "Rylik killed the king. And now, he plans to take the throne himself."

Leon leaned back slightly, his brow furrowing as he processed her words. For a moment, his expression was unreadable, his silence stretching long enough to make her uneasy. Then, to her surprise, he nodded with quiet conviction. "Good," he said simply.

"Good?" Aria repeated, her voice tinged with incredulity.

Leon's gaze met hers, unwavering. "The Sovereign will make a fine king," he said firmly. "I may not agree with everything he's done—hell, I don't think anyone does—but I've seen how he leads. He's sharp, ruthless when necessary, and strategic. He'll bring order, and that's what we need."

Maven nodded beside him, her tone equally resolute. "He's not perfect, but he's better than anyone else who could've taken that crown," she said with a slight shrug. "And heaven knows, it's about time someone competent wore it."

Aria's chest tightened, her heart a swirl of relief and trepidation. Their faith in Rylik brought a flicker of comfort, but it couldn't quiet the many questions gnawing at her. What would this mean for her? For them? For everything?

Leon stepped closer, his expression shifting to something raw, almost vulnerable. "Aria," he began, his voice low and thick with emotion. "I'm sorry."

Her brow furrowed, her gaze searching his. "For what?"

"For letting Orren drag you into this," he said, his words heavy with regret. "For standing by while you were put in harm's way. For not being the friend you deserved." His voice cracked, and he let out a frustrated sigh, raking a hand through his hair. "I should've done more—should've been there for you when it mattered. I failed you, and I don't know if I can ever make that right, but—" His voice softened, the weight of his remorse palpable. "I'm going to try. I'll do everything I can to protect you now. You have my word."

Aria felt a lump rise in her throat, her chest tightening with an overwhelming mix of emotions. She searched his face, seeing not just the man he had become but the boy she had once trusted so completely. His words carried a depth she hadn't expected, and for the first time in what felt like forever, she saw a glimmer of the Leon she used to know.

She stepped forward and wrapped her arms around him, hugging him tightly as her voice came out in a whisper. "Thank you," she murmured, her gratitude as sincere as his apology. She held on for a moment longer, letting the past and present collide in a bittersweet embrace.

As Aria pulled back, the warmth of Leon's embrace stayed with her, but it wasn't enough to keep the doubts at bay. They crept back in, shadowing the edges of her thoughts. How much longer could she expect to stay in the palace? If Rylik became king, would there even be a place for her here? She couldn't see herself—a mere peasant—fit to serve as a queen, and the idea of being reduced to a concubine who would soon be forgotten sent a cold ripple through her. That wasn't the life she wanted—nor one she could endure.

And worse still, what if Rylik didn't want her at all? What if she'd already served her purpose—healed him, inadvertently helped him seize the throne—and now he had no reason to keep her close? The echoes of last night's passion clung to her thoughts, but what if it had been a momentary pleasure with no lasting consequence? She couldn't bear the thought of being discarded, a mere chapter in his rise to power.

Her chest tightened, and the weight of uncertainty pressed down on her. She glanced at Leon and Maven as they continued talking, their voices a low hum against the storm in her mind. She forced herself to smile, nodding at their words as though she were present in the moment. But her thoughts churned, tangled in questions she couldn't yet answer.

What would come next for her? Would she remain in this place that felt both foreign and familiar, or would she return to the humble life she had once known? Could she even go back after everything? The answer eluded her, but one fear loomed larger than all the others: she might not have any say in it at all.

CHAPTER 47

RYLIK

The corridor stretched before Rylik like a gilded path to destiny, each measured step echoing in the silence. His thoughts, however, were anything but restrained. Last night lingered in his mind like the sweet burn of an addictive elixir. Aria, warm and tender, had been everything he wanted and more—soft whispers, stolen breaths, the enticing glow of her vulnerability. She'd been his entirely, and the memory of her lying in his arms sent a thrill of possession through him.

A crooked smile played on his lips, equal parts arrogance and menace. He'd tasted something intoxicating in her, a fiery depth that belied her outward gentleness, and he couldn't help but anticipate more. Tonight, he decided, would be even better. She would give him more—her voice, her touch, her submission—and he would take it all, reveling in the way she unraveled beneath him. Not even the throne he was about to claim stirred him as much as the thought of her. His queen, he thought idly, the idea simmering in the back of his mind like a dark temptation. She didn't yet know how thoroughly she belonged to him.

He reached the end of the corridor to find Thorian waiting, arms folded, a cautious smile curling his lips. The Shadow Knight inclined his head in greeting, his satisfaction barely concealed.

After leaving his suite that morning, Rylik's first order of business was to convene with his remaining two Shadow Knights. They had already been informed of the king's death in the dead of night, his body discovered by startled guards. Rylik's blade, still embedded in Kaldros's chest, had served as an unmistakable signature—less an accusation, more a declaration. As anticipated, no one mourned the tyrant, and no one dared to seek vengeance on his behalf. The dissenters had been dealt with, Orren chief among them, leaving no one to contest what was already inevitable. The path to power lay before Rylik, unobstructed and undeniable. Just as he had orchestrated.

Thorian and Kaelith had taken charge of assembling the court, ensuring that every noble, general, and courtier would bear witness to what came next. Rylik knew there was no time for hesitation—claiming the throne was not merely a necessity but a declaration of his superiority. Kaldros had ruled through fear, undefeated and unchallenged. But now, with Rylik's blade planted in the tyrant's heart, the message was clear to all: Rylik was not only stronger, but also cunning enough to seize victory where others would falter. He had proven himself a force to be reckoned with, a man no one would dare to underestimate.

Thorian leaned against the doorframe, studying Rylik as he approached. "General Hamish has arrived. He's inside with the rest of them—waiting, of course, for their new king to make his entrance."

Rylik arched a brow, a hint of teasing in his expression. "And here I thought they might want to grieve."

Thorian chuckled, a low sound. "I wouldn't count on it. Do you have a speech prepared?"

"I'm not much for speeches," Rylik admitted with a shrug, his voice casual, yet commanding. "But I'll address them. They deserve that much."

Thorian pushed the heavy doors open, the grand throne room unfurling before them in all its opulent splendor. Massive chandeliers dripped with crystal, casting shimmering light over marble floors and towering gilded columns. Velvet banners in crimson and black hung from the walls, bearing the sigil of Ravenhelm. The scent of wax and cedar filled the air, mingling with the quiet murmur of nobles gathered beneath the vaulted ceiling.

As Rylik entered, the room fell silent, all eyes turning to him. He strode forward, his gaze steady as he ascended the dais to stand before the empty throne. The silence stretched taut, anticipation brimming like a storm about to break.

Rylik surveyed them, his presence commanding. "The king is dead," he began, his voice cutting through the room like a blade. "May his memory rot where it belongs."

A ripple of murmurs passed through the assembly, rising like a restless tide before quieting under the weight of Rylik's unyielding gaze. The air seemed to still, tense with anticipation.

"For too long, Ravenhelm has suffered under his rule," Rylik began, his voice sharp and unrelenting. "His cruelty, his tyranny, his insatiable greed—he wielded fear like a weapon, silencing dissent and crushing the spirits of those he claimed to protect. Last night, I ended it. I drove the blade into his heart myself," he said, his tone steady, unapologetic. He let the words fall, their weight pressing down, daring anyone to flinch beneath their gravity. "Because he deserved no less."

He let his gaze sweep the room, taking in every face, every hesitant glance. "I will not stand here and promise perfection," he continued, his voice steady but edged with steel. "I am no saint. But I can promise you this: Ravenhelm will not bow to fear again. I will lead with justice, but do not mistake fairness for weakness. I am not a man to be trifled with. If any among you would challenge my claim, step forward now."

The silence that followed was deafening. No one moved. No one spoke.

Then, from the edge of the assembly, General Hamish stepped forward, his polished armor catching the light. Though his silver hair bore the weight of his years, his frame remained strong and steadfast, a testament to a lifetime of discipline and service. His face, lined with age, was familiar to Rylik—a memory of days long past. Rylik's father had often spoken of Hamish, had confided in him, trusted him as few others. Seeing the general now stirred a sense of loyalty within him that he'd thought long dead.

Hamish's stride was purposeful, each step resolute as he

approached. When he stopped before Rylik, his gaze was steady, the respect in his eyes underscored by a quiet resolve. "Your father, Rysandrian, was a good man," he said, his deep voice rich with the weight of memory. The name rippled through the room, drawing murmurs as those gathered were reminded of the fallen man's legacy. Once revered, Rysandrian's name carried both honor and sorrow, a lineage cut short by tragedy. Hamish cleared his throat, his composure wavering beneath the tide of emotion. "And I see his strength in you," he continued, his tone softening with conviction. "I believe you will lead us well."

With solemn reverence, Hamish dropped to one knee and bowed his head, the gesture unmistakably acknowledging Rylik's ascension with sincere respect.

One by one, the others followed, the nobles and advisors bending in reverence, their submission rippling through the room like a silent tide. Thorian and Kaelith knelt as well, their loyalty etched into their unwavering expressions.

Rylik stood taller, surveying the sea of bowed heads with a mix of pride and triumph. For the first time in years, a spark of something unfamiliar stirred in his chest—hope. Not just for himself, but for a Ravenhelm reborn in his image. This was only the beginning, and he would see it forged into greatness.

* * *

Once the court's affairs had been concluded, Hamish approached Rylik again, his expression grave but earnest. Their conversation turned to Rylik's father, dredging up the bitter memory of his execution and the tragic circumstances surrounding it. Hamish recounted how he had fought valiantly to save the man from the executioner's blade, only to be thwarted by Lord Eldric's treachery—a dose of poison that had incapacitated him at the crucial moment.

Now, Hamish stood before him, humbled yet resolute, pleading for Rylik's mercy and understanding. He sought Aria's unparalleled gift, hoping her healing touch could purge the poison that had lingered in his body like a curse for years, weakening but never fully claiming him. Rylik's gaze sharpened at the request, for he knew all too well the agony of such affliction, the way it clawed at one's strength and resolve. It was a pain he would not soon forget—and one he could not ignore.

Rylik had personally escorted Hamish to the apothecary, satisfaction gleaming in his eyes as Aria, at his urging, extended her hand with grace and healed the man with an almost divine touch. The poison that had ravaged Hamish's body was gone in moments, leaving behind a silent awe that filled the room like a palpable force. Hamish, humbled and visibly moved, knelt again and vowed his unwavering loyalty to Rylik and Ravenhelm. It was a pledge Rylik knew would carry weight; Hamish was not only a respected figure among the court but had also proven his unmatched prowess as a commander of the king's army many years ago, long before Rylik had taken up the role of Sovereign.

By the same afternoon, Rylik had reinstated him as a general, though not without a pointed warning. "I will always be watching," he had said, his tone edged with the subtle menace of authority. Trust was not something Rylik dispensed freely—character was fickle, but competency was undeniable. Hamish's abilities had earned him a place, but vigilance would ensure he kept it.

Rylik's mind was ever-calculating, ever-watchful. A kingdom was a fragile thing, a dangerous dance of loyalty and ambition, but he would reign with precision. None could contest his right, his strength, or his resolve to command. In his court, every step would be measured, every move carefully watched. No one— friend or foe—would dare question his power.

He let out a slow breath as he approached the door to his chambers, the weight of the day pressing against his shoulders. The hours had been long and filled with tedious court matters, but things were finally resolved and he could finally make his retreat. Now, with the business of the kingdom behind him, his thoughts drifted to Aria. The prospect of her warmth, her presence, was the only solace he sought tonight.

He recalled how she'd seemed at the apothecary—distant, her thoughts clouded with something he couldn't quite decipher. It wasn't surprising, considering what she had endured before he'd brought her back to his bed. She had been fragile then, shaken.

Surely, she would crave the comfort he alone could provide. A smile tugged at his lips, part fondness, part pride. If she needed reassurances, he would give them, though he couldn't deny the part of him that enjoyed her dependency.

Turning the handle, Rylik pushed the door open, expecting to see her waiting for him. Instead, he was met with silence. His brow furrowed as his gaze swept the room, taking in the neatly pressed bedding and the low, steady crackle of the fire in the hearth. It was all too tidy, too still.

His jaw tightened. He stepped inside, the door clicking shut behind him, and surveyed the space more carefully. Nothing was amiss, yet the absence of her presence unsettled him. She should be here. His plans, his evening, had revolved around her.

Suppressing a flicker of irritation, he crossed the room and headed for the adjoining door that led to Aria's suite. Perhaps she needed solitude—or perhaps she was brooding again, lost in whatever turmoil plagued her thoughts. Whatever the reason, he would find her.

Rylik pushed the door open and stepped inside. Her room was brighter than his, the light from the hearth casting a warm glow across the space. She was there, seated by the fire, her delicate frame outlined by the flickering flames. Her head was bowed slightly, her focus entirely on the dancing embers.

"Aria," he said softly, his voice low and steady.

At the sound of his voice, she looked up. Her expression was unreadable, her yellow eyes reflecting the firelight with an intensity that gave nothing away.

He approached her with even footsteps, his shadow stretching across the floor. "You should have been waiting in my bed," he murmured, his tone an intricate mix of teasing and reproach. "What kept you away?"

She smiled, though unease twisted in her expression. "Do you even have much use for me now?"

He scoffed, lowering himself onto the sofa beside her. The firelight cast flickering shadows across his face, lending his features an even sharper edge. "What kind of question is that?" he countered, leaning in slightly, his gaze steady. "I would argue that after last night, I have far more uses for you now." His tone was teasing, his lips curling just enough to soften the remark.

She stifled a chuckle, but her brows furrowed, betraying her inner turmoil. "You know what I mean."

"I don't think I do," he said, studying her intently, his head tilting just slightly to invite her to explain.

Her gaze locked with his, steady and unwavering. "You're a king now," she said. "I don't know if I should be kneeling at your feet, laying in your bed, or going back to my village."

His jaw locked with quiet defiance, and though his voice remained calm, there was a razor-thin edge of irritation. "You think I would send you away?"

She didn't answer, and her silence only stoked his annoyance.

Rylik's hand settled on her thigh, the touch firm yet meant to reassure. "I may be king," he murmured, his voice softening to a velvet tone, "but my title is all that has changed between us."

"Do I now address you as *Your Majesty*?" she asked, her tone hesitant, tinged with both shyness and defiance.

"You will call me by my name," he replied, meeting her gaze without flinching.

She blushed deeply, her cheeks flushed in the firelight as her eyes dropped to his hand resting on her thigh. Slowly, she laid her hand over his, her touch tentative. "I loved last night," she admitted cautiously, her voice barely above a whisper. "I loved everything about being with you, just as we were. However," Her eyes lifted to meet his, conflicted and hesitant. "I don't want to be just another conquest."

His brows drew together slightly, her words piercing through his usual armor of confidence. The idea that she might believe herself little more than a fleeting indulgence sparked a flicker of something unexpected — concern.

"I can't presume to want more, of course," she added quickly, though her voice wavered. "I'm not asking, either. But, I think I deserve to know what your intentions are for me. I need to know if I am just pleasant company you'll grow bored of next week. Perhaps I have no right to presume that I could possibly choose my own life, but—"

"You have no right," he interrupted sharply, his voice cutting through her words like steel.

Her chest rose sharply, her eyes betraying a stunned realization.

"You will remain here in this castle," he said, softer now but no less resolute, "and no amount of pleading to the contrary will sway my decision." His hand slid higher along her thigh, a slow and indulgent motion as he leaned closer, his lips near her ear. "I am your king, so let this be my first command to you, Pyra. You belong to me. I will not grow tired of you, and I will not cast you aside. You are mine. And likewise, I am yours."

Her body tensed, every muscle taut under the weight of his words.

"I have no desire to make you a concubine," he continued, his voice dropping to a husky whisper. "You will be my queen." He pressed a lingering kiss to her cheek, his hand tightening on her thigh for emphasis. "And you will serve me. You will satisfy me. You will submit to me," he said, his fingers threading through her hair with reverent care. "And I will give you everything in return."

Her breathing had grown shallow, her lashes fluttering as she struggled to maintain composure. He allowed himself a smirk, the dark pleasure of her reaction simmering under his skin.

"I hope my intentions are clear," he mused, pulling back just enough to study her face.

Her expression was unreadable for a moment, her lips parted as though she were searching for words. Finally, she spoke, her voice unsteady but threaded with longing. "You wish to make me your queen?"

"I do," he said with a smile that was both possessive and triumphant. "Though it is hardly a wish. I told you. *This* is my first command. You *will* be my queen."

She hesitated, her gaze flickering over his face. "So you've said," she murmured, her tone soft but searching. "And yet, you also said I must serve you, satisfy you, submit to you. Am I of no further value than what I can do for you in your bed?"

His smirk deepened, but his eyes softened, the intensity in them shifting to something undeniably tender. "Your value to me," he began, his voice rich with conviction, "is far beyond words. It is beyond any measure of gold, and far exceeds the need I have for the very air I breathe. You are my obsession, Aria. You are a necessity. You are everything that I want, everything that could possibly satisfy my soul."

He leaned closer, his lips brushing hers as he spoke. "Do not mistake this for lust alone. I would not make any woman my queen if she were any less worthy than you. I will never touch, or so much as look at another woman. I have no need. I have found something in you that I thought impossible," He paused, his voice dropping even lower before breathing the last words, "I found love."

Her breath caught audibly, her eyes glistening as her lips trembled. And then, without hesitation, she closed the gap between them, capturing his mouth in a kiss.

The moment their lips met, the world seemed to fall away. Rylik's hand moved to cradle her face, his fingers tangling in her hair as he kissed her deeply, possessively. Her hands gripped his shoulders, pulling him closer as though afraid he might disappear. He could feel her surrender, the way her body leaned into his, the warmth of her touch fanning the flames inside him.

When he finally pulled away, their foreheads rested together, their breaths mingling.

"I am forever yours," she whispered against his lips. "And you are mine, Rylik."

He muttered a curse under his breath as he kissed her again, his tongue gliding across her own with unrestrained fervor. His fingertips grazed her skirt, bunching the material up under his palm as he exposed her thigh. With a low growl, he tugged at her hips and pulled her swiftly on top of him, her thighs straddling his hips.

His kisses drifted lower, trailing down her neck as one hand pulled the front of her blouse down. He heard her gasp as he pressed his lips against her breast. His other hand unfastened the clasp at his waist, exposed for a moment before he drew in a breath and forced her hips down, seating himself fully inside of her.

Aria let out a sharp groan that quickly melted into that of yearning, her hips responding in rhythm with his own.

"I told you this morning," Rylik chided her with mischief in his grin. "I would show you what being *vulgar* really is."

He pulled her blouse down further, the fabric draping over her corset as her full breasts bounced softly with every undulation. She let out a quivering moan as she arched her back for him, savoring the feel of his mouth on her nipples.

"The things I want to do to you tonight, Pyra," his breath was cool against her glistening skin as he whispered, "are deeply, *deeply* vulgar. And I'm going to enjoy every sinful moment of it."

Rylik's hands wrapped firmly around her upper thighs as he lifted her off of him, turning her around. With care, he grasped the back of her neck and guided her down, easing her forward and away from him, until her hands were forced to the warm carpet below. He trailed his hands slowly down her spine, torturously so, before grasping her hips, her knees trembling as he lifted her skirt. Leaning over her, he curved his hand around her breast, squeezing as his words ghosted her neck. "Hold your breath," he purred, then buried himself inside of her with a deep thrust, relishing in the soft cry that wrenched itself from her lips.

Aria leaned her hips back against his own as he sank into her, every pound eliciting more of her tantalizing, desperate gasps for air. He was greedy, practically insatiable as he drove deeper and faster into her. She was bent over, her beautiful red curls spilling over her shoulder and glinting in the firelight. Her white hands were tense to either side of her, desperately trying to grasp onto the thick fibers of the rug to steady herself against his relentless pressure.

He savored the sight, reaching down to those lovely curls and threading his fingers through them. He gave a light tug, watching as she again curved her flawless back for him, taking him completely. He could feel his release approaching rapidly, and he slowed his cadence with agonizing pleasure. He was going to make this last a long, long time.

"Yes," Rylik said in a soft murmur, "submission suits you, my queen." He pulled gingerly back on her hair, ushering her upright on her knees, her back to his abdomen. His hips rolled into hers with a slow, steady weight. His hand trailed down her stomach and dropped to her sex, fingers nimble over the sensitive nerves there.

Aria panted breathlessly, soft whining sounds that were a blend of pleasure and impatience. "More," she begged him, the raw desire in her voice nearly making him succumb to his own peak. A low, ragged moan rumbled from his chest as fought to suppress his urges.

He pushed her back down again, dropping the both of them lower so that she was prone and splayed before him, propped up on her elbows. "I want to hear you say my name as you beg for more," he said in a hushed tone. "I want you to scream it."

Her moan was guttural, heavy with need. "More, Rylik!" she pleaded, her voice laced with longing.

Something instinctual rose up within him, unable to be restrained as he rammed forcefully into her. She was tight around his length, warm and wet as she embraced every inch of him. It was a primal hunger, a fire coursing through his veins as the sound of her screaming his name was all he could hear over the rhythmic slaps of skin against skin.

Euphoria washed over him in waves, shuddering through his body like an uncontrollable current. She gasped, a moan escaping her as though it were forced from her very soul. He pumped into her, filling her endlessly, melding himself with her as his seed began to spill out in droplets to the carpet. He could hear her as her orgasm coursed through her body, her sex trembling around him, trapping him in their shared moment of ecstasy.

The satisfaction of her release only drew more from him, his body quivering in pleasure as he rode the final waves of his climax.

She was a goddess. She was his *queen*.

He pulled out from her, still dripping, and turned her over so that she could lie on her back. Rylik marveled over beauty, the heavy rise and fall of her naked chest as she fought to catch her breath. His mouth closed over her own, passionately kissing her as he again immersed his length inside of her.

She choked out a breathy sigh, her hips again matching his own as if she were a slave to his whims. His lips curled in amusement as he watched her, feeling her squeezing around him. She opened her legs wider in provocation, and he drove himself in harder. They moved in harmony, saturated, their bodies so entwined that he could hardly know where he began and she ended.

She cried out again in pleasure, louder, her body shaking under another blissful climax as he pulsed against her.

A smug smile tugged at his mouth as he slowed his pace again, feeling her every trembling, involuntary shudder of rapture as he eased from her. "I hope you enjoyed yourself, Pyra," he cooed against her ear, "Because, you will submit to me again, and again, and *again*." He gave her only a short reprieve, his fingers trailing lightly over her dampened skin before sliding his length fully into her once more, over and over, his satisfaction blooming at her heady sighs of approval. "And just when you think you can't handle any more, it will be morning. And only then will I let you rest."

Aria's smile in response, so unguarded and bright, struck him like a blade sliding between ribs—silent, undeniable, and far too deep. Whether she thought him jesting or sincere, it no longer mattered. One truth shone with painful clarity: without her, he would never again grasp this fragile, incandescent happiness. She was the breath animating his soul, the unfailing tether anchoring him to this reality. And he knew with unshakable certainty—he could never, would never, let her go.

CHAPTER 48

ARIA

Aria awoke slowly, the first rays of morning light spilling through the gaps in the heavy curtains, painting golden patterns on the stone walls. She stirred against the solid warmth beneath her, her head resting on Rylik's chest, the steady rhythm of his heartbeat lulling her like a quiet symphony. His arm was draped protectively around her, holding her close even in his sleep, as if his subconscious refused to let her go.

She smiled to herself, her fingers idly tracing paths along the firm planes of his chest, savoring the feel of his skin beneath her touch. Memories of the night before coursed through her like a heady wine, her cheeks warming at the recollection. Fragments of the night resurfaced, of faint images of gasping by the fireplace, grasping the wall of the bathing room, panting as they'd made love on the surface of Rylik's polished work desk. Their passion had been wild and unrestrained, a tempest of emotion and desire. She hadn't known it was possible to feel so alive, so entirely consumed by someone else.

Across the room, she noticed the flowering plants blossoming in Rylik's windowsill, a reminder of the night she had given him the gift not long ago. Their petals unfurled in radiant splendor, catching the ethereal morning light, filling her with a sense of hope. For the first time in what felt like forever, she allowed herself to dream of the future—not in quiet dread, but with excitement. The idea of becoming his queen filled her chest with unbridled bliss, the word *wife* echoing in her mind like the sweetest melody.

She pictured Ravenhelm thriving, its people flourishing under their rule. No longer did the thought of a crown feel like a weight, not with Rylik beside her. He had laid bare his heart, admitted his love for her, and in doing so had stripped away her final defenses. She loved him, fiercely and completely, and the knowledge brought her a peace she hadn't realized she'd been searching for.

Her musings were interrupted as she felt his hand glide up her arm, the gentle motion drawing her from her thoughts. She glanced up to find him watching her through half-lidded eyes, his lips curving into a lazy, wicked smile.

"Good morning, my queen," he murmured, his voice low and rough with sleep. He tilted her chin up with his knuckle and kissed her softly, the tenderness of it unraveling her completely. When the kiss deepened, heat sparked in her veins, a vivid reminder of how restless their night had been.

By the time he pulled back, her breath was uneven, and she laughed softly, nestling closer to him. "Good morning," she whispered, her fingers resting against his jaw. "You're rather awake for someone who kept me up half the night."

He smirked, his fingers brushing over her temple as he kissed her forehead. "And yet you still wake looking like a goddess," he murmured, his tone holding that unmistakable charm she felt so drawn to. "If you knew what I see when I look at you, you'd never doubt how much I adore you."

Her heart twisted at the words, full and tender. "You mean that," she whispered, her voice soft as she searched his eyes.

"Without question." His tone was quiet but resolute, his gaze locked onto hers. "My soul is yours to keep, for better or worse." His hand slid to the back of her neck, his touch both commanding and gentle.

She smiled, her fingers grazing his lips. "You're going to ruin me for anyone else," she teased softly.

He tightened his grip on her arm, pulling her closer with a

slight, possessive pressure that sent her heart racing—exactly the reaction she'd hoped for. "Wicked girl," he purred, his voice a low threat against her ear. "It's almost as if you want to be punished for speaking such unforgivable words to your king." A sly grin curved his lips, and a glint of mischief sparked in his eyes. "And here I thought you might've learned that it's better to submit to me. You yielded to me so admirably last night. Continuously, as I recall."

Her cheeks burned as she tried to sit up, but his arm tightened around her waist, pulling her back against him. He wanted to continue the night before. She did too. But, how could she? She was pleasantly fatigued, and a little sore. "Rylik," she protested, though her laughter betrayed her.

He raised a brow, smirking down at her. "Don't tempt me, Aria. If I am to ruin you, I'd like to start now, and ruin you thoroughly. I ensured the day is ours, and I am more than willing to spend it exactly as we did last night."

"You're incorrigible," she teased, shaking her head. But when his lips brushed hers again, she found herself sinking into the kiss, unable to resist the way he made her feel—cherished, wanted, utterly adored.

When they finally parted, she rested her forehead against his, her smile soft and full of wonder. Silence settled between them, a language of its own, filled with meaning and tenderness. She closed her eyes, savoring the moment, the warmth of his presence and the steady rhythm of his breath mingling with hers.

She thought of all that had brought them here. The night she had walked into his suite, trembling with uncertainty, only to find her hands drawn to his wounds as if by some unseen force. She had been so naive then, unaware that she was healing more than his body—that she was mending something broken deep within him. Gratitude bloomed in her chest for that moment, for the path it set them on, no matter how treacherous it had seemed at times.

His protection came to mind, fierce and unyielding, even when wrapped in shadows and veiled threats. How he had guarded her with a possessiveness that might have frightened her had it not been paired with the tenderness he so rarely revealed to others. He was flawed, yes, but beautifully so, his love an all-encompassing fire that warmed every corner of her soul.

The man who had once been little more than a lethal, dangerous enigma now stood in her heart as her salvation, just as she had been his. She didn't know when, exactly, she had fallen in love with him. Perhaps it had been in the quiet moments, like the one now, when his touch was soft, his gaze unguarded. Or maybe it had been in the storm, when his ferocity had stood between her and certain ruin. It didn't matter. She loved him. She loved him utterly.

And finally, she reflected on the journey they had shared—a tempest of desire and devotion, of defiance and surrender. It had been a perilous gamble, one that could have torn them apart at any turn. Yet, against all odds, it had brought them here. To this bed, where their bodies rested entwined. To this love, fierce and unyielding, forged in fire and shadows. To this life, imperfect yet brimming with promise, a future she could scarcely believe was now hers to hold.

Aria opened her eyes, her gaze meeting his, and the quiet joy in her heart swelled. She leaned forward, brushing her lips against his in a kiss that spoke of hope and gratitude. For the night she had stepped into his suite and dared to reach for him. For the fierce protection he had given her, even when she didn't understand it. For the love they had unearthed in each other, a love she had never imagined but could no longer imagine living without.

It was all of it—every moment, every trial, every stolen breath—that had led to this wicked, wicked game of desire and devotion that had somehow become their happily ever after.

BONUS CONTENT

Need more content pertaining to A Wicked Game?

Please visit patreon.com/lifelight

For bonus scenes, artwork, trailers and more!